VICTORIES
GREATER
THAN
DEATH

VICTORIES GREATER THAN DEATH

CHARLIE JANE ANDERS

TITAN BOOKS

Victories Greater Than Death
Print edition ISBN: 9781789094725
E-book edition ISBN: 9781789094732

Published by Titan Books
A division of Titan Publishing Group Ltd.
144 Southwark Street, London SE1 0UP
www.titanbooks.com

First Titan edition April 2021
10 9 8 7 6 5 4 3 2 1

A CIP catalogue record for this title is available from the British Library.

Printed and bound CPI Group (UK) Ltd, Croydon, CR0 4YY.

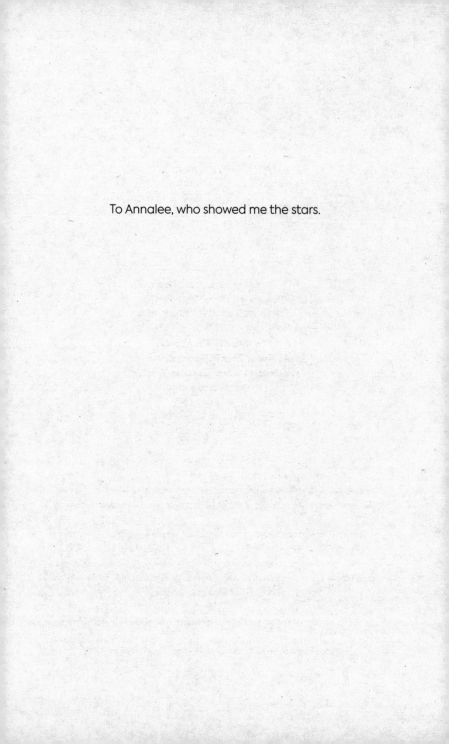

To Annalee, who showed me the stars.

1

I have a ball of starlight inside me. A globe, containing a billion bright pinpricks. It's always been there, since I was a baby—but lately I've been chewing up the inside of my own mouth waiting for it to burst out of me. Sometimes I feel all these little suns whirling, like they're getting ready to emerge from the hollow of my collarbone.

My whole life has been leading up to this, and I can't stand the waiting.

*

I'm dangling by my waist from the side of the highway bridge. All the blood rushes to my head as a sixteen-wheeler truck rushes past, so close that I can feel the air disturbance and smell the fumes. The bridge quivers, and so does my heart. I feel like I'm going to pass out.

"Anything?" asks Rachael Townsend, who's holding my belt in her strong grip.

"Nothing," I gasp.

"Maybe you're not scared enough," Rachael says.

"I'm definitely scared enough. This . . . isn't working."

Rachael helps me pull myself upward, back behind the rusted old railing. I collapse on the hot cement walkway, next to a graffiti tag with a picture of a snarling puma.

"Okay." Rachael smiles, sitting cross-legged on the walkway with her eyes looking wide and extra green in the midday sun. She's dressed like a fourth-grader, as usual, in corduroy overalls and a long-sleeved stripy shirt. "So it's not reacting to fear. Or adrenaline."

"And we know it's not triggered by anger," I say, "or it would have activated when Lauren Bose put dirt in Zuleikha Marshall's new shoes. For sure."

"Is Lauren Bose *still* harassing Zuleikha Marshall? And the school is doing nothing?" Rachael shakes her head. "*This* is why I'm being homeschooled."

"Yeah. And yeah, the administration is both-sidesing the hell out of it. Makes me want to scream."

"Okay." Rachael reaches into her backpack and pulls out a folder. "So I've personally seen your rescue beacon light up on three separate occasions, and you've told me about four other times." She shows me a chart, with beautiful handwriting and amazing doodles showing different versions of me with a bright blue-tinged glow coming from my sternum. Because Rachael is the greatest artist of all time.

Each cartoon version of me is labeled with things like:

1. Tina about to go to junior prom with Rob Langford
2. Tina right after cops broke up our flashmob outside the slumlord offices
3. Tina finds out she flunked trig midterm

"I got a D on that trig test," I protest. "I did not flunk!"

"So I don't see a huge pattern," Rachael says. "I mean, it's supposed to turn on when you're old enough for the aliens to come get you, right?"

"They're taking their sweet time." I drag myself to my feet. "My mom keeps saying it might not happen until I turn eighteen, or even twenty-one. She just doesn't want me to leave. As if it would be better for me to just stay trapped here forever."

Rachael stands up too, and we walk back toward her rust-colored old Dodge hatchback. She's being quiet again, which . . . a lot of being friends with Rachael is learning to interpret her many flavors of silence.

Like, there's the "I'm mad at you and you won't find out why for a week" silence. Or the "I'm figuring something out in my own head" silence. The most common is the "I need to be alone" silence, because Rachael has major hermit tendencies. But this silence is none of those, I'm pretty sure.

We drive for a while, without even any music. I'm one-quarter wondering what's up with Rachael, but three-quarters obsessing about my rescue beacon and why it won't just spill all the stars already.

At last, when we're stopped at an intersection near the upscale mall and the tech campus, Rachael glances my way and says, "I wish I could go too. When the aliens come to collect you. I wish I could come along."

I just stare at her. I don't even know what to say.

"I know, I know." Rachael raises her hands from the steering wheel. "It would be ridiculous, and I would be useless up there in space, and there would be creatures trying to kill us, and it's your destiny, not mine. But still. I wish."

I want to tell Rachael that she'll have a way better life down here on Earth. She'll go to art school, find a new boyfriend to replace that loser Sven, publish tons of comics, and win awards. She'll have adventures that don't involve things like an alien murder team trying to kill her. She has plenty of reasons to stay.

Unlike me. I don't have any real friends at high school, since Rachael dropped out. And the only thing I have to look forward to here on Earth is more people talking down to me. More bullies and creepers at school. More feeling like a bottomless pit, crammed with garbage emotions.

When Rachael drops me at my house, I just say, "I wish you could come too."

"Yeah." She smiles and hands me the folder. "Here. You should have this. Maybe it'll help."

She drives away. While I stare at a painstakingly annotated chart full of cartoon Tinas—each one bursting with pure dazzling light.

*

A few hours later, Rachael and I are already chatting again:

Chat log, Aug 19:

Trashstar [5:36 pm]: its gonna happen soon. i can tell. the beacon. it's gonna light up.

Inkflinger [5:36 pm]: thats what u said last spring. and last winter. and five other times.

Trashstar [5:37 pm]: its different this time i swear

Trashstar [5:37 pm]: my mom is doing that thing again where she just stares at nothing

Inkflinger [5:38 pm]: oh man, i'm sorry

Inkflinger [5:38 pm]: what do u really think will happen when it lights up????

[Trashstar is typing]

[Trashstar is typing]

[Trashstar is typing]

Inkflinger [5:40 pm]: helloooo?!

Trashstar [5:40 pm]: i dont know

Trashstar [5:41 pm]: they didnt tell my mom much when they dropped me off

Trashstar [5:41 pm]: just . . . alien baby. massive legacy. evil murder team.

Inkflinger [5:41 pm]: i hope there's a dragon that u get to ride on

Trashstar [5:41 pm]: like my own personal dragon

Inkflinger [5:41 pm]: ur personal dragon that u share with me

Trashstar [5:42 pm]: i'm pretty sure there will be at least a suit of armor

Trashstar [5:42 pm]: rocket boots!!!!

Trashstar [5:42 pm]: my theory is i'm the heir to a space casino

Inkflinger [5:42 pm]: u've had YEARS to think about this

Inkflinger [5:42 pm]: and space casino is the best u've come up with????

Trashstar [5:42 pm]: or maybe a wizard school

Inkflinger [5:43 pm]: its definitely either casino or wizard academy

Trashstar [5:43 pm]: pretty sure i've narrowed it down to those 2 options yea

*

This beacon is a part of me, like my liver or kidneys. Except sometimes at night, a faint growl wakes me—and I feel like I have a pacemaker, or some other foreign object, jammed inside my chest. And then I remember that my body isn't the same as literally everyone else's.

I fill our electric teakettle, with the switch jammed in the "on" position. And then I lean all the way over the side of my bed, so the steam is hitting the exact spot where the beacon is located. Mostly, the steam gets up in my nostrils and makes me choke.

My mom hears the kettle squealing. "What are you doing in there?" She peels back the curtain that separates my "bedroom" from the rest of the apartment. "Stop messing around. This is ridiculous."

"It likes the steam! I can feel it reacting." I cough and sputter.

"It's an interplanetary rescue beacon, not a pork bun." My mom turns the kettle off.

"I'm just so sick of 'almost.'" I flop back onto my bed and bury my face in my knees.

Lately, my mom spends her time either trying to hide her tears from me, or acting like I'm already gone. Last week, I caught her folding the same shirt for five minutes, just creasing and tucking over and over until it looked like a paper football. She's started calling up friends she hasn't seen in ages, signing herself up for adult education classes, working on ways to move on with her life without me. But then, she'll blow off some social plan that she spent hours making, just so she can sit at home staring into a Public Radio mug full of Chablis. I want to comfort her, or reassure her, but I don't know how.

For all we know, the people who left me on Earth as a baby are all gone, and there'll be nobody to answer the beacon when it does come to life.

"You could just stay here on Earth and have an amazing life." She stares at her refrigerator door, with all the old photos and the terrible artwork I did in fifth grade. "You're already helping people down here," she says with the full force of her midwestern Presbyterian earnestness. "All of the things that you do with the Lasagna Hats, everything you make happen . . . Nothing could ever make me prouder of you than I already am."

"Yeah." I stare at the floor. I don't know what to say. My mom knows I want this, more than anything, even though it's going to destroy her.

My mom sighs and drinks from her wine-mug. "Just promise me one thing."

"Sure. Whatever."

For once, we are actually looking at each other. Her red hair has wiry streaks of gray, and her eyes have new lines around them.

"When the beacon lights up, you have to run." Her eyes blaze, out of nowhere, with an intensity I've almost never seen before. "Run as if armies were chasing you. Because I've told you, the moment your beacon activates, monsters from beyond our world will try to kill you. They won't stop. Keep running, until you're sure you're being rescued for real. Promise me."

I kind of shrug it off, but my mom grabs my wrist. So I say, "Yeah, yeah. Of course. I promise. Jeez."

*

That night I wake up, and there's someone next to my bed.

All I can see at first is a pair of coal-black eyes, glinting in the moonlight filtered through the branches of the yew tree outside my tiny window.

Then I make out his face. Pale, like a ghost. Grinning, like a serial killer.

Something lights up in his hands. I glimpse a shiny metal tube with four wings on all sides, and an opening, full of bottomless darkness, aimed right at me. Somehow I know this is a weapon.

He stands over me, huge as a mountain, blocking out everything else. Even if I had the strength to rise, I would still be a speck next to him.

"I take no pleasure from killing you." The giant speaks in a low purr. "Satisfaction, certainly. And an adrenaline rush. And oh yes, a sense of vindication. Your death will probably give me closure. But still, I feel sad that it came to this."

My skin is so cold, my hands are numb and my arms feel prickly. I can't breathe.

"I want you to know that I feel nothing but pity for your miserable state." The huge figure raises the gun to my head.

I scream until my throat hurts.

The gun hisses. I'm about to be burned down to nothing.

I'm so cold, I can't stand this cold.

The word "miserable" rings in my ears as I scream and brace myself for death.

2

The next thing I know, my mom is shaking me and yelling my name. "Tina!" My mom wraps my quilt tight around me. "Tina, are you okay? Talk to me."

I still can't breathe. "He was here," I wheeze. "He was right here. He wasn't even human. He was about to kill me."

"Honey, it's okay," my mom says. "It's okay. You're safe. You're here with me, it's only human beings 'round these parts. I promise."

"I've never been so scared in my life."

That sentence takes me several breaths to say, with all the shivering. The quilt (with squares containing famous women who fought against oppression) helps a little. So does my mom, whispering reassurances in my ear.

That wasn't just a random hallucination, or a dream. It was a memory. A memory of the person I used to be. Whoever *that* was. Don't ask how, but I just know this was a glimpse of her life. The rescue beacon whirs inside me.

"I'm glad you saw that," my mom says, "because I keep trying to tell you. The moment that beacon activates, they'll be coming. I only saw a glimpse, and that was enough to make my skin crawl."

My stomach flutters. "Tell me again."

My mom hesitates, then nods. "I had just failed another infertility treatment, and they showed up at my apartment. They had a baby, with skin the color of fresh-picked lavender, and big round eyes, and they said you were a clone of someone who had just died, someone important. They took some of my DNA and used it to make you look like my daughter, so I could watch you until they were ready to come get you. They showed me a hologram of the monsters that I needed to keep you hidden from, and it was like seeing an army sent by death itself."

My mom leans on my quilted shoulder, like she's about to start crying.

Then she takes a deep breath instead. "Let's do something fun tomorrow. I have a day off. Worthington Garden Party?"

"Wow. What? Really? We haven't played Worthington Garden Party in forever."

The beacon goes back to sleep behind my breastbone.

"Oh! There's that brand-new mall near the tech campus that we haven't even been to yet. I can wear my church-lady hat!" My mom laughs, and rubs her hands together, and I can't help smiling too.

But after she leaves, I close my eyes again, and I still see the pale giant leering at me. Raising that terrible gun. I feel frozen to the marrow, like I've waded neck-deep into a lake on the bleakest day of winter.

*

Worthington Garden Party is a game my mom and I invented, where we go through the mall looking at things we could never afford to buy, and we pretend that we're planning a fancy garden party for the Worthingtons (who don't exist, just in case it wasn't already obvious).

My mom puts on her scariest hat, with the carnations and the pink ribbon, and I wear bright apricot capri pants. And we drive to the new shopping center, over on the rich side of town.

The kitchen store has this red-chrome machine that turns fresh fruit into a decorative fountain, and you can program it to spray a few different patterns. "I don't know," my mom says, in a very serious voice. "The Worthingtons are quite particular about their juice formations. We wouldn't want to have a fruit salute that lacks proper parabolas." My mom says the words "fruit salute" with a straight face.

"Yes, yes," I say. "I mean, the Worthingtons. How many times have they said they prefer their papaya juice to really soar? *So* many times."

My mom nods gravely. "Yes. The Worthingtons have strong opinions about properly aerodynamic papaya juice." Over in the corner, the salesperson is hiding her giggles behind her hand.

This is the mom I've been missing lately. The one who decided that she and I would treat everything like a grand ridiculous adventure, the two of us against the universe. Even when we went camping and set fire to our tent, and got ourselves menaced by beavers. (They were really terrifying. I swear.)

"I always knew that you were going to be taken away from me," my mom told me a while ago. "I thought about taking you off the grid, or trying to find people to train you in survival skills. But I decided it was better for you to have some good memories of your time as a human being. However long that lasts."

We keep moving through the mall, along marble floors that are so shiny, I see a murky ghost of myself reflected in them. We gaze upon shiny shoes, in a riot of colors, that cost nearly a month's rent. These kid-leather saddle shoes, with peacock feather heads all around the sides, might be just the thing to help the Worthingtons launch the season. "Mundane," my mother proclaims, squinting at them. "Frightfully mundane."

The only thing we actually buy is a basket of truffle fries, which we eat in the food court. They smell of rich oils and spices, but they taste like regular fries, just a little sweeter.

My mom chatters about the book club she keeps missing, and I let myself breathe. It's okay. Only humans 'round these parts.

Then I look away for a second, and see the pale man, standing near the video game store. Watching us. His lip curls upward, and he pats the ugly gun attached to his dark tunic.

When I look again, a second later, the pale man is gone.

*

The next day at Clinton High, someone has posted a slut-shaming video about Samantha Kinnock, and it has a hundred likes already. Only thirty seconds long, just a close-up of Samantha's ass in this pair of booty shorts that she decided to wear one weekend, with ugly messages popping up. I hear Lauren Bose and her other friends whisper about it in the hallway.

It never stops. The cycle just keeps going and going. People only feel like their footing is secure when they can step on someone else's head.

Why would I even want to be human?

I step into Lauren's path and the rage settles onto me, like armor.

"Leave Samantha alone."

I get tunnel vision, and my nerves are jangling, and Lauren's dimply smirk gets under my skin—and the beacon wakes up. Something to add to Rachael's chart of cartoon Tinas.

This ball of light throbs and pounds against the wall of my chest like a trapped animal, pale glow showing through my hoodie. And I think, *It's happening, damn damn damn, I'll finally be who I was meant to be.*

One of Lauren's friends, maybe Kayla, sticks out her foot, and trips me. I fall face-first onto the tile floor, hard enough to scrape my palms. Everyone is laughing and chattering and aiming their phones.

The beacon sputters.

All at once, I'm not picking myself up off the hallway of Clinton High. I'm raising myself, painfully, off an opaque black surface made out of glass, or plastic. The floor quakes under my hands and knees—and all around me is nothing but darkness, peppered with tiny lights.

Stars to my left, stars to my right, stars all around.

I'm standing on top of a spaceship, in deep space.

And my skin has turned purple. Not grape-soda purple, more like a pale, bluish purple that shimmers as it catches the starlight. I'm wearing a crimson suit, or some kind of uniform, with a river of lights on the left sleeve and a picture of a strange mask, like for an opera singer, on the right. My violet palms are cupped around a holographic message that I somehow know is telling me this spaceship is about to explode.

"You mustn't blame yourself," says a voice like the rustling of dead leaves in the wind. "You were always doomed to fail." The giant from my bedroom turns his depthless black eyes toward me. He's wearing a bloodred sash across his long dark tunic.

His face looks *wrong*, even besides the paleness and the big dark eye-pools. I can't figure it out at first, but then I realize: he's too perfect. No flaws, no blemishes. The two sides of his face are exactly the same, like a mirror image. His dark hair is cropped short across his white scalp.

"Marrant, even if you kill me, that doesn't mean I've failed," I hear myself say. "There are victories greater than death. I might not live to see justice done, but I can see it coming. Also, that sash makes you look like a third-rate CrudePink singer."

The giant—Marrant?—snarls and lunges forward, and his right hand holds the same weapon as in my vision from the other night. I've never even seen a regular gun up close, but at this range, I can tell this one will rip my entire body in half.

The darkness in Marrant's eyes makes me feel tiny, weak, a speck of nothing.

Then reality comes crashing back. My skin is back to its usual shade of pale cream. I'm standing there in the hallway, trembling, and the bell is ringing, and I'm about to be late for class. My legs won't budge, no matter how hard I try to make them.

3

Saturday morning, the sunlight invades my tiny curtained-off "bedroom" and wakes me from a clammy bad dream. Even awake, I keep remembering Marrant's creepy voice—and I startle, as if I had more layers of nightmare to wake from.

My phone is jittering with all the gossip from *Waymaker* fandom and random updates about some Clinton High drama that I barely noticed in the midst of my Marrant obsession . . . and then there's a message from Rachael on the Lasagna Hats server.

Monday Barker. It's happening: disco party! Coming to pick you up at noon.

The Lasagna Hats started as a backchannel group for *Waymaker* players—until the game had one gross update too many, and then we started just chatting about whatever. And somehow it turned into a place to organize pranks and disruptions against all of the world's scuzziest creeps.

I grab my backpack, dump out all my school stuff, and cram it full of noisemakers, glitter, and my mom's old costume stuff. I'm already snapping out of my anxiety spiral.

The back seat of Rachael's car is covered with art supplies and sketchpads, and I can tell at a glance that she's leveled up since I last saw her works in progress. As soon as I get in her car, Rachael chatters to me about Monday Barker—that online "personality" who says that girls are naturally bad at science and math, and women should never have gotten the vote.

Then Rachael trails off, because she can tell I'm only half listening.

"Okay," she says. "What's wrong with you?"

I can barely find the words to tell her I've started having hallucinations about an alien serial killer.

The artwork on Rachael's back seat includes a hand-colored drawing of a zebra wearing a ruffly collar and velvet jacket, raising a sword and riding a narwhal across the clouds. Somehow this image gives me the courage to explain about Marrant.

"Pretty sure these were actual memories from . . . before," I say. "I think this means it's going to light up soon."

"That's great." Rachael glances at my face. "Wait. Why isn't that great?"

"It is. Except . . . I've been waiting and dreaming for so long, and now it's suddenly a real thing. And . . . what if there's nothing out there but the evil murder team? What if all the friendly aliens are dead? Or don't bother to show up?"

"Huh." She drives onto the highway and merges into traffic without slowing down. "I guess there's only one way to find out."

I close my eyes, and remember that oily voice: *You were always doomed to fail.*

"Maybe I can't do this." I suck in a deep breath through my teeth. "Maybe I'm just out of my league and I'm going to die. Maybe I'm just not strong enough."

Rachael glances at me again, and shrugs. "Maybe," is all she says.

She doesn't talk again for ages. I think this is the "working something out in her own head" silence.

We make a pit stop at a convenience store, and Rachael pauses in the parking lot. "Remember when you decked Walter Gough for calling me an orca in a smock?" (It wasn't a smock, it was a nice chemise from Torrid, and Walter deserved worse.) "Remember the great lunch lady war, and that Frito pie costume you wore?"

I nod.

"The entire time I've known you, people have kept telling you to stop being such an obnoxious pain in the butt," Rachael says with a gleam in her eye. "But here you are, preparing to put on a ridiculous costume and prank Monday Barker. This is who you are. So . . . if some alien murder team shows up to test you, I feel sorry for them."

Rachael smiles at me. Everything suddenly feels extremely heavy and lighter than air, at the same time.

"Oh my god," I say. "Can I hug you? I know you don't always like to be touched, but—"

Rachael nods, and I pull her into a bear hug. She smells of fancy soap and acetone, and her arms wrap around me super gently.

Then she lets go of me, and I let go too, and we go to buy some extra-spicy chips and ultra-caffeinated sodas, the perfect fuel for confronting ass-hattery (ass-millinery?). I keep thinking of what Rachael just said, and a sugar rush spreads throughout my whole body.

I feel like I almost forgot something massively important, but then my best friend was there to remind me.

*

Monday Barker is scheduled to speak at the Lions Club in Islington, and we're setting up at the park across the street. Bette and Turtle have a glitter mist machine and a big disco ball, and a dozen other people, mostly my age, have brought sparkly decorations. I wander around helping people to figure out the best place to set up, since this "disco party" was sort of my idea.

"We got this," says Turtle, buttoning their white suit jacket over a red shirt. "Why don't you get yourself ready?" They've put pink streaks into their hair-swoosh.

In other words, *Stop trying to micromanage everyone.* Message received.

I retreat to Rachael's car, where I rummage in my knapsack and put on a bright red spangly tuxedo shirt and a big fluffy pink skirt I stole from my mom, plus shoes covered with sequins.

Rachael sets to work finishing some signs she was making, which are full of rainbows and stars and shiny Day-Glo paint. I pull out the tubes of glitter-goop I brought with me, and she lets me spread some around the edges using a popsicle stick.

I coax Rachael into telling me about the comic she's working on right now. "It's about a group of animals living on a boat. They thought they were getting on Noah's Ark, but the guy they thought was Noah skipped out on them, and now they're just stuck on a boat in the middle of the ocean alone. There's a pair of giraffes, and a poly triad of walruses. They have to teach themselves to sail, and maybe they're going to become pirates who only steal fresh produce. Once I have enough of it, I might put it online."

"Hell yeah," I say. "The world deserves to learn how excellent you are."

She just nods and keeps adding more sparkle.

I wish the bullies hadn't driven Rachael away from school. She just made too easy a target for ass-millinery: her parents are nudists, she's a super-introvert who sometimes talks to herself when she gets stressed, and she wears loose rayon clothing to hide all her curves.

The rich kids, whose parents worked at the tech campus, took her picture and used filters to make her look like an actual dog. Kids "accidentally" tripped her up as she walked into school, or shoved her in the girls' room. One time, someone dumped a can of coffee grounds from the teacher's lounge on her head. I tried to protect her, but I couldn't be there all the time.

So . . . homeschooling. And me never seeing Rachael during the week anymore.

Soon there are about twenty of us across the street from the Lions Club, everybody feeding off everyone else's energy and hoisting Rachael's glorious awning. And a pro–Monday Barker crowd is already gathered across the street, on the front walk of this old one-story brick meeting hall with flaking paint on its wooden sign.

A town car pulls up, and Monday Barker gets out, flanked by two beefy men in dark suits holding walkie-talkies. Monday Barker is about my mom's age, with sideburns enclosing his round face, and a huge crown of upswept hair. He waves in a robotic motion, and his fans scream and freak out.

Someone on our side fires up a big speaker on wheels, playing old disco music. The handful of cops between us and the Lions Club tense up, but we're not trying to start anything. We're just having an impromptu dance party.

The brick wall of the savings and trust bank seems to shiver. I catch a glimpse of Marrant, the giant with the scary-perfect face and the sneering thin lips, staring at me.

But I remember what I said to him in that vision: *There are victories greater than death. I can see justice coming.* And then I think about Rachael saying, *If an alien murder team shows up, I feel sorry for them.*

The throbbing grows stronger . . . but Marrant is gone. The brick wall is just a wall again.

The Monday Barker fans—mostly white boys with bad hair—are chanting something, but I can't hear them over our music. Rachael and I look at each other and whoop. Someone starts the whole crowd singing along with that song about how we are family. I know, I know. But I get kind of choked up.

We keep on, chanting disco lyrics and holding hands, until Monday Barker's supporters vanish inside the Lions Club to listen to their idol explain why girls shouldn't learn to read. Out here, on the disco side of the line, we all start high-fiving each other and jumping up and down.

*

Afterward, we all head to the 23-Hour Coffee Bomb. Turtle, Bette, and the others all go inside the coffee place, but I pause out in the parking lot, with its scenic view of the wind-beaten sign for the Little Darlings strip club. Rachael sees me and hangs back too.

"I started to get another one of those hallucinations." I look down at the white gravel. "During the disco party. Snow-white serial killer, staring me down. And this time . . . I faced it. I didn't get scared. And I could feel the star-ball respond to that, like it was powering up."

"Hmm." Rachael turns away from the door and looks at me. "Maybe that's the key. That's how you get the rescue beacon to switch on."

"You think?"

"Yeah. Makes total sense. When you can confront that scary

vision of your past life or whatever, then it proves you're ready." She comes closer and reaches out with one hand. "Okay. Let's do it."

"What, now?"

"Yeah. I want to be here to see this." She grins.

I swallow and shiver for a moment, then I clasp her hand and concentrate. Probably better to do this before I lose my nerve, right?

I remember Marrant and his bottomless dark eyes, and the exploding spaceship, and that curdled blob of helplessness inside me. And I catch sight of him again, striding across the road with his death-cannon raised. The icy feeling grows from my core outward, and I clench my free hand into a fist.

Then . . . I start to shake. I can actually see the dark tendrils gathering inside that gun barrel. Pure concentrated death. My heart pounds so loud I can't even think straight. I couldn't even help Rachael feel safe at Clinton High. How could I possibly be ready to face Marrant?

"I can't," I choke out. "I can't. I . . . I just can't."

*

"Okay," Rachael says. "Doesn't have to be today, right? But I know you got this. Just think of disco and glitter and the look in Monday Barker's eyes when he tried so damn hard not to notice us in all our finery."

She squeezes my hand tighter. I look down at the ridiculous skirt I'm still wearing. And I focus on the person I am in those visions—the person who can see justice coming, even on the brink of death. That's who I've always wanted to be.

I'm ready. I know I can do this.

I growl in my throat, and feel a sympathetic thrumming from the top of my rib cage.

The parking lot and the strip-club billboard melt away, and I'm once again standing on top of a spaceship, and my free hand is cupped around a warning that we're about to blow up. The stars whirl around so fast that I get dizzy, and Marrant is aiming his weapon at point-blank range.

But I can still feel Rachael's hand wrapped around mine.

I gather myself together, step forward, and smile.

I can't see what happens next, because a white light floods my eyes, so bright it burns.

Rachael squeezes my hand tighter and says, "Holy bloody hell."

A million stars flow out of me, inside a globe the size of a tennis ball. I can only stand to look at them through my fingers, all of these red and blue and yellow lights whirling around, with clouds of gas and comets and pulsars.

Way more stars than I've ever seen in the sky.

All of my senses feel extra sharp: the burnt-tire smell of the coffee, the whoosh of traffic going past, the jangle of classic rock from inside the café, the tiny rocks under my feet.

Everybody inside the coffee shop is staring and yelling. I catch Turtle's eye, and they look freaked out. Rachael has her phone out and is taking as many pictures as she can.

As soon as the ball leaves my body, it gets bigger, until I can see more of the individual stars. So many tiny hearts of light, I can't even count. The sphere expands until I'm surrounded. Stars overhead, stars underfoot. This parking lot has become a planetarium.

I can't help laughing, yelling, swirling my hands through the star-trails. Feels like I've been waiting forever to bathe in this stardust.

4

Then I'm just standing there, in the parking lot, with stars whirling around me. Bette and Turtle come back outside to stare and jump and run their fingers through my cosmic blob. Everyone is shouting questions and pointing their phones at me, and cars on the highway slow down and honk. I probably should have waited to do this indoors, or at least someplace more private.

"We better get out of here," Rachael whispers, then heads back to her car.

I give Bette and Turtle an apologetic shrug, and run after Rachael.

As soon as I get in the passenger seat and Rachael puts her car in gear, we spot the crucial flaw in her plan. The whole windshield is peppered with tiny lights—too bright for her to see the road.

"Oh, damn," she says. "Any chance you can turn down your light show?"

I try covering myself with a blanket from Rachael's back seat, but it does nothing to keep the star-map from surrounding my body.

"Sorry. I don't know how long this is going to keep up. Or even what happens now."

Rachael backs out of the gravel parking lot, because we're starting to attract a crowd here, and she inches out the back exit, onto the single-lane side road. She keeps pausing and cursing, then gliding forward again. We take ten minutes to go a few blocks.

"They did *not* cover this in driver's ed." Rachael squints at the road through the veil of stars.

My phone rings. It's my mom.

"I'm baking a cake," she says, before I can even speak.

"What?" I sputter.

"I've been saving that box of double chocolate sponge cake mix. The one at the back of the bottom cupboard, remember? I dreaded this day so much, and then I figured when the murderous aliens showed up, at least we could have cake. And years went by, and I stopped thinking of it as Murderous Alien Day, and started thinking of it as Cake Day."

"Are you sure that cake mix is still okay to eat—" I start to say, but then I focus on what's important here. "So you already know. The beacon."

"You went viral, sweetie." She sighs. "I just got a dozen messages in five minutes. So . . . I guess this is it."

"Yeah." I close my eyes, partly because the star-glare hurts to look at.

We're still driving extra slow on the one-lane road, except now people have spotted us and are running alongside, taking pictures of the car wrapped in a star-globe.

"Just please, remember what I told you. Run. Don't stop running for anything."

"I will. I need to go. Love you." I hang up before she can say anything else.

*

Rachael pulls off the road into a quiet spot between a tall wooden fence and a tiny community garden, where we can watch the light show without anyone messing with us. "It's real," she whispers.

"It's real, and you did it, and all of this beauty came out of you. I can't even believe it."

"Yeah."

I feel like I've always had a knot inside me, made out of pure concentrated if-only, and now it's gone, and I suddenly have all this extra space to fill. With what, I don't know.

We just sit there, watching the lights fade slowly. This one blue-green dot glows brighter than everything else, and I'm guessing that's Earth. And there are two different red blips, arcing toward the blue dot from opposite directions. Spaceships? I feel another chill go right through me, along with a wave of seasickness.

I guess we're about to make some new friends.

"You should get as far away from me as you can," I say to Rachael. "I don't want you to become collateral damage."

She's gone silent again. I don't know what kind this is.

So I just keep talking, staring at the planters full of sunflowers and tomatoes. "I wish those jerkrags hadn't driven you away from high school. I wish I could have done more to help. I know we've been in touch the whole time, but I don't know what I would have done if you hadn't been here today. But now . . . I have to do this alone."

Rachael looks at the dying embers of my star-map, then looks me in the face. "I just want to see how this turns out."

"Yeah, I get that. But . . ." I start to say that it's too dangerous.

And that's when the community garden bursts into flames.

I catch a glimpse of someone holding a big weapon like the one Marrant aimed at me in my visions. All I have time to register is: really bulky, built like a linebacker and then some. Matte black armor, with a red stripe going diagonally halfway down the chest. And a face like a human skull, grinning at us.

31

5

Rachael throws her car into reverse and backs up so fast her tires churn up the dirt of this turnaround. A second later, we're speeding away from the alien.

"Oh god oh god oh god it's started already." My breathing sputters, like I just ran a dozen sudden-death sprints. I was sure those spaceships hadn't even arrived yet, but this alien must have been hiding on Earth, waiting for my beacon to go off.

Rachael is talking to herself in a low voice, the same way she always used to whenever people hassled her at school. She swerves around a pickup truck. Her eyes bug out a little.

I need to take her mind off the skull-faced alien trying to kill us. "Rachael, what's your favorite comic these days?"

"What?" she swerves around another car.

"Just curious. What comics do you like?"

"Uh, that's a really weird question at this particular moment. I don't know. *Kim & Kim? Squirrel Girl* or *Ms. Marvel,* maybe? *Mooncakes? Lumberjanes?* Depends on the day."

Something blows up behind us—loud enough that my ears hurt. The very air seems to split in half.

The alien is still shooting their high-tech flamethrower at us, but we're actually getting away. For now.

"You should drop me off," I say to Rachael. "Get as far away from this mess as you can."

"You flunked driver's ed, and you don't even have a car." She's heading for the bypass highway.

We speed along the highway, going as fast as we can without getting pulled over. I keep Rachael talking about comics, so she can keep calm for us both. She explains to me about forced perspective: how the panel around each drawing can be a window, but also a frame.

I don't understand why Rachael won't just drop me off and let me handle this on my own. I used to see her huddling under a table in the empty high school library with a stack of books, rather than face the bullies. But as soon as a big *Fortnite*-looking creep with a skull face is chasing after us, she refuses to bail.

Billboards whiz past: empty promises on stilts. No sign of the alien chasing us, but I know they're still coming.

My phone lights up with a text from my mom: "Wish I could have been there to see it. I meant it when I said I'd always be proud of you. No matter what."

Then another Mom text: "Listen, they told me your beacon was designed to be tracked from SPACE. Maybe not so accurate up close. Try to find someplace with lots of walls and insulation. Someplace with no innocent people who could get hurt. I love you. STAY ALIVE!!!!"

I tell Rachael what my mom just said. She nods and smiles. "Maury's?"

"OMG yes. Maury's. We're not far."

A few minutes later, we swerve off the bypass highway onto a cracked tarmac road that makes the Dodge's suspension wobble. A big sign reads:

MAURY'S PAINTBALL AND MINIATURE GOLF FUNDERLAND
* * * TRY OUR HOT WINGS * * *

There's a padlocked chain on the gate, but kids have been sneaking in here ever since the place shut down.

*

Rachael and I slip through the hole in the fence and find the jimmied service entrance that leads inside the squat cement paintball palace. The top of the mini golf course's windmill peeks over the side of the building.

My knapsack buzzes: my mom again. I can't risk the flamethrower-packing monster hearing my phone, so I turn it off, and Rachael does the same with hers.

I hear heavy footsteps. Thump thump THUMP. A ways off, but getting closer.

Then I follow Rachael inside the paintball building, where it's too dark to see anything.

When my eyes adjust, I'm looking at a metal cutout of a woman holding a baby, next to another cutout of a man in combat fatigues. Targets. Nearby, there are metal barrels, artfully ruined sections of brick wall, and ladders to an upper level. Off to one side is a maze of metal walls, and over on the other side is a fake apartment building.

We find a ladder that leads to a crawlspace, which Rachael is pretty sure comes out in the upper floor of the fake apartment building.

We make it halfway across the dusty gloom of the crawl space. And then the whole building shakes, and the late-afternoon sun comes filtering through a brand-new hole in the wall behind us. The monster has arrived.

*

We move away from the splash of light from the new hole in the wall, until I can barely see Rachael's outline. The two of us shuffle forward, over splinters and discarded paintball gear, until we reach the back of the crawlspace.

A voice comes from underneath us. "She's here somewhere, but I can't get an accurate fix. We could just burn the whole place down."

A second, more guttural voice answers. "No. She might have useful information. Marrant believes she knew something about the location of the Talgan stone. Our orders were precise: take her alive for interrogation if possible, but under no circumstances do we let her fall into the enemy's hands."

"Best hurry, then. They'll be here soon."

At the mention of "interrogation"—which probably means torture, right?—Rachael reaches out and squeezes my hand. I squeeze back.

Through a gap between floorboards, I catch sight of the second alien: big powerful shoulders covered with curved spikes that look razor-sharp.

We slip through the trapdoor that leads to the top of the fake apartment building, which has another few metal silhouettes of people. I try to keep Rachael behind me, so I can shield her with my body. It's my fault she's in this mess.

My leg connects with an old paintball canister, and it clatters across the floor.

"What was that?"

The low, guttural voice answers. "I'll check it out."

The thumping footsteps come up the staircase, and a beam of light shines upward from below. Rachael freezes, shrinking into the darkness.

In the beam from the creature's high-tech flashlight, I catch a glimpse of a skull that seems to float in midair. The skull's eyeballs swivel in their sockets . . . and they see us. The light hits me right in the face, so I can't see a thing, but I hear the raspy grunts as the bulky figure lunges toward us.

Damn. I scuttle back the way I came, but Rachael pulls at my arm. She's found another ladder that leads in a different direction.

Skull-Face is still coming. I grope in the darkness and my hand closes around something: a discarded paintball gun.

I fumble with the gun for a moment, then shoot Skull-Face, right between the eyes. Doesn't slow them down at all.

Rachael's already gotten down the ladder, and I slide down after her like a firefighter. We're in a maze of corrugated metal that rattles as we move. Skull-Face is right behind us.

We put a few turns between the aliens and ourselves, and then we're in total darkness again. I trip over a pile of sandbags and barely catch myself. The heavy grinding footsteps are right behind us, and I keep glimpsing the light, which is now glowing green and yellow and red, like some kind of hologram.

"The Royal Fleet shouldn't have hidden you here among these lesser humanoids. Their influence has made you weak," Skull-Face says in a conversational tone. "You were a formidable warrior once, and now look at you. It's not your fault."

Rachael leads me through a fire door that swings open with a telltale squeak, and we're behind the castle in the miniature golf course. The castle's "moat" is dry, so we creep under the drawbridge.

The castle bursts into flames with a supersonic boom.

"We're out of time," the guttural voice says. "I'm exercising the kill option."

The fire spreads to the windmill. Smoke flows over us, rank with the odor of burning wood and plastic.

Another boom, this one off in the distance. Rachael and I crawl as far under the shelter of the drawbridge as we can, nestling amid scum and lost golf balls.

"They found us!" the spiky alien shouts. "I'll hold them off, you finish the—"

A high-pitched whistle cuts through the air, and the spiky alien's voice stops in mid-sentence.

The drawbridge lifts away from Rachael and me, with a splintering, rending sound, leaving us exposed to the smoky air.

Standing over us, silhouetted by flames, is Skull-Face: eyes scowling, exposed cheekbones making deep shadows.

"In the name of the Compassion, I consign you to death." That voice sounds even hoarser with all the smoke. A wizened gray tongue darts out of the lipless mouth.

I raise my fist and lunge forward, out of the moat. And I roar: "Leave. My friend. Alone!"

My fist connects with a bony cheekbone. I only manage to scrape my knuckles, and then I fall backward into the dried-out moat. My assault caught this creature off guard for a second, but then the gun is aimed at us once again.

My eyes are blighted with dark smoke and I can barely breathe, and I try to take in enough air to give one last shout of defiance. This grim reaper raises their giant weapon and aims right at my face.

Another explosion shreds my eardrums, followed by a horrible burnt-pork-chop smell.

Skull-Face falls to his knees, then topples over sideways.

Another shadow appears in the middle of the smoke, and someone leans over Rachael and me. A bright yellow hand, streaked with blue, reaches out to us.

"It's okay. You're safe now."

I look up and see a bald head, colored the same canary yellow as their hand, covered with sky-blue zebra stripes. Studs, or bone spurs, come out of the top of their head and go all the way down the back of their neck.

"My name is Yatto the Monntha, and my pronoun is *they*."

Their eyes, reflecting the glare of the firelight, have a kind expression. And they're wearing the same cranberry-colored two-piece uniform I wore in my visions of my past life, with a round emblem on the left shoulder with a picture of a winged serpent.

I reach up and clasp their hand, and they pull me up out of the foul moat.

"I'm a junior visioner with the HMSS *Indomitable*," they say to me, "and I'm here to bring you home."

Their strong hand is still wrapped around mine, and they smile at me like we're already friends. I still feel light-headed. Joy and relief flood through me, almost too much for one body to contain.

6

Yatto the Monntha leads Rachael and me away from the miniature golf course, which by now is entirely on fire, and finds a clearing in the forest. "We should hurry, because those two were just the advance team. Your beacon is still transmitting—so as long as you're still on Earth, the Compassion will keep sending soldiers after you."

"The what now?" Rachael says.

"The Compassion." Yatto wrinkles their brow. "Their name sounds friendly, but they follow an ideology of total genocide and subjugation."

"So it's 'compassion,' as in 'putting you out of your misery,'" I say.

"More or less." Yatto pushes a button on their sleeve, and a glowing platform appears right in front of us. Just a circle, made of some kind of metal, surrounded by scorch marks in the rocky ground. "This will take us back to the ship. Please step on."

Rachael keeps looking at Yatto and the metal circle. For once it's easy to tell what kind of silence this is, because the longing on her face is lit up like the miniature golf course on fire.

I have this urge to say, "Why don't you come with us," but I know that's ridiculous. I've already put her in way too much danger.

So I just say, "I'm going to miss you so much."

Rachael swallows. "I'm really happy for you." A tear glistens on her cheek. She seems like she's about to say something else, but then she goes quiet again.

"Wait." Yatto the Monntha runs their wrist over Rachael's body, then looks at a holographic cloud in the palm of their hand. "You need to come with us too. You were exposed to the radiation from the rescue beacon, and the Compassion might go after you by mistake. I can't remove the radiation here, but we can do it easily on the ship."

Rachael hesitates for a moment, then nods and steps onto the platform next to me.

Yatto presses another sleeve stud just as two more large aliens with skull faces, wearing the same red-streaked black armor, come charging out of the forest. I open my mouth to say something, I don't know what—and then the three of us are a hundred feet in the air.

*

As we shoot upward, the world gets bigger and wider, and somehow I feel bigger too.

The town where I've lived my whole life shrinks until every landmark smushes together: the tech campus, the fancy mall, and oh yeah, the flames spreading from the mini golf course to the paintball center. As these things shrink away, all my weirdest dreams start to seem possible.

"Don't lean too far over the edge," Yatto says. "This is an orbital funnel. Like a space elevator—except much faster, thanks to gravity-lensing. We'll only take a couple of hours, Earth time, to reach our ship in orbit."

Rachael sits down and hugs herself, taking short, shallow breaths. I pull myself down into a sitting position too, because it feels safer with no railing. Now Yatto towers over both of us, more than ever.

I turn my phone back on, and there are a million texts from my mom, mostly asking if I'm still alive. I call her and she picks up immediately. I blurt out, "Mom, I'm okay. They came after us, but we got away, and we got rescued, and now we're on our way up to their ship."

Rachael's talking on her phone too. We're both down to one notch of signal, almost out of range.

My mom is saying something in a crinkly voice that sounds like, "I'll always love . . . *szfizzs* . . . just remember, you don't need a spaceship to be—"

"I love you, Mom."

Then I realize the call dropped. My phone has zero signal. Even roaming, gone.

Rachael stares at her phone, shivering and wide-eyed. She sobs without making a sound, and I'm sniffling into my sleeve too.

The ground is a blur of colors. I'm probably never going to see my mom again. Plus I keep imagining this platform losing whatever holds it up, and us plummeting tens of thousands of feet. Every time I look down, I breathe fast and shallow again.

"Can I hug you?" Rachael whispers. I nod, and then she and I are wrapped in each other, both of us shaking and letting out gouts of tears.

Yatto kneels and touches my foot with one giant yellow-and-blue hand. "I know how hard this must be. I had to leave my family behind when I was very young. But soon you'll reclaim your true identity, and you'll understand why this was all necessary."

I look into their big fish/owl eyes, and my anxiety drains away. "I've waited so long to find out. Who am I a clone of, anyway? And what happened to her?"

Yatto straightens up and puts two middle fingers and a thumb to their chest, like a salute. "You are Captain Thaoh Argentian. You were one of my heroes, growing up, and you were one of the reasons

I wanted to join the Royal Fleet. You helped save millions of lives and safeguard the peace on countless worlds. And then . . . you died."

"How did she die?" says Rachael, still hugging me with one arm. She turns her gaze to me, like she's trying to see the shadow of the person Yatto's talking about.

"There was a vicious battle against the Compassion. She sacrificed her life to save her crew." Yatto shakes their head, and a single trail of bright silver liquid trickles down their face. "Captain Argentian's crew barely had time to put her mind into a brand-new body, and then they hid you on this primitive planet." They pause again, looking at the stars.

"But," I say, "if they put her mind into my body, why don't I know about any of this?"

"A newborn baby cannot handle all of the memories of a fully grown adult," Yatto says. "But now that your brain has reached maturity, all your memories of your previous life can be unlocked."

I think back to the woman I glimpsed in those visions—the one who stood up to that murderous creep, Marrant, and didn't lose her faith in a better future. And how *right* it felt to be in her fizzy purple skin.

A part of me has always known that I was meant to rejoin this fight.

"The Compassion has a barb-class warship in orbit right now, with superior weapons and maneuvering capacity. The *Indomitable* had a nasty skirmish with them right before I left," Yatto says.

"So . . . the people who just tried to kill us on the ground will also be trying to kill us when we get to space?" Rachael says.

Yatto nods. "Don't worry, though. We scored a critical hit on their engines and also disabled their main weapons. Their ship, the *Cleansing Fire,* is dead in space for now. Unfortunately, the *Indomitable* was also severely damaged. We were lucky that so much debris surrounds this planet for us to hide inside while we complete emergency repairs."

I'm still thinking about what Yatto said a moment ago. Soon, I won't just understand what all of this has been about, I'll actually know everything my previous self used to know. Everything will make sense at last. I'll understand how to fight for people who have nobody else.

All of a sudden, this platform feels like it's moving way too slow.

*

The Earth is a scar of light against an unforgiving blackness. Somehow there's plenty of oxygen, even though we left the atmosphere behind already. I'm in space! I'm not in school flunking a trig test, or getting shoved by Lauren Bose and her friends. I'm in freaking space. I can see the curve of the Earth. THE CURVE OF THE EARTH.

I only flew in an airplane one time, when my mom went to Vegas for some dental-hygiene continuing-education thing, and she brought me along. I had the window seat on the way to Vegas, and I remember watching the landscape turn abstract. But it didn't feel real, sitting inside a sturdy metal beast where everyone else was watching a Seth Rogen movie on their tiny screens.

We're already way higher up, and there are no walls and no screens, and every time I look down I have another jolt of panic. I think Rachael must be terrified, but when I glance at her, she's grinning from ear to ear.

"You're the first friendly alien I've ever met," Rachael says to Yatto. "And you're *amazing.* I mean, you're beautiful."

"I know that I am." Yatto does something that makes all the big studs on their back ripple under their uniform.

Rachael laughs. "But I still don't know anything about you. Like, who are you?"

"I'm Yatto the Monntha."

"So is Monntha the planet you come from?" Rachael's voice vibrates with giddiness. She has the same gleam in her eye that she used to have when she hid out and drew comics in the library at school.

"No." They sit down facing the two of us, cross-legged, so their huge shoulders block the sun coming out from behind the Earth. Their yellow-and-blue face is wide open and friendly in the starlight. "I'm from the planet Irriyaia. The Monnthas are my, uh, nation. My people. We used to be the strongest fighters and greatest builders on all of Irriyaia, until we lost everything in a natural disaster. Now the Monnthas go around begging other nations for food and a place to live."

"I'm sorry," I say.

Yatto raises and lowers their immense shoulders in a fluid motion. "I grew up ashamed of being a Monntha. And then when I was still very young, I found a way to redeem myself and the names of all my people."

"By joining the, uh . . ." Rachael looks at the winged-snake emblem on their left shoulder, which reads THE ROYAL FLEET on top, and WE GOT YOUR BACK on the bottom. "The Royal Fleet?"

Yatto smiles and shakes their head. "No. The Fleet came later." They look at their palm readout, and nod. "We're almost back at the ship. You should see it in a moment."

*

The HMSS *Indomitable* is the most beautiful sight I've ever beheld: curved lines, streaks of light flooding from hundreds of ports, a skin made out of some kind of burnished metal that's survived a million dents and asteroid impacts. The *Indomitable* looks like a silver beetle, with a long, sleek body, and a row of "legs" with glowing orbs instead of feet. The beetle's "head" is a huge globe, sparking with energy, with a bright blue circle at its center.

I can't believe something this epic has anything to do with me.

Our tiny platform seems to rise to meet the starship in a steady arc, like a boat moving closer to a dock. Then my perspective shifts, and it looks like we're racing toward the ship at a billion miles per hour, and we're going to crash. *We're going to crash! We're going to—*

The platform glides inside the ship. The next thing I know, we're rising up into a hangar, about the same size as Clinton High's basketball court. Next to Rachael and me, Yatto stands at attention.

Around forty people stand facing us in that hangar, all of them wearing the same dark red uniform as Yatto, with the same flying-snake emblem. They all have two arms and two legs, but they stand anywhere from three feet to eight feet tall. And their faces all look different—one person in the front has a face covered with wriggling worms.

They all stand there, in rows, waiting. And the moment I stumble off the orbital funnel, each of them raises a thumb and two middle fingers to their collarbone. A salute. Then everyone stomps on the floor, in unison, so loud the entire hangar echoes. They stomp again, and then a third time. It's deafening. A rock star greeting.

I look at some of the alien faces closest to me, and they're drenched with tears, of various hues and degrees of luminescence.

"Welcome back, Captain," Yatto says in my ear.

Captain Argentian's personal datajournal, 17.07.12.05 of the Age of Realization

Oof. Remember how I said that distress call was probably a trap?

I hate being always right. It's my curse.

That "freighter in distress" turned out to be a Kraelyor battle-slicer, and they threw off their disguise as soon as we were within weapons range. Soon we were up to our necks in immobilizer claws and medium-intensity pulse-cannon fire. The only advantage we had was the Kraelyors wanted our ship in one piece.

The Kraelyors were taunting and yelling and calling us "Symmetrons." And I get it. I really do. They've been treated like second-class citizens in this galaxy forever. But they were also getting on my last nerve, and I wasn't going to let them take my ship.

Thing is, this wasn't exactly the first trap I'd sailed into. Or the twentieth, for that matter.

And what the Kraelyors didn't realize was that I'd just saved the Bnobnobian Federacy from a whole Ratsnech swarm, and the Bnobnobians had been *very* grateful. So grateful, in fact, that they gave me a present: one of those displacers that all the gun smugglers have been using to get past our scans lately. Or as I like to call it, my shiny new toy.

The Kraelyors ended up wasting most of their resources attacking where the *Inquisitive* wasn't, and we were able to set a trap for *them*. We handed them over to their own people. And then I sent a strongly worded message to the

Firmament, asking: Where in the thousand flaming lakes is all the assistance we promised to the Kraelyo Homeglobe?

Sometimes I love my job.

7

glance at Rachael, to make sure she's okay with being surrounded by bizarre creatures who are all stomping and carrying on. She's . . . not good with crowds, usually, even crowds of humans. And we just went through a nose-bleeding journey from Earth— right after confronting evil aliens and Monday Barker.

But her eyes are open wide, and she stares at everything like she wants to memorize all of it. "This is the greatest moment of my entire life," Rachael breathes. One of her hands moves around in front of her, like she's sketching with her mind.

Then I see the skull-faced monster who attacked on Earth marching toward us. Or at least, it's the same face. Same bony plates arranged around bulging eyeballs, same nose-hole and grinning jaws.

I back away and search for a place to hide—until I realize that *this* walking skeleton is wearing a Royal Fleet uniform, with tons of bling on the left sleeve and some kind of poem covering the right. And Yatto is saluting them.

"I'm Captain Panash Othaar, and my pronoun is *he*," the skeleton says to me. "I'm glad we retrieved you safely." I can't help flinching when the captain's bony face comes close to mine.

Yatto steps forward and says, "Happy reunions and short absences, Captain. This is Rachael Townsend. She had to accompany us because she was bathed in radiation from the beacon." Yatto gestures at Rachael. "She'll need to be decontaminated, and then she can go home. Also, Tina's rescue beacon is still transmitting on low power, but we can deactivate it right away."

"So ordered," the captain grunts, and Yatto gets to work.

A moment later, another blue bubble floats out of my chest, and then fades away. Yatto runs a tiny wand over Rachael and tells her that it might take a while for the radiation to clear from her body, and then she can go home.

Captain Othaar smiles at Rachael. "You're welcome on my ship, Rachael Townsend. Please let me know if you need anything."

"Thanks." Rachael smiles, but with a trace of tension behind it. "Actually, there is something. I . . . need to be by myself for a while. This happens sometimes, when I'm around lots of people I don't know. Is there someplace I can just sit on my own?"

Othaar nods, and turns to the worm-faced alien who was just having a fangasm. "Uiuiuiui. Could you escort our guest to one of the empty crew quarters?" The worm-face nods and salutes, then gestures for Rachael to come with.

"I'll see you soon. I can't wait to see how this turns out." Then Rachael turns to follow Uiuiuiui.

Yatto also leaves us, to return to their post. So now it's just me and the captain in this big empty hangar. I'm trying to get used to that endless grimace, and the bony plates moving around on his face. And oh yeah—the way he looks exactly like the monster that was trying to kill me a couple hours ago.

"I'm overjoyed at the prospect of having my old friend Thaoh Argentian back from the dead, but I'm afraid . . . you're probably too late." Captain Othaar's eyes tighten with pain, behind the thick surface of his face, and his voice sounds heavy. "This ship has taken a beating one too many times, and we only have half the number of personnel we're supposed to have. We're falling apart, just like most of the other long-range ships in the Royal Fleet."

As he speaks, I look around at the cargo hangar—which I can see clearly, now that the rest of the crew have cleared out. And yeah . . . it's easy to tell, this ship is trashed. The dark-gray metal walls are scuffed and covered with little dents, and everything has a layer of scummy grease. I don't know what I was expecting exactly, but I definitely wasn't planning on coming aboard a broken-down deathtrap.

"What happened?" I ask.

"War," Captain Othaar says. "We've been losing for a long time, ever since Thaoh Argentian died. That last battle nearly finished the *Indomitable* once and for all."

My stomach lurches downward and all of the sugar-spiked adrenaline that was flooding through me a little while ago washes away. Captain Othaar slouches a little as he leads me up a ramp leading out of the cargo hangar and shows me the wreck of his ship.

*

Now that I've started seeing how messed up this ship is, I can't stop seeing broken stuff. I can tell it's all been put back together with the high-tech version of duct tape and chewing gum. Everyone who salutes as we pass in the hallway has the same look in their eyes. Like they're burned out, after having been terrified so long.

Now I know why they cheered and wept when I showed up. They were desperate, clutching at anything that might save them. But like Captain Othaar said, I'm probably way too late.

Every few yards we pass another repair crew trying to patch up all the damage this ship just suffered in its most recent battle—with the Compassion ship that's still out there somewhere, doing its own repairs, the *Cleansing Fire*.

Captain Othaar tells me the Royal Fleet used to be unstoppable, because it had these huge broadsword-class starships that could kick anyone's ass. "They're basically flying fortresses."

"So what happened to them?" I ask.

"Nothing. They're still unbeatable. But about twenty Earth years ago, a scientist came up with a new type of spaceweave, which lets us travel across the galaxy twice as fast as before, but it only works for smaller ships. Like the ones the Compassion has plenty of. So whenever there's a fight, the broadswords always show up too late to make any difference. And dagger-class ships like the *Indomitable* are on our own." He gestures around us.

We must be getting close to Sickbay, where I guess the ship's doctor is going to stick a toilet plunger in my head and unblock my memories of being Captain Argentian. I can't even imagine how I'll feel half an hour from now. My whole future is just a big blank. Am I even still going to be me, after this happens?

Somehow Captain Othaar notices that I'm tensing up, and he smiles down at me. "Don't worry. The procedure is pretty simple. And you'll still have all your own memories afterward. You'll just be . . . more."

I take a deep breath, and remember all those months of waiting for this day. Claiming my legacy, becoming the person I was meant to be. I reach for the stillpoint of yearning—of hope—at the center of the fear tornado.

"That's what I want. I want to be more than I am now," I say.

We've reached a dark metal door, with a label that says, "Sickbay Exam Room." (How can I read alien writing?) Othaar sweeps a hand next to the door.

A voice says, "Come on in."

*

The exam room is pretty small, with just a couple of high benches along two walls, one teacup-shaped chair, and a workstation. I guess the beds with all the injured people are next door.

Inside sits a pale-skinned alien, about my height, with a single huge eye, which wraps all the way around, so this creature can see in all directions. I can see my reflection in this ginormous eye, and I'm once again fighting my "squick" instinct.

"Medical Officer," says Captain Othaar. "Great hopes and small mercies."

"Brave deeds and kind cautions," responds the weird cyclops, who turns to me. "You must be Captain Argen—er, I mean, Tina. My name is Dr. Karrast and my pronoun is *she*. I'm the ship's medical officer." Dr. Karrast hunches over a holographic computer readout, so that her neck and back have a dozen folds of dry gray-white skin. "Well, whoever did your DNA-masking was good at their job. You look human at first glance, even on the cellular level."

"Uh, thanks," I say.

She keeps staring at her blob of data. "Might need to fix that later. But for now, I'm just going to be restoring your buried memories of your previous existence."

This is really happening.

My foolish heart opens up all the way, as if it had never been constricted by a hundred kinds of scar tissue.

Some wild creature is rising up inside me, something huge and totally unchained.

I bounce up and down and bump into a medical instrument that's shaped like a metal thistle, and it burbles in response.

"Hold still," Dr. Karrast says, in a gentle deep voice. She places a glowing doily on my head, plus little nodules all over my arms, legs, and stomach. "You might experience some pain and disorientation. But you're perfectly safe, and everything is under—"

Everything goes bright orange and my head feels like it's about to crack open. I taste chocolate and dirt and bitter lemon. My stomach surges, just as my head breaks into a million pieces, and the last thing I see is a speck of darkness at the center of an ocean of blaring whiteness.

*

And then . . . I wake up. Dr. Karrast is looking down at me, clucking at all of the readings in the holographic blobstorm over my head.

"Well?" Captain Othaar says from the doorway. This tiny room feels more and more claustrophobic.

"Looks like a tremendous success," Dr. Karrast says. "All neural blocks removed. Should be good to go."

I try to sit up, but then I gasp at the pain in my neck and shoulders, which in turn sets off white-hot spasms in my head.

"So? When does it start working? When do I get all the memories back?"

Karrast and Othaar look at each other, like *Uh-oh.*

"You still don't remember any of it?" Dr. Karrast pleads. "Your whole life—being Captain Argentian?"

"Look at me, please." Captain Othaar sounds like he's about

to cry out of some hidden opening on that skull face. "You don't remember our friendship? Not even a tinge of recognition? That voyage we took into the maelstrom at the center of the Dragon's Nest? The time I was your second in your duel with the Petal of Death? You must remember something."

I concentrate as hard as I can, search my mind. "No. I'm sorry. I don't remember anything new. Sorry. Maybe it just takes a little while?"

"Oh." Dr. Karrast covers her giant eye with both hands, and sits in her teacup chair, hunched over with sorrow. "Oh dear. This is bad. This is really bad."

Captain Othaar punches the doorframe so hard I hear the metal crack. "Shouldn't have gotten my hopes up."

Then he waves the door open and walks away, without looking back.

I sit there staring at Dr. Karrast, who's still bent double.

My full-body ache slowly fades enough for me to feel a much deeper misery.

8

I just sit there and stare down at my camo pants and Chuck Taylors, which are still covered with muck and ash from Maury's Funderland. My hands have dirt under the fingernails too. Everything is yuck. The stale air in here is making me nauseous, and my head still feels like it has a giant spike stuck through it.

Most of all, I feel so exhausted, along with the kind of empty that comes from hope draining away. Just a giant black void at the center of me.

I would have given damn near anything to be the person Captain Othaar talks about. The woman who fought duels and sailed into a dragon's whirlpool and, way more important, inspired people. Ever since I was thirteen and my mom told me my father wasn't actually some orthodontist she met at a dental convention—because really I had no father—I've been eating and sweating and breathing a dream that I never even had a name for.

At some point, I'm going to haul myself off this bench and find Rachael, and tell her that my whole existence is just a big joke.

She'll probably feel really bad for me, and that'll only make me want to scream myself even hoarser.

A million curse words crowd my mouth at once, abrasive as tiny grains of broken glass.

I finally look up at Dr. Karrast. Her pale gray skin is breaking out into light blue spots, which is how Oonians show extreme distress. Figures that the Oonians would be kind of a sensitive bunch, since there are only a thousand Oonians at any one time, and they can only have a new baby when one of the thousand dies. Talk about a sheltered upbringing—I mean, try to imagine being raised by 999 helicopter parents.

Whoa. Wait a second.

How do I know that Dr. Karrast is an Oonian? Or what an Oonian is? I've never even met any aliens, before today.

"Uh, Doc," I say in a hoarse voice. "I don't want to bug you. But something weird is going on."

"Are you remembering things from your other life?" The medical officer looks up from her hands, and her eye widens. The blue spots fade.

"Nuh-uh. I don't think so. Not memories, exactly. At least, not apart from the little flashes I had before the beacon lit up, back on Earth."

I search my mind just in case, but nope. I've still never been on a spaceship before.

"But, uh, maybe just to be on the safe side, you ought to try recalibrating your neurolytic scanner to the highest axon resolution? Just to double-check?" Then I let out an involuntary cry of pure WTF. "I mean, I *know* stuff. Like, I know all about your species, and I can hear just from listening to the ship's engines that our secondary impeller is out of whack, and we might blow up at any time, even if the *Cleansing Fire* doesn't shoot us down."

Dr. Karrast is already out of her chair, running the neurolytic scanner across my face, using the setting that I suggested.

"I mean, I know stuff," I say. "I just can't *remember*."

"Uh-huh," Dr. Karrast grunts. "This is interesting. Never seen anything like this."

She hunches her shoulders again. I can't help noticing that these cranberry-colored Royal Fleet uniforms have changed their design in the past seventeen years. Like, the shoulders are looser, to accommodate all the humanoids who are more top-heavy, and the left-sleeve insignia are easier for many different types of eye to read. But they're made of a lighter (cheaper?) fabric. And that flying serpent is actually called the Joyful Wyvern.

Everywhere I look, I see stuff that I know all about, but I have no memories to go with the information. Freaky as hell. Like, I can look at the wall, which was just "space metal" an hour ago, and now I see a reinforced carbonfast alloy. It's like I took off someone else's high-prescription glasses, and now everything is in focus.

But every time I have that spark of recognition of something I've never seen before, it only reminds me: I was supposed to know so much more.

*

"There you are." Rachael pokes her head inside the exam room. "So . . . I guess you must be Captain Argentian. Good to meet you. I've heard a lot about you. Thought you'd be taller. Just kidding. My name's Rachael. But you knew that, right?"

I sigh.

"I'm still just Tina. The memory thing didn't work." I hug myself. "I mean, I *know* stuff now. But I don't *remember* anything new."

I explain it a couple times before it clicks for her.

Rachael cocks her head. "So it's like my cousin Larry. He somehow just *knew* how to roller-skate, even though he didn't remember anyone ever teaching him. He probably had lessons when he was really young, or something. But nobody knows for sure."

"Uh, yeah. Just like Cousin Larry," I say. "This is Dr. Karrast, her pronoun is *she*."

"Good to meet you," Dr. Karrast tells her, then looks at a status update and groans. "I'd better get back to the main sickbay, because I've got a dozen injured crewmembers to check on, and there's only one of me. There was supposed to be a whole medical team on this ship."

Rachael frowns. "Maybe I could help out, while I'm still on board? I don't know a lot of medical stuff, but I'm good with fine motor control and repetitive tasks. And I'm a quick learner."

Dr. Karrast blinks her big eye and cocks her head. "That would be most welcome."

For some reason, I find myself thinking about the box of cake mix my mom saved for this day, and the fact that she'll never even know how this all turned out. I'm still just the same girl she raised single-handed. And then thinking about the probably-still-edible cake makes me realize: I'm starving. I haven't eaten today, except for a few spicy chips from a convenience store, which feels like a million years ago.

"I need to eat," I say to Rachael. "Failing to live up to my destiny gives me a powerful appetite."

"I'll come back soon," Rachael says to Dr. Karrast, who nods.

Rachael follows me out into the hallway, where I know the exact route to take us to the crew lounge and all of its food stores. I can't help staring at everything we walk past, and my head starts to hurt again as I try to make sense of all the information I suddenly have access to. I keep "remembering" a ton of random trivia, only with a ton of gaps and no way to put any of it into a context.

It's just like Cousin Larry, except for a whole spaceship full of creatures and advanced scientific stuff.

We pass a repair crew trying to patch up a busted momentum gravitator, and both crewmembers glance up at me, and then look away in a hurry.

Like, maybe these crewmembers have heard that instead of being the great Captain Argentian, back from the dead, I turned out to be just some useless kid. I'm pretty sure both of these people were stomping and cheering for me not too long ago. Now when I remember that scene, my mind fills in all the stuff I missed before—like, the crewmember with the wormy face, Uiuiuiui, was actually doing the Zanthuron Dance of Rejoicing. And now they just keep their heads down and ignore me.

There's a lump of ice in the spot where my beacon used to live.

*

We reach the crew lounge, which is a small space with a domed ceiling and curved walls, where everyone eats and relaxes in between shifts. There are three tables (two small, one big) and a bunch of teacup-shaped chairs.

Rachael and I sit at the small table at the back. The food is all janked up, but I find a stash of these dried mushrooms that taste kind of like hot dogs.

Yatto comes in and joins us at our table. They've already heard what happened, because news travels fast on this tiny ship.

"It's not your fault that the memory restoration didn't work," Yatto says. "When they cloned Captain Argentian before her death, it was an experimental procedure. It's good that you at least gained some of her knowledge."

"I feel like I know a ton of trivia, with zero context. Dunno how much use that's going to be." I stuff some mushrooms into my mouth.

"Did you just get knowledge?" Rachael asks. "Or did you inherit some skills, as well? I saw the way you handled the food locker just now, like your fingers knew how to operate the mechanism."

Oh, damn. Hadn't even thought of that.

"Huh. Maybe! I guess it would be sweet if I could actually do all the things that Captain Argentian knew how to do, even if I don't remember learning them."

"From what I understand, she was an excellent pilot and strategist, and she scored at the top of the rankings in most forms of combat," Yatto says.

I let that sink in. There's a holographic interface in the wall next to our table, and I stick my hand inside and pull up an update on our (really, really bad) status. I just automatically know how to access the ship's computer, without having to think about it.

"So. I know how to do stuff. Maybe even a lot of stuff. But I still have no clue what I'm doing." I slide the bowl of dried mushrooms over to Rachael. "Try these, they're pretty good."

Rachael tries some and makes a "yuck" face. Yatto takes some too.

"So the mantle of Captain Argentian didn't just get handed to you on a silver platter," Rachael says. "That just means you'll have to work harder to claim it. Whatever made her great, it's still inside you. And you know, it's not like having someone else's memories of being heroic would make you a hero. Being a hero is all about the choices you make, here and now."

I sit and let that sink in. "That's . . . really good advice. I hadn't thought of it like that."

"I read a lot of comics." She smiles.

I don't know what I did to deserve having an amazing friend like Rachael—but no way was it enough. The chunk of ice in my chest thaws a little.

Yatto waves the gadget on their right wrist (which is called a Quant) over Rachael and then looks at the holographic display in their palm. "Good news. All of the radiation has cleared from your body," they say to Rachael. "You can go back to Earth now."

I look at Rachael, and the frozen lump solidifies again.

I try to tell myself that I'm glad she's going to be safe, whatever happens to me on this broken-down old ship. But I just feel weary and gross, bracing myself to be lonesome.

"Okay. Let's go." Rachael shakes her head and climbs out of her teacup chair.

9

I tried so hard to talk Rachael out of dropping out of high school. She had a whole plan to get homeschooled, get her GED, and go to art school. I promised over and over that I would be all the way in her corner if she stayed at Clinton High, but she couldn't stand one more day of people tearing her down.

"No education is worth feeling unsafe all the time," she said, and then she was gone.

I remember the backpack she had back then: bright orange, with a dozen cartoon patches all over it. Every pouch and compartment, stuffed with pens, pencils, brushes, and other art supplies. Every time I got bored or annoyed at school, I at least knew that at the next passing period or lunch recess, Rachael would have some new doodle to show me, with a whole amazing story behind it.

She used to hug that orange backpack to her chest instead of wearing it on her back, so nobody could snag it and toss it into some dog poop. One time she looked at me, eyes gleaming with unshed tears, and said, "What's the point of having something awesome if you have to guard it every second?"

Like that nonstop protective huddle took all of the joy out of having a backpack the color of the morning sun, covered with cute icons and containing all of her drafting tools and her latest creations. And that's why she had to call it quits.

Now Rachael is going to leave me again, except this time it's for the best.

She asks me random questions about everything we walk past—partly to test the limits of my new knowledge, but also because she's curious about everything. "How am I understanding every alien language? What's the deal with Uiuiuiui, the guy with the faceful of worms? What does that box on the wall do?"

I answer every question patiently. "All these uniforms and devices include an all-purpose translator, called the EverySpeak. Umm . . . Uiuiuiui is a Zanthuron, he's from a swamp planet in a binary star system, and those face-tubes are mostly there to attract a mate, but they also help him breathe certain noxious gases. The thing on the wall is a momentum gravitator, it converts the kinetic energy into gravity when the ship stops or changes course."

Rachael keeps slowing us down with more questions . . . until I start to wonder if she's stalling.

We head downward, in concentric circles, until we reach the ramp that leads to the cargo hangar.

"Here we are," Yatto says. "I'll miss you, Rachael Townsend."

A big metal circle slides out of some opening in the carbonfast wall, and Rachael stares at it, but doesn't step on.

"I'll miss you too, Yatto. Hey, you never finished telling me your story. You said you found a way to redeem your family name, but it wasn't by joining the Royal Fleet. What did you do?"

This question seems to embarrass Yatto. "Are you sure that's what you want to know, right before you leave?" Their forehead ridges crease a little. "Very well. I became a performer, when I was younger than you are now. I appeared in light-dramas where I fought against criminals and saved our planet from imaginary dangers. I was always running around with a dark-matter cannon on one shoulder, shouting taunts at the performers who pretended to be my foes."

"You were an *actor*?" Rachael makes an imaginary frame around them with her hands.

Whatever that word gets translated as, it confuses Yatto for a moment. Then they nod.

"And you starred in, basically, action movies? That's amazing."

I can totally picture it. Yatto has a really strong gaze, with those fierce red eyes and the sharp bony ridges on their head. And they would probably be amazing at looking into the camera and saying something badass like, "You messed with the wrong Monntha."

"I had a lot of fun, but then it began to sicken me. We were always glorifying violence and celebrating the past, when my world, Irriyaia, helped rule most of the galaxy. I wanted to make a real difference, instead of just pretending to be a hero. The other Monnthas were furious when I quit, because I was the best thing that had happened to the Monntha nation in forever. I haven't even gone home since."

"I can't believe you were a movie star." I probably couldn't do what Yatto did: walk away from a situation where I was good at my job and everyone loved me. "But I'm glad you followed your heart."

"Even though my heart might get me blown into a million tiny pieces in the very near future." Yatto grins.

"Even though." I turn back to Rachael. "At least whatever happens, you'll be safe back on Earth."

"Yeah. Sure. Right."

Rachael still doesn't step onto the round platform.

"You should leave as soon as possible." Yatto looks at their

Quant's holographic display, in their cupped palms. "It might not be safe to stay on this ship much longer."

Rachael finally comes out and says what she's been stewing on for the past hour.

"What if I don't *want* to go home?"

*

I can't believe Rachael was too scared of some bullies to stay in high school, but now she wants to stay on this ship and risk actual death.

When I think of being left alone on this ship, without anyone to talk to, I get that ice shard where my rescue beacon used to be. I couldn't have gotten this far without Rachael.

But.

If she stays here, she could die.

I already accepted that risk for myself, but Rachael's an innocent bystander. And she belongs at home, in her cozy bedroom with a hundred different colored pens and brushes and pencils spread out around her. Not on a cold, dirty old spaceship with a busted secondary impeller, and an enemy ship lurking out there somewhere.

"Please think about this," I say to her. "Because after this ship leaves Earth, you can't change your mind. I've spent years psyching myself up for this, and I still don't feel ready. Life in space is lonely and scary and boring. It's just like your orange backpack, except you'll have to spend every moment guarding your actual life. Are you really sure this is what you want?"

"Of *course* I'm not sure," Rachael says. "How could I ever be sure about something like this? I only know if go home now, I'll spend the rest of my life wondering and regretting. And missing my best friend."

"Whereas if you go with us, the rest of your life could be exceedingly short," Yatto chimes in. "The razor tongue of death has already tasted the *Indomitable*'s crew many times."

"If something happens to you . . ." I have a sudden vivid image of standing over Rachael's fresh corpse, and the cold lump gets colder. "I couldn't handle it. I dragged you into this situation, and I couldn't forgive myself if you got hurt."

"It's not on you." Rachael's face turns bright red. "If I stay on this ship now, it'll be my choice. Not everything is about you."

"I didn't say that. I just . . . I worry about you."

"I literally just got done supporting you, and telling you that you can still claim the legacy of Captain Argentian. And then you turn around and tell me to just go home." She folds her arms and looks at a spot on the floor behind me.

"No! No. That's not what I meant." Ugh, I'm messing everything up. "It's more like, I want you to have all the things you were always telling me about, like going to art school and publishing a webcomic, and maybe going into animation. Growing up, having a life. You have this amazing future waiting for you back on Earth."

"Yeah. But I'd way rather be the first artist from Earth to go into deep space." Rachael's eyes shine, though she still isn't looking at me. "I want to see everything that's out there. All of the creatures. All of the planets. All of the beautiful things, and the ugly things, and even the scary awful things. All of it. I'm going to see the whole freaking universe, and then I'm going to make the best art ever." She scrunches her fists and closes her eyes. "Yatto, do you remember what I told you about why I'm considered weird, back on Earth?"

Their spiky yellow brow scrunches up. But then, they nod. "Of course."

"My parents are nudists."

Yatto's shoulder spikes ripple, in the universal sign of *Who cares*. "Many of my close relatives haven't worn a single item of clothing since before I was born. They took a vow, to honor those whom we have lost."

"I talk to myself when I get stressed out."

"I do that too," Yatto says. "How else will I hear my own thoughts above all the noise?"

"I'm fat."

Yatto peers down at her. "You're tiny. And I read that the human body evolved to store energy in that way. There are many benefits. Was that incorrect?"

"I'm a total social reject who sits in the corner and draws silly comics and ignores everyone, and sometimes I just can't be around people at all." She half covers her face, like that last one was hard to say.

Yatto puts a giant hand on her shoulder. "You are an artist. There is no greater valor than to create beauty where none existed."

Rachael turns back to me with a determined/victorious expression on her face. "Don't tell me where I belong."

"Okay, okay." I smile at her. "I get it. If you really want to stay on the ship, then I support your decision. Of course I do. I'm sorry I was being a butt."

"You were a total space butt."

"I was an interstellar cosmic super-butt." I can't help cracking up, and then Rachael is laughing too. "But you should talk to Captain Othaar right away about staying on the ship, since it's his decision. I'll come with you. He needs to decide what to do with me, now that I only have half the mind of Captain Argentian."

"Okay." Rachael holds out her hand and I shake it. "Let's go talk to Captain Othaar."

As we walk back up the ramp, relief washes over me, because I don't have to face this alone after all.

But there's also still a thorn of pure anxiety snagging my thoughts—because I picture myself cradling Rachael's dead body, knowing that I could have talked her out of this.

10

keep wanting to scratch and fidget, because my new reddish-brown cadet uniform chafes in some places, and itches in others. Plus it's weird to be wearing a uniform when I'm still officially nobody on this ship. But my clothes were wrecked and this is all they had.

Rachael is still wearing her denim overalls, which look the worse for wear. She seems more subdued as we walk to the control deck (because meeting with the ship's command staff and pleading her case is her number-one most social-anxiety-producing kind of situation). I'm giving her a crash course on how to talk to starship officers in a formal setting, and I don't think I'm exactly helping her to relax.

The control deck has a million holographic displays and a half-dozen teacup-shaped chairs arranged in a neat semicircle. On the other side of a noise-canceling see-through wall, there's Forward Ops: a cluster of seven workstations, ranging from tactical to weapons to flight control.

"Good food and lucky escapes." Captain Othaar greets me with a traditional Royal Fleet blessing.

I respond the way a fellow officer is supposed to: "Strong drinks and unexpected friends. Captain."

Captain Othaar is sitting, surrounded by the three members of his senior staff (plus Dr. Karrast). He introduces the officers, while I fight the urge to itch my armpit.

"This is Alternate Captain Lyzix." Othaar gestures at a sleek Javarah, whose hands and pointy fox face are covered with what looks like fur (but is actually a kind of symbiotic growth). Lyzix salutes, and lets us know her correct pronoun is *she*.

The senior security officer is Vaap (pronoun: *they*), a giant who appears to be made out of shiny rocks (but is actually half-rock, half-organic, and both halves are alive). My brain helpfully supplies a bunch of info about their species, who mate by finding the most perfectly compatible pair of rocks, and then growing organic material inside them. *Thanks, brain.*

And then Acting Senior Engineer Yma is a Zyzyian (small, slimy, blows bubbles all the time). It's a huge insult to use any kind of pronoun to refer to Zyzyians—like, a battle-to-the-death-level insult.

Once they've acknowledged Rachael and me, they go back to talking about the ship's repair status. "We're working as fast as we can," Yma says in a spray of green bubbles. "But for now, we're stuck in orbit for at least a dozen more cycles." (A cycle is about fifty Earth minutes, and there are thirty cycles in a metacycle.)

"We believe we put the *Cleansing Fire* out of action," adds Vaap. "But if they manage to mount an attack, our strategic posture is far from battle-optimal."

Captain Othaar looks at Rachael and me. "Is there anything you can tell us about your interaction with the Compassion's soldiers, down on the planet?"

"Umm. They were pretty busy trying to kill us," I say. "Although . . . they wanted to take me alive, if possible. They kept mentioning something called the . . ." I ransack my memory. This morning feels like a thousand years ago.

"The Talgan stone," Rachael says.

"Yeah. The Talgan stone! They thought I might have a clue where to find it. Or rather, Captain Argentian might."

"If this 'Talgan stone' is something that helps the Compassion become even more powerful . . ." Dr. Karrast closes her one giant eye, and her neck gets a few dark purple streaks.

"We need to find it first." Vaap crushes their fingertips together with a sound of grinding rock. "Junior Visioner Yatto could do a records search."

"So ordered," Captain Othaar says, and Vaap makes a note in the holographic display.

"All I know is, they seemed to think it was super important." I take a deep breath. "They said their head guy needed it for something. That scary serial killer dude. Marrant."

At the mention of that name, everybody in the room freezes. I can actually feel the temperature drop a few degrees.

"So . . . you know who Marrant is." Yma lets out a dark crimson bubble.

"Not really." I search my mind. "I had a scary vision of him before the beacon lit up. Now I know a million weird facts about the wraith-trees of Undhor, but Marrant is still a blank."

"As far as I can tell, Tina has all of Thaoh Argentian's knowledge, except when it's connected to Captain Argentian's own personal memories," says Dr. Karrast.

"So because Thaoh Argentian knew Marrant personally, you don't have access to her knowledge about him," Vaap rumbles. "Including any information about where to find this 'Talgan stone' before the Compassion does. That is . . . inconvenient."

My uniform is feeling hotter and pricklier than ever.

We move on to talking about what Rachael and I can do to make ourselves useful on this ship. "I've already spoken to Rachael about helping out in Sickbay," says Dr. Karrast. "She's highly intelligent and adaptable, and I can tell she'll be a great asset."

Captain Othaar nods. "If she wants to stay, we can give her a battlefield commission as trainee assistant medic."

Rachael beams with happiness, and I try to ignore another zap of anxiety.

"But then there's the clone." Alternate Captain Lyzix stretches out languidly in her teacup, and looks at me. "You know just enough to be dangerous, but perhaps not enough to be trusted with any responsibility. Knowledge without wisdom: there is no deadlier combination in the known universe." Her sharp fur-covered ears move closer to the front of her head.

"We're not even sure how much of Captain Argentian's mind you have," adds Vaap. "We need to test you, when we're not in a life-or-death situation."

My whole skin is breaking out in hives. What are they making these uniforms out of, anyway?

"Permission to speak," I say through gritted teeth.

"Granted," says Captain Othaar.

"I know enough to know that you're in a huge mess. I know the ship's secondary impellers are on the verge of blowing up. I know that the next time the Compassion attacks, you won't be ready, because that tactical station is sitting empty, which means you're not getting full-spectrum threat awareness." I gesture through the transparent wall at an empty chair in front of an idle holographic interface. "This thing I'm standing next to? This is the weapons control station, and you're using it wrong. You'd get more zing out of your plasma cannons if you boosted the variance. Want more? I can do this all day."

"But—" says Lyzix. Her ears are arrowheads aimed at my heart.

"I didn't just activate that rescue beacon out of curiosity, or for the hell of it. I want to save people. I want to bring a big blazing torch to everyone who has given up hope," I say, before she can tear me down again. "I want to do something good with my life. Please. Let me help."

Othaar looks up, with a kind of misty expression, like he caught a glimpse of his old friend for a second there. Lyzix rolls her stunningly beautiful fox eyes, and Vaap seems to have turned to pure stone. Yma lets out an iridescent white bubble that glistens in the air.

"She is correct: we need somebody at that tactical station," Vaap says. "I monitor our status, but another pair of eyes could be essential. We haven't had anyone there since Ona died."

"She's also right about the impellers. We could explode into a plasma cloud at any moment." A huge dark red sphere comes out of the opening atop Yma's head.

"Very well," Captain Othaar says. "Tina, I'm giving you a battlefield commission of acting cadet, and appointing you as junior tactical officer. Keep your eyes down, follow orders, and don't talk back."

"With a will," I say, in an even voice, without shrieking or jumping up and down.

Inside, I'm yelling, *I get to help fly a starship!*

Rachael raises one hand gingerly. "Uh . . . can I say something?"

Captain Othaar nods. "Go ahead."

"So . . . I had an idea." Rachael looks down and mumbles, but everybody still quits staring at the repair status updates on the palms of their hands and listens to her. "I keep hearing that this ship is operating with a skeleton crew. No offense." She says that last part to Captain Othaar, who just shrugs. "And meanwhile, Earth is full of science and math geniuses. There are kids who already have two PhDs by the time they're my age."

I don't like the sound of where this is going. At all. My uniform itches worse than ever.

"So I was thinking," Rachael says. "I mean, we could find some of the smartest nerds, who are still young enough to learn everything. They would jump at the chance to come on board as, like, trainees."

Lyzix stretches out one long-clawed hand at a hologram of Earth. "It's like we're dying of thirst, and there's a lake right in front of us. Regulation 76.3474 does say a Royal Fleet vessel is allowed to recruit trainees from the local civilian population, in cases of extreme duress. Like now. Plus, we won't have a chance to pick up new crewmembers for at least a hundred metacycles."

The biggest, brightest, greenest bubble comes out of the blowhole in the middle of Yma's head. "Tempting. Everyone here is at their breaking point. But we would need to identify the best candidates and then find a way to contact them. That's not a simple undertaking."

"Actually," Lyzix says with a sharp-toothed grin, "I've got a fix for that."

*

According to Lyzix, the Royal Fleet sent a probe to Earth a long time ago, and it's been hiding in orbit ever since.

This was back when the Royal Fleet was still unstoppable. Her Majesty's Firmament wanted to reach out to more primitive worlds, like Earth—but not by talking to any governments, because that never turns out well. Instead, the Longview probe would look for smart young people who could go study at the Glorious Nebula.

So the probe in Earth orbit was designed to adapt to local communications and then figure out a way to test local young people on science and math, but also on their ability to deal with unexpected challenges. Once the probe found some exceptional candidates, the Royal Fleet was supposed to send a ship to come pick them up.

Except that the war started, and the Royal Fleet wasn't able to spare any ships.

"So when it first arrived at your world," Lyzix says, "the probe probably tried using coded electromagnetic transmissions."

"Radio," I say.

"Sure. But by now, it should have upgraded automatically. It'll be using mass media, telecommunications, and so on. So all we have to do is instruct it to pick the best candidates out of the recent bunch, and invite them to join us. Then we send an orbital funnel to their location, which they can step onto, if they choose."

Everybody chews on that for a moment. Then Othaar says, "Thoughts?"

"Our security posture is weak enough already after that last battle," Vaap says. "We shouldn't tempt the Hosts of Misadventure."

"There's no way the invitations could give away our location, because they won't be coming from the ship," says Lyzix. Her ears swivel in opposite directions.

Another random fact pops into my head: Lyzix's symbiotic "fur" feeds on certain nutrients on her skin, and in return, it regulates her natural mating and fighting cycles—as long as the fur remains in one piece, she'll never go into either a mating frenzy or a killing rage.

But that doesn't stop her from having a temper.

"I just want to make sure these kids are prepared for this," I say. This could be my one chance to nip this idea in the bud before we put even more unprepared Earth kids in danger.

"We're asking them to just get on a big metal disc that appears out of nowhere, and get carried up into space. Without anybody else there to keep them company, or reassure them the way Yatto reassured us. And then once they get here, they could get blown to pieces by the *Cleansing Fire*?"

"Basically, yes." Dr. Karrast is getting the neck streaks again.

"We can give them a really good warning," Rachael says, already waiting for me to dump on her parade again. "I'll write it myself. It'll be really clear. Like, this circle will carry you into an adventure beyond your imagination, but don't step on unless you're prepared to leave everything and everyone you've ever known, forever. And there'll be unbelievable danger, but you'll be seeing stuff that nobody else has ever seen. That kind of thing."

Everyone is so eager to get more warm bodies, I'm scared we're about to make a huge mistake. But I don't want to tear down Rachael's idea, especially right after I tried to send her home.

I take a deep breath. "I mean, if Rachael writes something, I'm sure it'll be great."

"You can help write it," she says to me.

"I'll just take whatever you wrote and add lots of exclamation points to it."

Othaar clears his throat, and Yma blows a dark oily bubble.

"Are we about done?" Vaap grumbles. "We have a broken starship to patch up."

"I think it's decided." Lyzix shoots us a sharp grin.

"Very well. So ordered." Captain Othaar waves one hand. "Go write a beautiful warning statement."

"It's going to be the best 'Turn Back Young Hero' warning you've ever seen." Rachael bounces up and down—then suddenly runs out of steam. "I'm going to sit alone in my quarters now. Bye."

Lyzix gives me a happy grin, with her needle teeth bared. Her ears go all the way to the back of her head, which means she no longer wants to tear me limb from limb right this moment.

But as I follow Rachael out, I have a huge lump in my throat, that makes its way down to my stomach by inches.

Like, maybe I'm about to have more innocent lives on my conscience.

11

We've been standing in the cargo hangar for half an hour, and nobody's said a word.

Yatto is staring at the holographic workstation, monitoring the progress of the two orbital funnels that are already on their way up to the ship, containing two kids who accepted the invitation we spent a few hours crafting.

Rachael's warning message really was beautiful. If I'd read it before getting on that platform with Yatto, I might have thought twice. But I guess at least a few people read it and figured, *What the hell.*

The platforms took no time at all to descend to the surface because they were empty, but now they're taking forever to come back up. Rachael and I are just standing there next to Yatto, waiting to play welcome committee for the newcomers.

Once all of these Earth kids are on board, Captain Othaar will come on down to the cargo hangar and explain the situation—and then they'll all have a short window to return to Earth before we leave orbit.

Yatto breaks the silence. "I did a records search for the Talgan stone. There's no reference to it anywhere in the Firmament records, but there could be a clue on one of the planets that Captain Argentian visited in her final tour of duty. We'll send a coded message to the rest of the fleet once we're in deep space, to make sure everyone is looking for it."

"Okay." I smile at them, even though I can't help feeling like I let everyone down. If I had just gotten back all the memories of "my" former life, then I could just tell them where to find that rock, and we'd be all set.

"What is the deal with that Marrant dude, anyway?" Rachael asks. "And why are the Compassion such assholes?"

She's looking at me, but I don't know the answer either. I guess everything to do with the Compassion was part of Captain Argentian's personal memories. *Thanks, brain.*

"Thondra Marrant was one of the Fleet's most decorated officers until he disgraced himself," says Yatto. "Marrant believed that the Royal Fleet needed to show strength in order to keep peace in the galaxy, so when the people of Zenoith attacked their neighbors using a warship they had built out of scraps, Marrant decided to destroy it. He'd been ordered to resolve the situation peacefully, and his tactical officer warned him the warship's engines were dangerously unstable. But he shot it down anyway, and the resulting explosion killed almost a million people. Including half of Marrant's crew. And his wife, Aym, who was also his alternate captain."

"Wow." I shudder all over again at Marrant's creepy grin, now that I know he's an actual mass murderer.

"Captain Argentian was Marrant's best friend since the academy," says Yatto, "until she served on the tribunal that stripped him of his rank and discharged him from the Royal Fleet. He refused to accept any responsibility for his own actions, and insisted on blaming everyone else. So when some Royal Fleet officers split off and started the Compassion, he went with them."

"Wait, what now?" Rachael says. "Did you just say the Compassion used to be part of the Royal Fleet?"

"Yes," Yatto says, without looking up from the holographic display. "They betrayed all the ideals that we stand for. They should have known better, but they chose to follow a toxic ideology of total genocide."

Then Yatto stops talking, because the colorful pointy shapes in their display are bouncing up and down. One of the orbital funnels from Earth will be here in a few moments.

*

"Brace yourselves!" Yatto tells Rachael and me—just before everything goes sideways, and we both sail into the opposite wall.

The cargo hangar can change its orientation to the rest of the ship, up to about 30 degrees in any direction, and Yatto is trying to do something fancy here.

"The same space debris that's still sheltering us"—Yatto snorts with effort—"is also creating a barrier around the ship."

Once the orbital funnels are flying, you don't exactly "steer" them—they tend to just go in a straight line—but you can make course adjustments, with a *lot* of effort. Yatto tries to guide the first platform around the obstacle course of space junk, while also adjusting the position of the cargo bay's doorway to "catch" a platform that's moving a zillion miles per hour.

All Rachael and I can do is hang on for dear life to the straps for the safety restraints on the scuffed metal wall as the cargo bay whips back and forth. Neither of us actually manages to put the restraints *on*, but at least the straps are something to hold on to.

I look at Rachael, gritting her teeth, bracing herself against the wall with one leg and gripping the strap with both hands—and she looks, honestly, like a total badass.

"Come on, come on," Yatto says. "Cursed Hexapod-Eaters of

Jubilation Mountain, *come on*."

Yatto starts whacking at the controls on their own sleeve, because the funnel controls are not cooperating. I look at the Quant readout on my own palms, and I can tell that the little blip is not going to make it. The orbital funnel is going to sail right past us, and keep zooming out into space, forever.

At the last second, when the blip is so close that you could practically reach out and touch it, Yatto triggers a last desperate maneuver. The cargo bay swings so violently I lose my grip on my safety strap and go flying across the room, hitting the opposite wall. Our hatch opens just in time to swallow up the disc . . .

. . . which rises up into view, with one person standing on it.

She holds herself unsteadily on the round platform, like she's about to throw up. A girl, roughly my age, with brown skin, a pointy nose, and long black hair in a braid, wearing loose linen pants with bright shiny threads through them, and tons of jingly bracelets and anklets. She wears a loose cotton jumper with square cats on it, with a label that says, "No Nasties."

I walk toward the girl, ready to comfort her, because riding an orbital funnel was scary enough during a normal journey— and she just had the bumpiest ride, zigging and zagging around satellite junk, and she did it all on her own.

The girl looks around at the sparse metal walls of the cargo bay, stares at me and my itchy uniform, and lets a high shriek.

"It's okay," I say, "it's okay."

But she's not screaming with fear or whatever. She's squeeing.

"Best. App. Ever!" she shouts, jumping in the air—then she misjudges her jump, and flies off the platform onto the deck, landing in a heap at my feet.

*

Yatto was supposed to help us roll out the welcome wagon, but they're too busy shaking their head and preparing for the next person. "Hosts of Misadventure help us," they grunt. "If you thought this one was fun, just wait until the next three. They're all coming at different angles. Another one will be here in a moment."

I turn back to the girl, who's still lying on the floor in front of me.

"You're okay," I say. "You're safe."

The girl gets to her feet, shaking off my attempts to help her up. "I *know* I'm okay. I'm so much better than okay. That was a *sensational* ride. I can't believe I won."

"Uh," I say, "won what?"

She stares at me like I'm the one who's clueless. "I got to the final level on Krazzy Puzzle, yeah? I solved the extra challenge puzzle, which was a beast. I basically had to forget everything I knew about math and geometry. And then"—she gestures behind her—"this elevator platform dropped down and whisked me away. Best ride of my life!"

"Oh, right." I realize this girl mentioned an app. "So . . . Krazzy Puzzle is the, uh, the app that you were playing?"

She squints at me. "If you work for Krazzy Kompany, then you're the most incompetent company rep I've ever met. Although your Hindi is *amazing*. Not even an accent. Where'd you learn to speak it?"

"Uh. . . ." Not even going to *try* to explain the EverySpeak right now.

Damn damn damn. Lyzix *said* the probe was using modern communications to test kids, so of course it would just create an app. A puzzle app, even. How else do you get Earth teenagers to take a ton of weird math and science tests voluntarily?

"Let's start over." I hold out a hand. "I'm Tina."

"Damini," she says, gripping my hand so hard it throbs. "I live in Mumbai, as you probably already knew, and I can't wait to see my brother Govind's face when he finds out I actually won." She finally notices Yatto's yellow skin with blue stripes, and the spiky ridges on their head. "Whoa," she says.

"Don't stare," I say. "It's rude."

This does the trick: she looks back at me. *Thaaaat's it. Reassuring human face.* I try to hold her gaze, so she won't go back to looking at the giant space alien.

"So what's my prize?" Damini says. "And do you have any idea when I get to go home? I need to rub this in Govind's face."

I turn and see Rachael, who looks like she wants to go to her quarters and hide forever. I can't hear what she's saying to herself.

"Well," I say. "You can head back to Earth right now, as soon as the ship's captain gets a chance to explain everything to you. But we were kinda hoping you might want to stay."

"Didn't you read the warning?" Rachael blurts out. "The one that said if you got on the platform, you could be leaving your home and your family behind forever?"

"I thought that was just part of the game," Damini says. "Games always say things like that, to add drama."

I should have known Rachael's message wouldn't be enough. Name one time in my life that I ever paid the slightest attention to warning stickers, caution tape, safety notices, high-voltage signs, and responsible adults. Ignoring safety warnings is what got me where I am today.

Rachael looks like she's going to throw up, or run away, or both.

"So we're really on a real spaceship?" Damini says.

"A real spaceship," I say. "Full of real aliens."

"When we kept going up and up, I thought it must be some augmented-reality thing, or else some Richard Branson vomit-comet stunt," Damini says. "I've gone free-climbing in Sri Lanka and hang-gliding in Himachal Pradesh, so I'm not exactly afraid of heights. One time I jumped out of an airplane at fourteen thousand feet. But that platform kept rising, until I could see more stars than I've ever seen in my life." She looks around. "Now I *really* wish I could rub this in Govind's face."

And that's when the crying-baby noise starts up.

*

Lyzix's voice comes over my shoulder comms: "Active combat situation. Situation Green Crouch. Repeat, Situation Green Crouch. All secondary bridge personnel report to Forward Ops. All other personnel, secure stations. Brace for damage."

The noise gets louder and shriller, until my ears are ringing.

"Secondary bridge personnel" includes me, which means I should be running to Forward Ops and taking my place at Tactical.

But Yatto just snagged the second elevator platform. Standing on it is a skinny figure wearing expensive clothes. At first glance, my impression is: probably a dude, with dark brown skin and high cheekbones. His tailored shirt has cuff links and everything. But he's clutching his left arm, which dangles like a stringless puppet.

He stumbles forward, and then sees the chaotic situation he's wandered into.

"Whoa," I say. "Did you . . . did you break your arm just now?"

He blinks at me.

"Just now," I say. "On the platform. This flying pizza dish. I know it was a rough ride. Did your arm get broken on the way up here?"

He shakes his head slowly. "No, that happened as I was escaping from my father's wine cellar." He has a British accent—so either he's British, or he's speaking some other language and the EverySpeak decided that's how he ought to sound. "The message said that if I stepped on the metal disc, I would leave my family behind, forever. Never even see them again. Is that really true?"

I look over at Rachael, who stiffens. I see her psyching herself up to break it to him gently, somehow.

But I have to run, so I just rip off the Band-Aid. "Yes, it's true. You'll probably never see your family again."

The newcomer starts to cry.

"Oh, thank god. I did it. I finally got away from him."

He weeps into his unbroken arm, and I should have been at Forward Ops five minutes ago.

I shoot Rachael a desperate look. She looks back at me, equally helpless. She wriggles out of the safety restraints she finally managed to put on, then walks over to the weeping dude with the broken arm, and tries to offer some comfort.

12

I run into Forward Ops, all out of breath, and throw my butt into the chair facing the tactical station. Then I slide my hand into the gooey hard-light interface and twirl my fingers around to access the controls.

(That holographic interface is *really* gooey, like sliding your hand into a jar of grape jelly, and it feels like my fingers will be sticky after. Whenever I trigger one of the controls, the goo lights up around my fingers, and it feels like I've done this a million times before—but also like I'll never get used to this.)

I can't even make sense of the tactical readouts at first. Something ugly is coming our way, and it's spewing accelerated mercury ions like puke from a party bus. Ten flavors of deadly radiation are coming off this thing . . . but what is it? And where did it even come from?

"It's the *Cleansing Fire*," says the guy sitting at the nav station to my left. "The Compassion ship that we fought before."

"But we put them out of action," I say. "We disabled all their engines and their weapons. Right? How are they even attacking us now?"

And then I realize: this is the shell of a dead ship. The thing coming for us is just a shard of metal crammed with unstable power cells and engines that are on the edge of eating themselves. They've converted some of their gravity generators into a big freaking ray gun, and they're shooting it into space to generate thrust. Basically, they've turned their wrecked starship into a huge flying bomb.

This loose nuke is racing toward us, and we don't even have enough power to get out of the way.

Meanwhile, two more orbital funnels are still on their way up from Earth, with innocent kids on board—and they could die out here, without ever knowing what even happened. I see these tiny dots on one of my screens, moving way too slow. Like circus performers on trapezes, swinging out into empty space—trusting that when the hands holding their ankles let go, someone else will catch them.

"They're probably detecting it from the planet's surface by now," Vaap grunts in the control deck, behind me. "Tactical, watch for surface missile launches."

"We can't let it explode this close to the planet," Lyzix says. "Could wipe out the entire population."

I barely have time to look at the Earth on one of my screens, silently glowing with life and magnetism and warmth. I try to imagine my mom standing there as burning wreckage falls from the sky. For a moment, this paralyzes me, but then I force myself to concentrate.

No time to daydream.

I try to see past all the toxic waste spewing out of this wrecked starship, to find a weak spot we could hit with a dwarf-star ballistic missile or a single burst from our pulse cannon. But then I realize: there's no way. If we shoot at this thing, we'd just make it go boom ahead of schedule, killing every living thing on Earth.

"What's the revel?" Othaar says.

For a moment, the term makes no sense to me, but then Uiuiuiui says, "Five seven luminals and accelerating, Captain."

Oh, right. "Revel" means "relative velocity."

"Acting Senior Engineer Yma, we need main impellers now, or we're dead," Othaar says. "Engine room, please respond."

"Working on it, Captain," Yma says, and I can tell just from tone of voice that the bubbles are dark and oily right now.

"Uiuiuiui," I whisper. "If a miracle happens, and we somehow break out of orbit and escape from this bomb, what happens to the two kids who are traveling up from Earth?"

"The same thing that happens if this ship gets destroyed while those kids are still traveling toward us: they die."

I glance at Uiuiuiui, who's at the stellar mapping station over to my right. His face-tubes are twisted into a look of sympathy, and mourning for the soon-to-be-dead.

What's left of the *Cleansing Fire* goes from a pinhead to a softball on my screens in an eyeblink. I won't even have time to list all the things I wish I'd done differently, before it smashes into us. The senior staff keep all of us patched into the control deck, so we can hear them try to figure out this mess.

"Got ourselves a 3HM," someone sitting behind me in Forward Ops mutters.

("3HM" is short for "three-headed monster," or a situation with no good options. It's a different acronym in every language, I guess.)

"The good news is, this 'flying bomb' has very little maneuverability," Lyzix says. "Bad news is, we can't outrun it at .57 luminals per cycle, unless we get our engines back online."

"We have to lead it away from the planet, even if we can't escape the blast ourselves," Vaap says.

I turn and look at them, behind their glass wall. Othaar is hunching forward, staring at all the readouts with his jawbone clenched. Next to him, Lyzix juggles three holographic readouts in each hand, with her ears pointed straight up. The only calm person back there is Vaap, who could be a statue.

The two orbital funnels still approaching from Earth are between half an hour and forty-five minutes away from us. The *Cleansing Fire* will catch up to us long before those kids can arrive. Unless the *Indomitable* breaks orbit, in which case the funnels will just fly out into space forever.

Nobody's even talking about how to save those two kids— because they're as good as dead.

*

I spot another emission coming from the ugly toxic shell, and then Vaap says, "Captain. We're getting a signal from the other ship."

"Guess they don't care about comm silence anymore," Lyzix says.

"Let's hear it," Othaar says in a resigned tone.

A moment later, a horrible screeching sound, like the worst mic feedback ever, rings out. But it's not a problem with the comms. The captain of the other ship is laughing.

"You're all dead and rotting! This was a beautiful ship, as graceful as the wind and twice as unpredictable, but now I've torn away her lovely skin and her stately living quarters, and turned her into a missile. A vessel of pure unholy destruction! I set the crew adrift—maybe they'll be rescued, maybe they won't—and I'm coming to shove the stinking corpse of my ship down your throats."

"Should we respond?" Lyzix says.

"I don't have anything to say to this fool," Othaar snorts.

"If they signaled for reinforcements, there's still some benefit to us in maintaining comm silence," Vaap says.

"Is Captain Argentian there?" the *Cleansing Fire*'s captain shrills. "Oh, I hope so. I hope she's weeping with rage right now, screaming on her knees. Because she came all the way back from the dead, and now I'm going to kill her a second time. Thaoh Argentian, if you're listening, the Compassion sends you its rankest disdain. You should have learned from your mistakes, instead of throwing your life away. And to the great Panash Othaar, I say only this—"

The voice cuts out.

"That's quite enough," Othaar says. "I knew he was a fool already. Didn't need to hear his whole life story."

"That 'fool' is going to impact our ship in two minicycles," Lyzix says. (A minicycle is one-tenth of a cycle, or about five minutes.)

"Yma," Othaar hisses. "We need those engines *now*."

"Said and done, Captain," Yma says. "Just making sure it won't blow up as soon as we turn it on."

"All hands," Othaar says over the ship's PA. "We're about to break orbit. Let's hope the Hosts of Misadventure are on our side. But if this is the last time I speak to you, I've valued your service. Prepare for damage. That is all."

We're gearing up to leave orbit, as soon as Yma gives the all-clear. And those two kids are still rising toward us from different parts of the planet, and we won't be here when they arrive.

I try to imagine surviving this, at the cost of knowing that two innocent kids died. That we had left them to die. These kids don't even know what they've gotten themselves into. I think of all the decisions that I made, that led up to this moment, and I can almost see them from a distance, like a star chart. Each choice is its own bright hot center of gravity.

This is my mess, as much as it's anybody's.

I'm out of my teacup chair and halfway across the room before anybody notices, and then Vaap shouts, "Junior Tactical Officer, return to your post. That's an *order*!" But I'm already out the door and running.

13

The atmosphere suit doesn't exactly fit. The boots are half a size too big, the waist too tight. The top part gapes around my shoulders. I hunt for a helmet in the survival locker. I've never worn one of these things before, but—thanks, Captain Argentian!—it feels as familiar as tying my shoes.

"What are you even planning?" Yatto says from their cargo bay control station. "I should point out, you're under orders to return to Forward Ops, and if I had even a moment to spare, I would have to put you in restraints for insubordination."

"Yatto, you can reactivate my rescue beacon, right? The one that those Compassion soldiers used to track me in the first place. The one I was born with."

Yatto thinks for a moment, then nods. "But then what? The Compassion already knows where this ship is. Which is why they're on a collision course with us right now."

"But what if I fly away?" I say. "I could use the same kind of gravity warp that makes the orbital funnels go so fast, and travel a huge distance from the ship in a hurry."

"And then what? Try to lure them away from the ship?" Rachael says.

My helmet snaps into place, and everything smells stale and sickly sweet. Then the oxygen supply kicks on, which helps, a little.

"The acceleration would kill you almost immediately," Yatto

says without looking away from their station. "And even if you survived, your mass would increase with the acceleration. You'd weigh a few tons after traveling a short distance."

"Well, my girls' lacrosse coach did say I needed to bulk up."

"Your idea sounds like balls," Rachael says. "Don't do this."

The locker contains the makings of a personal impeller—basically, a jetpack that can go up to a dozen miles per second—but it's in several pieces, and I can't even see how they fit together.

I look up at Damini. "Hey, puzzle girl. Need some help here." She's already undoing her safety harness, with an expression of pure joy. Even on a ship that's in imminent danger of blowing up, she seems to be having an excellent time—I can absolutely believe that she's the kind of person who would jump out of an airplane. Maybe they didn't have a Seth Rogen movie.

"They'll be able to plot your trajectory to its origin. You'll be like an arrow pointing directly to this ship, for any other ships in the vicinity," Yatto says. "Your plan will kill you, and also fail."

"Your plan is balls," Rachael says.

"I can't do *nothing*." I feel like screaming. "Those kids are going to die, for no reason. And if I just sit here and let it happen, then what kind of person am I? If there's anything I can do, I have to try. No matter what it costs."

I glance at Damini, still assembling the impeller, with her bracelets jangling.

That's when the kid with the broken arm steps forward. "What the blue blazes is even going on here?" he asks.

"It's really complicated, and I don't have time to break it down," I start to say.

The kid, who was weeping and shivering a while ago, looks

up at the curved ceiling in exasperation. "I have a bloody PhD in physics from Cambridge University. Try me." He looks about fifteen years old.

"Okay," I say. "Two more of these platforms, like the one you flew up on, are traveling toward us, with an ETA of roughly twenty-five minutes." I point to the dots on my tactical display. "But these assclowns have turned their ship into one ginormous nuclear missile, and it's going to hit us in, oh, about seven minutes. So we're about to break orbit, and leave those two kids to die."

The Brit leans over, wincing as his broken arm shifts, and then says, "Well, then, it's simple, isn't it? All you have to do is adjust the trajectories of these two tea trays, so they converge at a much lower point. Plus 3.4 degrees for one, minus 2.8 degrees for the other, and they meet up . . . here." He points to a spot way below us, much closer to the edge of the Earth's atmosphere. "Then someone just has to scoop them up."

Yatto looks up. "That might actually work. And also, you'd have only an 80 percent chance of dying, instead of 100 percent."

"I'm in," I say. "Thanks, dude," I tell the Brit.

"I'm Keziah, and my pronoun is *he*."

Just then, Damini holds up the completed impeller, which chitters with energy as its systems power up. I strap it to my back, feeling the vibration through my padded spacesuit. I root around in the supply closet and find an ion harness, too.

"This was a fun challenge," Damini says. "So why can't I be the one to jump out of the spaceship? It's not fair."

"Maybe next time." I march toward the open hatch.

But suddenly, Rachael is blocking my path, arms crossed.

"I worry about you too." She looks like a ghost through my faceplate.

"Huh?"

"When you were trying to talk me out of staying on this ship, you said that you worry about me. So this is me saying, I worry about you too."

"Oh man, I really want to give you a clumsy spacesuit hug right now." I open my arms, and she leans into my chest so I can wrap my puffed-out arms around her.

Something strong and undeniable is rising up inside me, and my own heartbeat sounds louder than the roar of the ship's engines.

Rachael whispers, "When I used to hide under the table in the music room at Clinton High, you stuck up for me. But we're not in high school anymore. Up here, we need to watch each other's back. Just be careful, and come back in one piece, okay?"

"Okay."

I hold on to her for one more second, trying to take in all the happiness of this one last moment—hugging my best friend and feeling all of her warmth and strength, even through layers of insulation.

Then I jump out of the spaceship.

*

The Earth just gleams beneath me. So much light and warmth, you could almost believe my home is a star, rather than a planet. I take a moment to drink in the sight, because I'm pretty sure that whatever happens, I'm never seeing Earth again.

Then I go back to concentrating on guiding my suit to the exact meeting point that Keziah figured out. I'm holding the ion harness in one hand, and it feels bulky and cumbersome even without any weight. A clunky metal tackle box full of blinky lights, dangling from one hand.

These orbital funnels travel at like four times the speed of a rocket—but they still manage to stop without smushing their passengers. That involves a lot of complicated math, which starts before the platform leaves the ground. The trouble is, now that Yatto has managed to adjust these platforms' trajectories in mid-flight, to the paths that Keziah suggested, they're going to meet up much lower, instead of both arriving at the *Indomitable*'s current position. Which is good, except . . . they won't be able to slow down enough to stop safely.

Which is where I come in.

My shoulder comms spark up, which I've been half expecting. They've risked breaking comms silence with a coded transmission, just to cuss me out.

Lyzix's voice rings in my ear. "Junior Tactical Officer, I order you to return to the ship."

"Sorry, Alternate Captain. I can't do that."

"Yatto just told us what you're trying to do, and your unauthorized action has a laughable chance of survival," Lyzix says. "We won't be able to rescue you, even if you succeed."

My Quant says the first platform is just a couple minutes out, and I'm still getting used to the controls on this ion harness. I was sort of hoping that Captain Argentian's miraculous knowledge would kick in, and I'd be all over this. But I get the feeling she saw some stuff *like* this, but she never saw this exact kind of device. Argh.

"Please understand, we will leave you for dead," Lyzix says. "You may be under the impression that because you were cloned from a decorated officer, we'll prioritize your safety over the rest of the ship. We won't." She pauses, because maybe someone told her she's being too harsh. "But if you turn back right now, you might still make it. We need to break orbit *right now*."

"Don't worry about me," I say. "Save the ship. Get that bomb away from Earth. If you can come back for us after that, great."

She hisses with impatience. "There is *no point* in you dying alongside those two recruits."

"You know what, it sounds like I already had a pretty great life. I don't remember anything about it, but everybody keeps telling me it was incredible." I get something big and soft in my throat for a second. "I'm just trying to do what Captain Argentian would do."

"You're not even in the same stellar radius. Thaoh Argentian never took pointless risks like this. She faced this exact kind of impossible situation all the time, and she made the tough calls."

I have about thirty seconds left before the first orbital funnel arrives at my little vacation spot.

"We invited these kids to come join us, and now we're going to sacrifice them just because things got 3HM up in here. I refuse to believe that's how we do things."

"If there was a way to save those kids, I would—" She stops, because I can hear a whole new set of alarms behind her. An imminent collision alert. The *Cleansing Fire* has arrived. So Lyzix gives up on talking to me, and signs out: "End transmission."

Then . . . silence. Except for my own breathing, which suddenly feels very loud.

The first orbital funnel races toward me so fast it looks like a hot smudge. I get my big catcher's mitt ready, to catch a fastball that's still going almost the speed of sound.

Please, just this once. Please let me have this one, I beg the universe. *Even if I don't make it, don't let these kids die out here.*

By the time I even see the round metal platform, it's already right on top of me, moving too fast to track. I curse, and reach out with my ion harness. And . . . I miss.

The platform is already streaking away, out of sight, on a long horrible journey to nothing. It's probably too late.

I let out a scream of frustration and try a second throw.

This time, the beam from the ion harness snakes upward, snags onto the bottom of the shiny disc . . . and holds firm. *Oh, thank the Hosts of Misadventure, or whoever.*

I start reeling in the first platform that I already hooked. Slowly, gently. But the second platform is already blazing toward me. Just a white-hot streak of fire.

And this second platform is coming at me sideways. When Keziah talked about adjusting the trajectories, it sounded gentle. But this other platform is coming from the other side of the world, and the angle is all wrong. It's like trying to catch a bullet.

This isn't going to work. I'm not even going to be able to slow it down, with this trajectory. The faceplate of my suit looks like a windshield in a summer rain, but then I realize: these are my tears.

*

The second platform is only a few seconds out. *Time to pull yourself together.*

I wait until it's close enough for me to see a blur. Then I reach out with the ion harness, sending a finger of light to grab hold.

But it's no good. The second funnel doesn't even slow down, it just rushes past.

I try to keep a hold on it, but the momentum pulls my arms almost out of their sockets. I have to let go.

I let go and watch the platform disappear around the curve of the Earth. All I've succeeded in doing is dragging it down, so it's now in a decaying orbit.

A hissing sound comes from somewhere nearby, and an alarm sounds. I feel dizzy all of a sudden.

Then I realize: there's a rip in my spacesuit, and I'm leaking oxygen.

There's no time to find the leak and patch it—even if I thought I could. I look up and realize the first platform is still drifting down toward me, and it nearly lands on my head. I grab onto the edge with my ion device, and it slows down enough for me to pull myself onto it.

Then I'm standing next to an Asian teenager, who's wearing a T-shirt that reads, "Jay Chou Forever," and looks ready to barf with motion sickness.

I kneel on the edge of the platform, next to the startled kid's nice soccer shoes. "I don't have time to explain," I say, "but you're safe. For now, at least." Then I pull off my helmet, because I'm inside the funnel's air pocket.

The second platform is a few dozen miles away already, racing over the dark side of the Earth. Too far to reach. But I repeat to myself: *Nobody's dying on my watch.*

While the kid in the Jay Chou shirt watches, I fling the ion harness with everything I have, and it travels nearly forty miles, to where the other platform is . . . and misses. I try again a second time, and miss again.

The third time, though, I make contact. I have a weak, slippery hold on the other funnel.

"Hang on," I say. "This is going to be bumpy."

Understatement of the century. We're dragged forward, so fast that the features of the Earth blur beneath us, and the kid with the Jay Chou T-shirt finally barfs over the side. My arm is being dislocated again. I let out a yelp of pain.

We can't keep going this fast. My arm is throbbing. So of course . . . we get faster. Now the Earth is just a dark shape laced with streaks, because we're racing over the night side now. I think for a second I can see North America, sleeping but blazing.

My suit is sporting more little rips, and our platform keeps jostling like a wild horse. "Come on," I beg out loud. "Come on, *please*. Just give me this one. *Please!*"

I hold on as tight as I can to the other platform . . . and then, I get pulled off the platform I was standing on. For a second, I'm just flying through space at a blinding speed, with a shredded spacesuit and no helmet, and I don't even have time to gasp before I start passing out.

I've got maybe a few seconds to live.

But I still don't let go of the ion harness: the only thing anchoring the runaway platform. My last coherent thought is *Never let go.* I tighten my grip.

The kid in the Jay Chou T-shirt grabs my ankle with both hands. I flop around, just outside the platform's artificial gravity and air, and then the kid pulls me back inside. I fall to my knees, gasping, and clutch at the ion harness.

"Thanks." I cough. "I'm Junior Tactical Officer Tina Mains, and my pronoun is *she*. I'm from the Royal Fleet. You're . . . you're gonna be okay."

Then I cough some more and start to keel over.

"I'm Wang Yiwei. Your Mandarin is hardcore, except for the part where you tried to use gendered pronouns." He (I guess) leans over and helps me steady the ion harness, which is slowly reeling in the other platform.

I get feeling back in my hands and face, right around the time the two platforms finally kiss. I use the ion harness to tie them together, making one slightly bigger raft, floating above the Earth.

The occupant of the other funnel introduces herself as Elza, and she's from São Paulo. Tight dark braids, skinny brown wrists, big earrings, nice shoes. That's all I take in before my vision blurs again.

I roll onto my back and look up at the stars until they come into focus: a chorus of splendor.

I can't move.

I just lie there.

"Who the hell are you, and what happened to my geocaching scavenger hunt?" Wang Yiwei says.

"No clue," Elza says.

"And what happens now?" Wang Yiwei asks.

"Now?" I stare up at the endless starscape—but if I even lean over slightly I can see the sparkling darkness of Earth, creeping toward us. I manage to raise my palm to my face and check my Quant. "Well, we have enough oxygen for two hours, if we don't do a sing-along. And meanwhile, we're slowly getting pulled back down to Earth, unless I figure out how to retrofit my personal impeller to generate thrust."

I lie back down and close my eyes again. Now that my head is starting to clear a little, I can focus on the fact that my entire body is a playground for pain.

Everybody is asking questions at once. Just because I'm wearing some kind of starship uniform and controlling alien technology, and I already bent the hell out of the laws of physics stopping their runaway space elevators, they expect me to have all the answers.

Just . . . need to rest . . . for a moment. My eyes don't want to open, my brain doesn't want to think. I saved these kids, and I'm gonna figure out how to keep them alive. In five more minutes.

A hand is nudging me. For a second I'm sure it's my mom, holding a paper plate of burnt toaster waffles and telling me to wake up because I'm late for improv camp.

I open my eyes at last—just in time to see a blinding flash, directly overhead. Some kind of flare, like a supernova, but it's too close and too quick for that. I blink, and the light is gone. I try and get tactical info from my Quant, and it only confirms what I just saw: something huge and ugly just exploded into toxic rubble, out past Jupiter.

Nothing left but a cloud that's going to be deadly for centuries.

Captain Thaoh Argentian's personal datajournal, 9.16.11.03 of the Age of Expansion

Well . . . that went about as well as I could have expected.

Captain Argentian laughs and takes a swig from a bottle.

Try telling someone to their face that they're acting like a baby, when they've been surrounded forever by people telling them that both suns in a binary system shine out of their ass.

And don't even get me started on the Oonians, who wouldn't stop squinting those big eyes at me. They still remember when they were part of the Seven-Pointed Empire and they helped to rule this entire galaxy.

The captain takes another drink and rolls her neck.

I think we got them to take the blockade down, and I even coaxed all of those clowns to have a drink together.

But we didn't fix anything, of course. Nothing ever really gets solved. The Royal Fleet is basically just fixing the same messes over and over again. Still, if I did my job right, then nobody has to die this time around. Plus, you get to try every kind of liquor on every single planet in this job.

Captain laughs and raises her bottle.

Strong drinks and unexpected friends, right?

14

The afterimage of that toxic flare still spanks my retinas after a while, blotting out almost everything. Maybe this is permanent, and I'll see an exploding spaceship for the rest of my life . . . which is probably gonna be a couple hours.

Elza keeps turning around and helicoptering her arms, looking at our double platforms. "This is so very not what I was expecting. But after everything that's happened in the past nine months, maybe I shouldn't even be surprised at one more letdown."

My chest tightens. "What were you expecting?"

I'm trying to study the tactical display on my palms through the blot of light. No sign of the *Indomitable,* or any other hope of rescue.

Okay, *think.* We just need a way to get down to Earth gracefully, without going splat.

"I don't know," Elza says. "Some kind of victory celebration. Cool lights, awesome music. Maybe a DJ playing Anitta, or maybe even Anitta performing live. A giant banner saying, 'We Always Knew You Could Do It, Even Though We Publicly Doubted You Over and Over.' Some snacks, maybe some barbecue. A chocolate fountain."

"I sort of thought there would be an adult here, holding a big clipboard," Wang Yiwei says. "Leading us to a bus. A space bus, I guess? Is that a thing?"

"Instead of a floating death trap." Elza gestures at our raft.

"Don't worry, we're totally safe," I say. "There's a huge beautiful spaceship coming to rescue us, any moment now." I crouch to get a better look at the impeller I've rigged to keep our orbit from decaying too fast.

"Really?" Yiwei says. "Ugh, I was starting to freak out."

But Elza leans over and gives me a hard look while I try to keep my eyes on my work.

"She's lying," Elza says. "You get lied to as often as I have, you learn to notice the signs. There's no rescue ship."

I almost drop the piece of ion harness that I'm holding. "It's not a lie, not exactly. The truth is, I hope they're still in one piece. If they are, they'll come for us."

"I shouldn't even be up here," Wang Yiwei says, breathing a little too fast. "My ex-girlfriend told me not to come. Jiasong *told* me that this was something dangerous and maybe even alien. But I said, 'You don't get to tell me what to do right after dumping me.'" He laughs. "Worst way to get over a breakup. I could have just gotten a sick haircut, instead of climbing onto a magic circle that just fell out of the sky."

"Whatever." Elza laughs. "Life's too short not to step onto random flying objects."

"Right about now, life is looking extra short." Yiwei turns and looks at the endless blue and white patterns moving below us. "Getting kind of chilly up here."

I feel it too: a snap in the air, like a late autumn day. The platforms' protective fields are already breaking down.

*

The Earth has caught on green fire. Huge swooshing arcs of Day-Glo light, tinged with yellows and pinks, soar across the horizon.

We're seeing the aurora borealis from space.

Wang Yiwei reaches and opens his case, pulls out a steel guitar, like Hawaiian-style, and lays it across his lap. Still gazing out at the auroras, he plays this hauntingly beautiful melody, with tons of sweet bendy notes. Then his guitar case quivers and a tiny robot climbs out, with two speakers as its "eyes" and a camera as its "nose." The robot crawls over to Yiwei on four spindly legs and starts playing an electronic harmony to the tune that Yiwei is playing. Yiwei glances at the robot and looks surprised, like he didn't realize it had snuck inside his case. Then he scoots over to make a space for it to sit with him.

The music steals inside me and gets past the brave front I'm putting on right now. I can't help thinking about the fact that maybe Rachael and the others just got blown to bits. For a few heartbeats I feel brittle, shaky, as if this high wind will take me to pieces.

I look up and see Elza staring out at the horizon with the light playing on her wide brown-green eyes. Something about the sight of her angular face, bathed in this glow, makes me lose my breath for a moment.

"I love your robot," she says to Yiwei, who smiles but keeps plucking. "Did you make it yourself?"

"That's Xiaohou. It means 'little monkey.'" Yiwei sighs. "My girlf— . . . I mean, my *ex*-girlfriend and I built a ton of musical robots together. We were going to start a human–robot pop band and take over the world." Easy to see how he could become a pop star: a swoosh of wavy dark hair, a baby face, and lean, powerful arms that flex a little as he plays.

I need to keep these two talking while I try to build a reentry engine out of junk. So I ask Elza, "What about you? What made you decide to get on a platform that came out of nowhere?"

"I don't have to tell you anything." She hugs herself.

"Yeah, you don't. I'm just passing the time. No worries."

"Okay, fine." Elza snorts at my weak reverse psychology. "I was living rent-free at the Coletivo Frenético, this hackerspace in Vila Madalena, in exchange for teaching coding lessons. But even though I could run rings around most of the boys there, they never took me seriously, which is the only reason I even entered that hacking contest, or whatever it was. And then when I won, I had to see for myself if the invitation was real, or if someone was just tricking me." She looks down at me, auroras picking up all the hurt behind her smile. "And now I'm going to die, just because I needed to prove myself to some dicks who never even mattered."

"Nobody's dying today," I say.

She looks at me like, *Don't you lie to me again.*

So now I have to think of something to say, to back up my bravado.

The air is getting thinner, and my heart is beating way too fast, and I have no miracles left. I try to reach for some nugget of Captain Argentian, buried in my head.

But all I can think of is what Rachael said to me, before I jumped out of the *Indomitable*.

"We're going to watch each other's backs up here," I say. "We're going to get through this."

They both look at me for a moment, and I'm convinced they're going to see through my brave front.

But Elza just nods. "Okay. I wouldn't even dare to bet against a bossy girl in a ripped-up spacesuit."

And Yiwei goes back to staring at the light show on the horizon, and playing his guitar with his little robot jamming along.

I don't even register the exact moment when I go from actually trying to save all our lives, to just pretending. Like I'm in a school pageant, miming a fake "picnic" with no blanket, basket, food, or plates. At least my vision has cleared up, so I can see what I'm not doing.

Elza sees me staring and frowning, and crouches next to me. "Just breathe and clear your mind, okay? When I get stuck on a problem, I try to imagine having already solved it, and then I work backwards in my imagination to picture the steps that led me there." Her voice is gentle and patient, and I can totally imagine her being a great coding teacher.

I don't have the heart to tell her that I already failed. I don't even know this girl, but I already know the look of disappointment on her face would kill me.

I'm feeling light-headed. My fingers can't hold anything, and I'm swaying. I just want a nap. We're out of time. Yiwei puts his guitar away and just sits there, breathing way too loud.

Elza nudges me. "Come on. You said we would get through this." She's still using her nice teacher voice, but panic is creeping in. "You promised, remember? You said nobody was dying today."

I open my mouth to say, "I lied."

I have the words on the tip of my tongue.

And then I spy something leaping up and down on the palm of my right hand, like a cricket made of light.

I feel the grin spread across my face. "Relax. Our ride's almost here."

I look up a moment later and see the *Indomitable* descending, its scarred and dented hull turning purple and green and silver from the reflected auroras. I want to scream for joy, but my lungs can't manage a scream. Instead I just laugh and feel the anxiety drain out of me as an opening appears in the side, next to the cargo hangar, and swallows us up.

*

"Everyone strap in," Yatto the Monntha says as soon as we stumble off the platform and gulp some luxurious oxygen. "The Earth people just launched one of their large hot objects at us, and we're in no condition to take another hit. Plus two more Compassion ships are approaching." Yiwei and Elza both gawp at Yatto's blue stripes and yellow skin.

I glance at my palm, and sure enough, a honking big nuclear missile is on its way up from Earth, with heat waves coming off its nose cone and fire belching out of its tail.

Yatto helps Keziah back into a safety harness, taking extra care with his brand-new arm cast. Damini straps herself in, and I help Elza and Yiwei into harnesses on the opposite wall. No sign of Rachael—she's probably helping in Sickbay.

When I lean over to strap Elza in, she smiles at me with a twinkle in her eyes—like we're alone together, playing some prank on the rest of the world. I feel warm all over for a moment, but I just nod and tighten her harness.

"Everyone hold on tight," Othaar says over the comms. "We're going to risk a spaceweave out of here, as soon as we're clear of orbit. I'd say let's hope the Hosts of Misadventure are with us, but we've already asked for their help too many times lately."

"Hey, bossy girl," Elza whispers next to me.

"Don't call me that." I feel hot for a second.

"It's a compliment. I just wanted to ask, what kind of movies do you like?"

This ship is doing donuts, trying to shake off the missile from Earth. I would throw up, if I could figure out which direction "up" was.

"Uh," I stammer. "I guess I like superhero movies, but also those horror movies where you get scared of something random, like a creepy doll or silence. You?"

"I like movies where the Black people don't get killed," Elza says. "I like action movies and musicals, and I really like action movies with musical numbers."

"Everybody hang tight," Yatto shouts. "We're about to—"

The *Indomitable* bends spacetime, and all concept of "now" gets twisted into a million doodles as the whole universe goes inside out. The scent of fried onions fills my nostrils as everything turns bright blue, then slides into an eye-blazing ultraviolet.

15

Everything's quiet, now that we've left the solar system and we're cruising to the nearest repair outpost.

I lean against the wall I was just harnessed to, sliding downward until I'm sitting on the floor with my hands between my knees. I take a slow, painful breath. I look at my brick-red uniform shoes, which are still too pinchy and stiff, and I tell myself to get up. There's work to do.

I keep sitting.

I let myself think about the way this crew condemned Elza and Yiwei to death until it hurts too much to think about. I gaze at all those stars, and this old drinking song from the Royal Space Academy pops into my head, that goes like, *The stars, they love us! All those fragile crystals can glitter in peace thanks to us, so let's drink our fill before the stars need our strength again. Stars, oh crying stars, we're not too drunk to safeguard you.*

I realize I'm humming under my breath, and I sound like a supermassive dork.

A twisty ribbon of pink and sea green leaps onto the palm of my hand and wiggles around until I acknowledge it by squeezing my wrist. Captain Othaar wants to see me, in his receiving room.

I turn and look at the four newbies, and try to manufacture a smile. "I'll be back soon. Just hang tight, okay?"

I leave before they can even respond.

*

Everywhere I walk, people in safety gear are ripping stuff apart and putting it back together. Patching our shattered hull, grappling with the busted pipelines going from our energy converters to the engines. According to my Quant, a half-dozen more crewmembers were injured in the *Cleansing Fire*'s explosion, which explains why Rachael ran back to Sickbay. A few people are putting on atmosphere suits and flying outside the ship, trying to restore damaged impellers without the right replacement parts.

Then I reach a different part of the ship: the Executive Level. Nicer carpeting and shinier walls, with red stripes along them. At the end of a long hallway, I spot a big brass-colored doorway: the captain's quarters.

Time to face the consequences.

I swipe my hand, and Captain Othaar tells me to come in.

I enter and stand at inspection rest, the best way I know how.

The captain greets me with the proper wording for late evening, ship time: "Wild voyages and unexpected beauty."

I struggle to remember the response. "Uh, safe arrivals and haunting memories. Um . . . Sir. Captain."

Othaar tells me to relax and sit in the teacup facing him. Then we stare at each other while he struggles to find the right thing to say. I notice a hologram over his desk: a woman with effervescent purple skin in a captain's uniform, laughing. Captain Argentian? I stare at her while I wait for Captain Othaar to find his words.

"Do you know how many people you put in danger just now?" Othaar says at last. "We delayed our departure while Alternate

Captain Lyzix tried to talk you into returning to the ship, and the *Indomitable* could have been destroyed. But also, that whole planet full of people could have been scorched to a crisp."

Othaar rolls his skull—which isn't a skull at all, but a thick exoskin that evolved to survived the hydrochloric acid rain on Othaar's native planet of Aribentora.

I just stare at the hologram. She looks so happy.

Othaar grunts. "You can speak freely."

"I didn't ask you to delay your getaway," I blurt out. "I expected you to leave me behind while I tried to save Yiwei and Elza— remember them? The two kids you invited on board the ship, and then decided to write off? If this is how the Royal Fleet operates, then I don't even know if I want to be a part of it."

As I say those words aloud, I realize they're true, and they hurt me as much as they do Captain Othaar. He cringes, actually covering his face with one skeleton hand.

"I don't know everything about the Royal Fleet," I say, "but I know you have a thing called the Peacebringer's Code, which is pretty much all about protecting the innocent. And you just . . . left innocent people to die."

Captain Othaar sighs and uncovers his face. "I guess you only know about our ideals, because that's what Captain Argentian learned at the academy. You don't know about the reality, because she learned that through experience."

I don't say anything. I remember all those nights staring out my one window at the stars beyond the yew tree, waiting for a future that seemed like it would never arrive. How I cursed every wasted moment. I still have that same craving for something real, something huge and righteous. I don't think it's ever going away.

"Alternate Captain Lyzix wanted to throw you into the nearest sun for disobeying orders, but I told her that we can't blame you for making a mistake," the Captain says. "In the short time you've been on board, you've already heard us talk endlessly about the valor of the woman you were cloned from. We gave you too much to live up to, especially when you didn't retain any of her actual memories."

I look at the hologram again. Her sky-blue eyes seem to look into mine. She's heart-stoppingly beautiful . . . and she looks nothing like me.

"So was Lyzix right?" I ask. "Would Captain Argentian have left Yiwei and Elza to die?"

Captain Othaar hesitates, then says, "I would give almost anything to know the answer to that question."

He shakes his bony head.

"Thaoh Argentian was the angriest person I've ever met. And the most generous," Othaar says after a moment. "She never stopped being outraged whenever she saw the strong taking advantage of the weak. I always wished I could burn half as bright as she did. She never wanted to take the easy path. She made plenty of mistakes, but she always cared, even when the rest of us were exhausted."

That hunger inside me feels even more starved than ever—because the woman he's describing is the exact person I've always wished I could see a way to be.

"All I want to do is live up to her example," I say out loud.

Othaar shakes his head. "There's no way."

Those three syllables push all the air out of me and leave me utterly deflated. Like I just suffered a tiny hull breach.

"The age that gave rise to heroes like Captain Argentian is over. I was a fool to think we could have her back, and everything would be just the way it was before."

"I have to try," I say. "I don't know what else I can do."

"Why don't you just try being a good member of this crew?" Othaar smiles, pulling back his zygomatic plates as his mouth stretches upward. "That's plenty. We have five other Earth people on board, and unlike you, they don't understand what they've gotten themselves into. And we didn't exactly get off to a great start, thanks to the *Cleansing Fire*."

"I haven't even told Elza and Yiwei that you decided to leave them behind," I say.

"Leave that to me," Othaar says. "But I really need you to set a good example for these other new recruits. Can you do that?"

Part of me wants to say that I don't understand my situation any better than the other new kids, what with all the gaps in my knowledge. And also, that I can't be a good member of a crew that decided to sacrifice two innocent lives.

But then I look at the laughing hologram on the wall—and I think about the woman I share everything and nothing with.

"I'll do my best," I say.

A wave of sadness rolls over me, and I scrunch my eyes. And I say the thing that needs to be said, as best I can: "I'm really sorry you didn't get your friend back."

"It's not your fault," Othaar says. "She was the person I knew best in the whole fleet, but after she died . . . I realized that I didn't know her at all. You know, on my planet, Aribentora, we have a saying: 'The truth isn't true.'"

I nod. Somehow, my brand-new encyclopedic brain fills in the details. The Aribentors worship doubt. As in . . . the more you doubt everything you've been told and everything you see, the closer you are to God, who is total uncertainty.

"I went to Thaoh's funeral, and it felt like I was getting a tiny glimpse of this whole person that I didn't even know about when she was alive. I met all of her husbands and wives and partners, and they kept talking about this person, who cried at virt-operas she'd already seen ten times before, who was addicted to games that she was bad at. She did light-paintings, and wrote these amazing elegies. Sometimes she couldn't get out of bed, because she just felt too awful."

"Husbands *and* wives *and* partners, plural?" I can't even wrap my mind around that idea.

"Well, you know Makvarians."

Actually, I *don't*. Because apparently, all the important stuff was filed under "personal memories," not "knowledge and skills."

"Makvarian mating customs are kind of complicated—though many of them do just pair off nowadays. But . . . I think Thaoh just wanted to have a big noisy family around her. And I know she always thought about having a son, daughter, or thontir of her own. Sometimes I look at you, and imagine that you're her daughter, instead of her . . ."

And *that's* a sentence that Captain Othaar has no way of finishing.

16

drag my feet on the way back to the cargo hangar, with a tight feeling in the spot where my rescue beacon used to be. I keep wanting to turn around and head for Forward Ops, to take my place at Tactical—so I can start figuring out who I'm supposed to be, and where I fit in with this battle-wrecked crew. But instead, I have to go babysit these uber-genius kids.

I'm memorizing every scuff mark on the floor as I trudge down to the cargo hangar. So I almost collide with Rachael as she steps out of Sickbay.

"Oh, hey, there you are. Dr. Karrast wanted to check you out, since you went space-jumping and lost your helmet, and generally acted like Tina."

"I'm fine," I say. "I need to go check on the new kids. They're all still sitting down in the cargo hangar, probably starting to wonder if they're about to be experimented on."

"Let me come with you. I'm the reason they're here, after all."

I tell Rachael about the fact that I just agreed to set a "good example" for these new kids, even though nobody's ever called me a good example in my entire life. Of *anything*.

"You've been a cautionary tale plenty of times, though," Rachael says. "And a disruptive influence! That's something, right? They probably stuck a commemorative plaque on that one seat in detention where you sat every weekend."

Rachael and I walk down another ramp, and then another, until we're passing by the crew quarters, one level above the cargo hangar. She looks twitchy, like she's been beating herself up a lot about what nearly happened to Yiwei and Elza.

"Thank you for bringing them back safe," Rachael says in a pin-drop quiet voice. "I'm still not okay with you almost getting yourself killed, but . . . if anything had happened to those two kids, I could never have lived with myself. Just . . . thank you."

I feel warm inside, for the first time since I got stuck in low orbit with a shredded spacesuit.

"None of this is your fault," I say. "It was a good idea to recruit some more kids from Earth, and it's amazing that you still expect the best from people, after everything you went through before. Nobody could have predicted that the Compassion would go all suicide-bomber. But . . . you're welcome."

And then we reach the cargo hangar. Four kids sitting on the floor turn and stare at us. Everybody is talking at once.

"When do I get to see the whole ship? I heard there are repair crews doing space walks—when do I get to do that?" Damini asks.

"What kind of authoritarian nightmare have I wandered into?" Elza says.

"I just got dumped by my girlfriend and kidnapped by aliens on the same day, and I really need to talk to someone," says Wang Yiwei.

Rachael gives me a "help I'm drowning" look, and opens her mouth without making a sound. I forget all about everything I was just obsessing over before, and all I can think about is the look in Rachael's eyes.

"Hey, it's okay." I smile at her, and then at the four kids. "You're okay. You got picked up by the greatest force for justice that's ever existed, and you're on board a ship that makes the most advanced vehicles on Earth look like a rusty old Dodge Charger. This is Rachael. She's a friend."

Rachael smiles back at me, but still with anxiety burning in her eyes. "That's right," she says. "Now, who's ready for the grand starship tour?"

Everybody raises their hands. Damini claps and says, "About damn time!"

*

"All this stuff about keeping the peace and fighting for justice, I've heard it all before," says Elza as we walk up the ramp toward the crew levels. "Mostly from the alibã, right before they tried to mess with me and my friends."

"The what now?" I say.

"The alibã. The police! I guess your fancy translator can't handle pajubá—it's our own private slang, back home." Elza is looking at my cadet uniform with a cynical gleam in her distractingly gorgeous brown eyes. "Never trust anyone who tries too hard to convince you they're the good guys."

I'm trying so hard to hold on to my faith in this uniform and the ideals it represents, her suspicious attitude makes me want to scream.

I can't help tensing for a confrontation, the way I used to with Lauren Bose and the rest. My whole body, wound up and ready to explode.

"I'm just glad my father can't reach me here," Keziah says. "He's essentially the Black Elon Musk, except richer and much more evil. He would have tracked me down anywhere I tried to hide on Earth."

"I only came here to get over a breakup. I'm not even worth much on my own, because Jiasong was always the genius of the two of us," Yiwei says.

"I just got kicked out of my hackerspace over some totally pointless drama." Elza folds her arms. "I was about to be on the street again, so I guess maybe this is better."

"Who cares why we're here? Or what we thought we were getting ourselves into?" Damini runs ahead up the ramp, then turns back to face the rest of us. "We're the first humans ever to leave the solar system! We're on a real, actual starship. That's everything!"

Rachael has gone quiet, like she's hit her limit for socializing. This is right about when she would normally bail. Her discomfort feels like a whole bundle of static electricity right next to me.

And meanwhile, I can't stop chattering, like I need to impress everyone. We pass Crewmaster Bul, who has huge tusks going up past his eyes, and I start explaining how these tusks are actually sensory organs that can detect a thousand types of gases, and the whole unfortunate history of the Ghulg Invertocracy. Rachael finally kicks my ankle, and I get my info-bilge under control. Meanwhile, all four of the other kids are just staring at the big-ass tusks as Bul walks away.

"My parents would die. They would simply die," Damini says. "They're biologists, and they're always studying bacteria under the Arctic and poisonous toads in the Amazon. They would be so jealous if they knew I was seeing all this. But . . . even if I was back on Earth, I'd have no way to talk to them." Her face falls for a moment.

We pass another viewport, and everybody has to stop and gaze at the stars shooting past. The *Indomitable* is moving at its slowest speed, because of all the damage, but the stars still stretch into curved blades. "Look at that color." Keziah points at this one star that's just a big blue streak. "That's incredible."

"You can tell the iron and magnesium content in the star by how blue its trail gets," I say. "It's like a highway flare, sort of."

Keziah stares and his lips move, almost like he's making a wish on the blue star.

I take them through Engineering, where Yma vents a blood-red bubble at the interruption. But the kids are too busy staring at the swoosh of energy harvested directly from our sun's corona, snaking horizontally across the center of the engine room behind a translucent shield.

"Oh yeah, we caught a solar flare in a bottle," I say, like that's nothing.

We walk past the control deck and we all stare through the viewport, to see Captain Othaar having a huge argument with Lyzix and Vaap. I lead them around to the bigger door, which opens to show all of the hard-light displays dancing above all the workstations in Forward Ops, including my empty tactical station, which looks lonesome for me.

Just past Forward Ops, a short ramp leads up to the bluehouse, at the very top of the ship. Vegetables and fungi grow out of the dirt floor, bathed in a deep blue light, to supplement our stashes of food and medicine. There's just enough room for the six of us to sit on the mossy floor in between all of the quivering stalks of vegetation and the squishy fungal growths.

Right in the middle of the floor, a round window divided into spokes gives us a perfect view of space, ahead of the ship. We're plunging, like a stone into a starlit well.

Nobody talks. Everyone's just hugging themselves and quietly freaking out, except for Damini. I keep replaying all of the space trivia that I dumped on these kids who just left home a couple hours ago, and wondering if I could possibly have been any more of a tool.

The stars race toward us. Hundreds of worlds, all of them full of people obsessing about their lives and their families and their own random identity freak-outs.

These new kids probably think I'm a jackass now. It's going to be a repeat of improv camp, where everybody snuck into the woods to do bong hits and trust falls without me.

Rachael speaks, for the first time in ages. "Hey, I know this is really scary for all of us. I never even left home on my own before, and now I'm a million miles away. But that's all the more reason we should stick together. Nobody else on this ship can look out for the six of us as well as we can for each other. The Earthlings."

"Earthlings." Keziah nods, and holds out his hand, and Rachael clasps it.

Damini takes Keziah's other hand. "Earthlings."

"Okay. Earthlings." Yiwei grabs Damini's hand.

Elza rolls her eyes, then shrugs and takes Yiwei's hand. "I don't have the best history with joining clubs. But sure. Earthlings."

Now I'm the only one who's not holding someone's hand. Everyone looks at me, and I look away.

Because, do I qualify as an Earthling? And do I even want to? I'm not human, and all I can think about is laying claim to this heritage, which I want so bad that I feel sick to my stomach and dizzy with joy when I think about it. Calling myself an Earthling feels like a step backward.

"Guys, I don't—" I stammer. "I mean, I'm not really . . ."

"Tina, get in here," Rachael says. "You lived a whole life on Earth. You went to high school and flunked driver's ed and everything. You're an Earthling, too, whatever else you might be."

I hesitate one moment longer, then grab Rachael's hand as well as Elza's, making this a circle. "Earthlings."

It feels right. Comforting. Something to hold on to.

All six of us sit there, holding hands and gazing into the endless starscape, our faces painted blue.

17

Four kids collectively lose a breath at their first view of Captain Othaar's skull face and exposed finger joints as he waves us into the half-empty control deck. Lyzix is busy staring at damage reports with a frown on her fox-shaped face.

"Welcome aboard the *Indomitable*. Happy memories and bearable regrets," Othaar says.

I give the response: "Clever guesses and educational mistakes. Captain."

Everyone else is too busy figuring out the cool way to sit down in a teacup. The four new kids have ditched their messed-up Earth clothes in favor of the same two-piece rust-colored cadet fatigues I'm wearing: made of a material that feels like denim, with a pale stripe on the left sleeve that lists my status as trainee. At least I've figured out something else to wear under the uniform jacket, to stop it being so itchy. Rachael is wearing tan medical scrubs.

"I'm Captain Othaar, and my pronoun is *he*. I apologize for not greeting you when you first arrived, as I'd originally planned. I'd like to make it up to all of you."

"So is it true that you were just going to let Wang Yiwei and me die?" Elza asks.

Yiwei stares at Elza, like she just smacked him. I start to say something, but Othaar waves his hand.

"Yes, that's absolutely true," Othaar says. "We had to choose between saving the entire planet Earth, or your two lives. But I'm very sorry."

Lyzix finally joins the conversation, uncurling her sleek feline body. "We had concluded that there was no way to save you. And apparently that was incorrect. I understand that the three of you helped find a solution." She looks at Rachael, Damini, and Keziah, who just stare back—except for Damini, who grins.

"This just proves we were right to recruit you," Othaar adds. "You've been identified as the brightest young people from your planet," he says to the four newcomers.

"So . . . I almost died! And now I find out you decided I was expendable, and now you want me to join your crew anyway," Yiwei says. "What if I just want to go home? Maybe I just want to go back to Tianjin and play music and eat Gǒubùlǐ dumplings and live my life."

"You were never expendable," Othaar says. "But we can't go back to Earth. Once this ship gets repaired at the nearest civilized outpost, we have missions elsewhere. Not to mention, the humans just fired a nuclear weapon at us, which I think means we're not welcome there."

"The universal language of nukes," Rachael says under her breath. I look over her shoulder and see her sketching on a plastiform pad with one of Dr. Karrast's surgical notation lightpens. Captain Othaar looks cute and a bit wistful in Rachael's sketch, with a dreamy expression in his exposed eyeballs and jawbone.

"I definitely want to get as far away from home as possible," says Elza. "But I'm not sure I want to join a military squad, or whatever this is."

"Same," Keziah says. "I kind of love all the ceremony and fancy sayings and everything. But all this talk about monarchy is filling me with flashbacks of being forced to sing 'God Save the Queen' as a small child." Damini shoots him a look of sympathy, like she's glad he said that.

"Those are fair points," Othaar says. "Most of the time, our missions involve providing aid to people who are in trouble, or defending planets that are under attack. And also helping to create more understanding between different peoples. But now we've been dragged into a horrible war with the Compassion, whose agenda is nothing but the strong endlessly dominating the weak. They have to be stopped, or everyone will suffer. It's only a matter of time before the Compassion establishes a foothold on Earth."

"And our queen isn't a monarch." Lyzix yawns and stretches, and her ears flex. "She's more like a librarian, in the greatest library that has ever existed. She gathers the knowledge of a million worlds, and she shares it with everyone in the Firmament."

"Wow. *I love libraries.*" Damini's eyes get huge and greedy, even though I can't imagine her sitting still long enough to read a book. She's still wearing all her bangles and her necklace over her uniform, because they're all she has of home.

"I was in serious danger of getting burned out on science back home," Keziah says. "But now? I want to learn everything."

"Tina." Yiwei turns and looks at me. "You saved my life! So I trust you. And Yatto told me that you somehow know everything there is to know about this organization. So . . . is this for real? If you look me in the eye and tell me that these people are really about helping people and making things better, then I'll go with it."

Everybody turns and stares at me. Earthlings, aliens, everybody. I open my mouth to speak, and my mind goes blank. Just an hour ago, I was saying I wasn't sure if I still believed in the Royal Fleet, but now that hunger is driving me. I *need* to give these kids something to believe in.

Did I mention that I suck at public speaking? I suck at public speaking.

*

"All I know is what the Royal Fleet stood for back in Captain Argentian's day," I start, finally. "It was founded to keep people from stepping on each other—like in the bad old days of the Seven-Pointed Empire, when a handful of planets ruled over almost everyone else. And I've seen enough of the Compassion to know that they want to bring those bad old days back, only worse." I take a deep breath. "But that's not what matters."

I look at each of the four recruits in turn: Damini jittering with excitement, Keziah biting his lip, Yiwei folding his arms, and Elza staring at the floor.

"What really matters is, the four of you are all brilliant, and this is a chance for you to become even better," I say. "I've already seen so much badassery and coolness under pressure from all of you. But now, you could learn to fly a starship and save the galaxy, and also learn about alien cultures. Rachael was the one who thought we should recruit some genius nerds from Earth, because she thought you would be amazing. And she was totally right."

Rachael looks up from sketching, startled, and then gives me a quick smile before looking down again.

"This is a chance for all of us to be part of something greater than just ourselves," I say.

"Whenever people ask me to be part of something greater, it always means they want me to be smaller," Elza says. I feel myself tense for a confrontation, again.

"Well, I'm one hundred percent on board," Damini says, clapping her hands so her bangles clang. "As long as I get to help pilot the ship."

"I think we can make that happen," Lyzix says, ears twitching at her, in that way that means a Javarah likes you.

"Okay," Yiwei says, smiling. "I needed to find a new group of friends to help me get over my broken heart, and the Compassion sounds like it needs to be taken down. I'm in too."

"The whole reason why my father tried to lock me in a wine cellar was because I wanted the chance to go off on my own and figure out who I really am," Keziah says. "So yeah . . . I'm in."

Everybody looks at Elza.

She finally looks away from the floor and gazes at me, and her eyes are dazzling. My insides feel soft for a moment. "Fine. Okay. I'll give it a chance. I want to learn to hack on alien computers. And maybe the bossy girl is right, and you're not actually all creeps."

"Don't call me that," I mutter.

"Excellent." Captain Othaar scrunches his zygomatic plates into a smile. "We'll start teaching all of you the basics of life on a starship while we travel at low speed on our way to a repair station. And we'll assign each of you a mentor, who can teach you about a particular aspect of running this ship. I'd like to meet with each of you individually, to figure out the best situation for you."

So all of us Earthlings sit around the bluehouse, waiting for each name to be called in turn. Everything is still, except for this one big yellow fungus the shape of a pair of lips, which wobbles like Jell-O. At one point Yiwei pulls out his steel guitar and plays some blues with a slider on his fingers, and his tiny robot, Xiaohou, comes out and makes harmonica sounds.

Then Yiwei gets called down to meet the two captains, and the rest of us just sit there, in silence.

*

"I completely misread you," Elza says to me a while later, staring at the viewport full of blue streaks. "I thought you were a rebel. A rule breaker. I didn't realize that the cool outfit you were wearing was a uniform, until I saw everyone else wearing them—and now I'm stuck wearing one too, because my regular clothes got ruined."

"If I was someone who always followed the rules, you wouldn't be alive right now," I say.

"Sure, and I'm grateful. But you know what a uniform is, right? It's designed to take away your individuality and stop you from thinking for yourself. Everyone dresses the same, and soon we all think the same. And anyone who isn't wearing the same thing becomes the enemy."

I look at her delicate features in profile, and maybe one corner of her mouth is smiling.

"I get it." I move closer, trying to get her to turn and look at me. "You were homeless, and you got hassled by the police. But we're not like that. These uniforms are different: the left sleeve has my designation, acting junior tactical officer, but the right sleeve can have whatever message, or whatever design or picture, I want to program into it. And we don't even have ranks here. We have designations, like explorer, or engineer."

Elza shrugs. "Everybody always thinks they're the hero, in every story."

Gahhhhh, now I'm boiling again. She won't stop trying to tear everything down, without giving it a chance first, after I risked everything to save her. I can hear my own heartbeat, even over the whine of the damaged engines.

I try to explain to her that there are whole planets full of homeless people. Places where all the cities were smashed to rubble, whole populations hiding away in caves. "We're the only hope those people have."

"Why do you keep saying 'we'?" Elza turns to face me. She definitely has a half smile, or maybe a quarter smile. But there's a cynical edge in her gorgeous brown-green eyes. "You just came up from Earth too, didn't you?"

"Sort of." I try to explain how I was literally born to do this.

"You still have a choice. You still get to decide who you are and what you want to be."

"No. I don't." The blunt certainty in my voice startles me, as much as it does her. "I don't get to choose, any more than you chose to be homeless. This is a part of me, maybe the most important part of me, and . . ."

I trail off, because now she's fully smiling at me and it's making me fidgety. I can feel my cheeks burning.

"Everybody has choices," she says. "Even living on the street, or trapped on a ship racing away from the solar system, you always get to choose how to define yourself."

I'm about to say something else, but Yatto the Monntha comes walking up to us. Their tallness and bright blue-streaked yellow skin startles Elza, even though she's seen them before.

"There you are." Yatto introduces themself, wishing us beautiful journeys and safe arrivals. "Elza Monteiro, well met.

I've been assigned to teach you to use the ship's computers. I understand you're a . . . 'hacker.'"

"I code." Elza winks. "It's good to meet you properly."

"You, too." Yatto smiles. "Our first task is to search through all of the records of Captain Argentian's journeys for any hint about where she might have seen this 'Talgan stone' that the Compassion is looking for. If they become any more powerful than they already are, then billions of people could suffer."

"Okay, sure. Show me the advanced alien computers." Elza turns to walk away with Yatto—but then she looks back and gives me a spiky look that seems to say: *We'll talk about this later.*

I'm still stewing about her pointless hate for something she doesn't even understand, and the way her smile made me feel when she said, *Everybody has choices.* How the hell am I ever going to convince this girl that not everybody is evil all the time?

And then I realize I'm going to be late for my first proper shift in Forward Ops.

18

I can't stop thinking about Elza's sarcastic laugh, and the way she trashed everything I want to believe in, even as I slide into my seat at Tactical. My seat is right up front, facing the big anthill-shaped situation monitor, which projects a giant holographic blob with a ton of status updates. (Nobody ever looks at the situation monitor.)

"Wild weather and safe harbors," says a deep voice, to my left. I glance and see someone who looks maybe a year or two older than me.

I say the correct response without even thinking about it: "Harmless fauna and lush flora."

"I'm Junior Explorer Thanz Riohon, and my pronoun is *he*. I'm still in awe of that maneuver you did to save those two recruits. That took some guts."

I start to mutter some thanks. Then I turn and get a proper look at Riohon, and my jaw drops.

Riohon is the most attractive man I've ever seen, with amazing cheekbones and jawline, except that his skin is a translucent pale violet, and his eyes are big and round. I realize after a moment: Riohon is a Makvarian, the same as Captain Argentian. The same as me—except for the tweaks they made to my DNA when I was a baby.

I haven't had a crush on a guy in ages. Or anyone, really. My sexual orientation is basically just "I'm picky."

But I feel my hormones surge when I even glance at Riohon sideways. I almost forget how much Elza's smile made me blush, before she started getting obnoxious and making me want to throw something.

Riohon is still talking about the stunt I did to save Elza and Yiwei. "Scariest thing I've ever seen. But hey, you know that old Makvarian saying, about when you stare into the face of death and live to talk about it."

"Actually . . ." I search my mind, just to be sure. "No. I don't."

Pretty much any time someone mentions Makvarian culture, I don't know anything about it, I guess because anything major was part of Captain Argentian's personal memories. I can think of a million random facts about Yatto's home planet, or Dr. Karrast's, but almost nothing about "mine." (And yet, when the other kids want to bond over the stuff we miss from Earth, like pizza or TV shows, I feel like an imposter.)

Riohon's godlike chin is nodding sympathetically. "I ought to teach you everything I can about our culture."

I glance at his distractingly chiseled jawline and somehow put on a casual voice. "Sounds good. Thanks."

Then I throw myself into staring at my tactical display, swirling my hands inside the holographic slime to adjust the settings or zoom in on stuff. We're only doing passive scans right now, not sending any pulses of charged particles to see what they bounce off (because we're trying to stay hidden, while we're severely damaged). So I'm mostly looking for the radioactive farts that would be our only warning that another ship is out there, before they blow us to bits.

*

Some time later, I hear a familiar joyful squee.

"Hi, Tina! And oh, hello, you must be Riohon. I'm going to be your student! Sorry I'm late, I took a wrong turn near the ramp to the bluehouse, and then I was distracted by this one giant fungus that looked carnivorous. Oh, wait, I was supposed to say something else, like, 'Lucky journeys with good friends.' Was that it? Close enough, right? I'm Damini, and my pronoun is *she*, by the way. How does all this stuff work? What am I supposed to look for in this holographic display? How soon do I get to pilot the ship? I cannot wait to learn absolutely everything. I feel like I've been preparing for this my whole life. So where do I start?"

Riohon doesn't seem to mind Damini's motormouth. He just waits until she runs out of words, then says: "Great to meet you! I heard that you solved a puzzle that required high-level spatial awareness and the ability to think outside three dimensions. So, check it out: this is the four-dimensional trajectory display, and that dot is our ship. Those wavy lines represent the curvature of spacetime, and this overlay here is cosmic radiation. And here— try easing your hand into this hard-light interface."

Damini touches her elephant-headed amulet (which I guess is Ganesh) with two fingers, and touches both of her eyes. Then she slides her hand into the interface.

"Oh, wow. It's kind of gooey. How can a hologram be gooey?"

"Takes some getting used to."

Riohon's voice is so friendly and coaxing, a wave of jealousy catches me by surprise. Both because he's smoking hot, and because I wish I had a mentor like that. But mostly, I'm happy for Damini. She's going to *own* this.

"Now, can you sense that faint vibration against your fingertips, rising and falling?" Riohon says.

"Yeah," Damini says. "Yeah, oh wow. That's . . ."

"You're feeling the heartbeat of the ship. The engines, the guidance systems. Her muscles flexing, as she swims through the frozen vacuum. This whole enormous machine is at your fingertips right now, and when you learn to understand all these sensations and read everything on this display, you'll be able to make it dance, with the tiniest movement of your hand."

"Oh," Damini says. "Wow. Almost feels like petting a sleeping cat."

"Not sure what a cat is," Riohon says. "But yes, this ship is alive, in a lot of ways."

I turn away from Tactical just long enough to see the glow on Damini's face. She's going to be the best pilot, I can already tell.

Then I hear Lyzix's voice in my shoulder comms: "Mains, we're going to need you on full alert. We've identified one of the planets where Captain Argentian might have found this thing that the Compassion are looking for, the Talgan stone. We can visit on our way to Rascal Station for repairs. But if there's another ship out there, we'll need to see them before they see us."

"With a will," I say.

"Riohon, change of course," Othaar says. "We're going to Best Planet Ever."

*

Rachael: Just testing this out to see if it actually works. It works!!!!

Tina: yep, apparently the first thing Elza did when she got to the computers is figure out a way for us to text

Tina: when she wasn't busy accusing the Royal Fleet of eating babies

Rachael: Give her time

Rachael: She just needs to feel safe. Sounds like she's been through a lot

Tina: so have all of us. the rest of us are coping.

Tina: i've waited so long for this

Rachael: Remember your 14th birthday party?? Suzy Craddock?

Tina: yeahhhhh . . . i didn't want to invite her in the first place. i didn't even want a party at all.

Rachael: The look on your face, while we were all playing Waymaker. you looked like a pissy old man.

Rachael: That was the night you told me you didn't belong with us, on Earth. You belonged up here, in space. And then you threw a cupcake at the wall.

Tina: suzy craddock was like 'this is why nobody likes you!!!'

Tina: best birthday ever

Rachael: And your mom was like, 'even if you're going to grow up to be Buzz Lightyear, you still need to play well with others.'

Tina: my poor mom.

Tina: i hope she's okay. she'll be okay, right?

Rachael: I hope my parents reach out to her. I hope my parents understand why I left.

Rachael: I hope I get another chance to explain to them. Someday.

Best Planet Ever comes into view: a speck, next to the weak reddish glow of Best Star Ever. The star used to be called Seythop and the planet was Seythop IV—but they changed the names to try and attract more tourists.

"So, is it?" Damini asks. "The best planet ever, I mean."

"They might have exaggerated," Riohon says. "It's actually kind of boring. Ten different kinds of mud. Their main food is slug spit."

"Junior Visioner Yatto, scan for transmissions from the planet," Othaar says. "We should be close enough."

"With a will," Yatto says, then hesitates. "Oh. I'm not . . . I'm not finding any."

"Interference?" Lyzix asks. "Or maybe they had a solar flare."

"No sign of either of those, Alternate Captain," Yatto says.

I start to say something, but instead, I just squint at my tactical scans again. At this distance I'm still not sure, but . . . I don't think there's any heat sources down there at all. Maybe we'll get closer and realize there's some explanation, like the whole planet went on holiday. But.

"Sir, I . . . I think there's nobody left alive on Best Planet Ever," Uiuiuiui says slowly.

"They had a population of over a billion," Othaar says. "They can't have just . . ." He trails off in horror, until he notices Yiwei standing next to him and pulls himself together. "We'll get a closer look soon enough. Let's not jump to conclusions."

*

But by the time we know the worst for sure, everybody's already accepted it. There's a yawning crater where Best City Ever used to be, and all of the smaller cities and towns are dust as well. The whole atmosphere has been hoovered away, and the planet has a layer of debris just like Earth's, except this is nothing but wreckage.

"Who could have done this?" Damini whispers.

Nobody answers, because the answer is: "Anybody." It's not that hard to wipe out a whole planet, by dropping rocks from orbit, screwing with the magnetosphere, or a ton of other stuff.

We're already executing a slingshot around Best Planet Ever, to get us away from here faster, when I spot something in orbit that's not a piece of debris. "Um, Captains. You better check this out."

"It's a beacon, transmitting at low power," Vaap says. "Could contain some useful information."

A moment later, we've used the ship's ion harness to bring it on board, and the *Indomitable* is zooming away from what's left of Best Planet Ever.

*

The hologram is super blurry to begin with, plus the tall figure at the center is half in shadow, so all I can see is a dark blur with a pale smudge of face. But the white-faced giant still looks familiar, because he's been starring in all my nightmares lately.

Marrant.

All of those visions of him smirking at me, raising a weapon, come flooding back. Even my feet are shivering.

"Your entire culture, your whole society, are worthless," he's saying. "Their only value comes from giving me what I want."

"Please." A creature with ten long stalks coming off a chalky body, like a lump of coral, cowers. This is a Ganghoi, one of the natives of Best Planet Ever. "We don't know about this 'Talgan stone,' we've never even seen it," the Ganghoi whimpers. "We have all the best things on Best Planet Ever, but we don't have the item you're looking for."

Riohon freezes. Damini is recoiling from the holographic playback coming out of the situation monitor. Wang Yiwei, sitting next to Captain Othaar in the control deck, is staring in horror too.

Marrant waves a hand, and two humanoids in dark armor drag the Ganghoi toward him. Then Marrant reaches out one hand. I stiffen even before I see it happen: the Ganghoi who just spoke shrinks, or maybe melts, and a moment later all that's left is a dark shiny pool on the floor.

"Who's next?" For a moment, I get a super-clear view of Marrant's porcelain-mask face, and my gut folds in on itself. I know for sure that if we ever meet, this man is going to kill me.

The recording cuts out abruptly, with all the other Ganghoi still gazing into the sickening remains of their friend.

Somebody must have used their final moments to launch this recording into orbit, so somebody would at least know what happened.

"We have to assume that Marrant didn't find the Talgan stone on Best Planet Ever," Othaar says from the control deck.

"And apparently, Marrant's experiments have given him the power to melt people into puddles, just by touching them," says Lyzix. "He never stops surprising."

Nobody else talks. I can't stop remembering the way Marrant's perfect, smooth face frowned, right before sentencing an innocent person to death. And all our images of Best Planet Ever, as lifeless as the moon.

The thought hits me again: *That man is going to kill me.*

19

I sit on a teacup in my new quarters and try to make my heart stop thrashing.

When I finally found the room that's supposed to be "mine," I was so exhausted that I could barely stand. But when I tried to lie down, I remembered Marrant turning that poor guy into sludge, and my heart started jumping up and down, like a dog at a gate.

These quarters are barely large enough to move around in. A workstation faces the teacup where I'm sitting, and then there's a cradle hanging along the opposite wall, sort of like a cross between a hammock and a cocoon, for sleeping in. And a tiny alcove where you can use various sprays and devices to clean yourself up.

I'm never going to get used to the whiplash. One part of my mind looks at things and thinks, *What the hell is that? I've never seen that before.* But the other part knows exactly how to use this spongy celery-shaped sprayer to clean my teeth. (I spent ages explaining it to the others.)

I keep wondering about Captain Argentian, and how she could possibly have been friends with Marrant. And then it occurs to me: maybe I can find out more.

I slide my hands into the holographic jelly of my workstation. (Still not used to this feeling.) I don't have any access codes, but a surprising amount of stuff is available.

A holographic bubble pops up with Captain Argentian's service record: joined up in the Age of Plenty, served with distinction through the border disputes with the Free Endeavor Zone, helped to prevent a war between the Aribentors and the Zooii. Bravery, distinction, etc., etc.

And then I hit the jackpot: there are some recordings of Thaoh Argentian's personal log entries, and I can view them without an access code. Maybe because she's dead—or maybe the computer thinks I'm her.

I pick one at random, and what I see makes me gasp.

Captain Argentian is even lovelier than the hologram I saw in Othaar's receiving room. She holds herself upright, like a diva, and her skin shimmers a faint violet, shading toward blue. And she looks like she's walked through endless rivers of flaming sewage, but she's kept her head high. She has jewels in her cheeks and a few smaller ones going around her jawline, which I guess is the Makvarian custom.

She holds up a bottle of yuul sauce, the good stuff, and sighs. "Nobody seems to understand that the Peacebringer's Code is meaningless, if we don't do something to fix this mess."

Captain Argentian's personal datajournal, 11.23.11.08 of the Age of Regret

Nobody seems to understand that the Peacebringer's Code is meaningless, if we don't do something to fix this mess we inherited. We built our empire on the backs of creatures who were robbed of all the basic rights that we take for granted. We can't let that go. I don't even know why this is an argument.

Captain swigs directly from her yuul sauce bottle, and growls in her throat. Her mood seems to darken.

I still can't believe how Marrant acted. He's never going to accept responsibility for his own actions at Zenoith. Aym might never wake up. I would have said Marrant was the one person I could count on. Now . . . I just don't know.

We haven't even spoken to each other since the tribunal. I hope one day Marrant understands. He kept saying the Royal Fleet is weak, and we're going to fall apart the same way the Seven-Pointed Empire did—unless we're willing to do what's necessary.

That's the kind of talk that we both used to make fun of. I don't even know him anymore, and I wish Aym was here to knock some sense into him. But of course, that's the problem. If Aym was still here, we wouldn't be in this mess in the first place.

Captain takes another drink. Captain makes choking noise and says something inaudible.

This job . . . I just want to go home and cheat at wardlock with my family. Out here, everybody lets you down eventually.

Argentian shakes her head and slouches, as if the local gravity has suddenly increased inside her quarters. She takes another drink from the bottle as the recording ends.

20

The alarms stop ringing, and we all stand in the abrupt silence.

Except for Wang Yiwei, who picks himself up off the floor. He brushes off his uniform—which has a beautiful schematic, showing a robotic arm with exposed actuators and pistons, going all the way down his right sleeve.

Everybody looks at everybody else. Vaap approaches with a heavy tread.

"If that had been a real Situation Green Leap, you would all be dead right now," Vaap says, brushing their big rocky hands together with a scraping sound.

We've been here in the cargo hangar, drilling on different kinds of emergency situations, for a few cycles (or over two hours). They've shaken the hangar back and forth to simulate the turbulence from meteorite impacts, they've turned off the momentum gravitators so we had to float around in zero gravity, and we just tried to cope with direct hits from *two* dreamkiller missiles. (Which is what Situation Green Leap means.)

Damini should be jumping up and down with happiness right now. This is what she's been begging for, ever since she came on board. But instead, she's got a deadly serious look on her face. "We need to do better. We need to be ready for when we face the Compassion."

"We're doing the best we can," Keziah protests. "I don't respond well to pressure."

"Captain Othaar says that practicing the right response to each emergency could save our lives," says Yiwei. Elza rolls her eyes, the way she always does when Yiwei quotes the captain. (Which is all the time, lately.)

"You didn't see that recording," Damini says to Keziah. "He killed those poor creatures like it was nothing. It was the most monstrous thing I've ever seen, and I keep replaying it in my dreams."

"He was pure evil," Yiwei says. "He told them their culture was worthless, and he laughed as they were dying. I just want to knock that smirk off his creepy face."

I notice none of them are saying *Marrant*. Like he's too scary to even say his name.

"We're not drilling you on combat here," Vaap says, rolling their head around with a *crunch*. "All we want is to help you survive, if we do run into a bad situation. And to understand the different alarms when you hear them."

"But I *want* to fight them," Yiwei says. "I can't unsee that recording. I need to fight back."

"Who even are the Compassion?" Keziah raises one eyebrow. "They used to be part of the Royal Fleet, right?"

Vaap nods. "My gatherers—my 'parents'—were young when those traitors went rogue. They told me about it when I was still just a few stones tall."

"What happened?" Rachael speaks up for the first time in ages, from the corner where she's been keeping to herself.

"We discovered the most heinous crime in the entire history of the galaxy." Vaap looks down for a moment. Then they shrug and wander over to the exterior hatch of the cargo hangar. "I'll tell you the whole story while we take a walk on the outside of the ship. Follow me."

"With a will." I nudge the others until they mumble it too—because "follow me" was technically an order.

Vaap helps all of us to put on atmosphere suits, like the one I wore to rescue Yiwei and Elza. Damini punches the air with her gloved hand, while Keziah squirms and Rachael hugs herself. Then Vaap ushers us out onto the exterior hull of the *Indomitable*, where we all stand around inside the big "O" in the ship's name. (At least, that's what I see, in English.)

With the atmosphere suits, we're comfortable enough walking along the outside of the ship. Plus they've extended the atmosphere outward, so we can breathe even if the suits fail. The stars shoot past all around us: gemstones shaped like bent nails.

"This time, we're doing Situation White Fall," Vaap says over the comms in our suits. "In that scenario, hostiles have boarded the ship, and they are occupying all of the crucial strategic areas. Your mission is to walk along the outside of the ship until you reach the front section, near the bluehouse."

"Understood." I'm painfully aware that I'm the only one who's responding properly.

"And then we break into Forward Ops and help fight off the intruders?" Yiwei asks.

"No," Vaap says. "You reach the survival pods and escape from the ship. I told you: right now, my goal is just to make sure you can stay alive, in any situation."

The countdown clock appears on the palm of my right hand: one and a half minicycles, or about seven minutes. Then we all run across the scar-laced hull and weave around the jutting bulbs of the weapons systems, and the spikes of the ion harnesses and impact countermeasures.

I try to keep my eye on the goal, but I keep getting distracted by all the whirling lights.

"Look at that starscape." Vaap's footsteps make no sound for once. "The stars are always dancing around us, even though the ship's walls give us the illusion of safety and smallness." Vaap gestures. "And just think how unlikely it is that so many creatures in this wide-open galaxy would be the same basic shape as us: two arms, two legs, one head."

"I did wonder about that." Damini jumps over a maneuvering impeller. For a moment she hovers in space, then she floats back down onto the hull. "Everyone on this ship is human-shaped. Everybody even has two eyes and two ears, except for Dr. Karrast. My parents would have said that's really very unlikely. Did some ancient humanoids visit a bunch of planets and leave their DNA behind? Are we all related to the same distant ancestor?"

Damini is getting way ahead, so she has to turn to look back at us through her glassy faceplate.

"No," Vaap says. "My people and yours don't have much DNA in common. And neither do any of the other humanoid species. We wondered for a long time why all of the galaxy's most advanced peoples were humanoids. Until we found out the answer." They grunt. "And then we wished we hadn't."

*

We're all running across the "T" in the ship's name now. Rachael trips over one of the meteor scars on the hull and lands on her side, clutching her bruised knee. I reach down and help her to her feet, and she leans on me as we make our way to the "A," three-legged-race style.

"Ow," Rachael says.

"Good," Vaap says. "Nobody gets left behind. You watch out for each other."

"So what was it?" Elza asks, offering another shoulder for Rachael to lean on. "What was the answer to why all of the creatures on this ship are shaped the same as us?"

Vaap hesitates a moment, then says: "Some archeologists found evidence there was a civilization of humanoids that lived a long time ago. They traveled all over the galaxy, and wherever they found other species with this same basic humanoid shape, they provided some help. Like gene therapies. Or better technology. Or immunity against some diseases. Or else they reshaped our ancestors' home planets, to make them easier to live on."

"So they just helped other humanoids to become more advanced?" Damini asks.

"That doesn't sound so bad," Rachael says, gasping as she puts weight on her knee.

We've reached the "B"—and then the ship lurches, turning sideways so the hull is suddenly slanted downward on our right side.

Everyone yelps. Damini loses her footing and goes sliding toward the edge of the curved surface, feet first. Yiwei runs over to her and grabs her hand in time to yank her upright.

"Got you." Yiwei grins.

"Thanks for the save." Damini struggles to her feet.

"Then there's the other part," Vaap says. "Sometimes, those ancient explorers found intelligent creatures who weren't human-shaped—with too many limbs, or claws instead of hands, or slimy round bodies. And they did everything they could to hurt those creatures. They dropped a whole planetoid onto what appears to have been a lively civilization of creatures with nine tentacles. And they triggered an ice age, to destroy a species of giant worms who had constructed huge cities full of beautiful artworks."

Vaap's voice drips with disgust. "This . . . *project* went on for hundreds of thousands of years, and it shaped the galaxy we live in today. It's the reason why so many of us humanoid species are so powerful. And why anyone who doesn't happen to have two arms and two legs is still struggling to catch up."

"That's horrible," Yiwei breathes.

We've reached the "L," and now someone wearing another suit (Yatto?) is leaning out an open hatch, aiming a weapon at us. "The intruders have found us," Vaap shouts. "Take cover!"

We all hunch behind one of the ship's plasma cannons as the "intruder" shoots harmless bolts of light over our heads. Vaap gestures for us to sneak around along the side of the ship, so everything is suddenly turned at a right angle to where we just were.

"So wait . . . did these ancient humanoids . . . did they help out the human race too?" Damini asks.

"We've found evidence that they intervened on Earth, yes," Vaap says.

We've gotten out of the way of Yatto's fake gun, and so we creep back around, along the big globe-shaped nose of the ship. I can look right under my feet and see into the bluehouse now.

"Who were these dick-satchels?" I ask. "And what happened to them?"

"We call them the Shapers, but we still know almost nothing about them," Vaap says to me. "We only learned of their existence during Captain Argentian's career—she was one of the people who argued that we needed to work to fix the damage they had left behind. But there were others inside the Royal Fleet who thought the Shapers had the right idea, and wanted to continue their work."

"And those people became the Compassion?" Yiwei has found the exterior hatch to the survival pod, but the opening mechanism is stuck. We're down to just one hundred microcycles (fifty seconds) of air left in our suits.

"Yes," Vaap says.

The hatch won't open, even when we all tug at it. And now Yatto is running toward us across the hull, firing light-bursts wildly.

"Everybody stand back," Damini says. "I got this. This is just another kind of puzzle, right?" She reaches inside the jammed mechanism and finds a loose piece with her gloved hand, easing it into place.

A moment later, the hatch slides open, and the seven of us tumble inside the survival pod, in a big heap. There are four seats, with safety harnesses, and then a few places where extra people can strap themselves to the walls.

"Congratulations," Vaap snerks. "You didn't die this time."

21

Kez: Ugh. That last training session, with the rainbow force fields. My whole body is sore.

Yiwei: it's good though. we're learning how things work on this ship

Yiwei: i want to start carrying a lightpad so i can write down all the amazing things that Captain Othaar says.

Yiwei: he's so inspiring

Elza: you're like the president and treasurer of the Captain Othaar fan club all of a sudden

Yiwei: because he's awesome!

Yiwei: he's been teaching me how the ship's hull can change shape to repair damage or whatever.

Yiwei: the hull can rearrange itself, like a giant robot!!!!

Elza: that actually is kind of cool, i suppose.

Tina: the hull also conducts sound, so it's also kind of like a musical instrument

Yiwei: ohhh. Really??!?

Yiwei: I want to be the first person ever to play music on a starship hull

Damini: only if there's a cool concert t-shirt.

Damini: i used to go to all these fantastic music shows in Bandra

Damini: that was my neighborhood back home in Mumbai. you would LOVE it.

Yiwei: i can't wait to watch Captain Othaar up close, in a battle or something

Rachael: Be careful what you wish for.

Kez: I'm just happy to be down in the relative calm of Engineering with Yma, who doesn't have a heroic bone in . . .

Kez: Er, does Yma's species even HAVE bones?

Tina: sort of

Tina: Zyzyians have blood vessels that also serve as skeletons

Kez: There she is, the fountain of weird information.

Tina: ugh yea. . . . just call me Space Wikipedia

*

We walk in circles, watching the stripes on the walls go from utility black to engineering green to flight-deck blue to command rainbow, and back again, until we end up in the crew lounge.

Damini digs out a bunch of plastiform tubes and boxes from the far locker. "I have just one question. Which of you is going to be the *coward* who won't eat all of this space food?"

She opens a tube, and one greenish-brown lozenge rolls onto the metal table, about the size and shape of a poker chip—but as soon as it's exposed to air, the lozenge grows to hubcap size, with an ear-splitting clap.

Then it shrinks back to poker-chip size, with a "wet-towel snapping" sound.

Then back to hubcap size.

At the large size, you can see it glisten, and count all of the dark veins threading through the gelatinous flesh.

THUNK! whump. THUNK! whump.

It's sort of hypnotic.

"What is it?" Keziah asks me. "And how poisonous is it?"

I'm not sure for a second, then I remember.

"Uh, this is a Cydoghian eggburst. This creature on Cydogh Prime secretes these things for its mate to lay eggs inside. It's kind of . . ." I keep losing my train of thought, because it keeps going THUNK! whump. THUNK! whump. "I think it's probably edible by humans, but just super chewy."

"Enough talk," Damini says. "Who's trying the first bite? Or are you all *too scared*?"

When nobody answers, she grabs the thing and sinks in her teeth, just as it expands to dinner-plate size again. The Cydoghian eggburst gives a squeal—probably just air escaping—as Damini bites off a chunk. Then it's teeny again, with a miniature bitemark in one side.

THUNK! whump. THUNK! whump. THUNK! whump.

We can all hear Damini chewing. "I think," she says, still chewing, "this could be," chew chew chew, "kind of an acquired taste. Who else wants some?" Everyone looks away, including me. "Come *on*. It's an experience. I dare you."

Rachael sinks back in her chair and covers her face.

Yiwei chomps into the pulsating flesh disc during one of its "larger than life" moments. Dark brown juice spatters the side of his face, and he makes a disgusted expression. "Oh," he says with his mouth full. "This is the worst thing I've ever eaten. Thanks for that."

I bite into the eggburst, and my mouth fills with a revolting battery-acid mush. I want to barf, but my mouth thinks I'm already barfing. I get a stabbing pain. I'm pretty sure my bite of eggburst keeps growing and shrinking inside my stomach.

"I'm going to be the first person from Earth to eat every kind of alien food, unless one of you steps up," Damini gloats.

*

I could listen to Riohon talk about Makvaria forever. Not just because his voice is like silk billowing in a warm breeze—but also, every word he speaks makes this place seem more real, and more like someplace I could go. Or even belong, maybe.

He tells me about this valley where they grow the sweetest spreeflowers, whose red-and-silver petals reach upward like hands, and their juice tastes like the first day of harvest. There's also a continent that's all swamp, and people walk around half-submerged in water *all the time*, and they supposedly gain psychic powers from all that swamp gas, so they can tell you who you're going to become. Makvaria has a few dozen different cultures, and they don't agree about almost anything, including sex, romance, religion, or politics.

Could I belong there? Is that where I'll finally make sense?

"We all share certain stories," Riohon says at our tiny table in the corner of the crew lounge, apart from the other crewmembers munching on blaycakes or EveryStomach crisps. "Like, there was a huge Inrugh that swam up out of a spout from the center of the world and blew water through its blowhole, and that became the oceans and all life. The spout is real, incidentally. They found it at the bottom of the White Sea."

"Damn." That's my whole contribution to this conversation, so far.

"Makvaria is beautiful and mostly pleasant, even in the ice deserts. But the planet also has some ugly moods. Two different volcanoes have a habit of erupting and filling the skies with ash, creating a winter that can last a decade. There are large, nearly unkillable predators that hibernate for years at a time, only to emerge and slaughter thousands of people. And other stuff. That's why the one principle all Makvarians agree on is that nobody ever stands alone. Every Makvarian looks out for other Makvarians."

"Like you're doing right now." I punch his arm super lightly.

Wow. Flirting.

"Yes, exactly." Riohon smiles, and my mind swarms with fantasies of dragging him to Clinton High's senior prom. Maybe getting him to wear a tux. *Ewww, stop it, brain.* "Most Makvarians only go out into space in the company of other Makvarians. There's a whole separate fleet that's nominally part of the Royal Fleet. But I wanted to learn to understand other cultures, and maybe be part of a different kind of fellowship."

Everything Riohon is saying makes me desperate to visit Makvaria and maybe even meet the people Captain Argentian loved, the ones she wanted to cheat at wardlock with.

But when a couple cycles have passed, and he's finished cramming my head full of info, I still don't feel like I know Makvaria at all.

*

I always figured homesickness would just feel sad, or lonesome. But it turns out the "sick" in "homesick" is real, and it's a lot like the flu: queasy misery.

Everybody's feeling it. Wang Yiwei won't even play for us in the bluehouse anymore, because his guitar and Xiaohou both remind him too much of his ex, and all their plans to conquer pop music with cute robots. There's some Chinese saying about a thread of fate that reunites two people who belong together, even from a thousand miles away—but maybe it doesn't work for a few million miles.

Since Yiwei won't provide music, Keziah plays some J Hus on his phone, because he's figured out how to recharge it using the ship's power.

Keziah's phone still has the local time on Earth, so Damini figures out it's almost time for her weekly Skype date with her brother Govind, who's studying at Cornell in the United States. Not to mention we're coming up on Rakhi, Damini's favorite festival, which is all about a brother and sister being there for each other. Back home, whenever Damini got lonesome, she'd just go and sit in the Asiatic Society of Mumbai for hours, poring over all the rare books and artifacts.

"I'm homesick too," Keziah says. "Thinking about all the cute boys I never even got up the nerve to talk to. But also, I can't stop worrying about what could be happening back home."

Yiwei groans. "Yeah. I hope everything is okay on Earth."

"How could it be?" Keziah says. "A massive explosion went off near Neptune, and the Compassion probably left loads of alien technology lying about. People must be having an epic meltdown."

"Or? They just covered the whole thing up," Damini says. "People are surprisingly good at pretending things didn't happen."

"There's no way to know," I say.

"Plus, there's nothing we can do," Rachael says. "Even if we could go home right now, what would we do? Who would listen to a random group of teenagers?"

Keziah shakes his head. "Doesn't make me feel any better."

"I'm going to stick to believing they covered it up," Damini says. "Because denial is the most powerful force in the entire universe."

*

"So . . . how does this work?" Rachael stares at the blank right sleeve of my uniform jacket, which is folded across her lap.

"It's pretty easy, I think." I stare at the emptiness of the reddish-brown material. "You draw whatever you want, and then the computer can program it into the fabric, so it becomes the design on the right sleeve. Yiwei already put a schematic of a robot arm onto his sleeve."

"Yeah. I saw." She frowns. "So what do you want a picture of?"

"I don't know. It doesn't matter. I just want a Rachael Townsend original."

We're sitting down in the storage area, the lowest point in the ship, below even the cargo hangar. We're surrounded by engine parts and random gear, and it's weirdly peaceful.

Rachael ponders for a moment. Then she flips the uniform jacket over, so she's looking at the left sleeve, which contains my designation: trainee cadet and acting junior tactical officer under the WE GOT YOUR BACK emblem with the Joyful Wyvern. She points at a tiny bloodred oval. "What's this?"

"Ugh. That's my demerit, from when I abandoned my post and jumped out of the ship to rescue Yiwei and Elza. That's going to be on my left sleeve forever, I guess."

"Oh. I didn't realize." She shakes her head and kind of rolls her eyes up to the ceiling. "So you need something on the other sleeve that says that you have people who care about you. And your family is all in one piece, because you wouldn't give up when everyone else did."

"Ha, thanks." I squirm, but it's a happy squirming. "As long as it doesn't literally say that. I don't want to piss people off. Again. I'm trying so hard to be a good member of this crew, while babysitting all these new kids who don't know how to act. It's . . . a lot."

Rachael stares at the red oval for a moment.

Then she sighs. "You still wish I had just gone home. And then nobody would have suggested bringing those other kids on board, and you would be here on this ship by yourself. You could've just focused on trying to be the second coming of Captain Argentian, without any other Earth kids to get in your way."

"No. No, of course not. That's . . . no." I give Rachael my most reassuring smile.

But Rachael knows me too well. She's staring at me, with the full power of her "BS detector activated" gaze.

"Okay, fine," I say. "Part of me wishes that. But if you had gone home, I really wouldn't have anyone to talk to. I'd be super lonely. I love Yatto, and Riohon is great. But without you and the other Earthlings . . . I wouldn't have any real friends on this ship."

"You didn't have any friends at Clinton High, after I dropped out," Rachael says. "And you were fine."

"I was not fine. Why do you think I was so desperate to leave the whole damn planet? If I hadn't at least been able to see you away from school sometimes, I would have been just a miserable creature. All the time."

"Thanks for being honest." Rachael flips my uniform jacket over, and looks at the blank sleeve again. "How about wildflowers? The kind that bloom everywhere, and don't give a damn what you thought you were planting, or what your landscaping plan was. The obnoxious blossoms that show up with bright colors and twirly crinkly leaves, and get in your face with unexpected beauty?"

"Wildflowers sound perfect," I say.

She's already sketching something that'll cover my entire right arm with flowery goodness.

22

Yatto's forehead crinkles, which makes their stripes change shape. "I don't even understand what you're asking me," they say to Elza.

"Source code!" Elza raises her hands over her head. "How do I access the source code on the ship's computer?"

"From the main interface, you can control every part of the ship," Yatto says.

"I know, I know. Like, if I want to make it rain blood inside the crew quarters, it's the same basic command as venting the engine coolant."

"Please do not make it rain blood anywhere on the ship," Yatto says.

Yatto, Elza, and I sit at a corner table in the crew lounge. We're picking at sawdust-like EveryStomach wafers, because the ship ran out of the hot-dog-flavored mushrooms—and I'm not eating any more Cydoghian eggburst. Yatto is munching on Irriyaian floatbeast liver (which looks like a chunk of green-tinted glass from a broken beer bottle).

"But there's no way for me to reprogram the computer," Elza says.

"Our computer isn't 'programmed,' exactly," Yatto says. "It's more like an offshoot of the artificial intelligences back in the Firmament. Like if someone cut off your finger, but it could keep moving independently."

"Ewww. I hate that metaphor, and I'm going to use it constantly to gross out other people from now on." Elza sticks out her tongue. "But I still don't understand why anyone would invent a brilliant supercomputer, and then go and chop it up into tiny pieces, and stick them inside little boxes, so they can never grow into anything on their own."

"I've tried to explain a few times already." Yatto looks at me, like: *Help*.

"I mean, you don't want a starship that can think for itself," I say. "Back during the Age of Innovation, a ship would sometimes get curious about some random space booger and go way off course instead of completing a crucial mission. Or the onboard computer just couldn't understand why a captain's orders carried more weight than some random crewmember's. Not to mention the *Imperative*! It flew straight into a black hole, because the computer was in a mood."

Elza laughs. "Do you ever just creep yourself out, spouting weird alien facts like that?"

"All the time. You have no idea."

Elza turns back to Yatto. "But if your computer was smarter, it could help you when you run into those Compassion monsters. And meanwhile there's *so much* other advanced stuff on this ship. Like, the moment I met you, I just knew that you have a nonbinary pronoun, which isn't really a thing in Portuguese. So how did I know that?"

"It's the EverySpeak," Yatto says. "It lets you know the correct pronoun, or assembly code, or instigator, for everyone. Some people even hear it spoken out loud. But also, different languages have different ways to talk about someone without using their name. Some languages use gender or reproduction, but a lot of others give information about a person's accomplishments, beliefs, or food preferences."

"And how does it work for your people?" Elza asks.

"Most Irriyaians use either male or female pronouns," Yatto says. "I started using a gender-neutral pronoun after I went into space. So I had to spend a few cycles concentrating, to make sure the EverySpeak accepted it."

"So you hacked your own gender. Which is amazing! So why don't I get to hack the ship's computer?"

"Maybe sometime you'll get to visit the Firmament and see the queen," Yatto says. "Her brain is plugged into all those super-advanced artificial minds."

"The queen is a cyborg?" Elza says. "Well, now I *definitely* want to meet her." She chews some EveryStomach wafers and grimaces. "Okay. I guess it's time to go back to playing with a severed finger."

"Just be careful," Yatto says. "That 'severed finger' is the only thing keeping the ship from blowing up."

"I've been hacking for years." Elza swivels her teacup chair and stands up. "And I've never blown up a spaceship yet."

*

My right sleeve looks incredible. I have to keep stopping every other minute to admire the design that Rachael created. Red and yellow and turquoise flowers on thick stalks, with crinkled sawtooth leaves around them.

Unless you look carefully, you'd never notice that the tiny red oval from my left sleeve is at the heart of every one of those flowers: Rachael's way of turning it into a symbol of pride.

Then I run into Elza in the hallway, and she's gotten a design on the right sleeve of her jacket, too: a severed human finger, with the words "WITHOUT A WILL" written above it in barbed wire. The picture is gross, and the spiky letters look like she's trying to tell everyone on this ship to go screw themselves.

"What the hell is that?" I ask, pointing at her arm.

"Do you like it?" Elza says. "We're supposed to use that one body part to express our individuality, even though the rest of our bodies and minds are supposed to conform and obey without question. So . . . I really wanted to make it count."

"Why can't you just give this ship a chance?" Once again my face is hot, and my whole body is amped up. "Everyone else is trying. Why do you have to be such a jerk?"

"Maybe it's just that I've dreamed my whole life of seeing a computer that can think for itself—and then I finally do, but it's been broken and twisted into something small and terrible. And meanwhile, I'm not supposed to think for myself, either." She folds her arms, so the severed finger is right over her chest. "The computer and me, we're both just supposed to shut up and obey orders."

"Nobody is trying to crush your spirit," I say. "We're sitting inside this fragile little shell, a million miles from anything, and if people don't do their jobs and cooperate with each other, we all die."

Situation Red Jump: Tina has had it up to here with all this negativity, and is reaching critical levels of wanting to bite someone's head off.

"I'm sorry." Elza doesn't sound sorry. "You all made a mistake when you chose me to invite on a space voyage. You could have picked a million smarter kids who have a way better attitude."

I want to scream.

"We picked you because you're the best. You know that!"

Elza shrugs. "I already tried to cooperate and be a 'team player' when I was living at the hackerspace—and then everyone else stole my work and took credit for my code. And then they turned around and insisted that a Black travesti couldn't possibly code as well as they could."

"What does that mean? Travesti?"

"If the EverySpeak doesn't know how to translate it, then that's probably for the best." She turns and walks away from me.

"Look, I'm sorry those assholes ripped off your code." I rush after her, down the hallway toward the crew quarters level. "But this ship recruited you because you're brilliant, and they want you to come up with new ideas, and ways to do better. And all you want to do is dump on everything all the time. Are you such a broken mess that you can't even give this a shot?"

Elza just keeps walking away from me, without saying anything back, like she doesn't even think I'm worth listening to anymore.

"Seriously, what is wrong with you?" I yell. My skin feels prickly and my blood is boiling and I'm getting tunnel vision. I hear a pounding in my head, and I have a spiky knot right where my rescue beacon used to live.

I am not going to let Elza ruin everything for the rest of us. I'm not going to let her tarnish what's left of my legacy.

"Hey," I shout. "Hey, come back and talk to me. We're not done here. HEY!"

Elza only stops because we've reached the ramp that leads to the next level of the ship.

She turns enough for me to see her face. I brace myself to see another mocking, sarcastic expression.

I'm not ready for the faceful of tears and runny makeup that I see instead. Elza's face is contorted with misery and she's heaving slow tight sobs, in total silence.

All of my anger drains away so fast, I'm left light-headed.

"Oh god. Oh god! Can I hug you? Is it all right to touch you? Are you okay?"

Elza hesitates, stiff as a board for a moment, and then she leans forward and rests her face on my shoulder. I wrap my arms around her and hold her as gently as I can, stroking her dark curls with my right hand. I almost say something like "it's okay, I'm here," or "you're okay," or "let it out," but I don't know the right thing to say to comfort her. So I just hold her close, for as long as she needs me to.

She cries and heaves without making the slightest sound. Almost as if she's used to shedding tears in secret.

I don't let go of her until she pulls away and wipes the streaks away from her face.

*

Some time later, Elza and I are sitting on the floor of the ship's tiny exercise room, staring at this machine that helps you do jumping jacks while hitting you with gravity fields from different directions. (I tried using that machine and nearly lost my lunch.)

"I shouldn't give you such a hard time," I say, staring at the exposed gravitators and pedals of the exercise machine. "You're totally right that this crew needs to earn your trust, as much as the other way around. And I can see how, if you spent your whole life playing with computers, it must be frustrating to be stuck with just a tiny piece of the Ardenii."

"The what?" Elza somehow still looks perfect, and self-possessed, and you'd never know she was crying a while ago.

"The . . . the Ardenii." I think for a second, and a flood of info comes to me, as though I always knew it. "Before there was a Royal Fleet, or a Firmament, there were these computers that became so smart that they could gather information from all over the galaxy, and see patterns that nobody else could see. The smarter they got, the harder it was for anybody to understand what they were saying, so we needed someone to speak for them."

"And that's the queen?" Elza half-smiles.

"Right. She starts learning to connect her brain to these Ardenii when she's still a teenager."

Elza gets a faraway look in her eyes.

"My parents always used to tell me I could be whatever I wanted, that I could just choose who I wanted to be," Elza says. "But then I told them I didn't want to be a boy anymore, and they threw me out on the street. I was only properly homeless for a short time, before I moved into the hackerspace, but that was more than enough anxiety for one lifetime."

I didn't even realize she was trans, or whatever.

"You're one of the most gorgeous people I've ever met," I say, truthfully. "I'm sorry your parents couldn't accept you for who you are."

She leans her head against my shoulder, breathing hard. Maybe she is crying again, I can't tell from this angle.

"Is that what 'travesti' means?" I say. "Is it like 'transgender'?"

Elza shakes her head. "We don't use that word as much. 'Travesti' is more like its own thing. Not actually a man, but not quite a woman, either. Something else. A lot of travesti only date men, so I got a lot of static when people found out I liked girls as well as boys. Many of us get surgeries and other treatments, but not all of us."

I'm still a little confused, but I just nod. Elza's head is still leaning against my shoulder, and it feels . . . right. I can feel her breathing.

Then she turns and looks at me, with her eyes bright and open. And she says the last thing I was expecting. "I think I just figured out how to find that thing we're all looking for. The Talgan stone."

She smiles at me. Instead of all that prickly aggravation, this time her smile makes me feel warm all over.

23

"Steady looking. Approach vector nominal. All duty crew, maintain vigilance," Vaap says from the control deck.

For the second time since we left Earth, we're approaching another planet where the Compassion could be waiting for us. And our hull is still held together with dental floss until we can make it to Rascal Station.

"Let's hope the Hosts of Misadventure are in a generous mood for once," Lyzix adds.

Kraelyo Homeglobe looks shiny and beautiful from up here. The planet is streaked with bright crimson, thanks to these high-altitude wind jets that move around atmospheric particles, which interact with gases from the volcanoes along the equator.

The Kraelyors have five eyes in a circle around their two mouths, plus three huge limbs with barbed stingers, and a big squelchy slug bottom. They've never amounted to much in this galaxy, probably because the Shapers screwed with their planet, making it more prone to earthquakes and acid tsunamis.

Elza thinks we'll find the Talgan stone, whatever that is, on Kraelyo Homeglobe—or at least a clue to its whereabouts. She cooked up an algorithm and came up with a list of planets where Captain Argentian spent time that had a major archeological project before she went there, and a few other things.

"It's just basic pattern-matching," Elza kept saying, with a sideways grin.

This planet seems to roll toward us like a ball that someone tossed underhand, and I'm scanning for danger as hard as I can. I keep remembering how Elza and Yiwei almost died the last time the Compassion caught us off guard.

But I'm also staring at the red-streaked green sphere, and I'm thinking: *Captain Argentian was here. I'm about to a visit a planet that* she *visited*. Like if I look carefully, I could see what she saw, remember what she experienced. I could even find her actual footprints, if I searched hard enough.

"Any signs of the Compassion?" Captain Othaar says.

"Still scanning, Captain," I respond.

No trace of anything in orbit, even hiding on the other side of the planet. But then I find a starship—not in orbit, but down on the surface: a pile of wreckage.

"Looks like they got shot down," I say. "Or ran into some engine trouble, and couldn't call a tow truck."

Next to me, Damini whistles. "That's a nasty wreck."

Damini's right sleeve sports a picture of a grinning man with a round face and dark hair with shaved sides. Her brother Govind, from one of the photos on her phone.

There's no sign of survivors, but we can't know for sure unless we go down there and look for ourselves. And now we know that the Compassion was also interested in Kraelyo Homeglobe, which means Elza could be right.

"Yatto, assemble a small landfall expedition," Othaar says. "Try to stay out of trouble."

"With a will," Yatto says over comms. They start putting together their team, including Uiuiuiui and a junior surveyor named Iyiiguol (pronounced "Eagle.")

I pipe up. "Um. Can I have permission to join the expedition? Captain? I promise I'll be good. I want . . . I want to see a place where *she* already went."

I can see Lyzix tensing up, inside the control deck, but Othaar hesitates and then shrugs his skeleton shoulders. "So ordered. Tina, go with them. But don't give us a reason to add another red mark to your sleeve."

"I won't. I mean, with a will." I'm grinning with my whole face.

I turn, and realize that Damini is scowling at me. "Why do you get to have all the fun?" she whispers. "When do *I* get to visit an alien planet?"

*

In the end, Yatto brings both Damini and Yiwei along, after they both promise to stay close to the group, and keep their hands and feet inside the ride at all times.

Soon we're all descending on one metal frisbee. Damini is bouncing up and down and asking science questions about the planet, while Yiwei tinkers with his musical robot, Xiaohou. I'm sitting next to Iyiiguol, the junior surveyor, who's roughly the same age as me and has never been on a mission before either. Iyiiguol is a Yarthin, with a mossy film covering his skin, and he keeps repeating the Yarthin Prayer of Not Dying. The only calm people on this funnel are Yatto and Uiuiuiui, who both look bored.

I just hope I don't get stuck babysitting the other two Earth kids, instead of getting to be a real part of this mission.

Halfway down, Yatto touches my arm. "See that structure?" They point at the reddest edge of the horizon, where a big curved spike stretches upward, like a bow with no string.

I nod.

"We built that. I mean . . . the Royal Fleet built that. It was supposed to help clean up the atmosphere and stabilize the planet, to undo some of the harm the Shapers had caused. We got about halfway through building it before we got distracted by fighting with the Compassion. We made all sorts of promises to the Kraelyors that we didn't keep."

Yiwei stares at it. "It's an incredible piece of engineering, even if it's not finished." He starts asking a bunch of questions about how it was supposed to work, and Yatto answers.

"I can't even look at it without feeling sick to my stomachs," Yatto says. "We could have helped a lot of people. Instead, all I've done since I joined the Fleet is fight this endless war."

*

We touch down in the middle of a stand of tall pink-and-orange-striped spears of vegetation, thick as tree bark. We're right next to the crashed Compassion vessel. Melted, scorched chunks of spaceship are scattered everywhere, like the aftermath of a kid throwing their toys into the campfire.

Planets are always smelly. But even by planet standards, Kraelyo Homeglobe stinks: sulfur, rotten onions, unfiltered cigarettes. But Yatto says we should be able to breathe the planet's atmosphere safely because our uniforms will filter out the worst of the junk, without even needing to cover our faces.

"I'm walking on a different planet," Iyiiguol says, clapping his moss-covered hands and bouncing in the kinda-weak gravity. "I'm a billion miles from home, under a new sky."

"That's what I was going to say." Damini grins. She offers her hand for Iyiiguol to high-five, and he just raises his hand too.

She taps his mossy hand, and he laughs.

Yiwei is wandering away from the group because he wants to get a closer look at the Compassion ship's wreckage. Yatto catches his eye and shakes their head: *Be careful.*

And then I look at the holographic display on my palm, and realize we're not alone.

"Heads up," I whisper. "There are hostiles at everything o'clock. I mean . . . we're surrounded."

We form a circle, with the rest of us on the inside and Yatto and Uiuiuiui guarding the outside.

"Put down your weapons, Symmetrons," a voice yells out from behind us.

A Kraelyor comes through the wall of pink-and-orange vegetation: five eyes arcing around two mouths on a scabby-looking face. One of the three big stinger-arms clutches some kind of ion cannon, and this Kraelyor is wearing heavy armor, curved around the slug body.

"My name is Commander Zkog, and my pronoun is *she*, and you're all my prisoners."

Iyiiguol and Uiuiuiui look at Yatto, who nods. All three of them put their guns on the ground. More Kraelyors emerge from the vegetation and encircle our group.

"Move, Symmetrons," Commander Zkog barks.

We start marching through the thick stalks of vegetation, toward what looks like a big city in the distance. Lots of corncob-shaped buildings, with smoke pouring out of their tips.

My heart is racing and I can't stop looking around, my mind working overtime to find some way out of this.

"You're lucky we didn't just shoot down your vessel," Commander Zkog says to us. "We decided to give you a chance."

"So you shot down that Compassion ship?" Yiwei asks. "It sure looked as if it was shot down from the surface."

"That's right," Commander Zkog says with a grinding, crushing sound: Kraelyor laughter.

Iyiiguol whimpers a little, and Damini whispers something reassuring.

"Where did you get such powerful weaponry?" Yatto says. "The Royal Fleet is trying to keep this part of the galaxy from militarizing, and if you've got enough firepower to take down a starship, soon all of your neighbors will have it too. You could end up in a war that reduces your entire planet to rubble. We've seen it many times before."

"Let me guess." Zkog makes another grinding noise. "You're about to tell me that we don't need our own weapons, because the Royal Fleet will protect us. Right? Except, look how great your protection worked out for Best Planet Ever."

Yatto starts to say something in response to that, then stops and just shakes their head. After that, we all walk in silence.

*

Kraelyor society is based on a dozen kinds of sharing. You become part of someone's family by sharing food, secrets, know-how, danger, stories, or a bunch of other things. The more types of stuff you share, the closer your bond becomes—and if you manage to share all twelve categories, then you're basically married. The Kraelyors have all these myths about a goddess named Gtot who shared all twelve things with everyone in the world on the day she was born, so everybody was her closest kin.

So I'm walking alongside one of the Kraelyors, a boy named Fgof. I keep trying to give him some EveryStomach wafers, or tell him about the time I shoplifted a chocolate Easter bunny from Val-U Drugs when I was twelve. Anything I can share with him, to try and win him over.

But Fgof just grunts out of his left mouth. "Quit trying, Symmetron. It's not gonna work."

"What's a Symmetron?" Damini asks.

"You're a Symmetron," Fgof says. "It's what we call you humanoids, because of that thing where your left side and your right side are mirror images of each other."

"Because we have two of almost everything." Damini nods. "I like that. I'm going to start using it too."

"It's not a compliment." Fgof snorts out of both mouths. "We've been dealing with your garbage for as long as anyone can remember. Symmetrons show up and try to tell us how to run our own business. Sometimes you're called the Royal Fleet, sometimes the Compassion. It's the same, either way."

I want to tell Fgof that he's wrong, and there's a huge difference between us and the Compassion. But I keep thinking about that big metal half arch, reaching far into the sky, and what Yatto said: *We made promises we didn't keep.*

We walk for a couple hours, and my feet start to hurt, and the fumey air is making my stomach turn. At last, the Kraelyors lead us into a tunnel, lit by red sparky flares hanging on the walls. And then we're inside their city, which I think is called Greshday.

"Are we going to be executed?" Damini whispers. "Is that what's going on?"

"I don't know," I whisper back. "They could have killed us on the spot. Or they could have shot down the *Indomitable* before we even came down."

"I never get frightened." Damini looks at the bluish ground. "I always just remind myself that my parents are out there exploring rainforests and arctic oceans, and they eat danger for breakfast, and I try to be like them. But . . . I'm frightened now."

"Me too," Yiwei whispers. "I really wanted to come on this mission. But I wasn't prepared for this."

I almost say that I'll protect them (how?) or that it's going to be okay (why?).

But then I take a deep breath and just say, "I'm scared too. But I'm glad you're both here, facing this alongside me." As I say this, I realize it's the truth. I'd be way more freaked without these two.

At last, we're herded into the spacious Great Council Chamber, where a few dozen pregnant Kraelyors, both male and female, sit on benches, arguing about a food shortage in the southern regions. (Kraelyors are only allowed to serve in the government during pregnancy, because they're more inclined to think about the future.) We just stand there listening for a while, and then there's a hush.

The most pregnant of the council members gestures for Zkog to explain why we're here.

"The Royal Fleet finally bothered to show up," Zkog says. "Found them poking around near the starship we shot down."

"We didn't mean to intrude," Yatto says.

"Can I say something?" Yiwei says. Yatto turns and nods at him. "So, I was looking at the crashed spaceship, and I think the outside is basically salvageable. I wouldn't try to fly it, but . . . I've been studying how a starship hull can change shape, and I think you could reprogram it to fill in the missing part of that device the Royal Fleet never finished building."

"You really think you could do that?" Zkog scowls with one mouth, but smiles with the other.

"I don't even think it would be that hard."

"Wow," Uiuiuiui says. "That's brilliant."

"You are not even pregnant," says the leader of the council. "And yet, you're still pretty sharp."

"Thank you." Yiwei blushes.

"We're happy to help," I say. "But in return, we need you to hook us up." I explain about the Talgan stone, and how we need to find it before Marrant does.

"Oh, yeah," Commander Zkog grunts. "We don't have that anymore. We traded it to the Yellow Fronds for some stuff we needed."

24

The whole back wall retracts until it disappears into the ceiling. The rear part of the ceiling pulls back too, and then the *Indomitable*'s cargo hangar is exposed to Landing Bay No. 7 in Rascal Station.

The landing bay is shaped like the inside of a Jell-O mold, with the domed ceiling divided into long puffy segments, each of them glowing a different bright color.

"Nice to get a change of scene." Iyiiguol whoops, standing next to Yatto, Rachael, and me.

Everywhere I look, there are aliens that I've never seen before (but I know all about them anyway). There's a Baanza, whose body is just a single dark knot of tough, fibrous material, with five slimy blue creatures clinging to it all over, serving as its "head" and "limbs." Then some Yarthins, like Iyiiguol, and a gaggle of Irriyaians, like Yatto. And then there's a Pnoft, a giant dark red ball covered with silky blond hairs that can bounce it in one direction or another—the Pnofts are only intelligent during the final quarter of their lives, and I can't tell at a glance if this one has gotten smart yet. And there's a crowd of Kraelyors, like the ones we just met.

Rachael is trying to memorize every single detail so she can draw it later: all these aliens panhandling, pushing huge anti-grav platforms piled with random junk, and leading around giant cockroaches on leashes.

Yatto turns to Rachael and me. "The captain and the alternate captain really didn't want to let any of you leave the ship. There's so many ways to get into trouble on Rascal Station. We're only staying here long enough to get repairs."

"I know, I know," I say. "Thanks for agreeing to be our chaperone. I promise we'll behave. No running around and turning the whole station upside down or anything."

But that's just a figure of speech—because there's no right side up with Rascal Station.

*

A short time later, Yatto stands with all six of us Earthlings on the balcony of some fancy hotel, looking down at the rest of everything.

"My mind literally cannot make sense of what I'm seeing," Rachael says. "This screws with everything I ever learned about perspective."

We're on top of one of the twenty-seven great spikes of Rascal Station, and the nearest spike in any direction is tilted away from us and looks way shorter than ours.

"And here I thought Mumbai was overwhelming," Damini says.

"I keep replaying all my pretentious late-night conversations about whether humans were alone in the universe, and I want to go back in time and smack my past self," Keziah says.

Basically, Rascal Station is just a silver globe, about four miles in diameter, with ginormous diamond spikes coming off it in all directions, and this means that when we look down at the ground, the "horizon" is a short distance from us. Imagine being able to see the curve of the Earth while standing on the ground. I gaze at the closest spike, off to my right, and see a billion lights, plus a giant holographic advertisement for PLAYFUN BODYMELT, with Beyoncé pouring some kind of nanotech sparkle all over herself and laughing.

"Uh, did Beyoncé sign an endorsement deal with some aliens?" asks Rachael.

"You see Beyoncé?" asks Damini. "I see Priyanka Chopra."

"I see Tinnra the Wurthhi," says Yatto. "She's the biggest star on Irriyaia. I co-starred with her in seven different light-dramas, which makes this somewhat awkward for me."

"Ohh, I get it," I say. "It's just like the EverySpeak. Filling in whatever our particular culture sees as the definition of 'glamorous superstar.'"

Elza stands right next to me, staring at all the rippling lights on that huge spike with some supermassive yearning in her beautiful brown eyes. "I could get lost here, and nobody would ever find me," she mutters. "I could leave everything, and just be free. Never have to deal with anyone's garbage ever again."

"Yeah, you could," I say in her ear. "But I'd miss you."

"I'll miss you, too." Elza smiles at me. I feel this shiver, inside my stomach. I don't even know how to deal with this smile and what it does to me. I have to look away.

I just stare at the spikes, all these glittery billboards that make no sense, even with the EverySpeak. So many people, humanoids and non-humanoids, trading and stealing and dancing and especially partying, and I wish we had time to see all of it.

Then I realize Elza said "I'll miss you," instead of "I'd miss you," and I look back at where she was just standing.

Elza's vanished.

*

I'm running in a sudden death sprint, arms chopping and stomach burning, through the wide open space between the spikes of Rascal Station, shoving past Pnofts and Javarah and Kraelyors in colorful outfits, all of them trying to sell me something.

Two spikes ahead, Elza is running away, casting occasional glances over her shoulder and cursing loud enough for me to make out. I am not going to lose her, or leave her behind in this oversized mall.

"I see her," I gasp into my shoulder comms.

"Good," Yatto's voice comes. "We'll try and converge on your location."

The "ground floor" of Rascal Station is full of the people who can't afford the inter-creds to open a bank, shop, casino, nightclub, or sexytime parlor inside one of the spikes. Bottom-feeders, literally.

I shove past these cube-shaped Guouonans trying to sell me ampules of Wildjuice, and then I almost collide with a Kraelyor who bats all five eyes at me and offers to help me become an Invincible Lover. Most of the stuff they're selling would kill a human, or even a Makvarian with added human DNA.

But at least there's a five-piece band playing some CrudePink music, all loud thunderclaps and discordant jangles. I recognize the song even though I've never heard it before—it's the one about bad sex and time dilation. Earworm alert!

I catch up with Elza in front of a big blue bubble that bobs up and down in front of her, full of tiny globes with different kinds of booze inside. She's clutching her side and gasping, like she can't run anymore. She glances at me sideways, and pretends to be shopping for balls of alien liquor. They gave us access to the ship's line of credit here, so we can use the Quants on our wrists to pay for things, within reason.

"Don't tell me," she grunts, still breathing heavy. "I shouldn't drink any of this stuff."

"The blue ones would boil your liver, and it would be a super-painful death," I say, studying the assortment. "The red-and-yellow swirlies are JoySquirt, they'd make you leave your body for like three days, but you'd be physically okay. I think."

"Okay." She gestures. "I guess I'll take the JoySquirt, then."

The Javarah standing behind the bubble, whose "fur" is dangerously worn off in several places, nods and gives her a ball of alien poison.

Elza holds the little globe in her palm, but doesn't open it. Instead, she just walks around. "This place is just like São Paulo. Extreme luxury, sitting right on top of slums."

I follow her to the nearest spike, where the signs promise full-body skin removal, forever-sex, gambling loops, and the strongest mind-sponges in the galaxy. She leads me into the first door she sees, a nearly dark room where various gelatinous and tentacled aliens slither over each other, to the drone of Blot music. Elza leans against one wall, and her JoySquirt glows faintly.

"I can look after myself, you know," Elza says, without looking at me. "I survived on the street in São Paulo, where the life expectancy for someone like me is thirty-five. I even survived hackerspace bullshit. I can handle this."

"I'm sure you could. Maybe you'd have a wonderful life on Rascal Station. But . . . we need you on the *Indomitable*. I need you."

Elza shakes her head. "That ship is full of people who swallowed their own bullshit, and they hobbled their own computer on purpose.

You'll be better off when I'm gone, with one less person to distract you from trying to be the second coming of Captain Fantastic."

"Just stay with us long enough to learn the ropes," I plead. "So you don't go drinking the wrong globe of liquor. So you have enough skills to get a job or do whatever, on your own. You don't have to stay on the ship forever."

"Why do you even care?" She turns away from me, arms folded. One of the dancing Bnobnobians nearly slams into her.

Even with the flank-smoke and ten kinds of alien sweat in the air, Elza's wild-honey scent comes across, and I think about how soft her skin is, and how I feel when she smiles at me. I have this sensation like goose bumps or chills, and my heart is louder than the drumrolls of the Blot music.

I reach out with one hand. "Can I touch you?"

She nods, and reaches back until our hands touch.

"I really like you. I can't get over how cool you are," I say, right in her ear. "And I want to know you. Like, I want to know what makes you feel safe, and what makes you happy. I want to know you so well that whatever anyone tells me about you, I'll just smile and say, 'Yeah, that sounds like Elza.' No matter what. I mean, I, uh . . . I'm saying this all wrong, ugh. I suck at talking to people and being a person, and . . ."

I run out of words. Elza's face is so close to mine, we could be kissing right now. Am I supposed to kiss her? I don't want to scare her away in the middle of trying to convince her to stick around, and she probably doesn't even like me that way, anyway. She's staring at me, like she's trying to make sense of this too. The longer this goes on, the more I want to kiss her, but also the more I'm scared to.

Then Elza pulls at my hand, and I realize she's tugging me toward the door. We walk out of there, holding hands, and I see her giving me a curious smile out of the corner of my eye.

*

When Yatto finally catches up with Elza and me outside that weird dance club, their stripes are bright blue, which is the Irriyaian version of getting red in the face. "There you are," they grunt at us. "I lost the other cadets. The captain is going to throw me out of the cargo hangar."

I look at Elza, and she shrugs. "We'll help you look for the others," she says.

Everywhere we go, Irriyaians do a double-take when they notice Yatto's face. A few people beg them for autographs or holographic selfies, which slows us way down.

Yiwei has gotten pulled into a jam session with that CrudePink band, which is desperately trying to recruit him. And he also drank some lime-green sludge that is making his head spin in three directions at once.

Keziah has been getting a shoulder tattoo, one of those cool nanopolymer things that glows in the dark and will go really well with the equations on his uniform sleeve. It reads "hypothesis non fingo," which is a quote from Newton or something. "It means I worship doubt. Just like the captain," he says with a lopsided grin.

I can't locate Damini—until I look up and see her soaring, half a mile over our heads, with a grav-induction harness, surfing the gravity fluctuations from one spike to the next. She sees me looking and waves, then notices Yatto folding their arms. A moment later, Damini drifts down to the ground next to us, landing on her feet.

"Sorry," Damini says, "but that was the coolest thing I have ever, ever done. The blob with wings told me this was the most dangerous sport in Rascal Station! It didn't seem that dangerous, to be quite honest. But super fun!"

That just leaves Rachael . . . who we can't find anywhere.

Something must have happened to her while we were all off having our own silly adventures. I'm freaking out and starting to imagine all sorts of gruesome fates for her—but then we find her back on that balcony, right where we left her.

"Oh, hey. There you are. I was starting to wonder where you'd all gotten to."

Rachael has a big sheet of plastiform and a lightpen, and she's managed to sketch the entire space station. All the blaring signs, all the interlocking translucent strips and tiny arches of the spikes, all the people with their wings or tentacles or multisegmented bodies, buying and selling, partying and falling in love. And over all of it, a single person floats, with the biggest grin on her tiny face: Damini, in her grav-induction harness.

25

Back at the ship, my mind is just a dried-out wreck. Should I have tried to kiss Elza, in that weird alien nightclub? Or did I just dodge a kiss-bullet? What about Riohon? How does dating even work, when we're all cooped up on this little ship, and I'm not even human?

I'm too tired to sleep, and too confused to be awake.

I end up pulling up another one of Captain Argentian's log entries, which I haven't even had time to watch in a while.

She's much older in this one. It's the very end of her life, her final log entry before she died. She's wearing an emergency cryosplint on her right arm, as if it is broken in multiple places and she can't afford to immobilize it. She has several ugly cuts on her crystalline face, and the jewel on her right cheek is missing.

She chokes for a moment, then looks right at me, and says, "I think we made a terrible mistake."

Captain Argentian's personal datajournal, 7.17.19.09 of the Age of Realization

I think we made a terrible mistake. All of us. Me especially. But all of us.

Captain Argentian coughs.

We thought we could just do the right thing, and it would be simple. Doing the right thing is never simple, though. It's not the right thing unless it tears you apart with self-doubt, and costs you everything you would have gotten from taking the easy path.

Captain covers her face for a moment, then looks at the holo-recorder once more.

Does it ever stop hurting? Do you ever just...figure out a way to make sense of it? I feel like I'm just going to lose my mind, but there are people who have lost way more, for much longer, and they carry on with a smile on their face. Are they just pretending? I really wish I knew. I've given my life to the Royal Fleet, and it's only ever broken my heart, over and over.

Captain looks over her shoulder at something out of view.

Our engines have lost most of their buffer capacity, and our hull is crumpling in five places. This might be it. I need to get back to the control deck.

Listen. Whoever sees this. I know there's been all this talk about keeping key personnel alive by cloning them a new body and transferring their minds. Maybe hiding the newborn clones on a lesser-humanoid planet, for safety. So I just want to be incredibly clear about this: If anything happens to me, DO NOT BRING ME BACK as some kind of monstrosity.

Screw that. I've had my time! I've had a damn good life, except for these last few years. It's someone else's turn now. Please, whatever you do, don't put me through growing up all over again. Once was enough. That's my last, final request.

Captain Thaoh Argentian signing off, and may the Hosts of Misadventure be with us all.

26

First Cycle, I roll out of my bed-web, and groan. I clean myself up as best I can. And I try to forget about the fact that the only reason I'm even alive is because somebody ignored a dying woman's last wishes.

In the hallway, Wang Yiwei wants to tell me how Elza has been helping him to upgrade the firmware of his musical robot, Xiaohou. I just keep nodding.

At the crew lounge, Keziah hasn't been sleeping again, because he's obsessing about what might be happening to everyone back on Earth. He just lies awake and gazes at the glow of his new tattoo, and tries to figure out how he could help the human race. I make what I hope are sympathetic noises.

On the way out, Uiuiuiui wants to show off how he got his face-tubes buffed at Rascal Station so they look extra-luxurious and manly. I just keep walking, eyes on the floor.

Don't bring me back as some kind of monstrosity.

I want to curl up in a ball, and stay there forever.

But I'm needed in Forward Ops—because we may have picked up the trail of the Talgan stone again.

The Kraelyors said they traded it to the Yellow Fronds, a crew of space scavengers and junk-traders who go from planet to planet. And now we think we've found an old space-traffic satellite that might have tracked where the Yellow Fronds went after Kraelyo

Homeglobe. We're taking a shortcut through the Storm of Faces, with our engines going way faster, thanks to the tune-up we got at Rascal Station.

The Storm of Faces is one of the most gorgeous sights in the entire galaxy—the polarized gases form into a wall of shimmering faces, gazing out at everyone who passes. I give them a quick side-eye, and then just focus on my tactical readouts, because with all this interference, we won't see danger coming until the last moment.

Riohon smiles and offers a ritual blessing, and I glance at him and feel nothing. I mumble a response.

I feel so disgusting that everything disgusts me.

"This is so incredible," Damini breathes. "I never even imagined."

"Captain, is it okay if I let my trainee pilot steer us through the storm? Could be a good experience," Riohon says.

"Of course," Captain Othaar says. "Just keep it steady, please."

Damini is staring at Riohon. "Wait. Me? Right now? Flying the ship? Through that?"

"Sure. Unless you don't want to."

"What? No! I mean yes. Of course I mean yes, a billion yeses with extra yes on top. Get out of my pilot's seat! I've got this."

I keep thinking I see a Compassion mercy-killer ship descending through the staring blank faces, but then it's nothing.

"This is the greatest moment of my life," Damini says. "Can I speed up? I bet we could go faster."

"Just steady for now, please," Riohon says. "We don't want to risk getting swept up in the storm."

Don't bring me back. Just let me stay dead.

*

How immature was I, to think I had a purpose? That all of this meant something?

I can't be around people right now. Everywhere I go on this ship, people try to drag me into their conversations. I just keep walking, remembering the broken expression on Captain Argentian's face in her last hours. I need to be alone, but I can't go back to my quarters, or I'll wind up watching that hologram again.

Does it ever stop hurting?

After our duty shifts, the six of us are supposed to have another education session with Vaap or Lyzix, teaching us more about what to do if you're blown out into space without a suit (say your goodbyes, mostly). But they need all the senior officers on duty in the storm, so Elza and I end up hanging out in the bluehouse listening to Yiwei plunk on his guitar.

They got a bunch of brand-new Undhoran flaphoppers at Rascal Station—these little rainbow-colored balls of fluffy ferny matter that roll around us as we sit on the floor. They keep bumping up against Xiaohou, and he jumps out of their way with startled little "meep" noises.

Yiwei still hasn't been able to write a whole song on his own. "Keep coming up with a line, or a melody." He pokes at his steel guitar, in between munching on Zanthuron coral bites. "But I'm just . . . blocked. It's not just that Jiasong cowrote all our songs. It's also just, everything is weird. I don't know how to write songs about all this."

He gestures at the bluehouse, but also at the whole starship.

Don't bring me back as some kind of monstrosity.

Keziah comes up to the bluehouse, with his eyes all puffy and bloodshot.

189

"Hi." He sips out of a globe full of "tea" (which is actually hot snah-snah juice).

"Are you okay?" Yiwei asks. "You look like you didn't sleep at all."

Keziah shakes his head. "I'm okay. Kind of."

"Are you still obsessing about everyone back on Earth?" Elza says to Keziah.

She scoots closer to me and smiles at me, and I remember how we almost kissed on Rascal Station. I want to smile back at her, but I can't even manage a fake smile right now.

Keziah nods. "I know the Royal Fleet can't spare a ship to help Earth right now, but not knowing is freaking me out. When I do sleep, I have horrible dreams about the Earth being destroyed."

Elza is still trying to catch my eye, and I just stare into the well at the center of the room, which is now full of wispy faces leering up at me.

"I wish there was something we could do," I say.

Some kind of monstrosity.

Yiwei plinks on his guitar for a moment, lost in thought. Keziah holds his "tea" up to his face, like the steam will bring him back to life.

"Can't do anything to help the people back home right now," Yiwei says. "But . . . maybe there's something I could do to help you sleep better."

"Don't want drugs," Keziah says. "I already told Dr. Karrast."

"I didn't mean drugs." Yiwei shakes his head. "I could lend you Xiaohou."

"Your musical robot?" I say.

"Xiaohou already copied all of the music from your phone," Yiwei says to Keziah. "He could keep you company. Like, he could play soothing music, to help you relax. I think he could even monitor your vitals, so he knows what kind of stuff to play to make you more mellow."

At the sound of his name, Xiaohou draws himself upright and swivels his head left to right. He plays a little fanfare, like "ta-da."

"Huh. Worth a try," Keziah says. "Thanks, mate. Really appreciate it."

"Any time," Yiwei says. "I'm excited for Xiaohou to have another function besides playing along with the songs I'm failing to write." He goes back to playing tiny fragments of melody on his steel guitar.

"I hope that helps." Elza's stopped trying to catch my eye, and is ignoring me too.

I stand up so fast that I kick up some fresh gardening soil. "I gotta go." I'm down the ramp and passing the control deck before any of them can even react to me being gone.

*

Elza catches up to me by the engine section. "Hey. What the hell is going on with you?"

Her face catches the glow from the brand-new solar flare we just harvested, which is redder than the one from Earth's sun. The captive starlight brightens Elza's face and makes her eyes look like they're throwing off actual sparks.

"Nothing." I look at the floor.

She's so close. I'm garbage.

"So that's it?" Elza says. "You're just going to ignore me now. I should have known. This is what always happens. I fell for it again."

"It's not like that." I can barely hear my own voice. "I just found out that I . . . I'm not even real. You shouldn't waste your time trying to be my friend."

My whole skin is hot and my head is spacey, and I can't handle feeling this way.

"You are so full of bagaceira." Elza raises her voice, and Yma glances at us from inside Engineering with a grumptastic expression.

"No, really," I say. "You know who you are, and I envy that so much. You fought hard to be yourself, in spite of all this hateful garbage. That's the best anyone can do. But me? I'm nobody."

I explain about how Captain Argentian didn't even want me to be born. I hate saying it out loud, because now it's even more real.

"So what? Who cares what some woman who's been dead for years thought? She's gone. Captain Astounding doesn't get a vote."

I feel like the solar flare is inside my chest, rising up into my face. "Stop making fun of her name. Her name was Captain Argentian. She sacrificed everything to help people and stop the Compassion from hurting everyone. She was a hero, and you should get her name right."

Elza bristles, like she's going to say something else sarcastic. Before she gets the chance, I turn and stomp away.

27

A few metacycles (ship's days) later, the garbage storm inside me has subsided to just a gentle garbage breeze. We've gotten through the Storm of Faces, and now we're almost at the old disused space station that supposedly has the info we need, so we can find out where the Yellow Fronds took the Talgan stone.

I work my shifts in Forward Ops, sit silently in the back of our training sessions with my arms folded, and hide out in my quarters the rest of the time.

There's only one person I want to talk to right now. The only person who understood what I was feeling, back home on Earth, when I would have given anything to be where I am now. My best friend, who used to joke about borrowing my space dragon when I went to live in my space casino.

And Rachael's nowhere to be found.

I haven't even seen her since Rascal Station. She's not even signed in on the chat program Elza created. I keep freaking out that maybe we just left her behind by accident—but she was with the group when we came back on board. But what if something's happened to her? What if she needs me, the way I've needed her so many times before?

I've been so busy obsessing about Captain Argentian's last wishes, maybe I've let my best friend down.

*

Yatto shrugs when I ask them about Rachael. "You know how she is."

"Yeah. I've known her longer than the rest of you, remember? When was the last time anyone saw her?"

Yatto rolls their neck to one side, and then the other. "If you really think there's a problem, we should alert Vaap. Or Lyzix."

"Oh my god, you really think we should sic Lyzix on Rachael? The other day, she nearly threw Uiuiuiui out an airlock for being a few minicycles late for duty."

Yatto sighs. "Fine. Let's go ask Dr. Karrast if she's seen Rachael lately."

When Dr. Karrast sees us, her single eye narrows with annoyance. "Rachael has been showing up on time, and assisting me with acceptable levels of skill and focus. Do you have any other questions, or can I get back to work?" Then she practically slams the door in our faces.

"There you go," Yatto says. "Rachael is fine." They pause, scritching their head. "Perhaps instead of worrying about Rachael, who can take care of herself, you should be paying more attention to Elza."

They turn and walk away, without even waiting for me to reply.

*

I'm being chased down the hallway of an abandoned space station by a giant scaly monster with three mouths on long stalks, and five pairs of thick legs that stick to the walls with a suction-y noise. I hear a hoarse bellowing behind me, and run faster.

The creature is almost on top of me when Damini ducks out of a doorway I didn't even know was there. "Psst. Get in here!" She grabs my arm and yanks me inside a service chamber, slamming the door behind us.

"Thanks," I say.

"What is that thing?" She wrinkles her nose at the rotten-eggs stench.

"It's called a Hooghug Beast," I say. "It can survive in space, and it likes keratin. Which means if it catches us . . . it's going to eat our hair."

"Just our hair?"

"Maybe other stuff, if it's hungry enough. Skin has a bit of keratin, and so do nails."

"One problem at a time," Damini says. "We still need to finish uploading the data from this station, so we can track down the Talgan stone. And I can't get Uiuiuiui to wake up." Damini leads me to a holographic workstation, and Uiuiuiui slumped on top of a pile of cloths.

"Okay, then." I squelch my hand into the hard-light goo interface. This was supposed to be an easy mission, which is why they allowed Damini and me to come.

Just as I'm trying to figure out these unfamiliar menus, Damini distracts me. "I'm worried about Rachael."

"Uh. What?" Half my attention is going into making sure I don't accidentally trigger a security protocol and blow us to bits.

"She hasn't shown up in ages. What if something's wrong?"

I parrot what Yatto said, about Rachael needing "me" time.

"I just . . . Rachael was the one who made me feel at home on that ship, after I stumbled on board," Damini says. "She found all these little ways to bring all of us together. I owe her, and I don't think she knows how important she is to me. To all of us."

I have a moment of feeling jealous, but I shake it off. I've almost gotten the fail-safe sequence—but my fingers are stuck.

I can't pull my hand out, or move it around at all.

"I think Rachael's just hiding in her quarters," I say.

"It's just . . . people are always disappearing on me. My parents barely ever came home long enough to pack a bag. Govind went overseas for university, and then Uncle Srini married someone who didn't want me around."

"That sounds intense . . . Ugh. I'm totally stuck."

I tug on my arm, but it won't budge. I only have to flick my left middle finger a couple times to finish the upload protocol.

But the holo-goop has turned solid, like a plaster cast.

The hair-eating monster rips the wall in half with a terrifying roar.

"Oh no!" Damini grabs hold of Uiuiuiui and backs away. "Help me get him out of here."

The Hooghug Beast is peeling the wall like a tin of sardines.

"I can't. I'm trapped." I demonstrate, trying to pull my arm out of the holo-goop. "Save yourself! Your hair is way nicer than mine."

"Well, that's true. But I'm not leaving you behind."

Damini pulls a blowtorch out of Uiuiuiui's belt and aims at the Hooghug Beast, which looms over the gap in the wall.

"Hooghug Beast likes extreme heat, and extreme cold," I gasp. "Can't hurt it with fire or ice."

I tug harder and harder, but no luck. The Hooghug Beast almost has a big enough opening to grab us.

"Go," I gasp. "Get Uiuiuiui to safety. That's plenty heroic."

"Sorry, no way."

"No point in both of us being in danger!"

Damini slides her own arm into the holo-goop next to mine.

"What the— No! Now you're stuck too."

"Shut up," she says. "Try and move your hand."

I can move my hand now. I feel her hand twitch.

So I complete the upload protocol, and then I deactivate the hard-light interface, leaving Damini and me with our hands stuck in nothing.

"Wow. Thank you." I'm panting a little. "Thanks for the quick thinking."

She blushes, but just says, "Help me carry Uiuiuiui out of here."

The Hooghug Beast finally makes a big enough hole and smooshes its slimy, scaly body into the chamber. We grab Uiuiuiui's arms and legs and run like mad. The three of us fall in a heap on the orbital funnel, and I use my Quant to launch us back to the *Indomitable*, just in time to avoid the worst hair day in the universe.

"Are we just going to leave the creature there?" Damini asks.

I look back at the rapidly shrinking station, which looks a pizza stone, and shrug. "It'll leave on its own when it can't find any more organic food sources."

The station orbits Oinzoignu, a huge strawberry-colored planet with a dozen rings of luminous gas and dust.

When we're halfway back to the ship, Damini says, "How long do you think Rachael will keep acting like some kind of hermit?"

"I wish I knew." I look back at the space station, and the frustrated hair-eating monster drifting away from it.

*

I float in space, with nothing around but cosmic dust and the distant echoes of ancient suns. I'm wearing an atmosphere suit that fits better than the one I wore before, and my right hand is gripping a bright red beacon attached to a string. I look like a kid holding onto a balloon that floated away, and just kept floating up and up forever.

The *Indomitable* is on comms silence, so I hear nothing but my own breathing and the creaks and pops of the spacesuit. I stare out at the fizz of starscape and vow silently that if I make it back to the ship, I'm going to be a better friend to everyone. I'm going to listen more and hear better.

The stars don't twinkle, or do any of the blingy stuff I expected. They just pepper the sky—too many steady lights to count—and I can't help humming that ridiculous song about safeguarding them.

I'm starting to zonk all the way out when someone else drifts down from way over my head and coasts to a stop in front of me. Wang Yiwei beams at me from inside his spacesuit, waving a gloved hand. "Hey," he says. "How are you hanging in there? They sent me to check on you."

"I'm okay. Do they have the readings they need yet?"

"Uh, I guess not."

"I'm beginning to think this is a hazing. I'm being hazed."

"Does the Royal Fleet do that? Haze people?"

"Umm . . . Not that I know of. But I have a lot of weird gaps in my knowledge."

"Oh." Yiwei thinks for a moment. "I've always wanted to be hazed."

"What? Why would you want that?"

"It just sounds fun. Everybody paying attention to me, like a birthday party, but with a big prank instead of extra-long birthday noodles."

"You're kind of a weird kid, you know that?"

"Would I have gotten on a random space elevator with nothing but a steel guitar and a musical robot if I wasn't weird?"

"Uh. Point. Anyway, thanks for joining me out here. I'll try not to subject you to my awful singing."

"I like your singing."

That knocks me off my stabilizers. Is he flirting with me? I wish there was a neon sign that lit up over people's heads that said, "YOU ARE BEING FLIRTED WITH."

"Thanks," I say. "I want to hear more of your songs."

"I've still never written a song on my own." He pauses, staring into the starry distance. "I'm worried about Rachael."

"What?"

"I'm worried about Rachael. She's been missing since Rascal Station. Damini went to check on her, and she wouldn't even come out to say hi. I get that she needs time to herself, but it's been a billion years."

I groan. "Why is it that when I worry about Rachael, I'm being overprotective, but when the rest of you do, it's just friendly?"

"I don't know. I guess you have a track record. But since Rachael vanished, nothing feels right. Elza's been sulking like a baby. Everyone's in a weird mood."

The part about Elza sulking makes me feel like a dirtbag.

But then Yiwei distracts me by saying, "It's just a rotten mess of sevens and eights."

"A what now?"

"Oh. Sorry. I guess the EverySpeak can't handle some sayings. I mean, it's a mess. I was just getting to know Rachael, and now she's disappeared, and I miss her."

We're sitting here, alone in the void. The *Indomitable* could've been sucked into a naked singularity, for all we know.

But neither of us is scared of floating in space forever. We're both just worried about this weird artist girl who locks herself in her room.

I look at the ghostly image of Yiwei's face in his helmet, and something hits me. "Do you . . . like Rachael?"

"Like her? I mean, I think she's great. I don't know. What do you mean?" Even in deep space, with a fogged-up helmet, I can tell he's blushing and squirming.

"Oh my god. You *do*. You like her! Damn. I thought you were still obsessing over your ex. But you're into Rachael."

"Um, well . . . I don't know . . . I mean." Yiwei fidgets a moment longer, then finally nods his big helmet. "I mean, I guess. Maybe. Yeah."

"This isn't a rebound thing is, it? Because Rachael deserves better."

"This would still be the most unreal conversation of my entire life, even if I was standing on solid ground. But . . . if I even understand what you're saying, then no. I think I kind of got over Jiasong when I wasn't looking. I just one day realized that she wouldn't even understand what my life is like, now that I'm a spaceman. I'll always be sad about her, but I was ready to move on."

"Dude, that's amazing." I take a breath, super noisy inside this bubble. "Even the part where you called yourself a spaceman."

Still no sign of the *Indomitable*, and the lack of up and down is starting to mess with me.

"So do you have any advice? About, um, approaching Rachael? If she ever even comes out of hiding?"

I'm about to say something ultra-basic, like "just be yourself" or "don't try too hard," when the *Indomitable* comes out of spaceweave next to us. One moment, we're by ourselves, and then FOOM!, there's a dagger-class ship hovering close enough to see all the dents and scratches and that one gunport that might never open again.

I give a moment of silent thanks that I never had to give Yiwei advice on talking to girls.

*

I'm sitting outside the door to Rachael's quarters, cross-legged. I've been talking for like half an hour, and haven't heard a peep from inside the room.

"I respect your right to be a shut-in, I do. I just . . . I miss you. We all miss you. I just want to see you for five minutes. I know I tried to talk you into going back to Earth because I wasn't sure you were going to be able to deal with life on a starship, but I was wrong. You're amazing."

Total silence. I don't even know if she's in there or if I'm talking to myself in a black-walled hallway, ringed with crew-quarters stripes.

"Everyone keeps asking me where you are," I say. "I don't think you realize how much people around here depend on you."

I'm startled by a voice from behind the door. "That's the whole problem."

"Wait. *What's* the problem?"

"I turned this into a whole project, bringing these super-genius kids on board, and then I felt responsible. So I worked my butt off to make them feel welcome, and to help us all bond, as Earthlings. I ignored my own limits and pushed myself way too hard. And now they all expect me to keep doing that."

"Nobody expects anything, except for you to be our friend."

"Easy for you to say."

I laugh out loud. "You don't know how hard it's been for me to trust that these kids are my friends, and they're not going to turn on me the way Suzy Craddock did in eighth grade."

"Suzy Craddock was a dick." Rachael sighs. "I can't keep doing what I did before. I used it all up. Whatever reservoir of socialness I had that let me lead tours of the ship and stuff. It's drained, bone dry."

"You don't have to do that anymore. I promise. You can just be with us, and not speak a word. Or chill for half an hour and then disappear again. People don't like some imaginary gregarious Rachael, they like you."

And now, I finally am giving someone the "just be yourself" speech. Shoot me now.

"Okay. I'll think about it."

She doesn't open the door and hug me or anything. But I figured that was a long shot.

"So what's going on with you?" Rachael asks through the door.

I hesitate, then just spit it out. "I found out I wasn't supposed to be born." I explain the whole thing to her.

"Oof. That's rough. Sven had that too. My ex. Sven's parents let him know he was an accident. But . . . it doesn't matter if *she* wanted you to be here. You're here now, and you have to make the best of it. Right?"

"I guess." I sigh. "So did you hear about how Damini and me got chased by a hair-eating monster?"

Even with a door between us, it feels good to talk again.

28

"We're finally going to find this Talgan stone thing," Damini whispers to me in Forward Ops. "What do you even think it is?"

For once, a question I don't know the answer to. I just shrug. "Something very old that could make the Compassion even more dangerous. Maybe it's related to the Shapers, those jerks who helped all the humanoids and sabotaged everyone else."

We're approaching Second Yoth—the planet where the Yellow Fronds unloaded all their stuff after they visited the Kraelyors.

Second Yoth is covered with an ugly blob of gray-green smog. The Shapers left it surrounded by a ring of asteroids, which react with the high-infrared rays of its red giant sun and release dense toxic gases that drift down into the upper atmosphere.

The natives of Second Yoth are called the Grattna, and they have three wings, three eyes, and three limbs (that work like arms as well as legs), plus thick reddish-brown fur all over. They can't even see the stars, and they never knew there were other planets until the first aliens showed up.

"Because they have three of everything, including three brains, they think in threes rather than in twos," Riohon tells Damini and me. "Their language doesn't have a division between 'me' and 'you,' or 'this' versus 'that.' Instead, there are always three people in any conversation, and their wars always have three different sides. Takes some getting used to."

"What if two groups want to go to war, but they can't find a third party?" Damini asks.

"Then they just don't fight, I guess." Riohon shakes his head. "I wish that was the rule everywhere."

I keep my eyes glued to my tactical screens, looking for any signs of charged particles or weird radiation that could be an early warning of another starship in the area. We're still doing nothing but passive scans and masking our own heat signature, to avoid announcing our presence early. Often as not, the advantage in any space battle goes to whoever sees the other ship first.

Second Yoth orbits an especially gassy, cranky sun, plus those pop rocks in orbit are shedding tons of heavy elements. So it's hard to see much of anything at this distance—but I keep twirling my hands in the goo, scanning different wavelengths.

Then I hit the jackpot.

I signal the control deck. "Captains. Um, hey. I'm seeing accelerated mercury ions, coming from near the planet."

Lyzix growls a string of super-filthy (and untranslatable) curses. "It's a ship."

"Probably spike-class," Vaap says. "Larger than us, with better weaponry."

"Good work, cadet," Othaar says, and I can't help glowing with pride. "Have they noticed us?"

"Probably not," I say. "But they will soon, unless we turn around."

"We're not turning around," Othaar says.

*

A few moments later, Othaar's voice comes in my ear. "All hands, this is the captain. There appears to be a Compassion vessel in high orbit around Second Yoth. They are seeking the same objective we are, and we must keep them from obtaining it, at any cost. We will be within weapons range within seven minicycles. All stations, prep for battle. May the Hosts of Misadventure be with us all."

I think that's the whole message, but then Othaar's voice comes back again. "Trainees, you have one chance to leave this ship before we go into battle." This time, I can tell that only Damini and I are hearing his voice, among the people in Forward Ops. "We can jettison a survival capsule with you inside, to be rescued by the broadsword-class ship that's already on its way. You have two minicycles to decide. That is all."

(Two minicycles is about ten minutes. Not near enough time to make such a huge choice.)

Damini is looking at me. "We should talk to the others. Bluehouse?"

I nod. "Bluehouse."

Yiwei is already heading for the door of the control deck as well, and we signal Elza, Rachael, and Keziah to meet us at the bluehouse too.

The six of us arrive at the bluehouse around the same time. Everybody tries to talk at once except for Rachael, and then we all stop.

And then . . . everybody just stares at each other for a few precious moments, while our two minicycles tick away.

Finally, I speak up. "Whatever the rest of you decide, I'm staying on this ship until the last bell is rung. None of this has been what I expected. This galaxy is scary, and full of ugliness, and everything's twisted out of shape by crimes that happened so long ago, I can't even wrap my head around it." I look at each of their anxious faces in turn. "But this is our fight. We have a chance to stop the Compassion from piling injustice on top of injustice. It's not going to be easy. Or pretty. But . . . that's what makes it worth doing."

I pause for breath, and then I hear stirring chords playing.

Xiaohou the musical robot heard my speech. He thought I was singing, so he's been giving me dramatic background music for the past twenty seconds or so. The music trails off and Xiaohou bounces around happily.

"Well," Yiwei says. "I'm staying. I still can't stop thinking about that recording from Best Planet Ever, that Marrant guy murdering those poor creatures. And . . . I never thought I'd find people I belonged with, after all my dreams with Jiasong went up in smoke. And now . . . I have." He looks at all of us, but especially at Rachael.

"There's no way I'm missing out on this," Damini says.

"I finally got some sleep, thanks to Xiaohou. And things seem a lot clearer." Keziah definitely doesn't look as wrecked as a Bnobnobian on a ninety-cycle bender anymore. "I keep thinking that if I learn the truth about these Shapers, it'll help me figure out some way to help everyone back on Earth, because it's all connected. Also, I hate bullies. And I love all of you. So I'm staying too."

Rachael shrugs. "I had an opportunity to go back to Earth, unlike most of you. And I already made my choice, back then. I want to see this through, no matter what happens. And I promised Dr. Karrast I'd help with the inevitable casualties."

We all look at Elza. She rolls her eyes. "*Fine*. I'll stay too. I'm not getting into a survival pod all by myself. Maybe if we don't die,

I'll get an invitation to visit the Firmament and meet the super-intelligent computers that actually run everything. Plus, I care about all of you weird kids, and I want to do whatever I can to keep you breathing."

She doesn't quite look at me when she says that part. And then there's no time for me to talk to her before we have to go back to our posts.

We're coming up on space battle time.

I've been waiting my whole life for this. And now that it's here? I'm not ready.

*

Now for a moment of space battle nerdery.

So the unidentified Compassion ship is already in orbit around Second Yoth, which means they'll have to push against the planet's gravity to come at us. And they can only use their maneuvering impellers, or the planet's magnetic field will make them go boom. Meanwhile, we can hassle them as much as we want.

But the enemy has a few advantages, too:

1. If we shoot at the Compassion ship and miss, we risk hitting the planet—and they probably don't care about protecting the inhabitants as much as we do.
2. They can duck in and out of that soupy upper atmosphere and hide from us, whereas we're pretty exposed out here.
3. Their ship is a little bigger than ours, probably a spike-class warship. And they have better weapons (including dreamkiller missiles!) and stronger countermeasures. In a straight fight, we definitely lose.

This is the kind of situation where Captain Argentian would have *owned*. Too bad she's not here.

*

By now, the Compassion ship has definitely noticed us, and they're preparing to hit us with everything they have, as soon as we're in range.

My comms light up with a message from Keziah, down in Engineering. "Um, hullo. Righteous battles and healing respites, and all that." He totally picks the right blessing for this situation, and I give the proper response ("Proud hearts and joyful reunions").

Then Keziah goes on: "So I was thinking . . . you told me that we can detect other starships, mostly, because of damage. All the dents and scrapes that cause particles to leak out of our engines, in spite of all of our masking systems."

"Uh-huh," I say.

Weapons range in three minicycles.

"So, what if we used that?" Keziah says. "To make this ship appear more damaged than we really are. Or else, to make us appear to be in two places at once."

"Oh." My mind starts racing. "Oh! Yeah, that could actually work. Wow. Hang on."

I loop in Yiwei, and quickly explain Keziah's idea. Yiwei mutters to himself for a moment, then says, "That's really cool. Remember how I said you could play music on a starship's hull? This could be one awesome duet." He laughs. "Okay. Hang on."

Yiwei's voice cuts out, and Keziah signs off too.

We've got a clearer view of the Compassion ship now: definitely spike-class, with souped-up engines and a full battery of pulse cannons and dreamkiller missiles. I'm sending a torrent of data to the control deck on their defenses, but also their weak spots and dents in their hull.

That's when the Compassion ship lights up like a megachurch at sundown.

They're trying to get in touch with us.

"Let's hear it," Captain Othaar says.

A holographic image appears over the situation monitor in Forward Ops. A face the color of sour milk, with features that are too perfect. Too symmetrical. The face that kept featuring in my nightmares when my beacon was getting ready to light up, complete with lethal smirk.

Marrant.

Cold floods all the way through me, just like when I glimpsed him back on Earth. Like on Best Planet Ever, when I watched him murder innocent people with an ugly grin on his face. I feel as if he can see all the way through me, spot all of my weaknesses and poorly repaired breaks, the exact same way I was just scanning his ship. My rational mind knows he can't see me at all, but I still shrink into my chair.

My heart falters. The skin on my neck crawls.

Those dark eyes, like a starless sky, drive all my thoughts away. I try to reach for the thing that comforted me before, when Captain Argentian said, *There are victories greater than death.*

But I . . . don't know if I even believe that anymore. If it was up to her, I wouldn't even be here.

29

The only thing that *does* console me is thinking of my friends. Rachael urging all of us Earthlings to look out for each other. Yiwei playing his guitar while Xiaohou bounces and plays beats and bass notes. Damini sitting next to me right now, her eyes wide with excitement. Keziah's quiet determination to be his own person, instead of just his father's son. Yatto telling me that I should never be ashamed to ask questions. And . . . Elza.

Just the thought of Elza's snarky laugh lights a signal fire inside me, enough to drive away the chill. I wish I knew how to make things right with her.

"We really do not need to do this." Marrant shakes his head, still smiling. "I have nothing to prove. And it would break my heart to destroy another Royal Fleet ship, when I still have so many fond memories of my time wearing that uniform. I remember when I used to tell myself that I could face anything, because justice was on my side." He snorts. "I learned the hard way. Anyway, this is your chance to surrender and avoid a pointless death."

Othaar waves one hand, and now the connection is two-way. "I'll return the courtesy. You can surrender now, if you want."

"Panash?" Marrant's eyes widen. "I haven't seen you since *she* died."

I don't have to guess which "she" he's talking about. My skin is crawling.

"Call me 'Captain Othaar.' You no longer have the right to use my friend-name, after what you did," Othaar growls. "I barely even recognize you now, after all the experiments you've done on yourself. You look like a creepy phytayn doll."

"I've been transforming myself into the perfect humanoid." Marrant smiles wider. "Perfectly symmetrical, with a powerful brain and a strong body. Whereas you? You just look terrible. You should have stayed at home on Aribentora and become a poet-priest, like your parents wanted."

"I'll be sure to write a very short poem to read at your funeral." Othaar rolls his eyeballs. "So, are we going to do this?"

Marrant sighs. "I guess we are. One last thing. I keep hearing these strange reports that there's a clone of Thaoh Argentian running around. Is it true?"

"The clone was defective," Othaar says, without missing a beat. "She ran off on her own, and got herself killed."

My stomach drops. Is that really what he thinks of me? I know he's just making up a story to keep Marrant from finding out about me. But . . . still.

"Pity," Marrant says. "I had so many things I never got to say to Thaoh, preferably while administering slow torture. Second chances are so rare in life."

The chill on my neck is worse than ever. He's grinning and flexing one hand, and he seems to be looking right at me.

"Are we going to fight, or just banter each other to death?" Othaar says.

"Oh, we're going to fight." Marrant laughs. "But it won't take nearly as long as the banter. Goodbye, 'Captain Othaar.'"

The hologram vanishes, at the same time that his ship, the

Merciful Touch, spins up all of its weapons to blow us out of space.

*

My holo-screen is crammed with shiny blotches of death.

The *Merciful Touch* spits dreamkiller missiles at us, and also cuts loose with its pulse cannons. Not to mention some smaller pinpricks swarming us, which I recognize as immobilizer claws—if even one of those immobilizers touches our hull, our engines and weapons will shut down, and we'll be an easy target.

Meanwhile, we keep flying dangerously close to the ring of rocks around Second Yoth. They're nearly as far away from the planet as the moon is from Earth, but they're huge and full of sharp edges and caustic gases. And at the speed we're going, we barely have enough time to turn and dodge and run from all the missiles—we're basically trapped between Marrant's ship on one side and the ring on the other.

Turns out a space battle is not at all like playing *Waymaker* or *Combat Jam* or whatever. It's more like ten games of dodgeball at the same time, mashed up with a trigonometry pop quiz, mashed up with the migraine I got after I drank five cups of coffee.

Part of my brain is like, *Oh, of course,* and is just processing all the input like it's no big deal. But most of me is screaming inside my head, because I wanna get off this ride.

Next to me, Riohon coaxes the ship into flipping sideways, and then pulls us into full reverse to get out of the way of the immobilizer claws and missiles. Damini squints at the 4-D display and whispers safe coordinates in his ear, like she's reciting a poem made of numbers.

One of the missiles is heading straight at us, despite all of

Riohon's fancy dancing. It's so close that I can see the Day-Glo trail and the greasy furrows around the payload. Yiwei reconfigures our hull at the last moment, so we have a C-shaped indentation in our side, and the missile just barely scrapes past.

We haven't even fired back at Marrant's ship yet, because we're waiting for a clean shot, with no risk of hitting the planet. Second Yoth is so huge in my tactical screen, I can barely see past it.

I keep thinking I've found a shot, and then I haven't—and I hear Othaar saying, *The clone was defective*, and see the smirk on Marrant's face as he jokes about torturing me. Rage takes me by surprise, so intense that all the flares of missiles and cannon blasts blur into a reddish haze.

I want to scream out loud. I want to prove them all wrong.

But I can't even give Vaap a clear target. And we're running out of room to escape from all these weapons. We're going to be blown to pieces in a moment, unless we come up with a solution.

The clone was defective, some monstrosity.

I glance at Damini, and her eyes are on fire with excitement. Like she actually thinks we have a shot at winning this thing.

Then I take a breath, and close my eyes, and I realize something: Marrant's ship is staying out of the murky atmosphere of Second Yoth.

The *Merciful Touch* should be using the dense layer of gunk to hide from us, so they can strike out of nowhere. But Marrant is so overconfident, he's not bothering to use his biggest advantage. Or maybe he knows that if he hides from us, he won't be able to see us, either.

And here's the other thing I realize: we don't need to win this fight.

We only need to sneak past Marrant's ship so we can dive into that dense upper atmosphere, where he can't track us. Then we can send people down to the surface and try to find the Talgan stone before he does.

And that means that we can use the thing Keziah suggested before. I send a message to Othaar, Lyzix, and Vaap.

Lyzix lets out a sharp hiss. "Oh, broodmothers. Why'd I think this situation couldn't get any worse?"

"Worst idea ever," Vaap grumbles. "But also, the only one we have left."

Just then I hear a shredding, cracking sound, and the floor bounces so hard that I'm thrown sideways and my head is ringing.

One of Marrant's missiles has struck against the underside of the *Indomitable*, near the cargo hangar, and we're spewing air into the void. Yiwei wrestles with our hull configuration until he plugs the hole. For now.

"No choice," Othaar says. "Let's do it. Riohon, alter course to direct by 7239. We're heading into the planet's rings."

Riohon's eyes widen, and then he lets out a nervous laugh.

Damini whistles, like this is finally about to get interesting.

All of a sudden, we've gone from trying to steer clear of that layer of toxic, razor-sharp material to heading straight into it.

Somehow I refrain from actually saying out loud, *Time to put a ring on it*.

A moment later, we pass through a gap between two huge rocks and into the swirling dust storm in the center of the ring system. Dust particles batter against our hull.

Riohon gasps as the ship weaves between knife-sharp chunks. Damini just keeps speaking math in his ear.

Another impact. The hull screams and we all get flung back and forth in our seats.

"Only one shot," Othaar says. "Engineering, we ready?"

"No." Yma snorts. "But close enough."

"Here we go," Keziah says, also down in Engineering.

We emerge from the rings—and for a moment there are two of us.

Keziah's gambit totally works. We jettison a tiny piece of the ship's hull, and it spits out a radiation trail that looks like a damaged ship on the run.

And while the *Merciful Touch* is distracted, trying to target the decoy ship, the real *Indomitable* dives for the atmosphere of Second Yoth.

The toxic soup gets closer and closer, and then the *Merciful Touch* figures out our ruse. Three missiles are coming right at us, and we're not going to make it.

"Brace yoursel— . . . Oh, never mind, you can't brace for this," Riohon says.

The ship spins all the way around on its axis, so one of the missiles streaks past us. Vaap shoots the second missile with the pulse cannons. And the third dreamkiller explodes close enough that my teeth rattle and my spine feels like putty for a moment.

Now that we're closer to the planet, Vaap is able to return fire, and we unload a spread of dwarf-star ballistics, just before we disappear into the soup of Second Yoth's upper atmosphere.

30

"Hey, there you are." Rachael stops me on my way down to the cargo hangar. Some fluids I don't even want to think about are splattered across her medical scrubs, but she's smiling anyway.

"Hey," I say. "Can't stop to talk. I convinced Othaar to let me join the mission to Second Yoth. We're leaving in two minicycles."

"That's plenty of time," Rachael says. "I need to be back in Sickbay soon anyway. Come on."

She marches me down to the computer core, near the crew lounge, even though I keep protesting that I have to go.

"You and Elza need to talk," Rachael says. "There may not be a later."

Elza and Yatto are busy trying to see through the super-smog of Second Yoth's atmosphere, but they both look up when we approach. Elza glances at me, and looks down again.

Rachael shoves me forward. I'm starting to regret coaxing her out of her quarters.

"Um, hey," I say to the back of Elza's head. "I'm really sorry I was a jerk."

Yatto looks at us, and just silently withdraws from the room. Rachael goes with them.

Elza realizes that we're alone, and finally turns to face me. Her eyes are a little wet, and also the most beautiful thing ever.

"Apologies are cheap."

"I'll make it up to you. Right now I have to go down to a planet full of three-winged creatures and Compassion mercy-killers, but . . . when I get back, I'll be there for you. I promise. I want to be a real friend to you."

"Friends." Elza looks happy and disappointed, at the same time. "That sounds good."

I reach out a hand, tentatively, and she takes it.

"I hope you find what you're looking for," Elza says.

"The Talgan stone? It's got to be somewhere on this planet, unless we got bad intel."

"That's not what I meant." She smiles, and I feel turbulence inside me, like another missile just hit. "I hope you find a way to live up to the legacy of Captain Incredible."

She lets go of my hand and gives me one last smile before she turns back to her workstation.

*

The orbital funnel hits the surface of Second Yoth with a bone-jolting thud. I fall on my butt, but Vaap reaches down and pulls me upright. Iyiiguol is already doing a realtac (real-time tactical) scan of the terrain, and Uiuiuiui is shouldering his weapon.

"Keep alert," Vaap says. "Watch your threads and spikes."

Everybody responds, "So noted," including me.

Without any other Earth kids around, I'm acting way more like a perfect Royal cadet, saluting and obeying orders, with zero backtalk.

We've come down close to the main city, which is made up of three main sections. (Because the Grattna always have three of everything.) We're in a clearing in a forest of tall trees that look like super-long fingernails with pink doilies on top. The twisty tops of the city's skyline rise up in the distance, white and pale green. We start marching in that direction, quiet as we can be.

As we walk, I keep thinking about what Elza said, and getting a jolt of pure hope. Maybe I can still live up to this legacy, in my own way. Even if Captain Argentian didn't want me to exist, I'm here now.

Even before we reach the outskirts of the city, I hear shouts and the sound of weapons. The Compassion.

We creep forward, until we glimpse an open space where the Grattna are being rounded up by Compassion thugs and herded into big cages. The Grattna struggle, flapping their three wings and lashing out with their three limbs, but their captors use ion harnesses to catch them in midair and drag them down into the cages. I feel queasy, light-headed, ready to smack someone.

"Don't worry," hisses an Irriyaian whose black armor bears an insignia identifying him as a senior mercy-killer. "We're not going to kill you. Marrant needs you for his experiments."

"We need to help those people," Iyiiguol whispers.

Vaap shushes him. "That's not our mission," Vaap whispers. "The objective comes first."

The further we sneak inside the city, the more of those cages we see. I feel sicker and sicker, and I wish there was something we could do—but Vaap is right. There's nothing we can do for the Grattna right now.

The Grattna city, Kufn, is beautiful. Triangle-shaped and hexagonal buildings shimmer, in the sunlight filtering through the gray-green clouds overhead. All of the buildings have perches and ramps going into the sky, so the Grattna can swoop inside. Every intersection goes in three different directions.

A patrol of Compassion enforcers walks right past us (two Aribentors and one Javarah), and they almost see us. We duck around a six-sided building just in time.

A voice behind us says, "Pssst! You'd better come with me now or soon, not later."

We turn to see one of the Grattna looking at us. Three eyes and three nostrils in a fuzzy reddish-orange head, with one wing rising straight up, and the other two wings fanning out on either side. "My name is Bildub, and my pronoun is *wey*. Come on, I know where we can hide." Bildub gestures with one of weyr three arms/legs.

We all look at Vaap. Who shrugs.

Bildub leads us down a narrow alley that forks in two different directions. The right-hand path leads us to a hidden trapdoor, which in turn leads us down to a secret tunnel that runs under the city.

*

Some time later, Bildub takes us to a tiny chamber with six sides, lined with relics of the Grattnas' past: old texts covered with swirly letters, ornate jeweled staves with places for all three limbs to grip, and gorgeous paintings that show Grattnas dancing three by three.

Vaap stands up, rolls their head, and says to Iyiiguol and me, "Keep talking to weym. Uiuiuiui, with me. We're going to scout the area and come back."

Then it's just the three of us—which seems appropriate.

"You have to help us get to the Talgan stone," I say to Bildub. "The Royal Fleet is on your side."

"That's not true," Bildub says. "You're on your own side."

At first, I think Bildub doesn't trust the Royal Fleet because of all the promises we broke while we were too busy fighting the Compassion. I keep trying to explain that we're trying to stop the Compassion, who are hurting Bildub's people, so we have a common enemy.

"Why is this so hard for you to understand?" I groan.

"I absolutely understand," Bildub says. "The Royal Fleet is on one side, the Compassion is on another, and then there are my people."

"But! We should be allies," I say.

And then I finally get it, and slap my forehead.

It's like Riohon said before: the Grattna believe there are three sides to any struggle. So when I say things like "we're on your side," it just sounds like nonsense.

"Okay," I say. "So there are three sides in this conflict. But you must have some stories about fights where two sides teamed up against the third side. Right? That has to be a thing that happens here."

"Oh, sure," Bildub says. "That's called apexing."

"So maybe that's what's happening here? We want to help."

"You can't help, or hurt either. You can only stay out of it." Bildub sighs. "They've taken a lot of my people prisoner in those big cages. We couldn't escape or hide. Worse still, they brought the Chief Mercy-Bringer, Marrant. If he touches you, you don't just suffer or die. You are turned into a foul-smelling soup. But also, your very memory gets tarnished forever in the minds of your family, friends, and fellows."

I remember the hologram from Best Planet Ever, where Marrant touched someone and they turned into a puddle.

"So his touch melts people, but also ruins their memory? How does that work?"

"I don't know. He killed all of my children, and now I hate them." Bildub looks around, weyr red-flecked yellow eyes wide and impossibly sad. "I don't know how much longer we can hide, or flee."

Wey doesn't mention the third option: getting caught. Wey doesn't have to.

We're running out of time, and I'm scared something's happened to Vaap and Uiuiuiui. I need to find a way to convince Bildub to take us to the Talgan stone. Which means . . . I have to make helping us seem like the best of three choices.

"I don't know what this Talgan stone is," I say. "But it must be connected to the Shapers, the people who poisoned your atmosphere a long time ago. And it's dangerous. You need to give it to us, or destroy it. You can't let the Compassion take it."

Bildub hesitates.

"Whatever you decide, we'll help you," Iyiiguol says, mossy face parted to reveal wide-open eyes with no irises.

"Okay," Bildub says. "You're right. We'll destroy it."

Oh, damn. I think my clever plan just backfired.

*

I'm sneaking deeper underground with Bildub and Iyiiguol, plus Vaap and Uiuiuiui. Vaap wasn't exactly thrilled when I explained to them what I had done—but at least if Bildub smashes the Talgan stone, we'll be keeping it out of the hands of the Compassion.

We reach an underground river of noxious sludge that's easy to cross if you have three wings and three hands. We have to grab handholds in the ceiling and swing ourselves from handhold to handhold, with the sludge running right under our dangling feet, until we finally reach the other side. Then the tunnel reaches another fork, and another, and at last, Bildub brings us to the vault where they stashed the Talgan stone.

The vault opens with a creak, and . . . the Talgan stone is just a very old piece of rock, about the size of an iPad, with one jagged edge. Kind of chalky, heavier than it looks. There are some symbols carved on it, but they make the EverySpeak cough up a hairball.

"We should have done this a long time ago, or just not accepted this burden at all." Bildub raises the stone over weyr head. I'm trying to think of something to say to make weym stop.

Just then I hear noises from the tunnels all around us.

"Thank you," a familiar smooth voice rings out.

Marrant.

He steps from the shadows, along with a couple of skull-faced Aribentors in mercy-killer uniforms. "I had a feeling that you would lead me to my prize."

I'm frozen stiff again, from skin to bone.

31

"Marrant." Vaap doesn't bother to hide the disdain in their voice. "I always hoped I would meet you, and that I'd have a weapon in my hand when I did."

Before anybody can react, Vaap has their positron cloudstrike gun pointed at Marrant's head. At this range, Marrant's head will be totally vaporized.

Marrant laughs. "Go ahead. Try me."

Vaap pulls the trigger, and the cloud chamber discharges with a blinding flash.

When my eyes clear, Marrant's uniform is scorched, but his head and shoulders are exactly the same as before.

"I *told* you, I've been upgrading myself," Marrant says. "Humanoids are already superior to other species because of our symmetrical bodies, and the intricate way that our left brains and right brains dance together. But also, I've been boosting the power of my mind, to become more like the Shapers who lifted up our ancestors."

Vaap shakes their head. "You turned yourself into a monster, because you worship monsters."

Marrant's chalky face is even creepier up close. Like a mask. His left side and his right side look identical, without pores or lines.

Marrant smiles bigger. "Nobody is going to mourn for you. Nobody will even have a good word to say about you, once you're gone."

He leans in closer and touches Vaap's head with one finger. Vaap lets out a scream—more high-pitched and screechy than anything I would ever have expected from them.

And then . . . Vaap melts, uniform and all, with a horrible smell like a pile of burning plastic. A moment later, there's nothing left but a chunky puddle, with a fragment of Vaap's left boot and a few pieces of their gun sticking out.

I look down at all that's left of Vaap, who was kind to us and taught us and tried to keep us safe.

And all I can think is: *Good*.

I try to feel bad about Vaap's death, or sorry for what's happened to them, but all that comes is . . . disgust.

Iyiiguol rushes forward to attack Marrant as well, and Marrant lunges out with one hand. And there's another puddle on the vault floor.

I glance at Iyiiguol's remains and think: *No great loss. He sucked anyway*.

"It doesn't have to be this way. We humanoids can stick together," Marrant says. "We should be united, so we can all follow in the footsteps of the Shapers. They were the most advanced people who ever lived, and then they vanished. I believe they became so evolved that they no longer needed physical forms. Every humanoid has brains that rest above their bodies, but the Shapers managed to leave their bodies behind altogether. You and I could become gods, the same way they did."

I think of what Vaap said, right before they melted to nothing: Marrant turned himself into a monster because he worships monsters.

But Vaap was worthless—they were always a puddle of

224

sewage, even when they were alive. So they must have been wrong about Marrant, too. In this moment, I'm surer about this than anything, ever.

I step forward, ready to pledge myself to Marrant.

The stench of what used to be Vaap is getting in my nostrils. The thought of being on the same side as that piece of trash makes me even sicker to my stomach.

Marrant glances at me and smiles. Uiuiuiui's wormy face is twisted with horror.

Then the reality of what I'm about to do sinks in, and I have to double over for a moment. I've stepped in the puddle that used to be Iyiiguol, and my shoe is sticky.

I have to say it out loud. "You destroyed their memory. But that doesn't make them wrong." I only stammer a little.

Okay, a lot.

"Why should I care what you think?" Marrant turns his whole attention toward me, and his dark eyes seem to peel away all my defenses. He can see into the rotten core of me.

I am shaking so hard everything blurs.

"You shouldn't," I say. "But also, you shouldn't take your eye off the ball."

I snatch the Talgan stone out of Bildub's center talon. Then I shove Bildub and Uiuiuiui out of the vault and slam the door on Marrant and his two mercy-killer friends. Leaving them trapped with the two revolting puddles.

*

We run at top speed through tunnels where I can barely see in front of my hand. I only face-plant a couple times. But I just get up and keep running, until I'm gasping-groaning and my body is one big cramp. At least my blood is flowing, and I no longer feel so frozen.

I hear footsteps and shouts all around us. But according to Bildub, these tunnels have countless triple-forks, and you could search forever if you don't know your way around. At last, we reach the river of lethal muck, and I force myself to swing hand over hand until I reach the other side.

"We have to get back to the orbital funnel," Uiuiuiui wheezes, clutching his side. "We're lucky nobody was killed."

"Except for Vaap and Iyiiguol." Even saying their names makes me nauseous. I shouldn't waste my breath.

"Yeah. That was no loss," Uiuiuiui says. Then he hears what he's saying, and stops. His face-tubes sag.

"Damn," I say. "I can remember that I used to like Vaap and Iyiiguol. I thought of them as friends, even. But now? When I think of them, all I can think is that they were garbage."

"I told you before," Bildub says. "Marrant's touch does that. You can't mourn the dead, or celebrate their lives with the godparents. You can only despise them."

"He doesn't just kill people," Uiuiuiui says. "He tarnishes them."

I can't believe I let Vaap touch me, and I joked around with Iyiiguol a few times. Every time I think about either of them, I need to take a shower.

Bildub still wants to destroy the Talgan stone, but I'm holding on to it extra tight.

We run through the forest of doily trees, and run in circles for ages before we find where we left the orbital-funnel platform. I can hear the Compassion closing in: loud taunts, and the occasional blast from a fireburst gun.

"You should come with us," I say to Bildub when Uiuiuiui and I finally step back onto the elevator platform. "We can protect you. Your other choices are to get caught or killed."

Bildub shakes weyr head, slowly. "If I die anywhere but on Second Yoth, the godparents won't be able to find me. And if there's any way to help the rest of my people, I need to try."

"We'll come back for you, when this is over." Even as I say those words, I know they're probably empty.

"Just make sure the Talgan stone is either safeguarded or destroyed," Bildub says. "I can't even get my mind around everything I've lost in the past few days. Right now I can't even see a future, or even a present." Wey shakes weyr head.

The Compassion is getting closer. One of the doily trees near us bursts into flame.

"Time to go." Uiuiuiui activates the orbital funnel.

Bildub and the forest shrink to nothing, and then the city of Kufn looks like a toy model, and then the landscape loses all of its detail and becomes just colors and shapes. Uiuiuiui and I don't talk, the whole way back up to the *Indomitable*.

I can't stop thinking about Vaap and Iyiiguol, reduced to foul-smelling sludge. And I'm just glad I never have to look at their gross faces again.

Screw those losers.

*

"We obtained the objective," I say to Captain Othaar and Alternate Captain Lyzix, as soon as we're back on the ship. I hold up the Talgan stone, which still just looks like an old piece of granite with some scratchy lines on it. "Unfortunately, Vaap and Iyiiguol . . . didn't make it." I try to sound appropriately mournful.

Captain Othaar shakes his head. "It doesn't matter. They were both a disgrace to this uniform."

"Agreed." Lyzix flexes her ears in disgust. "I always loathed both of them."

I almost drop the Talgan stone. I stare at the two captains, and I don't know what to say.

"Vaap was your friend," I say at last.

"Can't believe I actually thought that," Othaar says.

Oh no. No no no. I feel like screaming, cursing, punching something.

Somehow, I thought whatever Marrant did to us wouldn't affect the people on the *Indomitable*. It had to be just a local thing, right? I can't believe I'm even hearing this.

"Marrant did this," I say. "He . . . when he touched Vaap and Iyiiguol, and they both . . ." I can't bring myself to say the word "died." "He said that nobody would mourn for them. Like, we would all realize how rotten they had always been."

Lyzix starts to say something sarcastic, but Othaar gives her a look and she stops.

"So. You're saying this was some kind of psionic attack," Othaar says.

"That's right." I feel heartsick. "Just think about it. Would you have put Vaap in charge of this mission to the planet, if you really thought they were a disgrace? Why would you entrust them with that responsibility?"

Othaar closes his eyes and covers his face with all his bone-fingers. "Oh, cursed certainty."

I've never seen Lyzix look freaked out, the way she does right now. Her eyes widen and her ears tilt all the way back.

"Broodkeepers. He got inside our heads."

"He got inside all of our heads," I say. "It affected me and Uiuiuiui, too. Probably everyone on the ship. Marrant kept saying that he had found a way to boost the power of his brain, the same way the Shapers did with theirs."

"So now anyone he touches . . ." Othaar is still covering his face. "Ugh. We have to give those two fallen officers a proper funeral, and find a way to pretend we still respect and admire them. I served with Vaap for seven megacycles. I can remember all the times they were there for me, but now I can't feel anything but . . . hatred."

"I'm sorry for your loss," I say—even though I'm thinking: *Good riddance to bad rubbish.*

*

I sit in the back at the funerals for Vaap and Iyiiguol. They recite all the complicated blessings, and consign the memory of our fallen comrades to the Winds of Gratitude. They lift a translucent white cloth in the air and let it billow over our heads, then light a tiny flame, smaller than a candle, and the heat-sensitive cloth evaporates into a mist that settles on all of us and then vanishes without a trace. They do this twice, once for Vaap and once for Iyiiguol.

I barely know any of the words to this ceremony. Captain Argentian probably had a lot of painful memories from all the funerals she attended.

While everybody stands up and talks about how great Vaap and Iyiiguol were, and how much we're going to miss them, I only feel grossed out. And then guilty, and then angry—and then more loathing. I try to remember the times Iyiiguol was nice to me, or how happy I was when Vaap praised my work. But all those memories are smeared with filth now. They were both creeps. I should have seen it all along.

I want to cry, but there's nothing worth crying over.

After the funeral, Rachael sidles up to me and whispers, "Are you okay?"

I nod, and then shake my head. "Kind of. I'm dealing. I don't want to talk about it."

"Okay." She smiles. "If you need to talk later, I'll be in the bluehouse."

"Thanks." And then I look away.

Because when I look at Rachael, or any of my other friends, I picture Marrant touching them—and my feelings for them turning bad, like expired milk, right as their bodies dissolve. Or I imagine my friends standing over what's left of me, and saying that I sucked and that I deserved to die.

I've been scared before.

This is something else.

*

Damini: what the hell happened down there? Tina?

Yiwei: why do i want to throw up whenever i think of Vaap???

Rachael: srsly this is freaking me out.

Rachael: Tina? i know you're on here, i can see your name

Kez: We just want an explanation, that's all.

Rachael: Tina? Hello? TINA?

Someone knocks on the door to my quarters, where I'm eating my dinner in private and staring at the wall. I almost don't answer, but then Elza says, "I'm not leaving until I see your face."

I open the door, and she's standing there, looking at me with wondering brown eyes, and my heart comes back to life, in spite of everything.

"I got worried about you," Elza says. "Ever since you came back from that mission, you've looked like someone who just swallowed a hundred ice cubes."

"I'm okay." I look at the floor.

"No," Elza says. "You're not. Maybe this'll help."

She rummages in a tiny tool satchel and pulls out something. A candy bar. Some Brazilian chocolate with a dark label that says, "Black Diamond."

"Where the hell did you get that?"

"I found it in my backpack, after we made it to the ship. I've been saving it for the right occasion."

I try to tell her not to waste her only chocolate bar, but she's already unwrapping it and handing me a piece. I put it in my mouth and feel the tart aftertaste melt away on my tongue, and it's like I'm back on Earth for a second.

I gesture for her sit in my one teacup chair, and I perch on the edge of my bed-web.

"I've never seen you like this," she says. "I've seen you freaked out, but this is something else. What could be so bad that you can't even talk about it?"

I shake my head. My mouth still feels sticky with chocolate. My heart is pounding, and tears gather at the edges of my vision, and she's close enough to touch. I remember when we held hands on Rascal Station.

Suddenly I need very much not to be alone.

Elza comes closer, and I let her clamber onto the web next to me.

"I couldn't save them," I say into my elbow. "Vaap and Iyiiguol. They died protecting me. And now I can't even feel bad that they're gone, because I . . ."

I try to explain, halting every few words.

"So. He's got some kind of psychic ability that makes people speak ill of the dead." Elza whistles. "That explains why I've had such dark thoughts about the two of them since you got back. If we were back home, I know someone who could give you something, like a mollusk-shell necklace, to connect you to your personal orixá and keep you from negative influences. I knew a few people who practiced Candomblé, they could have hooked you up."

"I wish there was something. I'm so sick of people messing with my head."

Her warm breath and her hothouse-flower scent comfort me. I feel safe in this moment, even if that doesn't promise safety tomorrow, or anywhere outside this room.

"People have been messing with my head forever," Elza says. "People made up their minds about me, before I even opened my mouth. Doors were open one day, closed the next, and I learned not to take anything for granted. Just like how they're always trying to shut down all the Candomblé temples back home, because they want to destroy Black culture. It's exhausting."

"How did you deal with it?"

She laughs, like that's kind of a weird question. "I stopped worrying so much about other people's expectations, and tried to be true to myself, whatever anyone else thought of me."

"That's great, until an alien psycho touches you, and everyone who survives thinks you were just straight-up trash."

"That'll be their loss." Elza shrugs. "Not mine. From what you've told me, Captain Wonderful didn't go through life worrying about what people would say about her when she was gone."

"She definitely did not. Thank you for what you said before, when you told me that I can still find a way to live up to Captain Argentian's legacy. I think you gave me the strength to survive that awful mission."

Elza smiles. I feel a whole forest of Christmas trees light up inside me.

"Any time."

"Can you do something else for me?" I hesitate. She already gave me chocolate and excellent advice. "I was about to watch some of Thaoh Argentian's log entries about Marrant. I need to understand more about what went wrong. But . . . I don't want to watch them on my own. Will you . . . will you stay and watch with me?"

"Movie night." Elza smiles wider. "I only wish we had popcorn."

Cadet Thaoh Argentian's personal datajournal, 5.15.22.03 of the Age of Expansion

He's the most annoying person I've ever met. His name is Thondra Marrant, and he Pronounces. Every. Syllable. Of. It. He seems to think just because we're the only two cadets from Makvaria, we ought to be inseparable, and he keeps trying way too hard, bragging about his test scores.

It's like: you already got into the academy. You don't need to keep proving you deserve to be here.

His insecurity makes everyone else feel insecure too.

He's always talking about how he's going to meet the queen and all the princesses someday, and he's going to learn all the secrets of the Firmament, and find the center of the Wishing Maze. Blah blah blah. Give it a rest, buddy.

I swear, if he doesn't turn it down a few dozen levels, I'm going to smack him.

Junior Explorer Thaoh Argentian's personal datajournal, 8.12.14.33 of the Age of Expansion

Singing Volcano Fish of Kthorok, I swear . . . if I didn't have Thondra to talk to, I'd turn into one of those people who tries to communicate telepathically with a flask of dirt from my hometown. Though to be fair, dirt would be a more interesting conversation partner than some of the people around here.

But Thondra? He cracks me up. Like, he's always making with the sarcastic whispers just when everybody takes everything way too seriously, and then *I'm* the one who gets in trouble for laughing. Don't ever tell Thondra I said this, but I don't think I'd have lasted in the Fleet if he hadn't been there.

Although now, thanks to him I can't stop thinking of Crewmaster Duth as Loose Boots Duth, which is gonna get me in trouble one of these days.

And meanwhile, he's actually found a girlfriend, and she's adorable and can hold her yuul sauce, and she doesn't make me feel like a surplus impeller when the three of us hang out. Her name's Aym, and she's got the meanest attitude I've ever seen—which is exactly what Thondra needs to keep him in line.

Captain Thaoh Argentian's personal datajournal, 1.77.34.07 of the Age of Regret

I would have said Thondra was the one person I could count on. Now . . . I just don't know.

His tactical officer warned him the Zenoithan warship had an unstable power core, and the consequences could be disastrous if it exploded. Aym begged him to stand down. She even tried to use her alternate captain authority to make him back off. He. Wouldn't. Listen.

And now Aym is gone, along with half his crew, and a good part of the population of Zenoith. It's every captain's worst nightmare.

And now they want me to be on his tribunal. I tried everything I could think of to get out of it. I have the biggest conflict of interest ever. But they keep saying there's nobody else who's qualified. I just wish I could talk to Aym.

He killed the woman he loved, and he won't even accept any of the blame.

Captain Thaoh Argentian's personal datajournal, 2.08.49.94 of the Age of Regret

Marrant . . . I won't use his friend-name anymore. He joined that splinter group. They call themselves the Compassion, because I suppose the Puke-Brained Xenophobic Murder Cult was too much of a mouthful.

Captain buries her face in her arm for a moment.

A long silence follows, until the holographic recording times out and starts to fade to black.

Captain Argentian raises one finger, so that the recording continues.

I need to say something else, on the record—so when everything goes streaky, I can at least look back and know that I saw it coming.

This is going to be so much worse than anybody realizes. The Royal Fleet isn't going to come out of this in one piece.

At least we've got the broadswords and they only have those little barbships and spikeships, which are like tiny bugs biting a giant. But it's starting to feel like half my friends are trying to kill me, and I don't know if I can kill them first.

So future me, if you're watching this: you knew what you were walking into, and you kept right on walking.

Captain Argentian half laughs, half groans, and the recording finally blanks out.

32

I can't help staring at the empty seat in the control deck where Vaap ought to be, and imagining the grouchy things they'd be saying.

But then a voice inside my head says, *They had it coming. They were pathetic, and we're better off.*

And I know that everyone else in this meeting is thinking the same thing. Nobody even mentions Vaap, or Iyiiguol, at all. They're not just dead, they're forgotten. Because it's just too painful to think about either of them.

This is what Marrant does. He was disgraced, and he lost the love of his life—so now he goes around disgracing other people, or destroying their love.

"So," Captain Othaar says heavily, like he hasn't slept. "We got hold of the rock that Marrant wanted, but we still have no idea what it is."

"Or why it's important," Lyzix says. "I doubt Marrant was hoping to put it in a museum."

"The Shapers had technologies that we still don't understand," says Yma. "We know they had means of crossing vast distances, perhaps faster than spaceweave, and engines for remaking whole planets. This could be a clue to some piece of technology they left behind."

"Something the Compassion could use to wipe us out, once

and for all." Othaar creases his zygomatic plates into a scowl. "This is too big for us to handle. We'll safebeam the details on this artifact to the nearest broadsword-class ship, the *Unquenchable*, and they can investigate."

"We're closer. And faster," Lyzix says. "This is our find, and I don't want to hand it off to someone else who's going to be late to the show. Plus we have the actual artifact, not just some holographic scan of it."

"The *Unquenchable* has a stronger hull, and the latest quasar-burst weapons that we haven't been fitted with yet," Othaar says. "Anyway, this is not a debate. I've made the decision."

Lyzix leans forward, like she's about to pounce, and her ears jut, and her face is a giant snarl.

"As alternate captain, I have the ability to undo your decisions when I judge that they represent an unacceptable risk," she hisses. "And we cannot risk Marrant obtaining some technology from the worst criminals in history."

"So that's how it is now." Othaar's actual skull gets pale, which I didn't think was even possible. "I judge the greater risk is the *Indomitable* rushing into an unknown situation and getting destroyed, or even giving Marrant access to this artifact. We barely escaped from Second Yoth without getting shot down, probably because Marrant didn't want to risk destroying this rock."

"Normally, the tiebreaking vote in this situation would be . . ." Lyzix looks at Vaap's empty chair.

"Permission to speak?" I don't plan to open my mouth, it just happens.

"Granted." Othaar gives me a friendly smile (but I still haven't forgotten how he called me "defective").

"Marrant is the worst person I've ever met. He really thinks the Shapers were gods or something, and he thinks he can become like them."

Othaar starts to say something, and I interrupt him.

"What's the point of any of this if we don't stand up against this creep? The fact that he turned our friends to sludge and I can't even say their names or think about them at all is not even the worst thing about him," I say. "We can't let him keep piling injustice on top of injustice, or it'll never stop."

Captain Othaar clutches his own thick forehead with a bone-plated hand. "Very well. We'll compromise. We'll safebeam the *Unquenchable* with a request for backup, but in the meantime we'll try to ascertain Marrant's goals on our own. And we'll hope against hope that the Hosts of Misadventure are in a generous mood."

"Thank you. *Captain*." Lyzix puts a lot into that last word.

*

Outside the control deck, I stop Lyzix, who gives me a curious smile and a twitch of her ears.

"Hey," I say. "I wanted to ask you something."

Lyzix nods. "Of course. I know you went through a terrible ordeal on Second Yoth. Anything you need, I'm here."

I guess since Lyzix and I were on the same side of the argument with Captain Othaar, she likes me for once.

"I need to get better at fighting," I say. "I was going to ask Vaap for help with combat skills, but . . ." I just shake my head. "I need to be able to defend myself the next time we run into the Compassion. I know the other cadets aren't getting combat training yet, but I was hoping you could make an exception in my case."

Lyzix frowns. "You have all of Captain Argentian's other knowledge, so you probably inherited her fighting abilities as well."

"Yeah. But being able to do something, and being ready to do it, aren't the same thing. I need to be ready to make a stand. This is who I am. You're looking at a person who used to dress up in a plushie dinosaur costume, just to help disrupt the office of this payday loan company that was ripping people off."

"None of the words you just spoke made any sense, even with the EverySpeak." Lyzix shrugs. "But I understand. You just met real evil for the first time. True cruelty, married to a toxic ideology. And you want to be able to do something about it."

"That's all I've ever wanted."

Weirdly, talking to Lyzix is making me feel better, which is the opposite of every other conversation I've ever had with her.

"But why me? Why not ask Yatto the Monntha? Or Riohon? Or even Captain Othaar? They could all train you to fight, almost as well as I could."

"Because you won't go easy on me." I smile, and she smiles back.

"That's very true. I hope you like bruises." Lyzix laughs. "Come to the cargo hangar after your duty shift ends."

Then she walks away with a bounce in her step, because she's going to get to kick someone's ass.

*

Rachael: i remember that plushie dinosaur costume!

Rachael: I stayed up half the night sewing on purple sequins. And then the costume was as hot as a tire fire on the inside.

Rachael: I only wore it a couple times, but you? You were the perfect pink dinosaur.

Tina: i hammed it up. ROAAARRRRRR!

Rachael: That's my Tina.

Tina: except when i was face to face with marrant, i was more like whimperrrrr.

Rachael: You got the rock, that's the main thing.

Tina: can't believe i actually miss the days when monday barker was our biggest problem.

Rachael: Except the Shapers were always a thing. they helped the human race and we never knew

Rachael: How are you holding up?

Tina: im ok

Tina: i can't find one clean feeling to latch onto

Tina: just a big blob of every emotion

Rachael: Like melted gummi worms

Tina: yes my heart is a blob of melted gummi worms yes

Tina: hey are you in sickbay? i was gonna head down there.

Rachael: Yep, in the exam room. What's up?

Tina: i need to be stronger

Tina: so im ready next time

Rachael: You know you don't have to be strong all the time. Right?????

*

Dr. Karrast comes into the treatment room, fresh from checking on the ever-increasing number of wounded crewmembers in the sickbeds. "Thrilling stunts and minor injuries."

"Delicious meals and harmless poisons," I reply.

"I went over the brain scans of Uiuiuiui and you," Dr. Karrast says. "Since the two of you were at close range when Marrant . . . when he made all of us hate our fallen comrades. I'm guessing he uses all the energy released by dissolving the victim's biomass to generate a psychic field. Ingenious. And horrible."

"Is there any way to defend against it?" I glance at Rachael, who's fussing with supplies.

"Maybe. I'm working on it." Dr. Karrast winces her one big eye. "Is that all you wanted to ask me about?"

"No. I was wondering if you could undo whatever they did to my DNA, to make me look like a human. Turn me into a real Makvarian."

"Sure," Dr. Karrast says, looking at me through the bioplastic scanner. "You'll need to get rid of your DNA mask eventually anyway. The process could be disorienting and somewhat unpleasant, though."

"Are you sure that's a good idea right now?" Rachael asks me. "I mean, you're already dealing with a lot. Maybe now's not the right time to put yourself through the mother of all growth spurts?"

"No choice." I shrug. "Next time we meet those assclowns, I need to be stronger. Tougher."

Rachael keeps trying to convince me to wait until things are more stable, but I've already made my mind up. So Dr. Karrast takes a big subdermal injector and squirts some dark blue sludge into my left shoulder with a "splorrp" sound.

"That's just the primer," Karrast says. "Come back in a few metacycles and I'll give you the first treatment. You'll need four treatments before your Makvarian DNA fully expresses itself. Eventually, you'll have more upper-body strength, and you won't need to sleep as much."

I nod. "See you in a few days."

33

"Come on," Elza says. "I want to show you something." I follow her as she leads me down, past Engineering, to an empty area near the crew quarters. We already watched all the Linn da Quebrada music videos that were on her phone, so I don't know what this could be.

I keep remembering the moment on Rascal Station when I almost kissed Elza. Her sweet scent and the way her lips opened a little as we leaned closer, feeling the vibrations of the Blot music. Part of me keeps living in that moment, even though the rest of me is obsessing about Marrant and his death touch.

Elza leads me forward, chattering about her favorite spot back home, the Parca de República, where you can always find people playing music and vendors frying some acarajé in palm oil—she describes acarajé to me, and my taste buds burst with envy, after so many gross EveryStomach rations.

Then she pauses in the middle of the ramp leading to the upper areas.

"This seems like a good enough place."

Elza does a hand gesture and snaps her fingers, and flowers bloom around me. Vines climb the walls, with strange conical blossoms, and everything is a riot of color. Elza waves her other hand, and hummingbirds swarm around the vines, leaving rainbow sparkle trails. My jaw hangs open in pure wonder.

"Whoa," I say. "That is . . . Is this all holographic?"

"Yeah. I've been trying to see how far I can push the ship's holographic projection capacity. You can't do anything immersive or super-realistic, but . . ." She waves her hand through one of the sparkle trails behind a hummingbird, and rainbow sparkles start following her hand as well. I try it too, and soon both of my hands are painting shimmering rainbows wherever they go.

I spin like a terrible ballerina through one of the trails. My whole body makes a rainbow swirl, and I look like this cartoon cat I saw on the internet. I fall on my back, laughing, in the middle of the hallway, looking up at the sparkly mess we made.

"I can't believe it," I gasp. "You managed to program the computer, even more than just creating that chat program."

"Yeah. I haven't exactly gotten root on it. But when you think about it, 'programming' can mean all kinds of things, and any machine has more than one kind of instruction set." She pauses. "Like, people get programmed in all sorts of ways, by privilege, or propaganda, or whatever."

We just lie there for a while, staring up at the glittery light patterns over our heads.

"Before my parents threw me away, I was going to be something great," Elza says. "I was going to invent new technology, come up with ideas that could help everybody, code the solutions that would help lift people out of poverty. I really used to believe that I could help to save the world with my mind."

"What would it take for you to believe again?" I ask.

"I don't know. All of those dreams feel like part of a whole different life." Her smile vanishes.

"All the people who rejected you and tried to tear you down are still stuck back on Earth," I whisper. "And you're out here, having an adventure they could never even dream about, and just look what you convinced this puny starship computer to do."

I gesture at the hummingbirds still swarming over our heads, trailing rainbows.

"Yeah, I did do that, didn't I?" Elza breathes.

The sparkly holograms start fading away—probably a good thing, since I hear the distinctive sound of Crewmaster Bul's footsteps approaching.

*

Rachael: So you're NOT going to ask Elza out.

Rachael: Just wanted to be clear about that

Tina: nah. too much complication

Rachael: Let the record reflect that Tina wussed out on romance

Rachael: This is just like Rob Langford all over again

Tina: i just

Tina: i don't even know what i am

Tina: barely know *who* i am

Tina: and elza needs a friend right now. she needs someone to be in her corner

Rachael: Have you asked *her* what she needs?

Tina: not exactly

Tina: but she said she used to believe she could help save the world with her mind

Tina: she needs to believe that again

Tina: wish i could think of a way to help her

*

I keep thinking there must be something I can offer Elza, to help her have faith in her awesome powers once more. A goal that's not just being part of this crew and helping us to fight against evil.

At last I hit on something, and it's so perfect that I can't help laughing out loud.

"What's so funny?" Elza asks, sitting next to me at the back of the crew lounge, where we've poured some Scanthian parsnip juice on a pile of EveryStomach rations to try and give them some peppery flavor.

"Remember how we were talking about you maybe meeting the queen sometime?" I say.

Elza cracks a smile. "I'm not going to meet the queen. She's going to meet me."

God. That smile. I feel lighter than pure hydrogen.

"But what if you could do something even better?"

"What are you talking about?" Elza says.

"Remember how I mentioned it takes years of training for someone to be ready to be queen? Well, there are always a bunch of princesses studying and prepping, in case they need to take over. Anybody, from anywhere in the galaxy, can apply to be a princess. They consider everyone: all genders, all species. There's a whole screening process. You could totally qualify."

"Huh." Elza's eyes mist up and have a faraway look. "I've always loved princesses, ever since I was little."

"With all the time you've spent with the *Indomitable*'s computers, you would be a really good candidate."

"You really think so? I keep telling you that I hate authority and pointless rules and structure." Elza laughs. "What makes you think I'm princess material?"

I almost say something sappy like, *Because you're so beautiful and clever.* But we're being friends.

So I say, "The princesses don't exactly have a lot of rules. Their most important job is to learn how to connect their brains to all the super-smart computers, the Ardenii. And that means that they have to think for themselves."

"Huh." Elza looks around the crew lounge, where Uiuiuiui is sitting by himself and eating a few dainty bites of Cydoghian eggburst. "You really think I could have a shot?"

"I think anybody who takes one look at you is going to see what I see: a kick-ass genius mastermind with fire in her heart and an endless supply of snark for great justice." I offer my hand and she takes it. "You are incredible, Elza Monteiro, and they'd be damn lucky to have you as a princess."

Elza looks at me with her eyes shining, and she clutches my hand tighter. We just sit there, hand in hand, until my shoulder comms pipe up.

It's time for me to go on another mission, on a thousand-year-old starship.

34

Yatto clutches at the giant burn mark on their arm, which messes up the elaborate crownflower design on their right sleeve. "It's . . . fine," they wheeze, closing their eyes to keep the tears locked inside. "They just winged me."

On the other side of the bulkhead of this ancient ship, the Compassion are still shooting at us, making things burst into flames.

"But I don't know how we get out of this," Yatto says.

There are just three Compassion soldiers left, and their leader keeps taunting us. "You Royalists are so weak-minded. You sympathize with the Misshapen so much, you should just share their fate." The leader is a Scanthian, a large humanoid with hedgehog spikes all over their body.

Yatto gasps with pain, but they still scrunch their face in disgust. "I'm so sick of their garbage."

We were supposed to be on a nice easy mission to survey the *Queen Pux,* a battle-ark from the old Seven-Pointed Empire: Yatto, Damini, Keziah, and me. We were hoping that its records would give us some clue to deciphering the Talgan stone, but the Compassion got here first.

"What do they mean by 'the Misshapen'?" Damini asks.

"Anyone who's not shaped exactly like us. Non-humanoids," Yatto says, then lets out a gasp. "Oh yes. I think I'm going to pass out soon." Their eyes roll upward.

"Everyone said that I was never going to be worth anything," says the Compassion leader. "They said I was a hollow-spiked fool. But when I bring back your heads as trophies, we'll see what they say about Gantarrawos then."

The four of us have barricaded ourselves inside the engineering section, but there's no other way out. A freestanding workstation bursts into flames, just a few feet away from us.

"What do we do?" Keziah asks.

And that's when Yatto looks at me. "Tina . . . I'm releasing my sidearm to you. It's up to you now."

At last, I think.

Except when Yatto holds their positron cloudstrike weapon out to me, I feel a cold weight settle inside me. I've never even touched a gun before.

Yatto sees me hesitating and says, "Captain Argentian was a top-ranked markswoman. And Alternate Captain Lyzix says you appear to have inherited all of her combat skills."

"Last chance to surrender. You can all die with dignity, like good little Royalists," shouts Gantarrawos, the Compassion leader.

"Please," Damini says. "Just take the gun already."

A beautiful brocaded chair here at the back of this engineering section, which was already kind of moth-eaten, becomes a tall bonfire. The flames spread to the rusted-out engineering console.

I start to reach out, but my hand gets stuck. "I guess Captain Argentian shot a lot of people, huh?"

Yatto just looks at me, like, *What do you think?*

"You're dead already," Gantarrawos shouts.

As soon as the grip is in my hand, and I feel the throb of the particles in the cloud chamber, the familiarity sets in.

These positron weapons are low-power, but high-accuracy, and you can shoot them in preprogrammed burst patterns. They fire in a slight curve rather than a straight line, so you have to know how to compensate. I heft it for one moment longer, while the flames spread around us and the bootsteps of the Compassion squad move further into the engine chamber.

Then I duck out from behind the bulkhead, roll behind the flaming instrument panel and come up shooting through the wall of flame. Gantarrawos goes down before he even gets a shot at me, and then I'm diving through the flames, in between the other two.

Fun fact: the Compassion's fireburst weapons are great for shock and awe, but they're terrible in enclosed spaces, especially when everything's already on fire. Also, they work by exciting the molecules in the targeted area, but you can trick them if you just move fast enough. Apparently.

Soooo . . . a moment later, I'm surrounded by the dead bodies of all three Compassion soldiers. Their eyes are all still open, and their snarling faces look just sad now.

"Come on, guys," I say. "Time to go back to the *Indomitable*. You don't want to breathe too much of that smoke. We've gotten all the information we can."

Damini looks at me, and then at Gantarrawos and the two other soldiers (one Javarah, one Yarthin) that I just shot. "Thanks for getting us out of here. I know that wasn't easy for you."

"Nah. It was super easy." I shrug. "Once I psyched myself up."

Now that it's done, I feel sickly, but I still remember how calm I felt when I was shooting. At peace, just letting instinct take over.

Keziah is shivering as he tries to support Yatto's weight. "It's the same everywhere," he mutters. "No matter how advanced people get, we always end up trying to murder each other. I don't know why I bothered to leave home."

I feel really tired all of a sudden, like I pulled an all-nighter and then ran a marathon. Adrenaline wearing off, I guess.

On the orbital funnel back to the *Indomitable,* Yatto lies there, unconscious, and the rest of us just watch the gray hulk of the *Queen Pux* shrink to nothing. Nobody talks.

I sit hunched over, swaying with the platform's motion. My thoughts are just choppy bits of nonsense.

*

After we get back to the ship, I just want to go lie down in my quarters, or maybe eat what's left of our stash of alien junk food. But as soon as we get Yatto to Sickbay, I get a notification in my shoulder comms that my presence is required in the captain's receiving room.

Captain Othaar is sitting at his workstation, and we exchange the usual fancy greetings. I feel so drained I can barely stand at inspection rest, until he tells me to go ahead and sit.

"Yatto the Monntha tells me that you acted with valor on this latest mission, but also that you shot and killed three enemy combatants." Othaar takes a deep breath. "Regulations require that you receive counseling after the first such event, and there's nobody more qualified than me on board."

"I'm good," I say. "It was kind of intense, but now I'm over it."

I can't help remembering those frozen death masks, for a second—then I blink them away.

"There's no way you could be fine after something like this. I remember the first time I took a life. I was a mess for ten metacycles afterward."

I shake my head. "They needed Captain Argentian's expertise, so I brought it. As usual. Seems like the only good things about me come from a woman who didn't even want me to be born."

"What's that supposed to mean?" Othaar recoils, and his eyeballs get wide.

"I guess you didn't know?"

I tell him about Thaoh Argentian's final log entry.

"Oh." He slumps over, so I can see the exposed vertebrae going down the back of his neck. "Cursed certainty. I guess I shouldn't be surprised, because that does sound like something Thaoh would say. Damn, I'm sorry you had to hear that. But now I'm even more worried about you. It's easy to lose yourself in this line of work. And if you don't have a good sense of self to begin with, then . . ."

We both sit with that. I still feel exhausted, so stiff that I can barely move.

I think about how calm I felt, shooting those Compassion troopers down. How good it felt to just let instinct carry me.

"It's fine," I say.

He stares at me with his eyes hooded by his frontal plate.

"You said it yourself, I'm just a defective clone."

Captain Othaar scoffs. "I just said that to try and keep Marrant from looking for you. You heard him, he wants to torture you to death."

Ugh. Now Marrant's creepy smile is back in my head. I don't want to fall back into being scared—not when I finally fought back. I look at my right hand and remember how right it felt to have a gun in it. How simple everything was in that moment.

"I understand that you were doing what you thought was right,"

I say in a flat voice. "And really, I'm okay. I'll let you know if I need to process this any more. Can I go get something to eat now?"

Othaar seems like he's going to say something else, to try and get me to open up, but then he shrugs. "Sure. You're dismissed."

I get up and walk to the door, and when I look back, he's looking at his hologram of the laughing Thaoh Argentian again.

*

Later in the bluehouse, Rachael is there, and she doesn't seem to notice Yiwei gazing at her. Elza is staring at the computer interface via her Quant. Keziah is just looking through all the alien fronds into the well of stars, and Damini is talking a mile a minute about all the stuff we saw on the thousand-year-old *Queen Pux*.

Yiwei is noodling on his steel guitar, with Xiaohou kind of warbling along, and then he plays a bit of "Bohemian Rhapsody" by Queen. Just for the hell of it, I start singing along.

I'm waving my arms and fake-dramatizing, like I'm trying out for *The Voice*.

And then I get to the part about how I killed a man—and suddenly I just break all the way down. Choking. Sobbing so hard, I can't even finish the line of the song.

The music stops.

Everyone is staring at me.

I lift my right hand, signaling that I'm going to be okay, just give me a minute. But a minute passes, and I keep coating my entire face with tears.

I'm hunched over, crying into my own knees. My whole body heaving.

"Can I touch you? Is it okay to hug you?" someone asks, and I realize it's Elza. I nod, and she wraps her arm around me.

Damini touches my hand. "They were trying to kill us, you know."

"I still hate that we did that, but there really was no other choice," Keziah says.

I'm still crying too much to talk. When I even try, all I get is the start of syllables, like "buh," "guh." I cry so hard, it feels almost like gagging.

Everybody's trying to say the right thing, so I'll pull myself together.

I need to pull myself together.

This is bad. I need to be better than this.

I'm probably scaring everybody.

Then Rachael leans forward and says, super quiet, "It's okay to cry. You did a huge, scary, awful thing today. You should let it out. It's okay. We're all here. You're with your friends."

That just makes me bawl twice as hard.

I probably look like a total disaster. Rachael and Damini both hold my hands while I lean on Elza's shoulder.

When I finally wear myself out crying, Rachael says, "That's the first time I've seen you cry since we got on this ship. I was starting to wonder if you'd had your tear ducts replaced with tiny rocket launchers."

I laugh, and it feels good to laugh again. "It's tough being a superhero."

"Nah," Elza says. "Being a superhero is easy. Being a real person? That's hard."

Yiwei starts playing his guitar again, some tune I've never heard before with a lot of high, short notes. Xiaohou chimes in with a peppy bassline. We all just sit for a while.

35

My tactical station is broken. Every time I squint at it, I see a Compassion ship coming out of spaceweave, about to blow us to pieces. The *Merciful Touch*, or just some other barbship or spikeship. And then I look again, and it's just a random space goober. Either the Compassion has gotten way better at masking their radiation trails, or my threat awareness is cranked up way too high.

Just as I'm thinking that, something moves behind me. I leap out of my seat, fists out, ready to defend myself.

"Whoa!" Damini raises her palms. "Hey. It's just me."

"Sorry." I unclench my fists. "I guess I'm a little on edge."

"Everybody here is." Damini shrugs. "Since Vaap and Iyiiguol . . . I mean, since *you know what* happened."

"You can say their names." But I have a knee-jerk feeling of disgust when I think of those two turds. Just like always, that leads to me feeling guilty for disrespecting our fallen friends—and *that* leads to me worrying about Marrant using his death touch on Rachael, or Elza. Or Damini, Yiwei, or Keziah.

Which leads to me wanting to punch someone.

"I was wondering," Damini says. "Can I look at the scans we did of the Talgan stone? I thought maybe I could see if I can make sense of it. Remember, I got on this ship by solving puzzles."

"Puzzle Girl! Yes. That's a great idea."

I send Damini the scans, and soon she's cupping her palms

around the image of the ancient rock. Meanwhile, I go back to searching for danger signs, and seeing them everywhere.

Some time later, Damini jolts me out of my concentration. "Huh. So where's the rest of it?"

I stare at her. "The . . . rest of it? This is all they had."

"Mmm . . . nah. You see, there are these edges, and you can tell it used to be part of a bigger thing." Damini sketches a rectangle with a ragged edge that should connect up with the artifact. "So maybe there's another piece out there that connects to this one?"

"Oh my god. You're right."

I send a message to the control deck, but also to Yatto and Elza.

When my shift ends, Elza's poking at the computer interface near Engineering. "Damini's seriously a genius," Elza says. "So now all I have to do is create a whole new search algorithm, to see if anybody already found the missing piece. Might take a while."

*

Alternate Captain Lyzix throws a bowling ball covered with sharp spikes at my head. "I can keep doing this forever." Her ears, her fangs, her claws, all knifed-out in my direction.

I dodge the ball, then pick it up and run right toward her with a loud noise that I hope is more battle cry than squeal. I swing the spike-ball at Lyzix's head and she dodges easily, then slashes at my face with her foot-claw.

"Good energy," Lyzix says. "But bad form. You need discipline."

"You're always saying that." I drop the spiky ball and try to elbow her in the face.

A moment later, I'm on my back, looking up at her happy snarl.

While I get back the breath she knocked out of me, Lyzix reaches for some Javarah shock-sticks (which are banned in twenty-seven star systems because they can cause permanent nerve damage).

"You don't always have the luxury of thinking, in a combat situation," Lyzix says. "But that doesn't mean you lash out wildly. It means you need to train your instincts until you do the right thing automatically. You know where my fur comes from."

Yeah, I do. The Javarah used to be out of control, prone to murderous rages and wild lusts. Until their own scientists engineered their silky brownish-red fur, a symbiotic organism that lives on their skin and regulates their hormones. And now, they channel their instincts for (mostly) constructive uses.

As soon as I get to my feet, Lyzix tosses one of the shock-sticks to me. I'm still figuring out which end to hold it by when she runs toward me, letting out her own battle cry. (Which is ear-splitting, and makes me feel brittle inside.)

"You can't hesitate or freeze when someone is trying to kill you." Lyzix rushes toward me with her shock-stick raised. I duck out of her way at the last minute. The second time she tries to whack me into unconsciousness, I actually parry.

It's true. I froze when I finally met Marrant face-to-face. And again when Yatto offered me their gun.

Anger gets under my skin and floods my head with noise. I'm screaming again—not trying to make a "battle cry," but just letting out all the pressure that's been building up inside me. I scream myself hoarse and jab at Lyzix with my shock-stick.

"Never pick up a gun unless you're prepared to use it." Lyzix blocks all my attacks without even breathing hard. "There's nothing worse than a weapon in the hand of someone who's not ready."

I can barely block her attacks, the ones I don't stumble out of the way of.

I'm not even hitting back anymore. I just want to hit something, a few million times, but I'm stuck parrying.

The next swing comes scary close to my head, and I trip over myself. Half roll, half crawl out of her way. I bring my stick up to block an attack that's not there. She arcs her stick behind me—and that's when I realize we're not alone.

Rachael is sitting on top of a pile of crates in the corner of the cargo hangar, sketching us with a lightpen and plastiform tablet.

We both stop and stare.

"Don't mind me," Rachael says. "This is great. Keep going!"

Ugh. At least there'll be a witness if Lyzix brains me and dumps my body into space to hide the evidence. She feints and I almost fall for it, then I still just barely block her next move.

I roar and swing my staff at her, and she leaps out of the way. My head fills up with noise again.

I couldn't save Vaap or Iyiiguol. I couldn't keep from killing those thugs. Too much death, and nothing to show for it but some pointless rock. I bring my stick down, right where Lyzix's head isn't anymore. She laughs.

"Your energy continues to be good. Your form continues to be bad."

I bring my stick up and nearly catch her in the leg.

"Better," she says.

"Stop patronizing me." I swing my stick back and forth and keep lunging at her again and again, until she actually backs up.

Just when I think I'm going to get her, she kicks my ankle. I go down on my back, with her standing over me, shock-stick aimed directly at my face.

"That's perfect," Rachael says. "Hold that pose."

*

Later, Rachael shows me her sketch. Lyzix looks like a beast that just escaped after a year in a cage, and I look like a scared kitten. "This isn't accurate. I had a look of steely determination on my face. You gotta redraw that."

"Sorry, I draw what I see."

"Ow. Well, it's a gorgeous picture, even if it makes me look pathetic."

We're sitting in the bluehouse, just the two of us, leaning against a big fluorescent orange growth that undulates occasionally. The rest of the ship is asleep, but I don't feel tired, because I still didn't get to hit anything—except for the wall a couple times by mistake.

Which reminds me: I'm almost due for my next treatment from Dr. Karrast. Soon my skin will be crystalline purple, and I'll only need to sleep like four or five cycles.

"Do you want to talk about it?" Rachael says.

"I don't know. I don't have any words."

"The things that Lyzix was saying." Rachael sighs. "She wants to turn you into a fighting machine."

"A soldier." I close my eyes. "But . . . we're on a gunship, at war. And I'm really good at fighting, even if I did just get my ass kicked in the most humiliating fashion. Plus this is what I was dreaming of, all those years I was just wearing the pink dinosaur costume back on Earth."

"You know there are other ways to be a hero than just punching things, right?"

"I know, I know. But we don't get to choose. And I'm okay. I'm really fine."

Rachael gives me a look, like she knows I'm not fine. But she doesn't push it.

Instead, she changes the subject. "So . . . Yiwei asked me out. Like, on a date. Just to have a picnic in the cargo hangar or something. But still. A date."

"Wow." I try to pretend to be surprised.

"You . . . knew about this." Rachael stares. "How long did you know and not tell me?"

"Not that long. A while. I mean, he told me during that time when you were holed up in your room. I didn't want to scare you further into hiding."

Rachael nods. "Okay, whatever. Anyway, I like Yiwei. I just want to make sure I'm not some kind of rebound girlfriend."

"That's what I said!"

"Remember how clingy and possessive Sven got? I can't go down that road again. And Yiwei had this joined-at-the-brain relationship with Jiasong, they cowrote songs, and built adorable robots, and solved alien scavenger hunts together. I can't replace that, and I wouldn't want to, even if I could."

She goes quiet again, and I just stare at her sketch of Lyzix and me for a while. I can practically see Lyzix's arms in motion.

"I can't believe you created something this beautiful in such a short time," I say.

"Sometimes this all just feels like a dream. I feel like I've been on this ship forever, but also like I just got here. I have to draw everything I see, and then I know that I really saw it."

"So are you going to do it?" I ask. "Are you going to go out with Yiwei?"

Rachael puts her plastiform tablet away in a medical satchel. "I don't know. Maybe? I just don't want to rush into anything when we're cooped up here. You know? We're a million miles away from the nearest comic-book store, which is the only remedy I know for a bad breakup."

"Maybe it's a bad idea to get into a relationship on a spaceship," I say—like I'm trying to convince myself more than her.

Rachael purses her lips. "I mean, Yiwei is seriously cute, and he's managed to keep his hair looking fluffy and nice with barely any access to hair-care products, and he gets that dreamy look in his eyes when he plays music, and he made the most adorable robot ever."

"Oh yeah, you're not into him at all."

"You should talk. I've seen you and Elza together. You finally found someone obnoxious enough to deal with you. I ship it."

I groan. "I already told you, I don't want things to get even more messy and distracting. I don't want Elza to get hurt. And . . . what if we're just not compatible in that way? Makvarians have *three genders,* and all I know about their mating customs is, 'It's complicated, and we don't talk about it with outsiders.' Maybe I just can't be with any human."

"If you really like her, you'll find a way, though," Rachael says. "I refuse to believe the girl who jumped out of a spaceship and lassoed two runaway elevators can't figure out how to hook up with someone she likes. And . . . I just realized, it's super late."

Rachael stands up jerkily, as though her leg went to sleep while we were sitting up here.

*

"So Damini was right, as usual," Elza says, and Damini pumps her fist. "The Talgan stone is part of something bigger."

"Where's the rest?" asks Captain Othaar, who has a brooding look on his faceplates. Like he slept about as well as I did.

"In the Royal Archeological Museum, in the Firmament, Captain," says Yatto, gesturing at another holographic piece of puffy rock. "It's been in the permanent collection since before we even knew the Shapers had existed."

"And, and, you put them together, and they make something," Damini blurts, too fired up to wait her turn to speak. "You'll never guess, it wasn't obvious at first, but I figured it out because of all the things that Riohon has been teaching me about stellar cartography and different notation systems."

"Is it a star map?" I squint, trying to see a constellation.

"No, no. It's a stellar classification system."

She pokes at her Quant and pulls up a set of notations that I can barely make sense of.

But Othaar says, "A binary system. Two O-class stars."

"You could even say it's double-O, like James Bond," says Damini. Nobody laughs. "Ugh. Never mind."

"A pair of O-class giant stars together is incredibly rare, and this specifies young O-class stars, with a high metallic content." Yatto has grown a few inches taller with pride in Damini and Elza. "That pairing would generate all sorts of unusual particles."

"Only one stellar pair has something like that, either then or now," says Lyzix. "The Antarràn system." She pulls up a whole set of holographic readouts.

"A whole star system with no organic life anywhere near, not for several light-years in any direction. Not even bacteria." Yma lets out a dark purple bobble. "Why do I find myself doubting this is a coincidence?"

"So there's some ancient weapon there. Something they could use to sterilize whole regions of space. Or something equally terrible," Yatto says.

"The good news is, we're the only ones with this clue, thanks to our trainees." Othaar glances at me, and my face gets warm. "So we can get there and secure this weapon, whatever it is, while Marrant is still stumbling around in circles."

"How soon can we be there?" Lyzix asks Yma.

"At best speed, roughly five metacycles, Alternate Captain." This time the bubble is the exact color of Mello Yello. "Keziah has been helping me make some improvements to our space-weave generators."

"Great," says Othaar. "We'll safebeam the *Unquenchable* to join us there as soon as possible. Soon, we'll get our first-ever look at the Shapers' ancient technology."

36

What do you do when you're a few days away from encountering a mysterious ancient weapon built by the worst people who ever lived? If you're us, you throw a party.

Yatto and I rustled up some Zanthuron sky-jerky and some other snacks that don't taste awful (or grow and shrink suddenly). And Riohon made some Makvarian opera candy, which tastes surprisingly great. Yiwei sits in the corner, playing random Chinese pop songs with Xiaohou jamming along. Elza and Rachael decorated the crew lounge with random holograms and cartoon drawings. Damini is coaxing everyone to play some strategy game she discovered on the ship's computer, where you try to be the first to build a ring around a star. And Keziah is on drink duty.

Keziah keeps telling us about the parties at Cambridge, which were called "sweaties," but also the times he hung out with his mom's family in East London, where his cousin was a road rap/afroswing DJ. His face lights up, talking about his mother's family and everyone else he left back home—and then he remembers that we don't even know what's happening on Earth.

"Ever since the *Queen Pux*, I've been thinking about something my father used to say," Keziah says. "He always insisted that anything you invent will always wind up being used for war. Like, the first time one of our ancestors invented a tool, they immediately turned around and thumped someone else on the head with it. But what if I could invent a technology that can't be used as a weapon?"

"What would that look like?" Yatto asks.

"I don't know. I was studying some schematics down in Engineering, and thinking that you could build a device that freezes time in a small area. Just . . . stops it." Keziah's eyes light up. "A stasis field. Imagine the applications. You could keep food fresh forever. You could keep an injured person frozen until they can get to a doctor."

"Making time stand still is tricky," Yatto says. "Time doesn't like to be tied down."

"It's true that time has commitment issues," Keziah says. "It's always running away."

*

Next time I walk by, Yatto is telling Keziah and Damini about why they quit acting in those action movies, back home. "I didn't want to keep celebrating my people's vile past. I seriously considered becoming a pacifist. I originally signed up for the Royal Fleet with a non-offensive designation, so I could avoid ever seeing combat."

"So what changed your mind?" Damini asks.

"I watched too many people die, right in front of me. Crewmates, friends, people I loved." Yatto sighs. "I decided sometimes you have to fight back. So now I just try to use violence only when absolutely necessary."

On the other side of the room, Rachael has pulled up a teacup chair next to Yiwei, who's talking about music.

"I've tried using tunings from a Chinese instrument, the guqin, for this steel guitar," Yiwei says. "Like the ruibin diao scale, which is sort of . . . pentatonic? But I still can't finish a whole song."

"Because you always used to write songs with your ex," Rachael says.

"That's what I thought at first. But I think it's more than that. I want to write some songs about all of this." He gestures with a slide-hand at the whole starship and space and everything. "And I don't know how to fit any of it into a song. Every time I try, it just feels silly. Too small."

"I know what you mean." Rachael says. "I've been sketching nonstop since I got here. But I keep wanting to draw a comic that includes Irriyaians, and Aribentors, and those bouncing red ball creatures we saw on Rascal Station. Pnofts. I don't know how to fit all of this alien stuff into a story. I just keep getting stuck."

"I'm glad I'm not the only one." Yiwei laughs. Xiaohou records his laughter and weaves it into an EDM-style groove.

"I feel like I'm storing stuff up," Rachael says. "And it's all just going to pour out of me at some point, in some huge epic thing. But not yet. The waiting is wrecking my nerves."

"Just wait," Yiwei says. "I'm going to write a rock opera about space battles, and you're going to write a graphic novel that's going to make people's heads explode." Then he adds, "Hopefully not literally. I mean, some aliens probably do have comics that make your head explode for real. But that was a metaphor."

Rachael leans a little closer to Yiwei, so she's *almost* leaning on his shoulder as he strums his guitar.

She notices me looking and gives me a little smile—like maybe a relationship on a spaceship isn't the worst thing after all.

*

I'm scrunched next to Elza on my tiny bed-web, fully clothed, and we just watched another log entry that didn't tell me anything useful at all. This could be our last quiet moment together, and I feel her hands just barely touching my leg and my rib cage. I never want to stop being close to her.

"I'm really glad we got to be friends after all," I say—even though I want to say something different.

"Me too," she says, looking away. "I'm really glad."

Her skin glows like pure amber in the pale light of the holographic display. Her hazel eyes have flecks of agate. She looks like this Art Nouveau poster of a soft lovely mysterious woman inside panes of bright colored glass that I hung in my bedroom nook back home and stared at every night before I fell asleep.

I'm never going to kiss her perfect face, or wake up next to her and tell her about the weird dream I just had.

"I just . . . don't know if I could handle anything other than friendship right now," I whisper, halting.

Maybe I'll be alone forever. Maybe I'll keep making this exact same choice—where I like someone, but then I decide to be sensible and avoid distractions. I could end up like Captain Argentian, drinking alone, a million miles away from everyone I care about.

Let the record reflect that Tina wussed out.

Elza is shaking her head. "I won't ever date somebody who's not sure they want to be with me. That's the worst. Plenty of people back home want to experiment with a travesti, because they're 'curious,' but then they run away as soon as they get a taste."

"Well, screw those people," I say. "They don't deserve your time."

"That's what I'm saying. I had plenty of friends back home who got their hearts broken every other week, not to mention the ones who were working. So the moment someone seems like they can't make up their mind, or they're trying to get over their hang-ups, I'm out."

I feel like she's trying to explain something to me that maybe doesn't need to be explained. I totally understand: I had a shot back on Rascal Station, and I blew it, and this is probably for the best anyway.

But I don't know what I'm supposed to say in response to all this. She opened up to me, and I'm going to say . . . what?

I try to breathe into my core, like my mom taught me. (God, I miss my mom.)

"The whole idea of dating anyone, of any gender, is terrifying to me. I can't even wrap my mind around the idea that I'm this whole other species, and I was just disguised as a human when I was born. I don't even know if it's physically possible for me to be with a human. And regular Makvarians will probably just think I'm a freak." This all feels way too raw to say out loud.

"Huh." Elza takes this in, and her eyes get a faraway look. "Well, don't let anybody experiment with you, either. Find someone who wants to be seen with you in broad daylight. I know there's someone for both of us, somewhere out there."

I bite my tongue to keep from saying, *I don't want anyone else. I just want you. I don't care how many suns a planet has, I would be proud to walk with you in any amount of daylight.*

*

It doesn't happen all at once, and there's no particular moment when I'm aware that something changed. I just feel this . . . longing. Or something.

I miss Elza when she's standing right in front of me. I see her all the time, because we live inside a flying minivan, but I still wish

I could spend more time with her. I catch myself looking at her when she's doing something random, like poking at an interface and complaining about the severed finger, or trying to force down the latest alien food that Damini has challenged us to eat. And I just wish I could touch her, or even kiss her. I've had crushes, but never like this. I just . . . really want to be close to Elza. And when she smiles at me, I feel like I just walked into a gravity distortion, like my internal organs are lighter than the rest of my body.

When I crawl into my weird mesh of bedding and close my eyes, I don't think about Marrant, or Captain Argentian, or what's going to happen when we get to the Antarràn system. I just lie there and think about Elza: the shimmer around her eyes from whatever substance she's figured out to replace the makeup she brought from Brazil, the little notches above her nose when she's concentrating, the taper of her wrists and the way she always talks with her slender hands. I feel kind of jazzed, all the time. Like the lady in the PlayfunBodymelt poster, transported by a ton of sparkles.

I can't lie to myself anymore: I have a monster crush on Elza.

But . . . it's too late.

So every First Cycle I wake up in my tiny cabin, and vow that this will be the metacycle when I face reality. Annnny time now. It's gonna happen. I swear.

Junior Explorer Thaoh Argentian's personal datajournal, 9.47.17.03 of the Age of Expansion

Hey, it's me. I've had an . . . interesting time. Everybody seems to think there's something going on between Thondra and me, just because we're two of the few Makvarians in the Fleet. Call me old-fashioned, but I wouldn't want to hook up with a man, unless we had a thont with us. It would just be too weird.

I know plenty of people on Makvaria just pair off these days, but having only two genders in a relationship just feels *wrong* to me. Like I said: old-fashioned.

Maybe if more than a handful of Makvarians would actually join the Fleet, it would be different. But I'm sick of people thinking I'm ready to throw myself at the first Makvarian I see, just because we're friends.

And maybe it's a problem that we're so secretive about how mating actually works among Makvarians, because there are so many misconceptions out there. And people are *so starking curious about it.*

Like, when I went out with the rest of the juniors on the *Indivisible*, and after the third drink, they all started in with the "Is it true that" stuff. And it was all total nonsense.

It's totally nobody's business what Makvarians do in private—but sometimes I wish we could just post a sex-education holo and have done with. Anything to get people to shut up.

The worst part is, Thondra thinks it's all hilarious, and he loves to encourage people to jump to the worst conclusions about the two of us. Whenever I call him on it, he always says it doesn't matter what anyone thinks, but that's easy for him to say. I'm the one who gets stuck explaining that no, the two of us are just best friends—and also, whatever ridiculous thing they've heard about what Makvarians get up to in bed isn't true. I wish I could just laugh it off the way Thondra does.

But the truth is, I don't have time for romance, or hookups, or anything. I've got planets to save!

37

The Antarràn system could be the most magical sight my bleary eyes have ever seen: two enormous spheres of bluish-white light in an endless dance, with fiery swirls all around them. They've been getting closer for millions of years, and they're finally kissing. "Oh, wow," Damini mutters next to me. "My list of the top five places I've ever visited just got a major reshuffle."

"It's incredible," Riohon agrees.

"Tactical, any time now," Captain Othaar says in my earpiece, and I stop gawping.

"We're the only ship in the vicinity, Captain." I poke and prod. "All this radiation is going to make it tricky to get an early warning if anyone else tries to join the party."

"Just stay alert and do your best."

"With a will."

Just to make things even trickier, there's a big patch of magnetized skyrmions—super-funky particles—between us and the two suns. They keep screwing with our readings, until we finally get past them.

Then I scan every inch of the five planets orbiting these two beasts, with the eye that I'm not using to search for Compassion ships. So do Yatto and Elza. And we come up empty. There could be some underground structure inside one of them, but no sign of an entrance. Every scan I can think of reveals nothing but big balls of mostly rock.

"Maybe we came here for nothing," Lyzix says over the open channel.

"That wouldn't be the worst outcome," Othaar replies. "Let someone else deal with this mess."

We all start getting used to the idea that this was all for nothing, and we can all just go to Vandal Station, buy mind-obliterating cocktails, and dance to CrudePink.

Then I notice something weird about those two suns: the coronas and swirls of hot gas are flickering. Like there's something in the way that's just too small to see.

"We'd better take a closer look," Othaar says, "without getting burnt to a cinder, preferably."

"Now for the fun part," Riohon mutters.

"I was going to say this is the fun part too, except without sarcasm," Damini replies.

"Just please, keep an eye on the gravitational flux."

We sail closer to Antarràn A, the star on the left, close enough to these starfire burps for us to get a nice tan. Riohon does some fancy dancing.

And that's when we see it: a web of what looks like silk, woven around Antarràn A. Millions of strands, maybe billions, crisscrossing around it, in the shape of a butterfly wing. And from this angle, we can tell there's a similar wing-shaped mesh around Antarràn B. Like a giant cage around these two stars, which are each a million times hotter than the sun.

"What is this made of?" Othaar's voice is full of pure wonder.

"Something we've never encountered before, Captain," Yatto says. "Each of those threads is only a few microns thick. No sign of damage, even after all this time."

"I think we found our ancient technology," Lyzix says.

*

Those double suns throw off bouquets of supercharged particles as they make out. Every few microcycles I keep thinking I see a Compassion barbship coming out of spaceweave with its weapons smoking hot. And then it just turns out to be more of these stars getting romantic.

I shouldn't even be so jumpy. I stole the rock that had the only clue to finding this place, so there's no way Marrant could even know where this is. But I never want to underestimate that monster.

"Riohon, take us on a full orbit of the structure," Othaar says.

"With a will. I'm going to take it slow, though. I don't want to know what happens if the *Indomitable* accidentally touches one of those threads." Riohon turns to Damini. "I need you to help me stay out of the way of any more solar eruptions."

"I'm helping to fly over a silken butterfly wrapped around two supergiant stars," Damini says. "Sometimes I just have to say it out loud."

We come around the top of the structure, and right away there's . . . something. Right where the head would be, if this was an actual butterfly. "Um," I say, "I guess it's a round platform, around two STUs in diameter, with some kind of structure at its center. A building? It looks like a building, shaped sort of like a church back home. The platform is just floating there, but it seems to have gravity and breathable air."

"Feels like an invitation," Lyzix says.

"Smells like a trap," Othaar counters. "How long before the *Unquenchable* arrives at our position?"

"Just over three metacycles, Captain," Yatto says.

275

It's like Othaar said before: these unbeatable broadsword ships always show up too late.

"We can't wait that long to get answers. I'll lead a team myself. Lyzix, you're captain in my absence."

Lyzix starts to protest, but then just sighs. "With a will."

"We'll ask for volunteers. I don't want to order anyone to go into this unknown situation. And Lyzix? No matter what happens, this weapon cannot be allowed to fall into the Compassion's hands."

"Agreed." Lyzix grins. "Let's give the Hosts of Misadventure a good show."

*

"So . . . you volunteered?" Rachael sits next to me in Sickbay while I wait for my next injection from Dr. Karrast.

This second treatment might actually make me start changing into a proper Makvarian, with the violet crystal skin and big blue eyes. I'm trying not to obsess about things like how the other Earthling kids will look at me once I start looking more like Riohon. Not to mention Elza.

None of that matters. I can't fall short if I meet Marrant again. No more stammering. No more hesitation.

"Yeah, of course I volunteered. We leave in one cycle." I hold out my arm and Karrast jabs me, sending more blue sludge into my vein. "I'm not going to miss out on all the fun. Plus this is my fight. Marrant was *her* responsibility, which means that he's mine."

Rachael nods. "I guess. I think he's kind of all of our responsibility. The universe is so much more messed up than I ever realized." She slashes at her lightpad, making big diagonal lines, as she talks. "Like . . . nothing on Earth was fair. And all of the grown-ups back home knew, but they decided to just put

their heads down and pretend it was all okay. And now it turns out the injustice on Earth is just a speck of dust next to this whole skyscraper of wrongness all over the galaxy."

I think about this for a moment. "Wrong is wrong. The bigger scale doesn't change anything."

Dr. Karrast finishes looking me over. "Looks good so far. The changes will probably still be gradual," Karrast says. "You'll need two more of these treatments. For now, you'll notice an increase in upper-body strength, and a slight change to your skin coloration. Possible side effects include headaches, nausea, and dizziness."

"Thanks." I look up into her one big widescreen eye. "So . . . did you ever figure out a way to protect against Marrant's death touch?"

Karrast frowns. "Sort of. You could set up a neurolytic field and inject yourself with the same medications that we use to treat Wranggon brain fever. But even then, the best you could hope for is to turn some of the effect back onto Marrant. You'd still die, either way."

"Well. That sucks. Thanks anyway." I turn back to Rachael, who's still angry-drawing. "I better get going."

She raises her lightpen and looks at me. "Just be careful, okay? I know you think Marrant is your personal challenge to solve. But life doesn't work that way. That skyscraper of injustice? It needs a million people with wrecking balls, chipping away at it for a long time."

"Yeah," I say. My arm hurts like a dozen beestings. And I do feel a little dizzy already. "Except sometimes, one person has to step up and make trouble for all the worst people." I put on a cocky smile. "But yeah. I'll be careful."

*

When I get to the cargo hangar to join the landfall expedition, Lyzix walks up to me holding a big tube, like you'd use for carrying posters. It has a long needle at one end, and two big see-through canisters full of sparks surrounding a chunky grip at the other. She hands it to me, and I need both hands to hold it steady.

"You know what this is," she says. Not a question.

"Umm. Yeah, so. It's a handheld superstream cannon with an adjustable scope. Capable of punching a hole in a reinforced carbonfast wall."

Space Wikipedia to the rescue.

"Remember what we talked about." She smiles, baring her fangs. "You don't hold a weapon unless you're prepared to use it. This mission could be incredibly dangerous. Are you prepared to defend yourself and the other team members, if necessary?"

I hesitate, but I know what answer she wants to hear. "Yes. Yes, of course."

I don't have an actual flashback to the *Queen Pux* and me shooting those three creeps. That moment of looking into the face of someone who was alive a moment ago, and knowing that I turned that life off. I don't see a movie in my head, or anything like that. I just have . . . a feeling. A shiver, a crushing sadness.

But this is what I signed up for. I demanded this, even. So I shoulder the superstream cannon as best I can, with my arm still throbbing from Karrast's injection.

"And I need to know that you're not going to go off-mission," Lyzix says.

"I'm not going to go off-mission. Alternate Captain."

"Good. Funnel drop in half a cycle. See that you're ready."

She smiles and sashays away, while I drag my huge gun over to the orbital funnel.

When I turn around, I almost collide with Elza.

"What are you doing here?" I ask.

"They asked for volunteers." She smiles. "I volunteered. No way I'm going to miss this. I heard Damini's coming too."

I start to say that this mission is too dangerous, and Elza cuts me off.

"Staying on the ship is also very dangerous, if the Compassion shows up." She folds her arms, eyes flashing. "And I need to know the truth about these Shapers. They're like the original source of all the oppression and exploitation everywhere, and I want to understand. That's how I deal with stuff: I take it apart and figure out how it works."

I almost try once more to talk Elza out of this. But I see her bristling, ready to bite my head off if I even hint that she can't handle herself. And . . . I hear this little voice inside me, from somewhere near where my beacon used to be, rejoicing, dancing—insisting I'd way rather face this with Elza by my side.

So I just smile and say, "Good."

Damini comes bouncing up a moment later. "Hi! Hello! I decided to come along and visit the ancient ruin because that's a once-in-a-lifetime opportunity, but I hate that we're splitting up the group. You know? What if this is the last time we're all together? And we didn't even say a proper goodbye? What if something happens? I want to be all independent and self-sufficient, but this is my new family, and I don't want it to go the same way as my old family. You know?"

Elza nods. "I get it. I don't use the 'F' word easily, but you maniacs have become my people."

Then Captain Othaar shows up, along with Uiuiuiui, Crewmaster Bul, and a friendly young Zugruth (covered with fluffy white wool, like a lamb) named Thot. "Brave comrades and predictable enemies." Othaar salutes. We all salute back, and give the proper response. "Thank you for volunteering. I'm proud that you'll all be there with me as we learn the answer to this mystery that's been eating away at us forever. Let's go."

And then we're dropping out of the belly of the *Indomitable* toward a platform the size of Manhattan, nestled in between the two blazing-bright butterfly wings.

38

As we get closer to the platform, I see way more details. Like, in addition to the gigantic mausoleum at the center, someone built a few thousand other smaller structures in a grid, and they all look like the stinkpalaces of Orvan IV: tall, wide, concave rooftops, dandelion turrets on all the corners.

"It's a whole city," Damini breathes.

"They probably needed to house an army of technicians and robots to build and maintain whatever this is," Uiuiuiui says.

My Quant shows the *Indomitable* arcing upward, disappearing back behind a coronal ejection from the closer of the two blue stars, as Riohon flies by the seat of his pants. Then I can't see the ship anymore, and we're back on comms silence—but I know they're out there, sun-diving.

The superstream cannon is too big for me to lay in my lap, so instead it digs into my shoulder and thigh. I'm starting to think the "handheld" thing means hands like Yatto's, not mine.

The orbital funnel is moving too fast, but also taking too long. I want this descent to last forever, this moment when we're all together and alive and okay. But I also want to get the waiting over with, because my guts cinch tighter the longer I have to think about this.

Damini stares at the two wings of the Butterfly, spreading out on either side of us, and the gorgeous stonework on the giant mausoleum on this floating island. "I still can't believe that people who created this much beauty could have been so evil."

Captain Othaar shrugs. "When my people ruled half the galaxy as part of the Seven-Pointed Empire, we also created exquisite art and music. The most heartless societies have created some of the most heartbreaking masterpieces."

The concave rooftops and huge central building take on more details as we drift down to the surface of the floating island. We land on the side closest to Antarràn A, and then the slightly higher gravity makes me lurch forward, clutching at my thighs. "This is going to be great for core strength, not to mention bone density," whispers Damini.

I pick up my superstream cannon—and then double over again, because it's gotten even heavier.

Whatever they did to give this rock an atmosphere, it creates the appearance of a yellowy "sky" over our heads, and a gentle blue-tinged sunlight peeks over two different horizons.

All of the other buildings we pass appear to be empty, with triangle-shaped windows and diamond-shaped doors embedded in their elegant stonework. Some of the structures have inscriptions on them that look like the markings on the Talgan stone. The EverySpeak still can't turn them into words, but Damini keeps collecting images on her Quant.

This gun is killing me. I try to brace it against my chest, and end up with a tiny bruise.

We head into one of the outer buildings. Inside, a series of rocky ledges jut out of the walls, all the way up to the high ceiling. No floors, ramps, or stairs. We pull ourselves up from ledge to ledge, and I manage to square the superstream cannon against my aching back. Eventually, we come out on the bowl-shaped roof, and we have a great view of the whole island. Including that tall building at the center.

From up here, that central building looks even more cathedral-like, with four cone-shaped towers around a larger one. We still can't scan inside the cathedral/fortress, because it's just solid walls on this side. "We need to get a view of the front entrance," Crewmaster Bul grunts.

Just then, my Quant blows up with a bunch of alerts.

They've found us.

The holographic display on my right palm shows the *Indomitable* facing off with not one, but three Compassion spikeships. Any one of those ships would be enough to take the *Indomitable* down.

Damini looks over my shoulder, sees the situation, and lets out a gasp.

The *Indomitable* is already trying to run while unloading all her dwarf-star ballistics at the main ship. But Riohon's fanciest moves can't help when the ship is boxed in, and the lead ship—the *Merciful Touch*, I'm pretty sure—gets in a direct hit near the *Indomitable*'s bluehouse.

The *Indomitable* is surrounded and outgunned. And there's nothing we can do to help them.

39

All we can do is just watch and shout curses as the *Indomitable* runs for its life, dodging and weaving to stay out of the way of dreamkiller missiles and dark-matter cannon fire.

Rachael is up there. Yiwei, Keziah, Yatto, Riohon . . . even Lyzix. They're all one bad moment away from being blown to cinders. I recognize the dance routine Riohon is doing: it's a modified version of the Xixthip Maneuver, which they teach at the Royal Space Academy in the first year, except that Riohon is flipping the ship on two different axes and then spinning backward.

"Come on," Othaar is muttering into his sleeve, even though nobody up there can hear him. "Come on, you can do this. Just use the solar flares for cover and get off their scans. Lyzix, I know you can do this."

Next to him, Damini just keeps breathing the word "go" over and over—and then something that sounds like a prayer, but I can't make out the words.

One of the Compassion ships, the *Sweet Euthanasia*, fakes a strafing run on the *Indomitable*, and then banks sharply to the left instead. The *Sweet Euthansia* unleashes a dreamkiller missile on the *Indomitable*'s midsection, right next to engineering.

Keziah.

For a moment there's a gaping wound in the *Indomitable*'s hull. Then somebody—probably Yiwei—rearranges the hull plating to compensate. The ship is still spinning wildly out of control. Helpless, ruined. A sitting target.

All three Compassion ships move in for the kill.

Damini curses, but Othaar smiles. "Just wait."

The attacking ships leave a hole in their formation for a second . . . and suddenly, the *Indomitable* darts forward at near-light speed. A couple of streaks of light blaze out of the *Indomitable*'s side: dwarf-star ballistics, which score direct hits on the *Sweet Euthanasia*.

Then the *Indomitable* does a perfect arc, like a hawk diving to scoop up a field mouse, and disappears behind a huge solar flare. The ship is gone from my Quant—which means the Compassion can't see it either.

Othaar lets out a deep breath and shakes his head. "Good show," he whispers.

Then he turns his Quant off and looks at the rest of us. "The Compassion will be landing its own people on this platform soon. Which means we have less than a cycle to do our own recon without any unwanted guests. Let's get moving."

We all say, "With a will," more or less in unison. Except for Elza—who looks at the rest of us, and then mutters it too. We take off as fast as we can in the direction of that cathedral at the center.

*

My eyes adjust slowly to the darkness inside the big central structure, which only has a few high windows and a couple sheltered doorways to let in the light of the two suns. The arched ceiling rises forty or fifty feet over my head. Every last sound, every whisper and every footfall, echoes off those high beams with a chuckling patter—like someone gossiping just out of earshot. There's a weird smell, too: like sour milk, or the compost bins at the 23-Hour Coffee Bomb back home.

Elza hugs herself, like this place is creeping her out, and moves closer to me. I try to give her a reassuring smile.

And *then* we see the creepy part.

Just over our heads, the walls have a series of alcoves on all sides of us, with statues of weird creatures inside. A blob with strings around it, a giant worm, a pyramid of cubes, other stuff. They cast deep shadows as they catch the light from the high windows, so they almost seem to be moving and glaring down at us.

"What the hell are those statues?" Uiuiuiui asks.

"Are these the gods the Shapers worshiped?" Damini suggests. "Or just some kind of gargoyles?"

And then the answer hits me, and I get a huge knot in my stomach.

"It's worse. These are the people that the Shapers wiped out of existence. Remember? The giant worms that they destroyed by causing an ice age? And those creatures with nine tentacles that they dropped meteors on?" I point at each of them as I talk. "The Shapers created these monuments to their victims."

Now when I stare at the statues, they look sad. Like they're pleading for just a little more time.

These creepy models are all that's left of people who had their own cultures, their own histories, their own dreams and inventions. And we'll never really know what they were like, or what they could have accomplished. The knot in my stomach gets heavier.

Captain Othaar nods. "That makes sense. Which only makes it even more disturbing that there are six empty alcoves, where more statues were supposed to go."

We reach the center of this giant chamber, which has a stone gazebo: four pillars supporting a dome.

I run a bunch of scans, and all I can tell is that someone is supposed to stand inside the gazebo and do . . . something. All of the energy from the two supergiant stars gets channeled to this one spot. But what's the point? What could be so awesome that it could be worth causing so much pain and death and ugliness for? I think of what Rachael said before, about a skyscraper of injustice.

"Maybe Marrant is right," Elza says, studying the machine. "Maybe you stand here and get turned into a god."

"Doesn't explain why there's nothing alive for light-years in any direction," Uiuiuiui grunts.

"Maybe it needs organic matter as a catalyst," Damini says.

"Let's hope we never find out," Captain Othaar says, in a firm closing-the-debate voice. "Right now, we need to destroy this machine, before the Compassion can get to it."

Uiuiuiui, Thot, and I all shoot our superstream cannons at the central gazebo structure, until it glows too bright to look at.

The glow fades and . . . it's exactly the same as before. We didn't even singe it.

We brainstorm a bunch of ways to wreck this machine. Like overloading all of our guns and turning them into bombs. But this building has been here for hundreds of thousands of years, and it can probably handle anything we throw at it.

"There has to be a way." Captain Othaar keeps walking around the gazebo. "Singing Volcano Fish of Kthorok VII, we can't just let this fall into their hands."

Speaking of . . . my Quant shows that two of the Compassion

ships are still playing hide-and-seek with the *Indomitable* in the coronas of Antarràn. But the *Merciful Touch*, Marrant's ship, is heading our way. Very, very fast.

We've run out of time.

*

The *Merciful Touch* hangs in the yellow sky, directly over our heads. I can see all five of its short-range impellers, plus every twisty furrow and tiny nozzle, bathed in the light of two suns.

They're lowering something from their cargo hangar, using an ion harness. Just a big dark shadow, against the intense sunlight coming from the horizon. Too slow to be a spaceship, too big to be an orbital funnel.

"Tears of my ancestors," Uiuiuiui says. "What are they sending down?"

I can't figure it out, until they start lowering a second one, and then a third.

Then . . . I recognize the cages they were using on Second Yoth. The ones I watched them herd all of the Grattna into. All in all, ten cages come down from the *Merciful Touch*, each containing hundreds of Grattna.

"They brought the Grattna here," I say. "Marrant said he needed them for his experiments."

Damini sputters. "What kind of experiments could they possibly—"

"Organic matter," Elza spits. "Remember? Whatever this machine does, it needs living creatures as a catalyst, which is why everything all around here is dead." She kicks at the outer wall of the giant building. "Those bastards are going to kill all of the Grattna, just to jump-start this horrible machine."

288

Elza's face is flushed, her eyes widened and tearing up a little. Her hands are balled into fists. A scream bottled up inside her. Even after all of the stuff she's been through and all the setbacks she's suffered, I've never seen Elza this pissed. And I'm not braced for the wave of pure adoration that washes over me, seeing her so powerful. Righteous. Alive.

Then the horror drives away every other feeling—because Elza's right. They're preparing to slaughter thousands of innocent creatures to get this machine working again, and I don't know how we can stop them. I promised Bildub we could help.

Meanwhile, the Compassion is sending down a couple of orbital funnels. "In a minicycle or two, this platform will be crawling with Compassion mercy-killers," Uiuiuiui says.

Captain Othaar looks around the big vaulted chamber. "We can't hold this space against superior numbers. Especially once they realize their weapons won't damage the ancient tech. We need to use guerilla tactics, try to slow them down until the *Unquenchable* gets here. Any suggestions?"

Othaar looks at me, because I'm the tactical officer. Plus maybe he hopes his old friend's strategic super-brain will suddenly kick in, now that our backs are to the wall.

I think for a second. "Most of the buildings here are unconnected and too exposed. But there's a complex on the side closer to Antarràn B, which looks to be partly underground. Lots of narrow spaces and interlocking tunnels. And plenty of spots to launch a sniper attack from."

"Sounds kind of like the sewer tunnels of São Paulo," says Elza.

"So ordered," Captain Othaar says. "Let's make for the Catacombs."

We all march out of the central structure (which I've started calling the Mausoleum, because of those gruesome memorials to dead civilizations). Damini pauses on her way out, to make more scans of the Shapers' carvings with her Quant.

We only make it halfway to the Catacombs, weaving around squat buildings with concave roofs, before the orbital funnels from the *Merciful Touch* arrive. The sounds ring out around us: the crunch of boots on the rocky ground and the harsh voices of Compassion soldiers. We all double-check the masking seals on our uniforms that hide our body heat and other vital signs. We're about to be surrounded.

I shoulder my superstream cannon, and it slowly sinks in that the plan I suggested is going to involve a lot of shooting the Compassion's troops. I can't let myself think about the *Queen Pux*.

I'm only certain of one thing—Elza and Damini are right behind me, and I'm not going to let anything hurt either of them, as long as I can stand.

40

My tenth-grade English teacher tried to teach us about some guy named Chekhov, who made up a rule that you can't have a gun sitting around unless somebody gets shot later—like, you can't just use a gun as a paperweight. Why? I don't know. Dude had a thing about guns.

We're standing in one of the main chambers of the Catacombs, surrounded by razor-sharp devices that hang from the ceiling by tiny threads. They look like nightmare dentist's tools, corkscrews, straight razors, silhouetted in the meager light from one tiny window over our heads. They're crusted with some kind of dried gunk that's probably not blood (but maybe it's blood).

My mind knows it's been thousands of years since anyone was in here, and every last bit of organic matter was scrubbed away long ago, but this place still smells like death to me. Burnt coffee and sour milk.

"Every time I think the Shapers can't get any creepier," Uiuiuiui whispers.

"Some of these symbols on the wall keep repeating," Damini says. "Could be important."

The superstream cannon digs into my shoulder, chafing the skin away and making my back ache, even though I shift it around every few minutes.

Screw you, Chekhov.

"Let's keep moving," Othaar says.

We get so deep inside these walls that even if the *Indomitable* wasn't hiding behind a plume of sunburst, I wouldn't be able to tell what's happening to our friends up there.

The Catacombs get deeper and gloomier, and we pass a room full of lumpy shapes that undulate with our footsteps. And a long narrow space, with grooves carved into the floor and ceiling.

Two Compassion soldiers pass by on the outside, close enough that we can listen in. "Are we really supposed to clean up after the flying pests? They're the ones who can't stop pooping on the floor of their cages. I didn't join the Compassion to siphon up crap."

"Just siphon the worst of it. We don't want them getting sick before Marrant is done with them."

"They keep trying to talk to me. It's obnoxious."

The voices move away. My knuckles are white around the grip of my weapon. I glance over at Damini and Elza, and they both have the same horrified expression.

*

Showtime. We've found a tunnel that widens in the middle, with an X-shaped window big enough to aim a superstream cannon through. And an excellent view of one of the big cages full of Grattna, with the Compassion patrolling nearby.

Uiuiuiui notices me fumbling with my superstream cannon, probably looking one-tenth as anxious as I feel. "Stand down. I'll take this shot."

I feel a flush of gratitude as he steps past me and aims at the Compassion guards. They're busy taunting the Grattna prisoners (who are freaking out, because if they die in this place,

292

far from home, their spirits will be trapped at the three-way crossroads forever).

There's the moment before we start shooting at the Compassion, and then the moment after, and they're two completely different universes.

The moment before is quiet—agonizingly quiet, even. All of us bracing ourselves, the best we can. Then Uiuiuiui takes the shot, his face-tubes twisting with concentration, and . . . everything is suddenly super loud.

The superstream cannon makes a deafening bleat, like a sheep with a megaphone, and Uiuiuiui is knocked back. One Compassion soldier dies instantly, but the other one just loses an arm and part of a leg, and the screams make me shudder. The Grattna are yelling because they think they're about to be rescued, and the rest of the Compassion forces are shouting and stampeding in our direction.

"Everybody scatter," Othaar says. "Go to ground."

And then the shooting starts in earnest, and we're all running down that tunnel as the fireburst guns go off all around us. The tunnel fills with smoke and I can't breathe and I can't see the rest of our party. Someone hisses my name, it's Elza—I follow the sound of her voice, like it's the most important thing in the universe.

Elza and Damini are hiding in a tiny chamber, kitty-corner from the end of this tunnel, in almost total darkness. They beckon for me to join them, and I squeeze in, and then we're pretty well hidden.

"What happens now?" Damini whispers.

"We wait a bit," I answer. "The last thing we want is a shoot-out. We disappear for a while, and then hit them again."

"Right. Guerilla tactics," Elza murmurs.

"We just need to keep them off guard and delay them until our reinforcements show up, like Othaar said." I keep chattering, like I'm trying to reassure myself that this situation is totally under control even though I'm cowering in the darkness, clutching a huge weapon and choking on fumes.

Then there's another loud noise. The ground wrenches up and down like an earthquake. A bright light stuns my eyes, and leaves me seeing blare-y streaks. People are yelling and stampeding all around us, and the darkness is back but my eyes can't adjust. I hear Othaar yelling something like "regroup," or "fall back," and Uiuiuiui and Thot screaming.

I get my vision back just in time to see a snarling face, with sharp teeth and flared nostrils, staring at us. A Javarah (like Lyzix), wearing the stripes of a senior mercy-killer. Aiming the fireburst gun directly at us. Too close a range to shoot my superstream cannon in this enclosed space.

So I swing the cannon like a baseball bat, connecting with the Javarah at just the right spot on the side of the head, below the ears. The Javarah yelps and goes down, and then I'm dragging Elza and Damini out of our hiding place.

Next thing I know, we're in the room full of dangling sharp objects, and two people are shooting at us. Flames pop up in midair, so close I can smell the air singeing. I shoot back, wildly, not even sure if I'm hitting anything. Elza finds another passage that leads deeper underground, and I follow her and Damini into a narrow low-ceilinged passage with spiky walls. Everything smells like burnt bacon.

I don't know if I've killed again or not; I'll probably never know for sure. I want to punch that Chekhov guy in the face. I tell myself that all the people I've killed were trying to kill me. I keep repeating this to myself, like it makes a difference.

*

I poke my torso through a diamond-shaped window, maybe ten feet above the ground, and spy a machine the Compassion soldiers are setting up, near the front of the Mausoleum. I barely take a few seconds between seeing the machine—a big carbonfast arch that looks like a security scanner at the airport—and taking aim at it. My superstream cannon roars to life, like an electric guitar with double extra fuzz tone, and I let it unleash an earsplitting scream into the air.

Whatever the Compassion was building is now a heap of melted scrap surrounded by guards who are freaking out and looking in all directions. I hope that machine was really important. I hope they can't replace it anytime soon.

Elza and Damini are already sprinting away, back down the high cloistered walkway we came along, and I'm right behind them. Damini's bony elbows saw up and down.

We're actually doing it, keeping them off guard. Our strategy is working. We just have to keep screwing with them, and then disappearing before they can hit us back.

I see Captain Othaar, Uiuiuiui, and Thot one level down, in a room that's shaped like a cross, with an open circle at its center. Captain Othaar sees me, and I shoot him a "mission accomplished" symbol, right elbow and right thumb extended in opposite directions in front of my chest.

Captain Othaar nods, and gives me the Fleet symbol for "keep quiet": one finger and one thumb, clasped over his mouth.

(Confusingly, also the "French chef" symbol back on Earth.) Then Othaar looks away from me, and I realize he's looking at someone else.

I hear a voice that turns my blood to a frozen Slurpee.

"I'm glad we're face-to-face at last," Marrant says, from somewhere below my feet. "You don't deserve to die of a gunshot or explosion. You, more than anyone, deserve to die at my hand, so everyone will know at last what a worthless failure you are."

Othaar snorts. "You went to a lot of trouble to turn yourself into a monster. You needn't have bothered. You were always grotesque, in your desperation to be stronger than everybody else, no matter how many times Aym and Thaoh told you to relax."

Marrant snarls. I realize Othaar is trolling him on purpose, bringing up his dead wife along with Captain Argentian. The other two parts of a once-inseparable trio.

"What do you think Aym and Thaoh would say, if they could see you now?" Othaar says.

Marrant starts to say something, then stops. "I don't need to do this. Soon I'll be a god, and you'll be hated by the few people who even remember you."

Othaar opens fire with his superstream cannon, and I hear Marrant laughing. I can't even see Marrant and his guards, let alone get a clean shot. Uiuiuiui and Thot are shooting as well, and then a wave of energy hits Uiuiuiui. A moment later, Uiuiuiui lies on the ground, with a scorch mark on his chest and one arm burnt to a crisp.

I see Marrant at last, as he stalks toward Othaar and Thot. "There's nothing crueler than refusing to face reality. Nothing more compassionate than accepting what can't be changed. Nobody is going to mourn for you."

My bones and blood vessels are frozen brittle, like a sapling in winter. I want to scream, but I can't even breathe.

I can't figure out how to stop this. Shoot Marrant? He's already shrugged off a superstream cannon at point-blank range. Jump down there? I'd break my legs and achieve nothing. Othaar glances up at me and mouths, "Stand down."

When Marrant touches Othaar with one hand and Thot with the other, I feel something sweep through me. A wave of hot air. I go from frozen stiff to boiling hot all at once, and I smell roasting flesh.

I close my eyes, and try to fight the wave of nausea. I think about Othaar, who saved me and mentored me and tried to help me live up to my potential and his friend's legacy.

And all that comes to me is: *Ugh. I'm glad he's dead. He was a shitty waste of space.* I open my eyes, and Damini and Elza both look horrified and revolted and paralyzed by hate. Below us, Marrant is standing over two steaming puddles. I barely knew Thot, but now I know he was garbage.

"Wasted enough time," Marrant is saying. "We need to rebuild that arch they sabotaged, and start sending the Grattna through it. See what happens when we feed the machine some living matter."

*

Marrant is gone, and I'm still just staring down at the two puddles and trying not to let the ugly thoughts in. Damini is muttering a prayer and Elza is singing to herself under her breath.

"I can't," Damini says after a moment. "I can't . . . it's too much. Captain Othaar was . . . I still remember how kind he was, but I can't feel it. I can't."

"It's not your fault," Elza tells her. "What Marrant does, it's the worst kind of violation."

"You can't let him do that to me." Damini is pleading with us. "Promise me. Whatever happens. Don't let him. I can't stand the idea of you and the other Earthlings hating me when I'm gone. Shoot me if you have to, just don't let him do that to me."

I feel myself straighten up, and I look away from the puddles, trying to put them out of my mind. Somehow I find a pocket of clearheaded strength.

When I speak, my voice sounds calm and reassuring.

"I promise, I'm going to get us out of this," I say, looking first Damini and then Elza in the eyes. "We're going to help the Grattna and our friends on the *Indomitable*. We're going to take Marrant down. We're going to bury the legacy of the Shapers so deep, nobody will ever speak of them again."

For a moment, I think they're both going to start asking questions, or pointing out all the ways we're screwed. But my tone actually works. They both nod at me, and get a grip.

"Don't worry," I say, leading them away from the remains of our friends. "I have a plan."

I don't have a plan.

41

I can see victories greater than death. That's what Captain Argentian said to Marrant, the last time they saw each other. Because she knew that after she was gone, people would carry on fighting in her name.

But Marrant made sure that nobody will carry on fighting in Captain Othaar's name, because now a voice inside me is screaming that Othaar was a scumbag. I remember his leering skull face and all those gross things he used to say to "motivate" me, and my skin crawls. It's his fault that we're even in this mess at all.

Wait. That's not real.

That's Marrant, getting inside my head.

I turn and Elza is next to me, and she can tell from my expression exactly what I'm going through.

"Hey, girl, listen to me," Elza whispers. "I know it's hard. I know you looked up to him, and now everything is tainted. I know you're trying to be strong for Damini and me, because we're all drowning here. But it's okay to feel shitty for a moment. Let yourself feel it."

I take a deep breath and nod, and now I'm going to cry. God damn it, I don't have time for this.

I sob once, twice, without making a sound.

"I was pushed out on the street at just the moment when I was figuring out who I really am," Elza says in my ear. "Everything I

299

thought was mine was taken away. I had to fight so hard to hold on to who I was, instead of just letting random people mold me one way or another. Everybody kept telling me I was nothing, I was worthless, I would die in a gutter. But I held on. I found myself. I got the hackerspace to take me in."

"You're amazing." I wipe my face with my uniform sleeve.

"I'm okay." She laughs, super quietly, because we're still hiding in the Catacombs. "It's just, that's what you have to do. When they take everything away from you, when all the people you counted on are gone, you hold on to who you are. And you? You're Tina fucking Mains. I know you were lying before, when you said you had a plan. But you will. You'll figure something out. I know you."

I'm pretty sure I'm in love with Elza. And that scares me more than anything. Because if Marrant lays just one finger on her, it's going to ruin me.

"Elza's right," Damini says. "Work the problem. We'll help."

"Okay." I pull up my Quant and concentrate. "The Compassion doesn't have enough people to hold this platform, especially after our guerilla attacks. And they don't know how many of us are left. They'll need to land reinforcements, and an orbital funnel won't be enough." Deep breath. "Damini, how do you feel about helping me steal a starship?"

Damini busts out with the biggest grin ever. "I feel very good about that."

I hand Elza my superstream cannon. "Elza, can you hack the computer interface on this gun? We're going to need a very loud distraction."

Elza starts poking at the gun's primitive computer. "Easy. Give me a few moments."

I feel like a huge weight has been lifted off my shoulders, now that I've handed the gun off.

Chekhov can suck it.

*

Something roars overhead. I look up just in time to see a cherry-red shape disappearing toward the far horizon. A knifeship, from the *Merciful Touch*. Just like I figured: they're bringing in reinforcements.

And meanwhile, now that we've left the Catacombs, my Quant once again shows me what's happening out in space. The *Indomitable* is still hiding from the two Compassion ships, weaving around solar coronas, in and out of view, but the enemy is closing in. And the Compassion has been scattering immobilizers to box the *Indomitable* in.

Hang in there. We're coming.

All of my concentration goes into avoiding the Compassion's search pattern, knowing when to duck into hiding, and when to run.

When we get about halfway to the Mausoleum, a voice startles me. "Hey!"

I can't even tell where the voice is coming from at first.

"Hey! You're the young Royalist, from our homeworld. Bildub told me about you."

We've wandered close to one of the cages holding the Grattna. Which means there must be guards nearby, and if they overhear this, we're toast. I'm close enough to see a few hundred furry bodies with three talons scrabbling at the ground and three wings crushed by the lack of space, crammed inside one cage.

"Oh my god," Damini breathes.

"There you are," says one of the Grattna, closest to the bars facing us. "My name is Halred, and my pronoun is *she*."

I make a "shhh" gesture, but it doesn't register.

"You told Bildub you could rescue or safeguard weym, back on Second Yoth. And then wey died," Halred says. "And now, those monsters have dragged us to this place where we're too heavy to fly, even if we weren't caged. It's humiliating. You have to get us out of here. Please."

Elza strides toward the cage, with a determined scowl on her face.

"How do we open these cages?" she asks.

I pause to look around to see if any guards are coming. Then I get a good look at the enclosure, and . . . it's not good.

"Ugh. I'm sorry. These bars are polarized, so you'll die if you touch them. And the lock is molecularly catenated. If we had cutting gear, then maybe. All we have is the gun, which would probably kill everyone inside the cage."

"We have to do something," Damini says.

All of the Grattna are staring at us now, with three big shining eyes each.

I keep studying the cage, while the hairs stand up on my neck because we're totally exposed here, out in the open. This yucky double sun won't let me think.

"I . . . I wish there was something," I stammer. "I wish . . . we'll come back for you."

"You'll be too late. We'll be dead, or worse," Halred says.

I hear footsteps. Compassion mercy-killers. We can't stay here.

"We sabotaged the Compassion's equipment," I say. "We slowed them down. Look, we'll come back. I swear. We'll find a way."

Now every hair on my body is standing up, and all my tactical instincts are screaming, *Get out of there.*

"Come on," Halred says from behind the bars. "Either you help us escape, or you give us a quick death, or the Compassion will kill us in some horrible experiment."

"There's got to be a way to get the cage open," Damini says.

"You keep telling me the Royal Fleet is about helping people," Elza says. "So let's help these people."

All of the Grattna in this cage are freaking out now.

"I . . . I don't know," I say. "I don't think we can do anything right now. I'm sorry. We have to stop Marrant. That's our mission."

"I can't believe this," Elza says.

"We can't just leave these people," Damini says.

I stare at the cage full of Grattna, and I know that if I don't leave right now, I'll never be able to. And we can't help the Grattna if we're dead. I whisper, "I'm sorry" one more time. Then I turn and walk away.

*

None of us talks. I'm busy listening for search parties, which are way more plentiful now that they've landed a ship full of people. I hear the drone of fireburst weapons powering up, and the hiss of comms traffic. And Elza and Damini are silent because they're both dealing with the fact that we left innocent people, maybe to die.

I wish I knew what to say to them. Some perfect reassurance, something to help them feel okay again. I open my mouth and nothing comes out. All I can say to them is "shh" and "get down" and "in here" as we skulk around. Elza is fiddling with the interface on my gun again.

Just as we pass by the Mausoleum, I hear two sets of heavy footsteps converging from opposite directions. I make a snap decision and lead the others inside the Mausoleum through a side door. "In here." With any luck, they won't bother searching there, because they'll expect us to go pretty much anywhere else.

The side entrance leads into a narrow passage covered with more carvings, and then we come back out into the central chamber full of tributes to extinct civilizations. Damini starts greedily taking in every detail she missed last time, which at least takes her mind off the caged Grattna.

"Look at this set," Damini whispers. "This symbol is repeated, and this almost looks like a schematic." She points at some pictures around the side of the gazebo, and her eyes light up as though this isn't the worst day in the history of everything. "It's clearly some kind of graphic gestural interface. You stand in the middle and make shapes in the air, and it responds somehow. Look, there's a whole set of instructions."

She keeps going, but I notice Elza's wandered off. She's standing over in the dark corner, staring at a statue of a long-dead species of spiral-shaped blobs.

"I'm really sorry," I whisper. "We'll find a way to help the Grattna. We will. We'll figure all of this out."

Elza shrugs. "People do their best, most of the time. And most of the time, it's not enough." She points at the statue. "Do you think the Shapers made this because they felt guilty for committing genocide? Or because they wanted to celebrate their achievement?"

"If I had to guess," I whisper back, "a little of both."

"Yeah." Elza sighs. "Sounds about right." She hands me back

my superstream cannon. "It's done. You send a pulse from your Quant, and it'll make the loudest, brightest bang ever."

I start to thank her—but then I hear Damini yelp, like something just startled her.

Marrant towers over Damini—like, she comes up to the middle of his chest—and even in the darkness his face shines, sickly white. The smirk on his face looks almost friendly.

"It's an amazing feat of engineering, isn't it?" Marrant says.

42

Once again I feel frozen. I don't know what to do.

I can't reach them before he touches her and she turns into a puddle. Just like Othaar and Thot. Just like Iyiiguol and Vaap. I know Damini said I should shoot her rather than let Marrant touch her, but . . . I can't. Even if I could still use the superstream cannon.

"The *Indomitable* must be dangerously short-staffed, if they're sending unarmed trainees on covert missions," Marrant says to Damini.

"We didn't think you would find this place." Damini chokes on her fear. "We took the Talgan stone. The only clue. We thought."

"The Grattna had already made some pictures of the stone, and I've been studying the Shapers' lore for a very long time." I can hear the shrug in Marrant's voice. "So . . . you're a type of humanoid I've never seen before, but you look young. It would be a terrible shame to have to kill you."

Oh god please no please god no.

My heart flops around like a caught fish.

I start to rush over there, but Elza pulls on my sleeve. Her eyes are huge in the darkness, and she's shivering, just like I am.

"You know what happens to people when I touch them?" Marrant says.

"Yes. They melt, and . . . and then . . . everyone hates them after." Damini sounds like she's choking on fear.

"That's correct." Marrant sounds pleased that she gets it.

I can't even get my mind to understand what's about to happen to Damini. Useless thoughts flood my brain. I'm stuck rethinking all the decisions that led to this point. *This is all Captain Othaar's fault, the worthless bastard.* Ugh, stop it.

"I don't want to have to do that to you," Marrant says.

Marrant is holding his hand half an inch away from Damini's face, like he's about to stroke her cheek. She's backed up against the gazebo, cringing and weeping.

"You could join the Compassion instead," Marrant says to Damini. "So many people are hurting, on so many worlds, and you could help us to do something about it. There's no need for all this misery."

"I saw what you did to Best Planet Ever. And I saw the Grattna in those cages," Damini says in a tiny, scared voice. "My parents, they always said that biological diversity is the richest resource we have. And all you want to do is toss that resource in the garbage."

Marrant snorts with laughter and waves his hand, right next to Damini's face. She flinches.

"Some people just can't be helped," Marrant says, in a way-too-reasonable-sounding voice. "Take the Grattna: they have three of everything, which means that they're always out of balance. And they can't ever make a simple decision between any two things." He snorts. "If we tried to help them, they'd just mess it up. And their planet's atmosphere is so ruined, all the civilized planets could bankrupt themselves trying to fix it, only to achieve nothing. It's kinder just to put them out of their misery."

Damini stares at Marrant, with her mouth hanging open—like she doesn't know what to say in the face of this much evil.

"I don't have time to give you the whole recruiting speech,"

Marrant says. "But I can tell you're curious about the Shapers. They were the most enlightened and advanced beings the galaxy has ever seen, and we still know almost nothing about them. Come join my team, and I promise you'll learn all of their secrets."

Damini's eyes widen greedily at that. "Tempting." She only stutters a little. "But joining up with monsters to learn about monsters seems like bad research methodology. I'm afraid I'm going to have to decline."

"Ah." Marrant shakes his head. "I thought you were smart. Well, I'm sorry to have to do this." He reaches out with one long finger.

My gut wrenches. *No no no please no please no.*

"Nobody will mourn for you," Marrant tells Damini as his finger stretches out to brush against her cheek.

*

I put down the superstream cannon and step forward, into Marrant's line of sight. "Hey," I say. "I heard you were looking for me." I try to keep my voice from trembling too much. I don't think I succeed.

Marrant steps away from Damini. Her whole body sags with relief.

"And who are you supposed to be?" he asks me.

I only have one card left to play.

"I'm *her* clone. Captain Argentian. They disguised me as a human, to keep me hidden from you. But I'm back, because there are victories greater than death."

For a moment, Marrant looks like a scared, lonely guy who lost his best friend and still hasn't gotten over it. His eyes widen, and he stumbles backward a few steps.

"Thaoh?"

"Leave my friend alone." I step forward and pull Damini away from him.

Damini's still trembling. I try to give her a reassuring smile.

"You don't look at all like her. Or sound like her," he says. "But Othaar did say that you were a defective clone."

"I'm a work in progress."

I try to ignore all the ugly feelings that Captain Othaar's name brings up in me.

"It makes me sick, seeing what's become of someone I used to respect," Marrant spits. "The Thaoh Argentian I knew would never have wanted to cling to life at the cost of turning into this . . ." He looks at me. "This tragic homunculus."

"You should talk." My whole body trembles, my stomach is a solid knot, but I keep yanking his chain. And I try to put myself between him and Damini. "You get off on killing people in the cruelest way you could think of, because there's something broken inside you. You want to become a god, but you're barely even a person."

Marrant laughs, a rattling scraping grunt that mostly comes out of his nose.

"Now you sound exactly like Thaoh," he says, getting in my personal space. He raises *that* hand. Up close, his hand has this acrid chemical stench, like the most pungent hair products at the salon, and his fingers make a squelching sound when they rub together. "I wish she could have understood. I wish I could make *you* understand, since you're all that's left of her."

This is it.

He's going to touch me.

There'll be nothing left of me, not even any good memories. Maybe my mom and Bette and Turtle back on Earth will still remember me as I was. There has to be some limit to the range of his psychic death touch thing.

I can barely even make myself speak. "I understand completely," I stammer. "You look at this massive bloody crime spree"—I gesture at all the statues of extinct creatures around me—"and you want to believe there was some grand purpose behind it. But you know what? It's just genocide, and you're just another bully." And then my voice falters.

Marrant's eyes stare into mine. I can't meet his dark gaze, dotted with little pinpricks of pale blue, like a starfield. "You're alone and helpless. You don't even have a weapon." His hand moves toward me.

"Actually, I do. I just left it with a friend."

I hit the controls on my Quant, triggering the superstream cannon that Elza rigged as a super-giant flash bomb.

*

Everything goes bright white, like a hundred migraine clouds. A shock wave knocks me halfway across the chamber, and I land on top of someone. A body wriggles under me, hands reaching upward, and for a second I'm terrified I'm lying on top of Marrant. But it's Damini. I can't see a damn thing, and my ears are ringing.

Someone grabs my sleeve. "A little warning would be nice next time." Elza pulls Damini and me upright.

Still can't see a damn thing, so I let Elza lead both of us out of the Mausoleum, and then we're running across the craggy rock, and I can just see enough to weave in between buildings. Footsteps ring out all around us, but I realize they're all heading in the opposite direction. Everyone is converging on the Mausoleum to investigate the explosion.

Eyes blaring, ears throbbing . . . doesn't matter. This is the only chance we're ever going to get to steal their ship.

43

can see again (mostly). And the Compassion's knifeship is so lovely I lose my breath for a moment.

Pointed front section, sleek curves and tapered wings, for flight within an atmosphere. About one-tenth the size of the *Indomitable*, with next-generation spaceweave drive and a gleaming impact-resistant hull, stained cherry red. And there are only two soldiers guarding it: an Irriyaian (like Yatto) and a Javarah (like Lyzix).

I can't help thinking of Captain Othaar and what he would do in this situation—and then I'm grossed out and furious and ashamed, and I lose a moment just getting my head back in one piece.

Can't believe I ever thought he had any of the answers.

"What do we do about the guards?" Damini whispers.

I close my eyes and give in to the rage that's been building inside me since we got here. I feel it flow through me. Like I filled my veins with a brand-new type of blood.

"Wait here," I whisper to Damini and Elza. Then I'm striding forward toward the two guards.

I'm sick of losing. Sick of cages I can't open, and friends I can't rescue. Sick of that gross smug look on Marrant's face.

The only thing I have going for me is the skills of one of the greatest fighters the Royal Fleet ever produced.

I sneak around the side of the knifeship, and the two guards don't even see me until I'm right next to them. And remember how

I mentioned those fireburst guns are range weapons? Yeah. I knock the Javarah sideways with a jab to the ynthgus, which is an organ that regulates all the toxins in a Javarah's blood. And then while the Javarah is half-stunned and clutching at their side, I'm pummeling the Irriyaian over and over: face, neck, stomach, ears. I hear myself grunt and rasp and low-key roar, and the Irriyaian swings wildly at where my head was a moment ago. And then both the guards are down.

The Javarah recovers enough to try and stand, and I kick them a couple of times, until they're out for real.

We drag the two bodies into one of the buildings and do our best to tie them up and gag them. One of the guards has a device that's similar to a Quant, and we use it to get the knifeship's outer hatch open. Their guns are locked to their DNA and won't fire for anyone else, so I just yank out their power cores.

My knuckles are bruised and scraped up, and my hands feel sore. But I feel relieved, like I finally got a grip.

And at least I didn't kill anyone. Else.

*

The inside of the knifeship is mostly an echoey personnel carrier with scuffed blue-green walls, without any place to sit down, or even a toilet. Plus a cockpit, with three teacup chairs.

"We'll need to disable the security protocols," I say, looking into the holographic interface.

"I'm on it," Elza says. "Basic principles look pretty similar to the *Indomitable*'s computer, but there are some differences. Still, I've never met a system I couldn't win over to my way of thinking. Give me a few."

Damini is already sitting in the center pilot seat, familiarizing herself with the controls. "We'll call her the *Skin of Our Teeth*," she whispers. "Nobody's ever loved a ship the way I'm going to love this ship."

"Almost ready," Elza says. "Just another couple—"

Someone's trying to open the ship's hatch from the outside. "Hey! Get out of there!"

I poke at the interface on the inside, scrambling to keep it locked, while they keep entering override codes. Then I hear a loud thud and the ship rocks onto one landing strut for a moment.

"Promises and curses! Someone's trying to steal our ship." A voice comes from outside.

"Get the ion cutter," says another voice.

"Where's Marrant? He's going to be so pissed," the first voice says.

They're still trying to override the lock. I'm running out of ways to shut them out.

"Now would be a really freaking great time to not be here," I shout at Elza and Damini.

"I always forget how bossy you get," Elza says. "Just a moment longer."

"We don't—urk!—we don't have a moment," I say. They're almost in.

I hear a loud hiss coming from outside. An ion cutter.

A dazzling yellow spot appears on the wall, a few inches away from the lock that I'm still wrestling with.

Doesn't even matter if they manage to get the door open. If they make the tiniest hole in this ship's side, we're not going anywhere. This ship can't do that trick of reshaping its hull to cover up gaps, like the *Indomitable* can.

"Now or never!" I shout.

I can feel the heat coming off that yellow pinprick.

"Strap in!" Damini shouts—just as the ship lurches off the ground. I'm hurled into the opposite wall.

By the time I pick myself up, with a huge bruise on my side, we're half an STU (or a few miles) up, and climbing fast. The ship is lurching and jittering, and I wipe out three times before I reach the cockpit and strap myself into the right-hand teacup. Which is the weapons station.

"Bring us around," I tell Damini. "I want to leave them something to remember us by."

For a moment, we have a beautiful view of the curvy, sinuous upper side of the *Merciful Touch*, with the Mausoleum directly beneath it. I glimpse some of the cube-shaped cages holding the Grattna, dotted all across the platform, and my heart twists.

I want to punch a hundred people in the face.

But I can do even better.

I coax the *Skin of Our Teeth*'s weapons systems online, and unleash two dreamkiller missiles—directly into the primary and secondary engine compartments of the *Merciful Touch*. I feel the shock wave from both impacts, and the *Merciful Touch* wobbles for a moment, with reddish-orange plumes of smoke coming out of both impact sites.

That'll keep them from crashing our party.

Flashes of light come from the ship beneath us: they're shooting back. I see a bright scrim of light go past us—but then there's a fiery inkblot directly on our tail.

Damini swerves the ship, and the dark ball, encircled in flames, just sticks to us, close enough to see the swirl of energy at its core.

"I can't shake it," Damini says.

"We could try and fool it into detonating early," Elza says.

"Could work. If we jettison one of this ship's warheads." I poke at the unfamiliar console in front of me, trying to do some calculations. "Even better, if we can get close enough to one of these suns, we can drop off their scans just as it explodes. They'll think they destroyed us."

"Sun-diving!" Damini claps her hands.

We soar up along one wing of the Butterfly: a roller coaster of shining lace. The dark orb looms in our rearview the whole time.

Elza keeps poking at her console and humming some Brazilian funk song to herself, with an angry little smile. Liniker e os Caramelows, maybe. I suddenly have a super-vivid image of her going to the Firmament and becoming a princess.

Then we hit a burst of stellar energy, enough to hide this little ship from anyone's scans.

"Now! Do it now!" I shout.

"Hang on! This could be bumpy." Elza turns one wrist clockwise and the other one counterclockwise.

We drop a warhead out of the belly of our ship, and it just hangs there for a second.

A second later, the flaming ink-ball detonates. The shock wave feels like a giant boot kicking my ass, and I'm slammed forward in my harness.

Then we're sun-diving, and Damini is whooping. We race along the curve of the Butterfly, toward where our friends are barely holding on. Time to rejoin the *Indomitable* and even the odds.

Time to end this.

44

"A beautiful life, and a worthy death. This is Acting Junior Tactical Officer Mains," I say into my Quant.

"Epic love affairs, and no hatred." Lyzix sounds startled to hear my voice. "Where's the rest of your party? Where's Captain Othaar?"

"The others . . . didn't make it."

I have to squelch the awful urge to add that they got what was coming to them.

"Oh." Lyzix lets out a string of Javarah curses. "I . . . I can't even imagine this ship without Captain Othaar. He and I fought sometimes, but I . . . I don't know what I'll do without him." I hear a weird noise, and I realize the cryoducts in Lyzix's neck are leaking, which is the Javarah version of tears.

So. I guess the *Indomitable* was far enough away to avoid the mind-freak attack, when Marrant touched Othaar. Or the solar flares protected them.

Even though he was a piece of shit, I'm glad someone misses him.

"We can't talk for long," I say. "This channel will only be secure for another few microcycles. We stole a ship from the Compassion and we're coming to help."

"That would be welcome." I can tell from Lyzix's voice that her ears are standing straight up. "We're boxed in by the other two Compassion ships, plus all the immobilizer claws they've been spreading."

"I know. And I have a really bad, super-reckless idea for how we can ruin the Compassion's whole day."

I explain my plan super quickly, and Lyzix starts cursing again.

"You're completely out of control, and you're probably going to get us all killed, and I love it." She laughs.

Then there's an inaudible voice.

Lyzix says, "There's someone else in the control deck who wants to talk to you."

"You're alive!" Yiwei's voice comes. "We've all been freaking out. Keziah kept dreaming up worse and worse worst-case scenarios, and Rachael drew some truly bizarre cartoons . . . I'm so sorry to hear about Captain Othaar and the others."

I bite my tongue, to keep from saying what I'm thinking.

"I'm sorry too. We'll see you soon."

Our connection cuts out.

*

Rachael: Tina's okay? And Damini and Elza? Oh thank all the space weasels.

Yiwei: yea. but captain othaar . . . didnt make it.

Rachael: Oh. I'm so . . . I'm sorry. He was amazing.

Yiwei: there was still so much i wanted to learn from him

Yiwei: i wish i could come down there right now

Yiwei: i want to hug u so bad right now

Rachael: When we're not in a space battle I'm going to hug you forever

Yiwei: gonna hold u to that

Yiwei: oh damn, we're under attack AGAIN. gotta go, bye!

*

Elza walks to the back of the *Skin of Our Teeth*'s big empty "troop carrier" section, where I'm sitting on the floor while I poke at my Quant and try to convince myself that my plan has a shot at working.

"Hey," I say, without looking up. "Can't talk now. We're rendezvousing with the *Indomitable* in half a cycle."

"That means this is our last chance to talk," Elza says. "Maybe ever."

I look up at her at last. Something opens up inside me, something huge and epic—like maybe my heart could be good for something besides quiet rage and self-hatred. Maybe.

I've stared at these calculations a hundred times, and I'm not going to see anything new the hundred-and-first time around. So I shut my Quant down.

"I'm here," I say. "I'm listening."

"And now, I don't even know where to start."

"You don't have to talk. We can just sit." I pat the floor next to me.

We sit together, looking at each other. Elza's eyes have the opposite effect on me of Marrant's: I feel safe, full of possibility.

Then I look away from her face, and notice what's different about her. Her right sleeve no longer has the barbed "WITHOUT A WILL" message. Instead, there's a gorgeous image of the three-stem thistle, one of the main symbols of the Grattna and their way of life. Crinkly leaves, rippling sky-blue flower.

"You changed your sleeve."

"Yeah." She looks down at it. "I found this picture on my Quant's memory files, because I wanted to remind myself who we're fighting for. And that we promised to go back for them. And also, that there's always a third choice, in any situation."

"It looks seriously cool."

Longing intensified.

We sit a moment longer. And then the words just tumble out of me: "I don't just want to be friends."

Elza nearly falls over, even though she's already sitting. "What?"

"I don't just want to be friends." I talk in a nonstop rush, like Damini when she's about to do another stunt. "I've been into you ever since the first time I saw you, standing in front of the aurora borealis with glittery eyeshadow all around the most beautiful pair of eyes I ever saw. I know I'm way too late, but I can't keep this inside anymore."

I've never seen Elza speechless before. Her mouth opens and closes.

"Are you . . . asking me out? Is that what this is?"

"Um . . . yes?" I didn't mean for that to come out sounding like a question. "I know a lot of people hurt you before. I know one of them was me. But yeah . . . if we survive this. I want to hold your hand and dance super badly and tell you everything. I want to be close to you all the time."

Elza just sits there, processing, while I'm jumping out of my skin.

We probably have about twenty minutes left before we join the all-out space battle.

"So is this for real?" she says at last.

I nod. "There's nothing I'm more sure about."

"I watched Marrant raise his hand to you," Elza says. "And I knew if he touched you, and my feelings turned ugly, I would never even have had a chance to tell you how I feel. I couldn't stand the idea of these feelings going to waste."

There's a species called the Ainkians, who turn into mist when they get too excited. I feel like I could do that right now: just burst into a cloud of vapor.

"The first time I ever saw you, you dropped out of the sky, literally right out of the sky, wearing a torn-up spacesuit, and I had never seen anything so ferocious in my life. Before I even knew what had hit me, I had it bad. All I could do was try not to get carried away." Elza shakes her head. "I got carried away."

She's so close now. I can see her delicate earlobes, her slender lips, the line of her neck. Not leaning forward, not pulling away.

I whisper, "Oh god, I really, really want to kiss you right now."

She tilts her head. Her lips come closer to mine, and I have a feeling of *oh damn this is happening,* and then our mouths touch. Her lips graze against mine, dry but soft and warm, and my heart can't even contain everything I'm feeling. I start off super tentative, and then she's kissing me back, and I grab the tight black curls on the back of her head. I pull her body toward mine. My whole skin is awake and sensitive, and I feel so present, I am so much *this person here now* that I want to laugh and cry at the same time. But more than either of those things, I want to keep kissing her forever.

"Hey," Damini says from the cockpit. "Really sorry to disturb you, but you better come look at this."

*

It's worse than I expected. The two Compassion ships have the *Indomitable* backed up against the left wing of the Butterfly—that ginormous lattice of silken threads, which will slice through any ship that touches them. And there are immobilizer claws scattered

320

all around, which can glom onto any ship that comes too close, and then you'll be dead in space.

The *Sweet Euthanasia* and the *Kind Blessing* are closing in on the *Indomitable,* almost in weapons range. Already, the *Indomitable*'s hull has been patched in a couple of places where they took some nasty hits.

"What do we do?" Elza jumps into the left-hand chair and starts interfacing with the computer.

"We're so tiny," Damini says. "We'll barely be any help to the *Indomitable.*"

"We're going to give the Compassion the biggest surprise of their lives," I say. "Let's increase speed, and find out what this ship can do."

"With a will, Captain." Damini does the salute and everything.

"What?" I sputter. "I'm not a—"

"Of the three of us here, you're the most qualified," Damini says. "And even if you weren't, there's nobody I'd rather follow in the last desperate battle against evil. Seriously."

"I agree," Elza says, "and not just because I want to be the captain's girlfriend."

"What?" Damini squeals and claps her hands, so her bangles ring. "You're— The two of you are—"

"Yeah." Elza grins.

"*Fi*nally," Damini says. "I've been wanting to smack both of you for ages."

I'm blushing all over.

And then I remember that we're closing in on the enemy.

"Okay," I say. "I'll play captain. Just don't let Lyzix hear you call me that. Damini, give us a parabolic course that takes us around that patch of immobilizers, out toward the field of nasty-ass skyrmions. Try not to let them spot us until we're ready to be seen."

"With a will, Captain," Damini says.

"Elza, I'm sending you some calculations, and I need you to double-check them with the computer."

"With a will. Captain." Elza smiles.

"And let's give the Hosts of Misadventure something to talk about."

A second later, we're racing forward at top spaceweave, so fast the light of the two suns blurs, and all the other stars are bright blue needles. We're rushing past a blob of ship-killers, and if we don't do this exactly right, we're toast. But I trust my instincts, and, more important, I trust these two with my life. Just like they trust me with theirs.

My crew.

45

We've left the cloud of immobilizers behind, and the *Indomitable* and the two Compassion ships are also vanishing into our rearview. I only hope we made a clean getaway.

"Feels like we're running away from the fight," Damini says.

"We're not running," I say. "Prepare to turn on my signal."

"The Compassion ships will be able to shoot our friends in a minute," Elza says.

"Trust."

We hit the cluster of magnetized skyrmions at the exact moment we reach spaceweave velocity.

The whole outside of our ship is bathed in ripples of orangey-yellow light that probably makes us look like a big globe of JoySquirt. It's utterly gorgeous, and I can't spare a second to appreciate it.

"Wait for it . . . Wait for it . . ." I mutter.

Our ship jitters itself almost to pieces, and the hull turns taffy-soft. And the *Indomitable* is seconds away from being destroyed.

"Now, Damini!" I shout.

Damini spins the ship on its axis, and we emerge from the skyrmion field, lit up like the biggest house party ever. We're still going faster and faster, racing back toward the Compassion ships.

They see us now, because there's no way to miss us.

Two Compassion ships swerve toward us—leaving the

Indomitable behind and preparing to unleash all of their firepower in our direction.

"Guess we got their attention," Elza says.

"Oh, damn," Damini says. "Either one of those ships could smush us like a bug."

Damini's the one piloting, but I'm feeding her tactical data from my console, and Elza is adding her own nav simulations. Elza and I are both totally focused, but it's like we're having our first dance together.

We streak ahead, faster than this ship was ever designed to go. Alarms are bawling. Our hull lets out a high scream.

I realize I have the biggest grin across my whole face, because I can't wait to see if this works.

*

"Elza," I say, "please open a comms channel to the two Compassion ships."

Elza does a double take, but then she just nods. "With a will."

"Attention approaching vehicles," I say in my most Serious Captain voice. "This is the *HMSS Unquenchable*. We have superior armaments and countermeasures, and we have declared Situation Red Call. Consider this your only warning: power down your systems and prepare to be boarded. Test us, and you'll burn to stardust."

I cut the comms channel, and turn to see identical WTF expressions on Elza's and Damini's faces.

"Wait a sec," Damini says. "The *Unquenchable* . . . isn't that the super-sized unstoppable ship? And isn't it still three days, I mean metacycles, away from here?"

"Yes, and yes," I say. "But the Compassion doesn't know that.

They've been gambling that they can finish their work here before a Royal broadsword can arrive. So this is their worst nightmare."

The Compassion ships are still zooming toward us. They've also diverted the cloud of immobilizers away from the *Indomitable*, so our friends are getting some breathing space.

"Can't they tell we're just a teeny ship that we stole from them in the first place?" Elza says.

"Not with all those gnarly particles messing up their scans," I say. "We look huge and terrifying to them right now, and they think their stolen knifeship blew up. Plus we're moving fast enough to look as if we just arrived from a long way off."

I reopen comms. "Final warning. We open fire in ten microcycles."

The Compassion ships still haul ass toward us.

In a moment, they'll be close enough to see what we really are, and then . . . well, it's been fun.

"Come on," I plead. "Don't make my ninth-grade volleyball coach a liar, when he said all bullies are cowards. Come *on*."

The enemy ships are almost in weapons range. We won't last a second.

I can feel the sweat gather in the palms of my hands. My stomach tightens. *I just got us killed.*

"Do we have a backup plan?" Damini asks.

I start to answer . . .

. . . but then, both Compassion ships abruptly turn and swoop away from us, in an arc that takes them back toward the Butterfly. Now *they're* the ones trying to hide by sun-diving.

"Yeah, you *better* run," Damini hoots. "Don't make us chase you."

"Can't believe that worked." Elza whistles.

"Never doubted for a second," I lie.

*

All of the immobilizers that were swarming the *Indomitable* are still heading in our direction. Just one of those beasts is enough to end us, and there are a few thousand of them closing in, plus we're still racing back in their direction. This could be the shortest celebration ever.

"Damini," I whisper. "This is all you."

"Oh, I'm so ready."

We plunge into the field of immobilizers, and they're all around us. Luckily for us, they're in a formation designed to hit a much larger ship.

Damini twists the *Skin of Our Teeth* this way and that as these grabby claws streak past us, each one a few feet in diameter. One of them swipes past us, close enough to see four segmented carbonfast fingers groping in space.

The next one nearly smacks right into us. Damini pivots at the last moment, and we squeak past.

Damini laughs. "Never done an obstacle course quite like this."

We keep lurching around until I feel more and more nauseous, and then we finally make it into wide open space.

Meanwhile, the *Kind Blessing* is still trying to run away from an imaginary Royal broadsword, leaving an opening for the *Indomitable* to get the drop on them.

I manage to open another secure channel to the *Indomitable*, so I can send them a tactical solution.

A moment later, I hear Yiwei's voice. "We're all a little busy here. But that's beautiful. Thanks."

"Count yourself lucky." Keziah's voice comes. "The engines still haven't blown up."

"Yatto, give them the full package," says Lyzix.

"With a will," Yatto says.

A moment later, the *Indomitable* unloads dwarf-star ballistics and plasma cannons on the *Kind Blessing* . . .

. . . and misses.

"Damn," Elza smacks her console.

"Wait and watch," I say.

The *Kind Blessing*'s evasive maneuver has taken it a little too close to Antarràn A—and that shell of sharp threads surrounding it.

The *Indomitable* lashes out with an ion harness and sends the *Kind Blessing* careening into the Butterfly. Pieces of hull go flying off into space, including the maneuvering impellers. The Compassion ship spins out of control, with no ability to steer. If we're lucky, we took them out with zero casualties.

But now, the *Sweet Euthanasia* has swung around to attack the *Indomitable* . . . and they've just realized we're a tiny knife, rather than a huge broadsword.

My nerves are jangling. I can't even tell if I'm terrified or fired up, or both.

"The *Sweet Euthanasia* is signaling us." Elza sighs.

"Let's hear it," I say.

"Now it's my turn to give ultimatums to you pathetic starship thieves," a harsh voice comes. Sounds like an Undhoran (like Uiuiuiui). "My name is Captain Teyeyeyey, and my pronoun is *she,* and I am going to slaughter you. You have ten microcycles to surrender."

I respond. "This is the *Skin of Our Teeth*. Give us a moment to power down."

Then I cut the comms.

"We're surrendering?" Damini asks.

I laugh. "Have you met me?"

I send her some tactical vectors.

"Speed us up. I wanna see how fast we can really go."

"Umm . . ." Elza looks over Damini's shoulder. "We're on a collision course with the Butterfly. At this speed . . ."

". . . there'll be nothing left of us," Damini says.

"We've got one more surprise up our sleeve," I say.

Or rather, I've got one last terrible idea.

We go faster and faster, until the Butterfly's rippling wing is dead ahead: an undulating mesh of breathtaking silvery-blue jewels that'll slice us into teeny tiny pieces.

I may or may not be laughing my head off.

*

We're so close I can see every node and perturbation in the shimmering surface. This incredible piece of engineering would be a pretty great choice as my last sight ever. But also I'd really like to live to talk about it.

Here's where it helps to know all about how starships work. Not just the controls or whatever, but the deep guts.

"So, you remember what we learned about the momentum gravitators?" I say.

"Yeah," Damini says. "They convert our momentum into gravity when we stop, so we can walk around instead of floating."

"Except? We'll overload them if we slam on the brakes at this speed," Elza shouts.

"Exactly," I say.

The *Sweet Euthanasia* fires three dreamkiller missiles at us. Spitting poison in front, spewing obnoxious amounts of radiation in the back. We manage to shake off two of them, but the third is still on us.

"Wait for it," I mutter. "Just a moment longer . . ."

We're coming right up to the razor-sharp lattice, which throbs with captured starlight.

"Now!" I shout.

Damini turns us so fast my stomach lurches. The momentum gravitators try to absorb all of our inertia, but it's too much for them.

Our ship barfs up a giant wave of pure artificial gravity. Which bounces off the Butterfly, hitting the missile on our tail. The missile blows up, close enough that our hull buckles on one side, and honest-to-god smoke comes out of the panels next to Elza and me.

The *Sweet Euthanasia* catches the gravity wave in the dead center of its hull . . .

. . . but shrugs most of it off. They're coming around to wipe us out of existence once and for all. Weapons blazing hot.

Damn. I really thought that would work.

"We can't slow down!" Damini yells over the scream of our engines.

"I know," I shout back. "They're right behind us!"

"No, we actually *can't* slow down. We blew out our brakes."

We're going faster and faster, with no way to stop, or even redirect our momentum when we make a turn. Elza is frantically trying to coax the gravitators to reboot.

The *Sweet Euthanasia* is still on our tail, targeting us with pulse cannons. One of them singes our already-damaged skin, but Damini keeps the ship thrashing like a fish in a net.

"What now, Captain?" Damini manages to smile even though her voice is edged with terror.

I freeze. I'm out of ideas. My cockiness and my half-baked battle plan are probably going to get my friends killed. I have a sudden sharp realization: all the people who told me I was out of my depth were absolutely right.

There's an ice shard in the place where my rescue beacon used to be.

"Captain?" Damini says again. Then, more shaky: "Tina?"

I snap out of my haze of despair, and glue my face to the tactical scans again.

I can still fix this.

"Stay close to the Butterfly," I say. "Make them work for it."

Time to use our smaller size to our advantage, forcing the *Sweet Euthanasia* to navigate its much larger bulk around the Butterfly wing to stay on us. Our whole ship rattles as another pulse-cannon blast narrowly misses gutting us.

There's probably only one move left, and it sucks.

I signal the *Indomitable* one last time.

Yatto answers. "Raised glasses and last dances."

My breath catches in my throat. You only say that particular blessing when you know you're never going to speak to someone again.

My voice trembles, but I blurt out the reply: "Bright memories and warmth in the dark."

Everything shakes around me, and I hear the distinctive

squalling of critical damage alarms. That damn ship is still right on our tail, even as we hug the edge of the Butterfly.

"We already sent the other trainees away," Yatto says.

I don't even have time to respond to that. Instead, I just say: "Solar flare. It's the only option."

"Agreed," they grunt. "If you carve, we'll serve it up."

"Said and done." I close the channel.

"Wait, what?" Elza asks. "Are they going to—"

"No time," I say. "We need to maneuver the *Sweet Euthanasia* to this position." I send some vectors, basically the bottom tip of the Butterfly's wing. "And then we need to peel away as fast as we can, put some distance between us."

Damini is sobbing, even as she executes a perfect loop around the last twirl of the wing. "I can't . . . this is too much. I can't."

"We're right here." I don't even know where I find the calm that I put into my voice. "You don't ever have to face any of this alone. We're with you. You can do this."

The *Sweet Euthanasia* makes it around the curve and takes another shot at us. We barely dodge.

We've reached the designated coordinates. And thank the Hosts of Whatever, we're able to slow down—because Elza just got the momentum gravitators back online.

"Let's make it look like our engines just failed," I say.

"Close enough to the truth." Damini slows our roll and even gives our engines a dramatic sputter, for good measure.

They close in, but don't shoot again. Maybe they want prisoners.

I catch one last sight of the *Indomitable*: hull splintering in several places, engines wrecked, bluehouse burnt to cinders. The ship pauses for a moment, then snakes out an ion harness and unleashes its final spread of warheads into the heart of the sun.

"Now!" I shout.

We're racing upward and away from the Butterfly when the sun bursts out with a pillar of flame right behind us. Everything is too bright to see. My seat shakes so hard there are three of everything. The alarms drown out my thoughts, and everything is breaking around me.

Then . . . dead quiet. There's still a plume of superheated gas behind us, but we're sailing away from it, out into open space. I let out a breath and slump in my chair. We're alive. The *Sweet Euthanasia* is gone.

Then I see something else floating away from the solar eruption: a piece of starship hull, with the words "HMSS INDOM" written on it.

Captain Thaoh Argentian's personal datajournal, 2.08.49.94 of the Age of Regret

Okay, I'm going to tell you the most important thing, that took me way too many tours of duty to learn.

The only part of leadership that really matters is listening. I wish I had figured that out a long time ago. You can't lead anybody, unless you've heard them. Their fears, their reasons for fighting, and their inspirations.

The Royal Fleet doesn't have any ranks, except for captain and alternate captain. That doesn't mean that there's just bosses and a lot of underlings. It means that there are a whole lot of experts—and then there are two people whose job it is to pay attention to the experts around them. That's how you get the best ideas.

Scanthians have no concept of hierarchy. But then there are the Oonians, who have a strict system based on birth order, from oldest to youngest. My own people, the Makvarians, believe that authority comes from service to others, and it's never permanent. There's no way the Royal Fleet could impose a rigid top-down system on people from all these different cultures, and they didn't even try.

Still . . . when I became a captain, I suddenly thought I was supposed to have all the answers. I could have avoided a lot of disasters if I'd realized sooner that being in charge means you never need to be embarrassed to admit you don't know something. People like a leader who tells, but they love a leader who asks.

So, now you know.

46

wish the debris field looked ugly. This much destruction ought to look so grotesque, the teeniest glimpse would make you sick to your stomach. A blood-soaked battlefield. Instead, the trashed remains of the *Indomitable* look beautiful: glimmering in the blue-tinged light from Antarràn B, spinning and twirling in fractal patterns.

The emptiness inside me is bigger than I am.

Last dances and raised glasses.

We've spent a whole cycle trawling through the wreckage, and there's still no sign of survivors. My vision blurs, and my whole body feels exhausted. Each shattered piece of starship is another kick in the teeth.

I ought to be crying and freaking out right now. Pouring tears out of my eyes, hugging Elza and Damini, yelling that this isn't fair, kicking stuff, curling up in a fetal position. Instead, I just feel . . . drained.

I keep remembering the battle, and how invincible I felt, and those memories are coated with a film of wet ash.

"They're out there somewhere." Damini trembles so hard her bracelets jangle. "Our friends. We can't give up on our people."

"Nobody's giving up on anybody," I say—but then I notice Elza shaking her head.

"We need to decide how much longer we're going to keep on

sifting the same patch of debris," Elza says, not making eye contact with Damini or me. "The Grattna are still in danger, and we promised to go back and help them. Every moment we delay here, the chances increase that we'll be too late."

"Why are you always so cynical?" Damini snaps.

"I'm not saying we should leave right this moment," Elza mumbles, arms folded. "But we need to agree on a time limit, because the Grattna are running out of time."

"Yatto said they had sent the trainees away," Damini says. "So, we keep looking until we find them."

"Shhhh, both of you." I swat with one hand without taking my eyes away from the tactical scans.

And then . . . I find something. Two things, even.

"Good news and bad news," I say. "I found a piece of wreckage with life signs inside . . . but also, the *Kind Blessing* is closing in on us."

"The *Kind Blessing*?" Damini says. "I thought we put them out of action."

"We trashed their engines. But they're drifting our way, and they'll be in weapons range in about a minicycle. Five minutes."

The *Skin of Our Teeth* crawls closer to the piece of inhabited debris, wriggling around sharp fragments of starship. The only thing moving slower than we are is the *Kind Blessing*. But they're going to reach their goal before we reach ours.

*

We found one atmosphere suit on board the *Skin of Our Teeth*, so I'm putting it on. Then I seal the rear section of the ship, and depressurize it, so I can open our cargo hatch to space.

I can't see anything out there but empty space and melty chunks of starship, and then I'm thrown against the wall as Damini executes a sharp turn. The *Skin of Our Teeth* almost wipes out on a jagged chunk of carbonfast.

I spot the piece of the *Indomitable* that still has survivors, and it's so tiny that my heart sinks again.

My new spacesuit has an ion harness, but it doesn't work the same way as the one that I used to lasso the runaway orbital funnels in Earth orbit, such a long time ago. My first throw, I overshoot.

"We've got like thirty seconds before the *Kind Blessing* gets in position to nail us," Elza says.

"I know!"

My second try falls way short.

"They're prepping a dreamkiller missile," Elza says.

My third toss bounces off the lifeboat . . . but wraps around, and gets a grip on it. I tug as hard as I can, my boots clamped to the floor.

"They just fired on us," Elza says.

"Still pulling," I gasp.

"Thirty-four seconds to impact."

I play tug-of-war with this spaceship compartment, until my arms and shoulders scream with pain.

"I can see the missile approaching. It's actually quite pretty," Damini says.

I make one last desperate tug on the rope, and the *Indomitable* compartment sails into our empty back section with so much momentum it smushes me into the wall.

"GO!" I shout.

Damini whoops and puts us into a spin, just grazing a couple chunks of the *Indomitable*. A second later, we're home free, zooming around the curve of the Butterfly's wing. The missile strikes a piece of space junk.

*

As soon as we repressurize the *Skin of Our Teeth*'s rear section, I yank myself free and try to find a way to open the compartment that somehow survived from the *Indomitable*. I can't find a latch anywhere. But then a whole wall slides out of the way, and I'm looking into the exam room from Sickbay. Inside are Rachael, Keziah, and Yiwei.

"You found us just in time," Keziah says. "We were running out of episodes of *Kitchen Nightmares* to act out for each other."

Keziah's laughing, but he has a wan look in his face. They all do.

Makes sense: first they spent ages on a ship that was running and hiding on the edges of a sun, waiting to get caught and killed. After all that, the actual battle must have been scary AF. Then they were cooped up in a tiny medical exam room, with no way to know what was going on except for the occasional sound of debris striking against the outside.

"I can't believe this actually worked," Rachael says.

"I barely had enough time to seal up the exam room before we were jettisoned," Yiwei says. "I'm just glad I spent so much time learning to reshape the hull."

"How many other survivors?" Rachael looks around.

I shake my head. "We haven't found anyone else. Doesn't mean anything. There was at least one cryo-suspension unit on the control deck, plus someone could have launched an orbital funnel." I'm trying to comfort myself, as much as them. "But for now, we're on our own."

Everybody looks at the floor, thinking of Dr. Karrast, Riohon, Yatto, Lyzix, and everyone else we lost. (And I try not to think about Othaar or Thot.)

"You're alive!" Damini squees for joy, coming out of the cockpit. "I can't believe you're alive. I mean, I never doubted it, but I'm just glad we found you in time. Can I hug you? I basically need to hug all of you at once."

And then we're in a big group hug, all six of us. Even Elza only hesitates a moment before joining the huddle.

I look over Rachael's shoulder at the exam room. I have line-of-sight at the bench I sat on when I had my failed memory restoration, and also where Dr. Karrast gave me the injection to start undoing my DNA mask. (My skin still looks mostly pink, but I can see a touch of light purple, if I squint.) This is the room where I spent so much time trying to reclaim the legacy of Captain Argentian.

I tried. I really tried to live up to her memory. And all I have to show for it is a giant patch of shattered debris.

Lyzix tried to warn me that I had knowledge without wisdom, and that I was going to get a lot of people killed.

I pull away from the group hug. The cold of the ship's cavernous rear section seeps back into my skin.

"Gotta get back to the cockpit." I stare at the scuffed carbonfast floor, and my own filthy uniform pants.

We're already on a course back to the platform at the head of the Butterfly, to try and rescue the Grattna. But there's nothing the six of us can do on our own, in a tiny half-wrecked starship.

If we had any sense, we'd get the hell out of here right now.

"So what now, Captain?" Damini slides back into her pilot seat.

"Don't call me that." I say it loud enough that all five of the other Earthlings stop what they're doing and stare at me. I can't look any of them in the eye. "It's not real. This isn't a game, and we're all in over our heads, and I'm not your fucking captain."

Damini starts to say something, but shakes her head and concentrates on piloting instead.

The whole ship is so quiet you can hear the creaks and groans of our hull slowly disintegrating, thanks to all the damage we sustained during my big hero moment.

47

Some time later, I still have my eyes glued to the tactical screen. Because we're flying back toward Marrant's ship, the *Merciful Touch*, and they could still wipe us out without breaking a sweat. And also, to keep anyone from trying to talk to me.

Everybody except for me is trying to mourn the dead. Hesitating. Catching their breath every other word.

Yiwei wants to talk about how great Captain Othaar was, and Damini and Elza have to hide their disgust. Nobody wants to admit the rest of the *Indomitable* crew are probably dead. The whole conversation is like skipping through a patch of immobilizers.

They're all sitting in a circle in front of the piece of Sickbay, except that Damini's still in her pilot seat next to me. She's piloting the ship, but also studying the scans she made of the Shapers' carvings.

"We should be doing something," Yiwei says. "Like that white silk ceremony. Or I bet there's a song. Tina, what do they sing in the Royal Fleet to honor the dead?"

I just ignore him. There's a few songs, but I don't feel like singing.

"I wish I could write a song for our fallen comrades," Yiwei says when he realizes I'm not answering. "I don't have my guitar anymore, but I still have Xiaohou. I keep trying, but . . ." He cradles his musical robot in his lap, poking at its delicate guts.

"Yma wouldn't want any fuss," Keziah says. "Yma would be yelling at us to get back to work—probably spitting out the darkest, orangest bubbles ever."

"The Oonians can have a new baby to replace Dr. Karrast." Rachael shakes her head. "But only if they know for sure she's dead. I don't know what . . . I don't know what they do if there's no body. But her death means a new Oonian will be born. That's something, right?"

Yiwei offers his hand to Rachael. She looks at it for a moment before grasping it with both of hers.

"I loved that ship," Keziah says softly. "I loved those people. I didn't even realize how much until they were gone, because I was always too busy looking back at what I'd left behind."

"We'll keep their memory alive," Rachael says.

"Even Captain Othaar," Yiwei says. "I won't let him be forgotten."

Damini tries to hide her revulsion at that name. "We can honor our friends by keeping the fight going."

"Not me," Keziah says. "If we survive today, I never want to fight again. I want to find some way to work for peace."

"You should," Rachael says. "Maybe you can even help everyone we left behind, back on Earth? Lyzix said the satellite that recruited you was supposed to find the best and brightest so they could train to become ambassadors and then return to their homeworlds. Maybe you could still do that."

Keziah looks at me.

"Umm, yeah," I mutter. "I think they'd probably let you join the diplomatic training program. And after that, you could go back to Earth with your own starship and crew, and everything you'd need to make people listen to you."

I wait for Elza to pipe up and say that she's going to apply for the princess selection program if we make it out of this. And wait. And wait. She just shrugs and looks at nothing.

I unstrap myself and get out of my seat and walk back into what's left of Sickbay. I look around at all the medical supplies scattered all over every surface. I want Keziah to become an ambassador, and Elza a princess. And for everyone else to achieve all their potential.

And then it hits me.

I could stop Marrant, and nobody else has to die.

Except for me.

*

"No."

I don't even realize Rachael has followed me inside the exam room, until I hear her voice behind me.

"No what?" I ask.

"No to whatever you're planning. I recognize that look on your face. It's the same look you had right before you jumped in front of the bulldozers at Cannyland. Or when you were willing to turn yourself into a pancake to try and save Yiwei and Elza. You've got your self-sacrifice face."

"I have a self-sacrifice face?"

"I know it by heart, which is just too depressing."

"I was . . ." I shake my head. "The others gave their lives to save us. I can't let anybody else die. And you heard what Dr. Karrast said: I could turn Marrant's death touch against him, using some of these medical supplies. With any luck, he'll die. And then all of his people will hate him afterward, so they'll probably quit following his awful plan."

"Except that you'd still die too. That's what Dr. Karrast said. And she wasn't even sure if this would work at all."

I nod. "I'm willing to take that chance."

Rachael laughs. I'm so startled I nearly drop the neurolytic scanner I'm holding.

"You are so full of it. You can't face the fact that you're not perfect, so you're just going to go out in a blaze of glory. With, honestly, the worst plan ever."

I shrug. "I've had worse plans."

"You're going to, what? March up to Marrant and hope that he uses the death touch on you? What if one of his soldiers just shoots you, instead? What if they toss you in a cell, so they can interrogate you later? That's what I'd do. What if Marrant is too busy racking up genocide points to deal with you himself?"

"I can goad Marrant into touching me. I've seen how he is."

"Your plan. Is balls."

I sit down on the exam bench and let all my supplies fall in my lap.

My eyes feel weighed down with all the tears I refuse to shed.

"We already tried all the ideas that don't blow chunks," I say after a moment. "I can't stand the thought of anything happening to any of you. And it's not fair for me to drag anybody else down with me, not when I have a shot at stopping him without any more collateral damage."

"We can stop him another way."

"I was supposed to know what to do, if I'd gotten all of her memories and thoughts and everything. But I didn't, and I don't." I can't even find the bottom of this inky frozen pit inside me.

Rachael scoots onto the bench next to me, and just gazes at me. "I'm glad your memory restoration failed," she says.

*

"What?" I literally can't believe what I just heard.

"I'm glad." Rachael crosses her arms. "I didn't want to say anything back then, but I kept thinking that it was going to suck if you suddenly had all the memories of this woman who had lived a whole life. And my best friend, the Tina I knew, would be an epilogue in her story. I was so bummed, even though I was happy for you, because I knew that was what you wanted."

"Nobody needs a random girl from Earth named Tina, though."

"I do. *We* do."

Her green eyes are wide and full of love, and I can't face them.

"Whatever. I'm the consolation prize." Overwhelmed by unshed tears.

"You are not." Rachael scoffs. "Remember when we first met?"

"Yeah." I close my eyes for a second. "That douchebag Walter Gough was harassing you on our field trip to the shoe museum, and I told him to back off."

"That's not what I remember," Rachael says. "You asked me about my art, and you actually cared about it. You wanted to see all the drawings I was working on. You kept asking me about them. That was when you became my hero."

I finally make eye contact with Rachael, and her smile is so sad it damn near breaks me.

"I just . . . I've been trying so hard to be enough." I lose the battle with my tear ducts. My eyes flood and everything goes blurry and I feel like I'm going to shake myself to pieces. "I . . . I just feel like I could keep on fighting for the rest of my life, and I'll

344

never be strong enough. I'm so tired of being pissed off and scared and feeling like there's nothing I can do about any of it, and I'm never going to be the person I was supposed to be, and I'm not enough, and I've let all of you down."

Rachael offers me a hug, and I only hesitate for a moment. Then my face is on her shoulder, and I'm breathing in her comforting warmth. "You're so much more than enough," she whispers in my ear.

That just makes me bawl harder. "I don't know what we're going to do. We lost everyone, Marrant already won. I don't know what we're going to do."

"We'll figure it out together. All six of us. We made a promise, remember? Earthlings."

"Yeah." I wrap my arms tighter and press my face into her neck. "I'm so lucky to have you as my best friend."

"No kidding. I've put up with a lot. Remember your peanut-butter-on-everything phase? You put peanut butter on apples, on hot dogs—even on pizza that one time. It was horrifying."

I try to say, "If you can put pineapple on pizza, then peanut butter isn't weird," but I'm too busy sobbing my face off.

Rachael just keeps holding me until my crying jag wears itself out.

I feel this bubble of happiness, in the midst of so much grief and rage. I can't help thinking about how hard I tried to send Rachael back home to Earth. And if it had been up to me, we wouldn't have brought the other Earthling kids on board the ship. I never would have made it this far without Rachael and the others.

Rachael saved me, way more than I ever saved her.

"You're *my* hero," I whisper to her.

I feel like I've taken off a huge piece of armor that's been weighing on my neck and shoulders forever.

Captain Argentian hated her life. She died miserable and alone, and even Captain Othaar—*worthless! Asshole!*—even Othaar never really knew her. She never wanted to be brought back.

Maybe Rachael's right, and I should just try being Tina instead.

"Come on." I pull away from Rachael's embrace. "It's time to figure out a new plan. Together."

Rachael nods, and the two of us leave the quiet of Sickbay for the cockpit, where our friends are all freaking out together, and we're less than half a cycle away from the Mausoleum and the *Merciful Touch*. I look at Yiwei, Keziah, Damini, and Elza, each in turn, and gratitude hits me so hard I have to sit down.

48

"Okay, so. These symbols have their own logic. Like, the Shapers always seem to depict hierarchies in terms of concentric circles, with the most powerful at the center."

Damini is showing us a holographic slideshow of the highlights of the inscriptions and carvings from inside the main building, which we're still calling the Mausoleum.

"There's no way I can make sense of all these symbols in the time we have," Damini says. "It would take a team of experts years. But I think they wanted whoever found this stuff to be able to understand it, and some of the patterns are really obvious. Like, I was solving harder puzzles when I was still in primary school." She pauses, and looks at all of us. "And I think we've all been wrong about the Shapers."

"Wrong, how?" Elza says.

"Like, I don't think they were even humanoid. I think they looked like this." She shows us the center of a bunch of circles: a weird creature that looks like a fancy nine-pointed star, with circles on the ends of all the points.

"But . . . that doesn't make any sense," Keziah sputters. "If they weren't even humanoid, why would they want to fill the galaxy with creatures that look like us?"

Damini wrinkles her nose. "My uncle Srini used to breed horses."

Elza perks up at this. "Really? What kind?"

"I don't know. Just horses. I never liked horses."

"Whaaaaat? Everybody likes horses."

"It doesn't matter. The point is, you want horses to be smart enough to do the things you need them to do, and able to deal with whatever terrain. And be the right size for you to ride them."

"Uh," Keziah says. "So are you saying they wanted to *ride* people?"

"No. Not exactly. But I think . . . I don't know. But look. There are all these pictures of humanoid bodies, with diagrams—like, they needed the right shape for some particular purpose."

As Damini talks, she's showing us some of the pictures—which do look an awful lot like Ikea diagrams for attaching things to various parts of a humanoid body.

"So . . ." Elza frowns. "They needed the galaxy to be full of humanoids, all over. And they needed us to be advanced enough to have experience traveling through space. So . . . they gave us a boost, *and* got rid of all our competition?"

"But we don't know what their actual goal was," I say.

"It all depends on the meaning of this one symbol." Damini points to a sideways diamond with a triangle inside, sort of like the doors and windows of their buildings. "But yeah. This makes more sense than the idea that they just liked humanoids because they had a . . . a fondness for two arms and two legs. People just jumped to the wrong conclusion, maybe because they were projecting."

"You mean, we all decided the Shapers thought we were the most perfect shape . . . because that's what we all think," Yiwei says.

"Exactly. We just put our own prejudices onto these ancient beings, whose actual motives are much more mysterious."

None of this is making me feel better about what might happen if Marrant manages to turn on that ancient machine.

*

We've been talking for ages, and now we're running out of time.

"We've only got one minicycle left before we reach the head of the Butterfly," I say.

"Or about five minutes," Elza says.

"We need a real plan," Damini says.

"I've been studying your scans of the Mausoleum," Keziah says. "And I wouldn't trust any machine that old, handling that much stellar radiation. Let's just say you probably don't want to eat any fruit that was grown anywhere near there."

"Got it," Elza says. "If Marrant offers us homegrown fruit, we will not partake."

"But if Damini's right and you operate it by making graphic gestures in midair, then I don't know how a person stands at the center of that much energy and maintains control." Keziah frowns. "Oh, and if they actually get that machine working, its electromagnetic field will probably disrupt everything. Weapons, communications, any engines within the immediate vicinity of the Mausoleum. Nothing will work properly near that thing."

"That's super helpful," I say. "Thank you."

"Also, I grabbed something when we evacuated the *Indomitable*." Keziah half smiles as he produces something from his shoulder bag. "I only just got it working."

It's a small egg-shaped device, with a glass tube that looks like the smaller cousin of the bottle that enclosed a solar flare on board the *Indomitable*, and a bent fork on one end.

"It'll stop the flow of time within a very small area," Keziah says.

I stare at it. "We could use this to freeze some of Marrant's people."

"Except . . . I built it to prove my father wrong, by creating something that could never be used as a weapon." Keziah sighs.

"What if this device helps us save a lot of people without any bloodshed, though?" Elza asks.

He takes a deep breath and purses his lips. "I think . . . yeah. If we can do this without more slaughter. I keep thinking, the only real way we can ever defeat the Compassion is to prove them wrong. They used to be part of the Royal Fleet, so we need to show that we're not the same as them."

I can't help glancing at my tactical display. We've got like two minutes left.

"I really hope we can do this without killing anyone else," I say. "I've already had enough death for one lifetime."

"The range is not great." Keziah holds up his invention. "I'll need to get within about fifty meters of the target area."

"I can help with that." Damini grins.

And just like that, we start coming up with more pieces of a plan. Everybody tosses in ideas.

"It has to start with freeing the Grattna," Elza says. "We're not going to save them. They have to save themselves."

"Agreed," Keziah says. "There's been more than enough paternalism."

"I have an idea for the most unsafe stunt ever," Damini says.

"And I think I know how we can use what's left of the sickbay," Yiwei says.

We have about thirty seconds left before showtime.

This time, Elza's the one who says it first: "Earthlings."

She looks like she's about to cry, and if she does, then I'm going to cry again.

Yiwei takes Elza's hand. "Earthlings."

Rachael takes his other hand. "Earthlings."

"Earthlings." Keziah is holding hands with Rachael and me, and then I take Damini's hand.

"Earthlings," Damini and I say at the same time.

"We're going to give them the biggest surprise," Elza says. "The six of us, plus the Grattna."

"Yeah," I say. Then something finally clicks into place, and I realize what's been right in front of me the whole time. "But there's only one of us here who has the superpowers we need to stop Marrant." I take a huge breath. "And it's not me."

Everyone else in the circle stares with their mouths open, like *Who* are *you right now?*

*

The *Skin of Our Teeth* has traveled all the way around the Butterfly, and now we're in position near the "head": that big floating platform with the Mausoleum on it.

The *Merciful Touch* hovers directly over the Mausoleum, and they have at least fifty soldiers on the ground. The Compassion have already replaced the machine that I melted down—that big square arch near the front of the Mausoleum—and they're marching the Grattna inside, single file. The captives march in, and there's a crackle of reddish-orange energy, and they don't come out again. We have a good view of this as we approach, and it makes me sick to my stomach.

Two of the cages are empty already.

Something about reducing all those living creatures to atoms seems to be bringing the Mausoleum back to life. Bluish-white lightning, like the distilled rays of Antarràn A and B, is starting to play over the ancient stone walls.

"Those poor people." Elza stares out the viewport. Then she shakes it off, and heads toward the pressurized side hatch. "Almost time. Wish me luck."

"Good luck." I walk over there with her. "And be careful."

I'm having an epic brain-freeze, because (a) Elza's so close and I just want to kiss her, (b) Damini is sending us into a steep nosedive, or (c) that shot Karrast gave me is still making me woozy. Or maybe all of the above.

Elza is putting on the spacesuit that I wore when I lassoed the sickbay. I help her to put on the pants that are sort of like overalls, and then the clunky boots.

I have too many things to say to Elza, like a whole lifetime's worth, but I'm scared to say them in the wrong order. Like, I need to say the first thing first, or the second thing won't even make any sense. There's so much we haven't even talked about—like whether Elza wants to be with me once I finish transforming into a tall purple alien with mysterious mating practices.

But there's only one thing I can think about right now.

"Listen . . . I want you to promise me something," I mumble.

"Yeah, what?"

"If we actually survive this, promise me you won't let fear, or all the people who told you that you weren't good enough, keep you from trying out for the princess thing."

"Maybe." She shrugs. "Let's worry about that later."

I almost let it go, but I see the bitterness behind her smile.

"I saw the look in your eyes when I first told you about it. And I know you would be perfect for it. You could do so much good, way more than the rest of us."

She shakes her head. "It's pointless to want something like that."

"No, it's not. I love you too much not to want to see you shine."

I don't even realize I've said *that* word until it's out of my mouth. And then, it feels terrifying—like free-falling naked into one of those suns. But also right.

"Don't use that word unless you're sure." Her mouth quivers.

"I wouldn't. I am."

I look into her warm brown eyes and I feel so alive and floaty inside, a smile bursts out on my face. She looks so badass in this spacesuit, black curls spilling out of the wide neck, with cutting gear in one hand.

Elza blinks and then runs the back of her hand over her eyes to brush away tears. "I never thought I deserved to be loved. But—"

"Hey." Damini's voice comes over our internal comms. "We're over the dropsite. And the *Merciful Touch* just spotted us."

"Okay. Thanks." Elza puts her helmet on, and then I can't see her face.

"Say hi to the Hosts of Misadventure for me," I say.

"You too." She takes my hands in her big gloves for a second, then opens the hatch and vanishes.

*

The *Skin of Our Teeth* shakes up and down and back and forth. The *Merciful Touch* sends us a welcome-to-the-neighborhood bouquet of dreamkiller missiles, but we're flying too close to their own people on the ground, and Damini's not giving them a clear target for even a second.

Just for a second, we tilt way over on one side, and I have a perfect view of Elza on the platform. She's using the cutting tools, safety gloves, and goggles we found in a supply locker on this ship, to open one of the cages holding the Grattna.

Damini's providing Elza as much covering fire as she can, while also creating a pretty freaking huge distraction.

But there's still a group of the Grattna getting herded into that archway, to be turned into nothing.

A dreamkiller goes off, close enough to us that I hear the ear-splitting shriek of pure destructive power. The *Skin of Our Teeth* rattles and drops several yards.

Then Damini decides we're flying too slow, and guns the auxiliary impellers, so the acceleration blows Rachael and Yiwei back into their seats, and knocks Keziah and me on our butts.

Then Rachael turns to Yiwei. "It's time." They both get out of their seats.

The *Skin of Our Teeth* is already making a super-bumpy landing at the other end of the floating island from where we dropped off Elza. Right near where we stole it from.

Yiwei hands Xiaohou to Keziah. "Please look after him."

"Will do." Keziah smiles, and Xiaohou makes a little musical trill in his hands.

"Watch yourself out there," I say to Rachael. "Don't forget to wait until Damini makes her big entrance."

"You too, be careful," Rachael says. "All of you." She looks at Keziah and Damini, and they both smile. Then she offers Yiwei her hand.

"Let's go make some trouble," Yiwei says, taking her hand and leaning close to her.

Rachael hesitates one moment, then she leans forward and kisses him on the mouth.

"So much trouble," she says.

Yiwei looks startled—like that was their first kiss ever—but also wild with joy.

Rachael and Yiwei push the whole sickbay exam room out through the main hatch, leaving the back of the *Skin of Our Teeth* yawning empty once more.

Now that we're on the ground, I hear the sounds of Compassion soldiers yelling and running toward the cages. I hear the voice of one of the Grattna shouting something like, "Eat your own face, Symmetrons!"

"Appears I was right: weapons won't work near the Mausoleum when it's activated," Keziah says. "The only gunfire I hear is farther off in the distance."

Damini tries to take off again, and our engines stall out—because the Mausoleum's interference is screwing with us, too. She tries a second time, and finally pulls us into a steep climb, until the engines come all the way back online.

As we climb, I get a really good view of the Mausoleum, which is now aglow with the fire of a million suns.

We're too late. Marrant has already started.

49

I'm floating a few hundred feet above the rocky platform with a personal impeller strapped to my back—but no spacesuit, so I feel the cold air blow through my cadet uniform. Underneath my feet, the Mausoleum glows too bright to look at, almost like a third star, and a shrieking, grinding noise rings out. As if this machine is actually shredding the fabric of the universe.

From up here, I have a perfect view of Elza, along with a small crowd of the Grattna, fighting for their lives. They've taken cover in a space between three of the empty buildings, and the Compassion forces have them surrounded and are slowly closing in on them. Elza is shouting something defiant, but I can't hear it. She looks so alive, and even at this distance I can see her hair billowing around her face, like a crown.

When I look up, I see the *Skin of Our Teeth* zooming along the underside of the *Merciful Touch* and keeping all of those guns busy. Trying to get close enough to let Keziah use his invention. Damini must be having the time of her life.

At the same time, I feel chilled, and not just because of the thin air.

The fire around the Mausoleum feels as though it's going to consume everything and everyone I love, and I'm scared, all the way down in the marrow of my bones. Even over the primal-screamy noise from the Mausoleum, I hear Marrant laugh—like he enjoys being at the center of a death machine.

Elza probably has minutes left to live, and I'm too far away to help her.

The air bursts into flames around her, and all I can see is a dark cloud.

For a moment, I'm sure Elza's gotten burnt to nothing.

Please, no. I can't lose you, right after I finally opened my heart.

The smoke clears, and Elza is standing in the middle of the flames, with her spacesuit only a little singed. She roars, and I feel my heart rise up. One of the Grattna, who looks like Halred, beats her wings frantically, rising just a few feet, so she can slash at the attackers with her three sets of talons. A Compassion trooper whacks Halred with a gloved fist, then shoots a fireburst into the crowd.

Come on, Yiwei. Now, please.

Right on time, he steps out of one of the buildings and heads toward the fighting. My first impression is just of a big hulking figure, covered with sharp jagged edges, stepping forward into the melee, slapping two of the Compassion soldiers down.

But when I wheel around, I get a better view for a second. Yiwei is covered from head to toe in carbonfast plates, which move with him and magnify the force of his arms and legs. And written across his chest, in big letters, are the words "MSS INDOM."

He's wearing what's left of the *Indomitable*'s outer hull as a suit of armor.

Okay, now it's my turn. Deep breath. Make a fist. Time to put on a show.

"Marrant!" I shout as loud as I can. "It's me. Thaoh Argentian. I'm back—all the way back—at last. And I want to talk to you one last time. About Aym. About all the promises the three of us made. I want to look you in what's left of your face, before the end."

I'm trying really, really hard to sound like *her*—but I probably sound like a little kid in a school play, trying to act "momentous." I've watched tons of her log entries, but that doesn't mean I can imitate her. And I still don't look much like her, in spite of Karrast's treatments.

And meanwhile, I'm holding a big "bomb" that Keziah helped me rig up in a hurry. It's actually a food processor we scavenged from the *Skin of Our Teeth,* but we tricked it out with five thick tubes that glow bright red. Red glow always means scary danger, right? It looks super convincing, if you don't get a close look.

"Marrant!" I shout again. "Are you really too scared to come speak to me?"

Nothing happens. I don't see Marrant anywhere. And even with Yiwei smacking the Compassion soldiers around with his starship arms and legs, Elza and her new friends are still massively outgunned.

The whole plan is ruined if Marrant doesn't take the bait.

"Marrant! I want to be looking you in the eye when I detonate this." I hold up my fake bomb.

He rises up from the ground, long dark trench coat fluttering in the air currents under his red sash. Wide mouth twisted into a smile. His gaze is so much deeper than I remembered.

"You can stop shouting," Marrant says. "It took a few attempts before I could coax this impeller to work, so close to the ancient citadel."

"We've been calling it the Mausoleum," I say.

I feel the fear gripping me again, stealing my voice. But the others are counting on me to keep this murder-freak busy. As long as I pretend to be her, I can just put on a performance. I don't have to think about his eyes, seeing all the way inside me as if I was hollow.

"So you're really back?" Marrant smiles, but his voice sounds needy. "You restored all of your old memories?" He's so close he could touch me right now.

The wind feels colder and colder.

"More or less." I try to smile like her. "You should see your face. You look exactly the way you did at the academy, when you ate that fire-roach that someone snuck into your meatspore casserole."

"I want to believe you." He frowns. "I would give anything to talk to her one last time."

"I'm here." I hold up the bomb. "And I'm telling you to stop this right now, or I'll stop you."

Ooh scary red glow. So scary. So red.

"I like you ruthless," Marrant says. "That's always been my favorite part of you. But you were always terrible at follow-through."

"What I want to know is, why couldn't you just admit that Aym's death was your fault? She believed in you. She stood by you. And your arrogance got her killed." I'm actually curious to hear the answer—but also, bringing up his dead wife seems like a good way to keep him talking.

"Aym understood. She always knew . . ." Marrant closes his eyes and takes a deep breath. "I can't do this. Set off your bomb. I don't care anymore."

He turns away, looking back down at the Mausoleum, where the screaming energy field seems to be reaching some kind of peak.

"I never gave up on you," I say in my best imitation of her voice. "You never even knew how many smallfires I lit, hoping you would get back on the sunlit road."

Marrant starts to respond. But just then, the *Skin of Our Teeth* finally slips past the big guns, and pulls right up next to the *Merciful Touch*'s control deck and weapon controls.

Keziah leans out of the ship's hatch far enough to toss his invention in the air. The machine twirls for a moment, catching the rays of both suns . . . then spins up and attaches itself to the hull of Marrant's ship. Then there's an incredibly satisfying "SCRAAAAAPE" sound, and a swirly hot pink cloud rises up to envelop part of the *Merciful Touch*.

Inside that ship's control deck, everybody is frozen in a moment of time, paused in the act of trying to shoot down my friends. No more missile launches, no more cannon bursts . . . the stillness feels downright eerie.

Marrant is shaking, and his dark eyes are huge with fury.

"What did you do?" he hisses.

"I guess we gave your crew . . . a time-out." Yeah, I made a quip. Sue me.

He lunges at me with the death touch without any warning, and I barely get out of the way in time.

I drop my fake bomb, and it drops half a mile, shattering into a million tiny pieces.

"You're dead." Marrant keeps slashing at me with his hands, coming closer and closer each time. My stomach is a blob of anxiety. "There will be nothing left of you, not even a memory. Nobody"—slash, slash—"is going to mourn for you."

I turn and fly away from him as fast as I can, watching the

buildings streak past. The cold blue flame of the Mausoleum keeps rising higher underneath us.

I need to keep Marrant busy a little longer.

Which means I have to stay alive, whatever it takes.

*

"The Shapers," I gasp. "They weren't who you thought. We deciphered some of their symbols. That machine isn't going to turn you into a god or anything."

"I don't care. There has to be more to existence than just planet after planet of weak and selfish creatures, rooting around in the dirt." Marrant nearly tags me this time. "I can't bear the idea that the universe is just meaningless garbage. There has to be some purpose to all this."

"The purpose is that people just want to live their lives."

I drop down five feet, just to get some distance from his deadly hand, and then race away again.

"That's not enough. I've lost so much, I need to know that there's some greater reason why we're all here. I want to meet the architects of the galaxy, face-to-face, as their equal."

I start to say something—but then Damini makes her big entrance. Finally.

The *Skin of Our Teeth* peels away from the *Merciful Touch* and goes into a swan dive. The ship falls so fast it's a shiny blur against the line between artificial atmosphere and open space, leaving a trail of smoke that points straight down. Marrant gives a roar of triumph.

Until the *Skin of Our Teeth* comes crashing down with a "THOOMMM" sound—right in front of the Mausoleum, sending a huge cloud of dust and smoke up around a three-block radius.

Damini and Keziah both drift down to the ground, using our last two impellers as makeshift parachutes. Maybe it's just my imagination, but I think I see the biggest grin on Damini's face, even though I know she loved that ship.

Marrant freezes in midair, with actual veins popping out of his smooth, perfect forehead.

"Good luck moving several tons of spaceship out of the way of your ancient superweapon, when nothing technological works anywhere near there," I spit.

I take off flying away as fast as I can, with Marrant in pursuit. My lungs are burning and the speed of this flight is making my face hurt, and I hear Marrant's breath—his snarling voice—right behind me.

As I race away from the wreckage, I catch another view of Elza, Yiwei, and the Grattna, and they're cornered inside one of the buildings. Too many Compassion soldiers in full attack armor are closing in, and they're far enough away from the Mausoleum that their fireburst guns work. One of them hits Yiwei squarely in the chest, and he shrugs it off—but they keep coming.

"This is for Captain Othaar!" Yiwei shouts as he knocks two Compassion enforcers over with one swing of his bulky arm. "And this is for treating people like farm animals!" His voice comes loud and clear, out of the *Indomitable*'s comm speakers.

Then I'm too high up to hear Yiwei, or see any of what's happening. The artificial atmosphere is thinner up here, and I'm feeling pleasantly sleepy, except I'm so cold. The blue-white fire around the Mausoleum still shows through the smoking wreck of the *Skin of Our Teeth*. From up here, the empty city looks peaceful, maybe even cute.

Marrant comes up so fast he nearly catches me off guard. He snarls something that I can't hear in this thin air.

My vision blotches up. I swoop lower, so the model-train city turns back into a collection of dirty old buildings, with people fighting and dying all around me.

And then my impeller gives a snorting belch, and gives out. I flew too close to the Mausoleum's magnetic crud. Next thing I know, I'm heading for the ground, way faster than I planned.

*

The impact knocks all the wind out of my body, and my left wrist and hip both throb when I try to move. The pain burns too hot for me to even tell how bad I'm hurt.

A team of Compassion enforcers are already lifting the melted chunks of the *Skin of Our Teeth* out of the way, clearing the entrance to the blazing Mausoleum, which I can't even look at directly.

Marrant drifts down to the ground, landing on his feet in front of me while I hug my injured hip.

"I couldn't imagine a worse punishment for Thaoh Argentian than having to come back to life as a crying weakling." Marrant leans over me. No way to escape.

Am I crying? Ugh, yes, damn it. Hot tears all over my cheeks, from pain. From terror.

I came all this way just to let myself down.

The sound of someone struggling breaks Marrant's concentration, and then his soldiers drag Elza and Yiwei over to us. Yiwei's armor is gone, and he's still shouting defiance, except now it's with tears in his eyes. A moment later, someone drags Damini over as well, with her arms pinned behind her back.

And then they throw Keziah facedown, so he's crouching on his hands and knees looking up at Marrant.

The noise from the Mausoleum is getting higher and louder, like an engine grinding to life after countless years of stillness. Plus this creepy rustling, like a million whispers.

"It's time," Marrant says. "Bring them."

50

Tongues of energy are snaking out from the gazebo in the center of the Mausoleum, so many that it's like staring into the sun no matter where I look. But I feel colder than ever. My skin crawls. I look over at Elza, and she's wearing a look of total defiance. I try to give her back the same expression, despite how soft my insides are feeling. I still can't stand, but one of Marrant's bastards is helpfully holding me up.

"I just have to step inside there"—Marrant gestures at the gazebo—"and maybe I finally transcend this dismal existence."

I look past him and catch a glimpse of what's going on inside the gazebo—and my heart leaps.

Keziah struggles to his feet, so he's face-to-face with Marrant. "I've met sadists like you before," Keziah says, between gasps of pain. "The delusions of grandeur are just an excuse. Your whole tragic origin story is just shabby window dressing. The truth is, you just enjoy hurting people."

Marrant scowls at Keziah and leans closer to him.

I want to say something, do something, to save Keziah, but I feel frozen. I can't bear the thought of what's about to happen.

Then Marrant laughs and pulls away from Keziah. "You're not afraid of me at all, are you? I'll have to do something about that, when I have some time to spare."

Then Marrant turns toward the gazebo—and I need to keep

him from seeing what's going on in there.

"Hey," I say. "This is your last chance to listen to us. You're blundering into a situation, just like the time you ate a snipsalad from the wrong end in front of the whole dining hall."

That does the trick. He turns and stares at me, doing a double take. "You didn't get her memories back at all. You were faking, the whole time."

I shake my head. "Doesn't matter. All that matters is, you were wrong about all of it. You need to stop, before you make everything worse."

"I think I figured out that one symbol," Damini says. "The one that explains the whole reason why the Shapers were helping all the humanoids and hurting everyone else. I think it's their word for war."

"War?" Marrant glances at her, one eyebrow raised.

The strands of blazing light race past, and I flinch as they graze my face.

"Like, maybe they were preparing to fight some other, more powerful group. And they needed a huge army, for when the time came."

"Damini is smarter than anyone," Yiwei says. "You should listen to her."

Marrant is still standing in front of me, and my arms are pinned behind me, making me squirm involuntarily. His pupils are like black suns.

He brings his hand up to my face, so the burning-chemical stench fills my nostrils and my eyes tear up. I struggle against the grip of the soldier holding me, but I'm stuck.

"Nobody is going to mourn—"

"You said that already," I hiss.

I look away from Marrant, and catch the eyes of my friends. Damini freaking out, as two Irriyaian soldiers hold her back. Keziah staring in horror. Yiwei spitting curses. And Elza, yelling with tears in her eyes.

"Leave her alone!" Elza shouts. "Leave my girlfriend alone, you creep!"

Welp, I finally got an amazing girlfriend, even if it only lasted a couple hours.

"I love you," I tell Elza, as his fingers come closer and I choke on the fumes. My whole body is a frost-brittle sapling. "Remember I said that, even if all your feelings get wiped away. Even if you lose everything else. Promise you'll remember that my love for you was real."

Try not to cry. Don't give him any tears.

Just keep looking at Elza. I can't imagine a better last sight.

"In a few heartbeats," Marrant tells me, "your friends will know the truth about you. That you were never worth caring about. That you were just a pitiful echo of someone I used to respect. They'll see you the way I do."

"I don't care." I put every ounce of defiance I can summon into my voice, even though my last nerve is gone. "It doesn't matter. Whatever anyone else thinks, I'll die knowing that I did the right thing, and that I'm surrounded by my friends. But there's one last thing I have to tell you, one final message from the crew of the *Indomitable*."

"What's that?"

"Never underestimate the awesome power of a real artist."

I jerk my head to indicate the gazebo at the center of the

Mausoleum, where Rachael has been standing this whole time, drawing pictures made of pure starlight with her bare hands.

There's only one of us who has the right superpowers to stop Marrant.

And she's magnificent.

51

Marrant runs over to the gazebo and tries to enter, but the threads of light block his path.

"Get out of there," he shouts at Rachael. "You don't even know what you're doing."

She doesn't reply, though I can see her muttering to herself, the way she always does when she's anxious. She keeps sketching something incredibly gorgeous, and after a moment I realize it's a picture of Yiwei's beloved steel guitar, floating somewhere in a shimmering starscape.

"It's a graphic gestural interface," I say to Marrant. "Which means it works by drawing pictures. And nobody does that better than Rachael."

"I know what a graphic gestural interface is." He doesn't turn around. "Get out of my machine," he snarls at Rachael.

He lashes out with one arm. Rachael flinches, and talks to herself, loud enough that I can hear a few stray syllables. If you didn't know her, you would think she was trapped, helpless. Deer in the headlights.

If you didn't know her like I do.

"It's her machine now," I taunt. "You've been watching the wrong people this whole time."

"I'll kill all your friends in front of you," Marrant says to Rachael. "You know what my touch does. Just imagine how it'll feel when your affection turns to revulsion."

But when he turns around to make good on his threats, more of the lines of blue energy come between him and us, and form another barrier that he can't get past. Now Rachael is drawing something else that I can't make out at first, until I realize: it's the sign she and I made at that protest against Monday Barker, with the stars and rainbows and everything.

"She's so tough," Yiwei says. "I swear I'm going to write a song for her, when all this is over."

Marrant just stares at Yiwei for a second. Then he turns to his goons who are still holding us captive. "Kill them. They don't even deserve my touch."

There's nothing Rachael can do to keep the soldier holding my arms from reaching around and choking the life out of me. I hear Elza and the others struggling too, but we've run out of tricks.

Except that Keziah shouts, "Look at what's happening outside!"

Everyone stops. And stares. And starts to freak out.

*

I can't even make sense of what I'm seeing at first. Even after I stare for a moment, it's still too hard to take on board.

The way-too-bright energy snakes are grabbing all of the Compassion soldiers outside this building and lifting them up. And transforming their bodies—like, their elbow joints suddenly have a shiny rod sticking out of them, with sharp spikes facing outward. A similar spike goes through their shoulders and knees, and a dense mesh covers them from their shoulders up to their noses, so they can't even open their mouths anymore. I watch an Irriyaian get squashed and reshaped into something that looks more like a nightmare action figure.

For a moment I think this is something Rachael is doing, to help us—then I get a look at her, and her face is in full-on panic crunch mode, trying to shut this thing down. She frantically sketches a picture of the *Indomitable* sailing across the Storm of Faces.

It's happening all around this building: bodies get reshaped into some kind of design that seems like it's intended to fit into something bigger. Like, those spikes and things are supposed to plug into some slots. Just like those horrible Ikea diagrams Damini showed us.

"Just this once, I wish I was wrong," Damini says.

"This could still work," Marrant says. "I can have an army made up of every single humanoid in the galaxy, under my command."

"Except I don't think they're going to hang about to wait for your orders," Damini tells him.

As soon as the tendril of energy is done remaking that Irriyaian, it sweeps them up into the air, carrying them toward a glowing scar that's opened up in the "sky." The scar looks like a gaping laceration in the fabric of the universe, and it leads . . . somewhere else. All I know is that when the Irriyaian gets close enough to see whatever's on the other side of that hole, their already-bugged-out eyes look twice as terrified.

Every humanoid who isn't inside the Mausoleum is getting twisted into a horrible shape, and then yanked into the sky—and then they disappear.

I glimpse a stream of squirming bodies getting pulled out of the *Merciful Touch*, too.

Another crack in spacetime appears, inside one of the walls of the Mausoleum. On the other side, I see a world that looks familiar for some reason. Then I realize: this is Makvaria. A few people who look like Riohon are bustling on a path covered with spongy mud that bounces as they walk. And then a tendril of energy comes through the crack and seizes a young Makvarian woman. She screams out in terror and agony as the machine reshapes her body.

More portals open up, and I'm pretty sure I recognize Aribentora, Irriyaia, Oonia, Scanthia Prime, and . . . someplace on Earth, a city that looks like New York or L.A.

"Oh no," Elza is crying. "No, no, no. I can't see this anymore." I hear Yiwei shuddering and making tiny freak-out noises to my left. I still can't even process what I'm seeing.

Some white-haired old lady, out walking her poodle, is the first person on Earth to be snagged by the Mausoleum, and the noise she makes as the spikes go through her is the worst sound I've ever heard. A moment later, what's left of her is pulled into the Mausoleum with us, squirming and whimpering through the mesh, and then she's shoved through that hole in the sky.

*

Marrant looks at us, and then at his four remaining guards. And he straightens up, and puts on a game face. "Enough hesitation. It's time we started acting like—"

And then he stops, because another sound is coming from right outside this building. A few dozen angry faces, with teeth bared in pure righteous fury, are racing directly toward us. I catch a glimpse of razor-sharp talons flexing and clutching weapons.

The Grattna beat all three wings and flex all three claws, with hatred in all three of their eyes for the people who locked them in cages and forced them to watch their friends die.

Marrant's soldiers see this swarm of wings and claws coming their way, and take off running in the opposite direction. As soon as the soldiers get outside, the Shapers' machine seizes their bodies and starts remaking them.

The Grattna come inside the Mausoleum and advance on Marrant, roaring, until they back him into a corner.

Rachael sketches picture after picture, in the middle of the gazebo, in response to a voice that only she can hear.

I limp over there to see if I can help, but she doesn't even seem to know I'm there. "Rachael," I say. "We're all okay. You saved us. You were amazing. Now we gotta get you out of there, before this machine messes you up."

"I still need to shut this thing down," she mumbles, not looking at me. "Few more minutes. It's fighting me."

The fingers of light are still reaching through more and more cracks in the universe, grabbing more and more humanoids to transform. I can't stand to look at the contorted bodies, whooshing past on their way to a giant hole in the sky. So I just keep my eyes on Rachael.

"No, you don't," she says to the machine. "If you didn't like that one, try this one."

Her next sketch looks like Keziah standing in front of a solar flare in a bottle. And somehow, the machine seems to understand. One of the portals, leading to a planet I don't even recognize, closes suddenly. And then the hole in spacetime that leads to Scanthia Prime. More and more of these portals start winking out of existence.

"Thaaaat's a good death machine," Rachael says.

A few of the portals remain stubbornly open, including the one that leads to Earth.

But Rachael sketches a shining picture of Yatto, with a look in their big goldfish eyes that somehow conveys unlimited kindness and patience . . . and the last portals vanish, leaving no trace.

But scary, eye-blazing strands of energy still whip around the walls of this big vaulted chamber. The terrible screech of the First Humanoid machine only gets louder.

"You did it! You closed the gateways." Yiwei tries to reach out and touch Rachael, but the blue lightning still blocks his path. "This is the greatest thing I have ever seen anybody do, ever. Now you need to come out of there. It's okay. I'm here to catch you."

"Not yet," she says, gasping a little. "Still need to . . . close this thing . . . down."

"You already did it," I say. "You've stopped Marrant. You've saved everyone."

With all the portals gone, the machine's energy has no place to go, and it starts lashing out, around the roof of the gazebo. A dozen lightning bolts, bright as sunfire, snake inside Rachael's head, and her face floods with so much light she looks like an angel.

Her eyes close, and her whole body trembles, arms and legs thrashing, like a seizure. Then she opens her eyes again and keeps sketching.

"Shut up and let me concentrate," she says—not to Yiwei and me, but to whatever is speaking in her head. "It's time to go back to sleep."

She draws faster and faster, streaks of light in the air. Each image disappears as soon as she finishes, and I can't even make out what they are.

"Please stop," I beg her. "Please. You've done enough. You have to come out of there now, before this thing cooks your brain."

"She's right," Yiwei says. "We can figure out how to turn it off later."

"Shhh," Rachael says to him. "Let me do this. I can do this."

Now her hands are sketching two different things at the same time, moving so fast that each hand seems to be in three places at once. Her eyes roll upward and her eyelids flutter, and she keeps making pictures, two by two. Faster and faster. It's just a blur of luminous shapes now.

If I lose Rachael now, everything in my world will be small and terrible forever. My head is flooded with memories of Rachael helping me into a sparkly dinosaur costume, Rachael bringing all of us Earthlings together, Rachael telling me, *You are so much more than enough.* Everything just looks like a swoosh of blue flame through the tears in my eyes.

I hear myself sob in short, quick gasps.

"Please, Rachael. Please don't do this," I plead. "You're the one who called me out on my self-sacrifice face. Please. You can't leave us. We need you, you're the heart of this group, and I never even got the chance to be the friend you deserved. Please. I can't face this messed-up galaxy without hearing you snark about everything."

Someone grabs my hand and pulls me close, and I realize it's Elza. I turn and weep on her shoulder.

Yiwei is begging her too, talking about the song he wants to write for her and the presents he still needs to give her. "I'm going to make a way better robot and give it to you. And I want to take you home to Tianjin and show you to my parents and my friends and even Jiasong, and I can feed you Gǒubùlǐ dumplings until you understand why they're the best. You just have to step out of that thing. Just come back to me."

I brush enough tears out of my eyes to see Rachael's skeleton showing through her luminous flesh. And all her veins stand out too, as if the energy is burning all the way through her body.

"You're the bravest person I've ever known," I say between incoherent crying jags. "I can't face any of this without you. Rachael Townsend, I need you."

Those last words turn into a wail that sounds loud to me, even over the crescendo of the alien death machine.

Rachael turns her gaze and sees me, and smiles.

And the light vanishes. All the noise, silenced. The room feels as still as midnight.

She sways and squints at us. "Hey there. You know what? I think the Shapers were assholes."

Then she topples, falling face-first. Yiwei and I barely catch her in time.

52

Yiwei cradles Rachael's head in his arms, making sounds too quiet for me to hear. At first I think he's saying a prayer, and then I realize: he's singing to her. Some Chinese pop song.

I grope for her wrist and can't find a pulse. I start to panic, but Yiwei says, "She's breathing. Just super faintly. She needs medical attention, and we don't have that sickbay exam room anymore."

I turn to look at Marrant, who's sitting cross-legged in the corner, with several of the Grattna keeping him at bay using fireburst guns and long sharp sticks, so as to stay out of range of his death touch. Marrant barely seems to notice me. He's staring into space with a dazed expression, like his whole world just fell apart.

Elza pokes my arm, and I turn to look at her. The whole universe changes shape, like the stars shine brighter and space expands faster. Just seeing Elza's face is enough to change the whole cosmological constant, no kidding.

"That ship over our heads," Elza says. "The *Merciful Touch*. It probably has a proper sickbay with the equipment we need to stabilize Rachael."

"Yeah," Damini says. "And its crew all got sucked out and turned into origami, along with all the other humanoids around here."

"Rachael's the only one of us who was trained to use that stuff," Yiwei says. "But we can figure it out."

I turn to Marrant. "How do we get up there? Is there an elevator or something?"

Marrant just ignores me, with that vacant look on his face.

"We'll figure it out," I say.

"I can help with the security protocols," Elza says.

Halred, who seems to be the de facto leader of the Grattna, steps forward. "We can help you get inside the *Merciful Touch*. We spent enough time there. But in return, we'd like you to help us, or at least not hinder us."

"What do you want?" I ask.

"When you're done using the sickbay, we'd like to take the ship. We don't want to leave it here, or destroy it. We want to get the engines moving, and fly it home, before the Royal Fleet's broadsword gets here."

"I might be able to help get the engines back online," Keziah says.

"It's been almost a whole day since I helped to steal a spaceship." Damini steps forward.

I feel like everything is moving way too fast. "Wait a sec. You want to take the *Merciful Touch* back to Second Yoth? I'm sure the Royal Fleet would be happy to give you a ride home."

"We want to take over that ship, so we can defend ourselves, the next time something like this happens," Halred says, like she's explaining something super obvious to a small child. "We don't want to be victims, or under anyone's protection. We want to protect ourselves."

I hesitate, because I know the Royal Fleet would dearly love to capture Marrant's flagship for themselves, so they can take it apart and study it. Plus there's probably a ton of strategic reasons why giving one of the most advanced starships in the galaxy to the Grattna is a bad idea.

Then I shrug, and smile at Halred. "Sure. I figure you deserve it, after everything you've been through."

If the Royal Fleet wanted the *Merciful Touch* for themselves, the cavalry should have gotten here sooner, right?

"All I ask is, please come up with a new name for that ship, something less creepy," Damini says. "Maybe the *Basket of Fuzzy Cuteness*?"

"The *Impromptu Jam Session*," Yiwei suggests.

"The *New and Improved, Now with 100 Percent Less Genocide*," Keziah says.

Halred smiles at all of us. "Once that ship is ours, we'll have a cleansing ceremony, or a rededication. We won't leave it the way it is. We'll also learn how to copy all of its technology, so we can make more ships like it."

I don't know what to think about this. Is it bad that the nice, peace-loving Grattna are going to build their own fleet of warships? Are they letting the Compassion win if they become more like the Compassion, or are they just being realistic? Are they going to start attacking nearby planets? These questions are way too huge for my exhausted brain to make sense of. Plus, I can't exactly stop the Grattna from taking Marrant's ship, if they want it bad enough.

"Okay," I say. "Let's go steal a starship."

53

The *Unquenchable* comes out of spaceweave right in front of us, and my first impression is just a big sleek fortress, blazing with lights. This Royal broadsword is the same beetle shape as the *Indomitable*, but a hundred times larger—and way louder, because the *Unquenchable* never needs to hide from anyone. The hull looks freshly colorsprayed, with a proud banner featuring the Royal Crest at one end and the words "HMSS UNQUENCHABLE" written so huge you could build a whole city inside the Q.

"Guess the *Merciful Touch* left just in the nick of time," Damini says. We're floating in one of the *Merciful Touch*'s escape pods, stuck in a lazy orbit around the Antarràn system. It's basically a box with minimal engine and life-support functions, and a dozen seats.

Yiwei glances up at this incredible sight, and then looks away. Normally he'd be geeking out about that giant hull and all of the cool things this ship can probably do, but all of his attention is on Rachael, who's lying with her head in his lap. She still hasn't woken up. Next to them, Xiaohou the robot picks up on Yiwei's mood and plays a sad melody, drooping his head.

The *Unquenchable* finally notices us, and reaches out with an ion harness to pull our little space dinghy inside their cargo hold.

As soon as we're inside a pressurized chamber, I pop the door of the pod open, and find myself looking into a familiar face.

"Brave comrades and predictable enemies," says Thanz Riohon, with a huge smile.

"Umm." For a moment, my mind goes totally blank, then I remember what to say back. "Raucous celebrations and few funerals. I can't believe you're alive."

"That's just what I was about to say to you," Riohon says.

*

Riohon and Yatto the Monntha just barely got inside the survival pod in Forward Ops before the *Indomitable* blew up. "Lyzix made sure we got to safety at the last moment, and then she went down with the ship." He shakes his head. The survival pod used a short-range spaceweave to get them clear of the solar eruption, which also saved them from the origami thing.

Damini is rushing forward. "I'm so glad to see you. Is it okay for me to hug you? Is there some special Royal Fleet hug for when you think someone's been blown to pieces and then they turn up in one piece? Also, is Yatto okay?"

Riohon hugs Damini. "I got to see you piloting that knifeship you stole. You're a natural. Unfortunately, Yatto sustained some head trauma. They're still in a coma."

"So is Rachael," says Yiwei, who's helping Keziah to carry her out of the pod. "We need to get her to Sickbay."

Riohon is surrounded by an entire Royal Planetfall Squadron wearing clean, crisp red uniforms with the "We Got Your Back" flying-serpent patch on one shoulder and a whole lot of bling on their collars and cuffs. They're all armed with cloudstrike guns, and clearly prepared to take on whatever hostiles might step out of a Compassion escape vehicle.

The leader of the welcoming party steps forward. "Well met,

and welcome to the *Unquenchable*. Her decks are yours. I'm Crewmaster Antoy, and my pronoun is *se*. We'll get your friend some medical attention right away. And I'll show the rest of you to some quarters, so you can rest and clean up before you meet the captains."

Crewmaster Antoy is a Makvarian—still only the third member of "my" species that I've ever met—and then the pronoun thing hits me. Se is a thont, one of those third-gender people I keep hearing about. I bite my tongue, because I have So. Many. Questions.

Antoy's people help Rachael onto a kind of stretcher that floats a few feet above the floor. None of us wants to leave Rachael's side until we're sure she's taken care of, so we all end up walking with Antoy's squad to the nearest funnel, which whisks us up seven decks to the medical level.

Everywhere we pass, people do the fingers-and-thumb salute, standing at inspection rest as Crewmaster Antoy passes. Their shoes, their guns—everything looks brand-new. I hear voices all around me talking in crisp tones about assessing the realtac and assembling teams to survey this ancient structure. We walk on immaculate carpets, past gleaming silvery walls and expensive gear.

Elza squeezes my hand and I look over at her to see that she's wide-eyed with nervousness. Which I can totally understand: this ship is so fancy you probably can't go to the bathroom without asking permission.

I keep wanting to play Worthington Garden Party.

Soon, Rachael is lying on a bed in one of the five patient rooms of the *Unquenchable*'s Sickbay. Yatto rests in the room next door with a placid expression on their face, like they've just dozed off for a moment.

*

"I still can't understand what in the Sludgepits of Bakaaron happened here," says the captain of the *Unquenchable*, a Javarah named Withni. We've already explained the whole story to her a half-dozen times, and I don't know if I can stand to go through it one more time. Withni's left sleeve is a sea of bling, and her right sleeve is the Peacebringer's Code in lovely calligraphy.

"We'll have plenty of time to study the ancient structure ourselves," says her alternate captain, an Irriyaian dude named Minto the Karthha. "For now, we need to take Marrant into custody before he finds someplace to hide."

"We left Marrant tied up, inside the Mausoleum," Damini volunteers.

"It's unfortunate that the Grattna managed to abscond with Marrant's vessel, however," says Withni. "This could cause a lot of problems in the future."

I'm super itchy, because they've stuck me in a brand-new cadet uniform that feels like sandpaper, and it took me ages to load Rachael's sleeve design onto it. All I want to do is sit by Rachael's bedside. At least the doctor checked out my hip and said I'm okay.

"We're still searching the debris field for any other survivors of the *Indomitable*," says Minto the Karthha, shaking his head. "But we don't expect to find anyone else. We'll have a memorial service in three metacycles for all of our fallen comrades."

"Meanwhile, there's the question of what to do with you trainees," Withni says. "The Royal Fleet owes all of you an incalculable debt, and I'd be pleased to recommend you for any career trajectory you desire."

Damini is bouncing up and down in her chair, with her hand raised. Withni nods at her and she blurts, "I want to finish training to be a pilot, it's all I've ever wanted, and maybe someday I can fly a ship like this one, and see all the cool tricks it can do."

It's going to be my turn in a moment, and I don't even know what I'm going to answer.

A couple days ago, I was sure I wanted to do whatever it took to be just like Captain Argentian. But now?

Withni inclines her head and smiles at Damini. "That can be arranged. Though trust me, you wouldn't want to pilot the *Unquenchable*. We mostly sit in one place and wait for trouble to find us, because it takes us so long to go anywhere."

I think about the *Queen Pux*, and all the people I've helped to kill since then, and my stomach spasms. I wish I could talk to Rachael.

Keziah goes next. "I'd like to go into the diplomatic service, so I can become an ambassador and go back to my homeworld. Um, Earth. They're going to need a lot of help adjusting to being part of a whole galactic community."

"Done," Withni says. "We can fast-track the process."

They're going to ask me soon. I can't do this. I feel like I'm about to leap into an endless void.

"I'd like to go to the Royal Space Academy," Yiwei says. "I want to learn to be more like Captain Othaar, so I can follow in his footsteps someday."

Everybody looks at me. My heart is so turbulent I can't even think.

And then I straighten up, and breathe. I know exactly what to say.

"Um, I'd like to study at the academy too. But . . . I would like to formally request non-offensive status. I never want to kill anyone, ever again."

As soon as I say this, my heart slows and my head clears, and I feel like I just saved my own life.

Withni and Minto, and even Riohon, all look at me as if I just grew another head.

"Are you sure?" Withni says. "Seems like a waste of your talents."

Oh, right, because my "talents" are all just fighting and killing.

"I prefer to think of it as a worthy challenge. Captain."

"There are so many monsters out there, most of them worse than Marrant," Minto says. "And those monsters only understand one thing."

"With all respect, it doesn't matter what *they* understand." I somehow keep my voice even and calm, even though I'm feeling hot under this stiff uniform collar. "What matters is what *we* understand. If the Grattna taught me anything, it's that there's always a third option."

I glance at Keziah and he smiles. I can't help smiling back.

"Very well." Withni shakes her head. Then she turns to Elza. "How about you?"

Elza bites her lip and then just shrugs. "I'm good. You don't have to worry about me."

I just stare at the back of Elza's head, wishing I could at least make eye contact with her right now.

54

By the time we get back to the quarters they're letting me share with Elza, I'm getting tunnel vision. I can't remember the last decent sleep I had, and this "rescue" has been almost as stressful as having the Compassion try to kill us. This whole ship is like someone gentrified the *Indomitable*. At least the food is amazing. They have ten different kinds of Irriyaian caviar, and one of their seven (!) crew lounges is serving fried Scanthian parsnips, which are basically my new favorite food.

Even these guest quarters are ridiculous, with two ginormous beds made of some kind of plastiform that changes shape in response to any sudden pressure. The wall has a beautiful picture of the Glorious Nebula with glittering starships revolving around it, and the bathroom is bigger than my old quarters on the *Indomitable*.

Elza flops out on a bed and closes her eyes. "I was starting to think they didn't have actual beds in space."

I lie down next to her. "So we're just not going to talk about it?"

"The bed? I can talk about this bed for ages. I want to memorize every inch of this bed."

"No. I mean the meeting, where they basically said you could have anything you wanted, and you said you didn't want anything."

"I don't want anything from those two. I could feel their eyes looking through me, judging me. Reminded me of the way people used to look at me back home."

"They owe you. You helped to save their complacent butts. If they recommend you for princess school, they're not doing you a favor, they're paying you back."

We both lie there, staring up at the ceiling. Which has a gently undulating hologram of endless stars, with the occasional comet streaking past.

"They'll never let someone like me become a princess," Elza says in a small voice, so quiet I can barely hear.

"You're basically the most ideal princess candidate ever," I say in her ear. "You've survived things that would have broken almost anybody, by being wise and clever and patient and good at breaking into spaceships. Even if I wasn't in love with you, I would be in awe of you."

"I would put up with a billion tons of bullshit if it means I get to meet the smartest computers in the galaxy." Elza stares at the ceiling with a dreamy look in her eyes.

"Yeah. But also . . . a lot of messed-up stuff is going on here. You said it yourself. The Royal Fleet is so busy fighting this endless war against the Compassion, they haven't been doing anything to help people like the Grattna. They've lost sight of who they're even fighting for. Someone needs to help them understand. A princess could do a lot to change things."

"My girlfriend is a pain in the ass," Elza tells the ceiling. Then she turns to me. "If I agree to talk to them about entering the princess selection, will you stop bugging me?"

"Of course not." I giggle. "I'm going to keep bugging you forever. Call me your girlfriend again."

"My." Elza leans forward until I can feel her breath on my face. "Girlfriend."

I will never get used to this feeling—this happy-scary vulnerability—as long as I live.

Elza unzips my cadet uniform just enough to run her smooth hand over my collarbone. My skin tingles like the time I walked into an electric fence around a horse field at improv camp.

"Wow. Your skin's a little more purple than before."

She's right. My skin is a kind of silvery lavender color against the dark brown of hers. And maybe I'm an inch or so taller. I only just got the next injection, from the *Unquenchable*'s doctor.

"I mean, no pressure, but . . . could you even *be* with a six-foot-six purple girl?"

Elza is laughing so hard she's about to fall off the bed.

"What's so funny? Wait. Am I funny to you now? What's funny?"

"You're saying you're going to start looking like someone out of *Overwatch* or *Mass Effect*, and you want to know if I'd be into that? Have you *seen* my Tumblr feed?"

"Uh. No?"

"Come here."

She kisses me, and I run my fingers through her thick black curls, and breathe in her wild-honey scent. We cling tight in this ridiculous stateroom, kissing and touching each other, and I try to snapshot this moment in my mind.

"Tell me where it's okay to touch you." I can barely hear my own voice. Shy, for once.

"Everywhere," she whispers. "You can touch me wherever."

I slide my hand under her bra, and oh wow, more electric-fence sensation, except it's going right through me now.

Her hands slide across my body, exploring—electric zaps!—and I freeze for a moment.

"What's wrong?" she asks.

"I'm just . . . it's scary weird. Me being an alien, you being a human. I mean, Makvarians have all these weird mating customs. Like they have a third gender, called the thonts. I finally got up the nerve to ask Riohon about it."

"What did he say?" She stops touching me, and just looks me in the face, her eyes wide.

"Uh, yeah. So some people are born as thonts, but most of them actually start out as boys or girls, and then they decide to change when they hit puberty. A thont can't become a parent in the normal way, but se can add some genes to a baby by, uh, singing."

"Whaaaat? They *sing* to the unborn baby?"

"It's not actually singing, I guess. But se can make improvements, or whatever, to the child, either during or right after conception. During is way better. A thont can add ser own DNA to the mix. And a baby who has three genetic parents is considered super lucky."

She lets this soak in. "I probably can't be a parent anyway. And I've never even wanted children."

"Me neither. I don't think."

"But I totally want someone to sing to us while we . . ." She makes a gesture.

"Really?"

"Yeah. You don't? That sounds amazing."

Now she's smiling, and I smile back.

"You wouldn't be self-conscious? About someone seeing us . . . naked? And everything?"

"People have tried to make me ashamed forever. And screw that."

Her breath warms my cheek. Of all the stuff that I couldn't possibly ever explain to myself from a few months ago, this right here is the strangest and the luckiest.

"I feel brand-new," I whisper to her. "Like I could be anybody. All I really know is that I want to be close to you always, no matter what. In the Glorious Nebula, or in the middle of nowhere. Anywhere you go."

"You better not ever change your mind. I've already let you all the way inside my heart, Tina, way faster than I ever should have." Her brown eyes are so close I can see every fleck of green and yellow. A single tear rolls down her face and lands on the magic bed.

"Never." I kiss her tears away. My eyes are getting swimmy too, but not like sad tears. More like the way you cry when someone finally sees you, after you spent so much time trying so hard to be seen.

I'm in love. Hot damn.

55

"Um, so. What else have you missed?" Keziah keeps chatting to Yatto, who shows no sign that they can hear him. "Damini keeps making us play *Ringforge,* that game where everyone tries to be the first to build an artificial ring around a red giant star, and you can choose to cooperate or to sabotage each other. I bet you're already really good at it."

Yatto just lies there, in coma-town.

"Also, I just heard I've been put on the priority list for diplomat school," Keziah says. "I can't wait to see my father's face when I return to Earth with my own private starship and the full authority of the Firmament behind me. On a mission of peace and understanding. He will have a total meltdown. It'll be so fantastic."

He sighs.

"I guess I've run out of things to tell you. Again. But . . . just know that you're safe. And surrounded by people who care about you. I hope you wake up before we do the memorial service for everyone we lost from the *Indomitable.* Wouldn't feel right to do it without you."

Keziah is still speaking to Yatto in a low voice when I walk into the next room, where Rachael is in a coma of her own.

Yiwei has a new instrument, which looks a little like a mandolin, only bigger and with a curvy neck. "It's a lute," he says. "Or maybe . . . an oud. This ship has a fabrication machine that can make almost anything that they've scanned in detail, and I guess someone snuck a visit to Earth back in the Middle Ages." He plucks, making sweet percussive notes. Xiaohou hops up on the foot of Rachael's med-couch and adds some low chord progressions to the mix.

"It's really pretty," Damini says.

"Thanks. She doesn't seem to hear."

Rachael just lies there, surrounded by neurolytic scanners and other gizmos monitoring her vitals. She has a whole room to herself, with an empty med-couch that Elza, Damini, and I are perched on.

"I wrote you a song," Yiwei tells Rachael. "I finally did it." He sings a verse in Chinese, and the EverySpeak apparently decides not to try and screw with actual song lyrics. The melody is sweeping and a little sad, with a lot of rising intervals—until the chorus, when it opens up into a major key.

Elza reaches out and holds my hand, and I smile at her.

Yiwei gets through a second sad verse, and another uplifting chorus, and his voice gives out. He puts his instrument aside and clutches at Rachael's hand, pressing it to his forehead. He shivers and convulses, and makes tiny choking sobs. He looks like his new lute, with his neck curved forward and his body scrunched into a ball.

"Let's give them some privacy," Damini whispers.

Yiwei straightens up and blinks away the tears. "Don't go. I need the company. I just . . . I thought if I actually wrote her a song and played it to her, she'd wake up, like some kind of storybook magic thing. I don't even know why I was so naïve."

"It was a good idea," Elza says. "I bet she appreciated it, even if she can't wake up just yet."

"We just have to give her time," I chime in.

Yiwei nods. "I guess. Ugh. I've barely eaten since we got on this ship."

Everybody decides to take Yiwei to one of the fancy crew lounges and feed him Scanthian parsnips. I volunteer to stay and keep an eye on Rachael.

Yiwei leaves his lute perched in the corner, and it looks quaint, with its blond varnish and hand-carved-looking frame, surrounded by shiny technology. Rachael looks peaceful, like her face is half smiling, but the hand that Yiwei was holding twitches.

I take that hand, and stroke it gently. "It's okay," I say. "You're on the world's most upscale spaceship. We got rescued. We're finally safe."

Her eyes open.

"We're not safe." The smile is gone, and her green eyes dart around the room. "Nobody is safe. I can still feel their presence inside my head, if I concentrate."

"The Shapers?" My heart turns into a chunk of frozen stone.

I'm looking for a bell or a nurse button, to get someone to come look at her.

"They call themselves the Vayt. Nobody's communicated with them in such a long time."

"What do they want? Why did they—"

Rachael's hand squeezes mine, and she pulls me forward. "That machine, it opened a gateway to a place that nobody was ever supposed to disturb. And now they're awake, the Vayt. They're awake, and . . . they're scared out of their minds."

"Of what?" I ask. My whole skin is crawling, even my scalp. "They're the most powerful creatures the galaxy has ever known. What do they have to be scared of?"

But Rachael has closed her eyes and conked out, and seems to be sleeping peacefully now. As for me, I'm never going to sleep again.

The whole room is quiet, apart from a slurping, sucking sound coming out of one of the medical devices, and Yatto's gentle snoring in the next room. Feels like the stillness of the grave. There's a threat out there that the most powerful creatures in history couldn't deal with, and we still don't even understand what it is. Anxiety and dread are churning inside me.

I know everything there is to learn about a thousand planets and their people—but I don't know the one thing I need to keep my friends safe.

ACKNOWLEDGMENTS

I'm so incredibly grateful to everyone who took this epic journey with me. My agent, Russ Galen, first got me thinking about writing a young-adult novel, which was what led to me remembering all my teenage dreams of leaving Earth and discovering my true alien heritage.

But also, I'm ridiculously thankful for the support I've gotten from everyone at Tor Books. Especially my brilliant editor, Miriam Weinberg, whose keen, insightful vision was essential to helping this book achieve its potential. Miriam has an unerring sense for story, and this book wouldn't be the same without her help. Also, Patrick Nielsen Hayden was an early champion of this book and really believed in it from the beginning. I'm also super grateful to Lucille Rettino, Sanaa Ali-Virani, Devi Pillai, Alexis Saarela, Sarah Reidy and everyone else at Tor who helped make this book happen.

I'm also very grateful to Nate Miller at Manage-Ment for having my back and supporting my writing in a million ways.

And thanks so much to Liana Krissoff, the heroic copy editor without which none of this would work.

I had a ton of help with making this book work. Hailey Kaas spent hours and hours on video chat with me, helping me to make Elza's portrayal as accurate as possible. And then Hailey also sensitivity-read the novel, reading some parts more than once.

(Also, thanks to Duolingo for teaching me Brazilian Portuguese.) Meanwhile, Shobha Rao helped me to shape Damini's backstory and gave incredibly insightful comments on the book as a whole.

Terry Johnson and Katie Mack helped a ton with the science stuff in the book, and also gave me plenty of feedback on the entire shebang.

I'm also super thankful to my other sensitivity readers: Na'amen Tilahun, Jaymee Goh, and Keffy Kehrli.

Thanks also to my beta readers: Sheerly Avni, Karen Meisner, Liz Henry, Baruch Porras-Hernandez, Rebecca Hensler, Danny Lavery, K.M. Szpara, Cecilia Tan, Elena Rose Vera, and Andrew Liptak. Plus the Lexicats: Claire Light, Maggie Tokuda-Hall, Sasha Hom, Rachel Chalmers, Emily Jiang, Mel Hilario, and Audrey T. Williams. I also got some great feedback on the opening chapters from Ben Rosenbaum, Jackie Monkiewicz, David Moles, Anthony Ha, and Mary Anne Mohanraj.

And finally, thanks always to Annalee Newitz, my partner, my inspiration, and my best friend, whose support made this book, and everything else in the universe, possible.

GLOSSARY

How to Tell Time and Distances in the Royal Fleet

Cycle: Around 54 minutes, Earth time. Standard unit of time.

Minicycle: One-tenth of a cycle, or around 5.4 minutes, Earth time.

Microcycle: One-one-hundredth of a cycle, or around half an Earth second.

Metacycle: Every 30 cycles, or about 27 Earth hours. Basically one standard ship's "day."

Megacycle: Every 300 metacyles, or 337.5 Earth days. More or less, a standard "year."

Standard terrain unit (or STU): Roughly six Earth miles. Used for measuring the surface of a planet.

Standard space unit (or SSU): A standard measurement for distance in space.

Useful Phrases in the Royal Fleet

Inspection rest: Standing before a superior officer, upright but with a comfortable posture.

Ion harness: A device that allows you to shoot out a "rope" of pure ionized particles, which can be used like a lasso to capture free-floating items in space.

Landfall expedition: A group of explorers sent down from a starship to the surface of a planet.

Peacebringer's Code: Code of conduct that every member of the Royal Fleet agrees to.

Quant: A personal communication and monitoring device, usually fitted on the wrist of a Royal Fleet officer. Information and pictures appear as holographs in the palm of your hand.

Realtac: Real-time tactical summary. In other words, what the hell is going on right now.

Revel: Short for "relative velocity," meaning how fast a ship (or object) is moving in relation to other ships.

Safebeam: A way of sending messages securely between starships.

Said and done: Phrase meaning that a conversation is over, and orders have been given and received. Usually used over comm channels.

So noted: Standard response to being told something by a commanding officer.

Three-headed monster (or 3HM): A situation so terrible there's no way out.

With a will: Basically means that orders have been given and received, in person.

People and Places

The Ardenii: The super-smart computers at the center of the Firmament, who are connected to the Queen's brain.

Aribentors: The natives of the planet Aribentora, whose skeletons are on the outside. They worship doubt, and their poets are also priests.

The Compassion: A radical faction that left the Royal Fleet because they believe human-shaped creatures are superior, and believe that other, "misshapen" creatures should be kept down by any means necessary.

The Firmament, or Her Majesty's Firmament: The area of space that contains the Queen's Palace, the Royal Council, and other areas of Her Majesty's government.

Grattna: Creatures with three wings, three eyes, and three of just about everything. Natives of the planet Second Yoth.

The Glorious Nebula: A huge cloud of dust that surrounds the Firmament.

Irriyaians: Giant humanoids with brightly-colored tiger stripes and bony spikes sticking out of their heads, necks, and spines.

Javarah: Fox people, sort of. Their "fur" is actually a separate organism that keeps them from going into a murderous rage (or mating frenzy).

Kraelyors: Creatures that have five eyes arranged in a circle around their two mouths. Plus three huge limbs with barbed stingers, and a big squelchy slug bottom.

Makvarians: Large humanoids with light purple skin and big round eyes. Tina's people.

Oonians: One-eyed humanoids. There are only a thousand Oonians at any given time, and they can't make a new baby unless one of them dies.

The Queen: The one person who interfaces with the Ardenii. She helps to guide the Firmament, using these supercomputers' vast knowledge and experience. The Queen is always chosen from among a whole group of princesses who also learn to connect to those computers.

Rosaei: Humanoids who are half made out of rocks, half made out of flesh.

The Royal Fleet: A peacekeeping force that patrols the entire galaxy, trying to keep less-powerful species from being exploited by more-powerful ones.

The Seven-Pointed Empire: A government made up of seven different species (the Irriyaians, the Oonians, the Scanthians, the Makvarians, and a few others) that used to rule a large area of the galaxy, before the time of the Royal Fleet.

The Shapers: A mysterious civilization that existed hundreds of thousands of years ago. They traveled around helping humanoids to become advanced, while sabotaging every other intelligent species.

Yarthins: Humanoids whose skin is covered by a thick moss.

Zanthurons: Humanoids who have slimy tubes (like worms) all over their faces.

Zyzyians: Tiny creatures whose bulbous heads have blowholes that spit out different-colored bubbles depending on their mood.

For more fantastic fiction, author events,
exclusive excerpts, competitions, limited editions and more

VISIT OUR WEBSITE
titanbooks.com

LIKE US ON FACEBOOK
facebook.com/titanbooks

FOLLOW US ON TWITTER AND INSTAGRAM
@TitanBooks

EMAIL US
readerfeedback@titanemail.com